The Profit Dilemma

The Profit Dilemma

Dr. James Doran

ISBN: 1530440971
ISBN 13: 9781530440979
Library of Congress Control Number: 2016904353
CreateSpace Independent Publishing Platform
North Charleston, South Carolina

This is a work of fiction but the research, premise,
and implications are built upon actual academic works, true market
events, and potential economic outcomes. Enjoy.

For Heather

The number 4 express was uncharacteristically empty at six o'clock as it rattled pass the Canal Street Station. The general condition of the Lexington Avenue line was plush compared to the Nassau Street lines, as was to be expected. The floors were not sticky, and the seats were clean, but Dr. Michelle Lancaster was not inclined to sit. She had been attending discussions in Midtown all day, listening to and assessing projections on the potential dangers of deflation like that experienced in Japan in the early 1990s. Her focus had been elsewhere. In fact, it had been squarely on the meeting she was about to attend—not on the potential damages to personal-wage growth and real-estate prices if interest rates continued to persist at close to 0 percent. She had known this final meeting was coming, and the anticipation had been building ever since her mentor had sat her down last month in his office. While the impact and reality of what was discussed in seclusion had shocked and decimated the fundamental core beliefs she had grown to both love and defend, the real impact of what she was about to enter into was only now just formalizing in her mind. There was little choice; in fact, it was now an obligation and her duty to join a small group of individuals that had more power than any other group had possessed since the birth of modern-day capitalism.

The train rumbled along with the typical side-to-side jerkiness that all commuters are used to and hardly notice, having learned to transfer weight from left foot to right in a natural, innate movement. Michelle stared blankly at the advertisements for cologne, jeans, and legal services that are ubiquitous on all subway cars. She rarely let her mind wander to the vagaries of life, but now seemed like the most appropriate time to relax and reflect on how she had gotten to this place. She had gained an acute understanding of herself in junior high. That had been when her interests had deviated greatly from those of her peers'. While her friends became interested in standard teenage fare, she found herself consumed with stock quotes, articles in the *Wall Street Journal*, and economic policy. It was not that she had been an outcast or had not enjoyed what her friends liked. She just knew what her passion was. From this point of self-awareness, there had been only one course her life could have possibly traveled. The path to success was never preordained but had been driven by her own self-belief and unyielding desire for success. Of course, with all great successes come sacrifices, and Michelle allowed herself a brief and unsatisfying smile at the thought of these sacrifices. Was it worth it? It was a question that any highly motivated, highly successful person asks himself or herself without ever really knowing the answer.

She caught a reflection of herself in the window and noted the face looking back appeared slightly older than she would have liked, but on the whole, she still felt attractive and knew that men still paid attention. There was the occasional gray in her chestnut hair, an extra line around her large brown eyes, but the positives outweighed the negative. Assets were assets, and any asset had value. She always dressed conservatively but made sure the outfit highlighted a figure that most women would be jealous of.

Michelle's thoughts had drifted to the past, but a quick jerk of the train returned her to the present. She couldn't quite believe that she was making this journey, but success and choices can lead you to places that you least expect. Maybe if she was tougher, she could have walked away, but the internal drive for power was too strong. This thought was sobering. It reflected all the good and bad Michelle thought about herself.

Only a few passengers remained after the Brooklyn Bridge station, and she hardly noticed the train pause at Fulton Street. When the Wall Street station was announced, her daydreams vanished, and the rough exterior that she had built up through years of academic and political maneuvering bristled to the surface. The train doors opened, and she headed for the stairs that led up to the entrance to Trinity Church on a cool April evening. The sense of wealth and power was palpable upon exiting the subway station, and Michelle felt it every time she walked these streets. Today as she walked away from the subway station, she felt an unaccustomed and altogether bone-chilling sense of anticipation. Normally she would walk down Wall Street and take the left down Nassau and the right on Liberty Street to her office. Today she would continue down Wall Street, heading toward the corner of Wall Street and Broad Street and that famous market corner.

She had been informed that this morning someone would be there to meet her. She would not know this person but was to follow his instructions to the letter. For a person who typically gave orders and was used to hearing information first, this degree of uncertainty was uncomfortable. Of course she understood that there was nothing she could do about this and thus could only follow the instructions and hope the actions she was, and would be, taking were the right thing.

The walk down Wall Street was quiet. On a Friday at six in the evening, it was probably the quietest place in Manhattan. The employees of the New York Stock Exchange and the traders who worked the floor were mostly done for the week. Most of the married investment bankers were on the trains back to Rye, Greenwich, or one of the lush suburbs in Fairfield or Westchester County, while at some Midtown or Upper East or West Side bar, the overworked single analysts unwound from another ninety-plus-hour week. The tourists always left by early afternoon, and nobody lived in this part of the island. Michelle could hear the click of her heels reverberating off the walls as she made her way down the street. She was always careful not to wear too high of a heel, since looking down on male colleagues was one of the best ways to hamper a career. It felt bizarre walking alone into a life-altering meeting with people unknown, in the epicenter of the financial world. It was causing her heartbeat to accelerate.

Calm yourself. Stand tall. Remember who you are. Michelle uttered these words quietly to herself, steeling her nerve. She had repeated this phrase every time she had presented a paper as a graduate student at Michigan, and from then on, it had been her go-to saying to quash nervous butterflies.

At the corner of Wall Street and Broad Street, a man in a black suit and tie was standing conspicuously alone. He looked like a secret-service agent, except that there were no sunglasses or obvious earpiece. Michelle saw him and noted the lack of distinguishing features. He wasn't especially tall or handsome and had a bland, disinterested expression on his face. If she were to describe him, the best adjective would be to say he was plain.

As she approached, he addressed her with a flat, unemotional greeting. "Good evening, Dr. Lancaster."

"Good evening." She met his eyes and tried not to look away first.

"I'm glad to see that you're early, as I was told to expect, since you have a reputation for promptness. The meeting is scheduled for six thirty, and everyone is waiting. My name is Mr. Jones. Please follow me."

She nodded in response. There was little point in small talk. The man named Jones turned on his heel and walked down Broad Street without glancing at the exchange. From one of the surrounding skyscrapers that had a view of the street, two men followed the movements of Michelle Lancaster. One was watching through binoculars, while the other viewed her through the scope on his SR-25 sniper rifle. A shot from this distance with this caliber would make any facial recognition impossible. His orders were to wait unless summoned. At present his earpiece remained silent.

Broad Street's wide avenue, combined with the towering skyscrapers, focused the setting sun's light into a concentrated hue of red and orange, causing Michelle to squint as the reflection of the glass shimmered down the road. April was always a pleasant month in Manhattan, assuming there was no rain. Winter had passed with its typical unpredictable snow flurries and biting wind, and there was always a sense of renewal when the days were once again longer than the nights. They crossed over Exchange Place and walked next to the renovation work being done on the facades of most of the surrounding buildings. The nondescript Mr. Jones stopped at the entrance of 60 Broad Street, a thirty-nine-story tower located in the heart of the financial district. One of the first modern skyscrapers in New York's financial district, 60 Broad Street was home to a number of government and city agencies, accounting and insurance firms, and the International Securities Exchange. Historically, it was probably best known for being the home of Drexel, Burnham, and Lambert, Michael Milken's firm, the junk-bond kings.

Michelle followed Mr. Jones into the building. She had been there many times before, admiring the understated but clearly expensive lobby with its black marble floor and handsome elevator cabs, but this evening she was taken aback by the lack of security personnel fortifying the entrance. Mr. Jones preempted her thoughts.

"Dismissed for the evening. Take the elevator up to the thirty-seventh floor," he said.

He pushed through the gate and pointed her to the elevators. Jones took up the seat behind the security desk and stared out the main entrance. Michelle walked to the elevators on the right and pushed the button. The nearest elevator opened, and Michelle entered and selected the thirty-seventh floor. She didn't look back at Mr. Jones, so she didn't notice his subtle hand movements sending an encoded message. The doors closed, and the elevator ascended swiftly. She kept her breathing slow and controlled as the elevator stopped and the doors opened.

"Hello, Michelle," said the warm and infectious voice of Dennis Haybert.

"Hello, Dennis." She was unable to hide the shock and relief in her voice. "I didn't think you were coming tonight. At least that was the impression."

"I know. However, I felt that it would be best. This transition and responsibility isn't easy. I want to help you through this, since I'm responsible in part for you being here."

Michelle noted that his eyes reflected the same emotion that his voice relayed. Dennis's affection for her was apparent, and while nothing had ever happened between them, there was an attraction that bubbled just below the surface. He had been a significant part of her life for close to twenty years, and now she was ready to assume the mantle and title he had groomed her for.

"OK, Michelle, follow me," he said. The lobby lacked the glass security doorway that was so common on many floors of New York's commercial buildings, so they were able to walk directly into the interior lobby. The thirty-seventh floor was home to an insurance company, the name prominently displayed on the glass doors of the front conference room and carpet of the waiting area. Michelle wasn't familiar with this company, but that didn't mean much. Dennis led Michelle down the corridor to the right, past a bank of cubicles and a conference room, until they reached what appeared to be the extension of the concrete wall. Upon closer examination Michelle noted that there were doors, but she had to look carefully to notice them. They were located in the middle of the floor, away from the windows, and surrounded by thick concrete and not the standard drywall that typically separated one office from the next. Dennis pressed his hand next to the door, and a panel with a small ten-digit keypad revealed itself. He punched the keypad seven times, and a small click sounded the release of the lock. The door opened outward, and he led Michelle through.

They stepped into a single room that was barren except for a stock conference table and six surrounding chairs. There was no artwork on the walls, no minibar, and no sign that anyone occupied the office throughout the year. Michelle looked around the room and saw five of the seats were occupied, and four of the faces were recognizable. While she had been aware that the group she was meeting with was powerful, she had not known who the members were. Seeing the faces in person for the first time crystallized the notion of what she was about to enter. These people controlled an unparalleled amount of wealth and with it, power. As she walked in, none of the people seated got up.

"Dr. Lancaster, please be seated. My name is Frank Lyman," said the man across the table from her. His tone was short and perfunctory. His was the one face she didn't recognize.

She nodded and took the seat directly in front of her, while Dennis stood behind her.

"Dr. Lancaster, you're here for a reason, and your presence here confirms that you accept this reason and the task in front of you," Frank said.

"I understand and accept."

"Good. You understand that the duty in front of you, in front of all of us, isn't easy and has to be done in absolute secrecy. In this duty, we must not fail. We mustn't deviate from the plan outlined, and we must perform the duty selflessly," Frank said.

"I agree."

"You understand that any action that will cause undue harm to the natural order of things, purposefully or accidentally, will be met with dire consequences. This isn't a veiled threat but a statement of fact."

"I agree and understand."

"Good." Frank looked around the room. He looked at the faces of the four men who had been members with him for over five years, and finally at Dennis. "We've all agreed that Dr. Lancaster is going to be the new member of the Markov Group, replacing Dr. Dennis Haybert."

There was a nod of assent from the others in the room. At this Dennis nodded to the other members of the group. He took out a card, which had the code for the security pad, and placed it in front of Michelle. She looked up at him and held his eyes just before he pulled on the handle, opened the door, and vanished. Michelle had seen that look before. It was one of concern. However, at this point it was too late, and both Michelle and Dennis knew it. She had been informed about a month ago, and there was no turning back. He had made the initial move, and she had followed. In the end, it was a choice that she had wanted, and, as with all the hard choices before, she did not allow regret to cloud her future thinking. The past was just that; all that mattered was the future.

There was no sound of footsteps retreating down the corridor, but neither Frank nor the other members said anything for several minutes. Michelle waited patiently with her hands folded in her lap. She looked at nothing in particular, keeping her eyes focused on the grain pattern cut into the mahogany conference table. The quiet lingered until a small beep echoed from inside Frank Lyman's jacket.

"We're officially alone. No one is on our floor, and the security personnel in the lobby know the location of all others present in the building.

Dr. Lancaster, welcome to the Markov Group. Before we start, let me remind you to meet with Mr. Jones so he can scan your handprint for access to this room. Now I'm going to explain what your role and contribution will be to our small group."

Michelle listened without saying anything. There was no job title with the Markov Group, no paperwork, no public appearances, no salary, nothing. But the job required decision making and influence greater than her actual job. That was saying something, given that she was about to be announced as the next president of the Federal Reserve Bank of New York.

CHAPTER 2

Jake Chamberlain stood with his back against the glass of the main atrium of McCombs Business School, watching the four newly accepted PhD students getting their pictures taken for the finance department website. He could see in their eyes the dreams of future chair positions and academic success, and he envied and pitied their naïveté, remembering his own innocence four years ago. Jake had come into the PhD program at the University of Texas with only his college degree and some years on Wall Street, and the transition had been eye opening. College had been a blur of good times and athletics prowess, mixed in with some minor studying. Graduate school had been the complete opposite.

The four who stood by the old ticker-tape display, getting their photos taken, came from diverse backgrounds but were armed with serious pedigrees, as was typical with finance PhD candidates. Three guys and a girl, all from Ivy League undergraduate programs; three had their master's in business administration (MBA), and one had a master's in statistics. Jake knew that only because his advisor had mentioned the new crop that was coming in over the summer. At the time Jake had thought little of it; new graduate students were hardly seen until after they had passed their qualifiers after the second year, but mild curiosity struck him now as he was walking through the main lobby. As a student in his fifth and hopefully last year, his memory of standing in this building and getting his picture taken four years ago was as clear as ever.

That whole day, including meeting with the department chair and the newly minted PhD graduate who had taken a job with New York University, was so memorable because of that feeling of being a third wheel. They were speaking a language that was completely foreign, and while it was in English, it made no sense. Jake laughed to himself at the memory as he crossed by the business-development offices to the bank of elevators and pressed the button for the sixth floor. To think that terms such as *Black-Scholes equation, jump processes, adverse selection,* and *quasi Monte Carlo* were unknowns to him then, when they now made up a core component of his being.

The McCombs Business School was two parts, old and new, or the undergraduate and graduate schools, although classes were not separated by the buildings. While not the newest or nicest building at the University of Texas, the business school felt like the heart of campus, as it sat at the corner of Speedway and Twenty-First. The argument could always be made, and justifiably so, that the clock tower that housed the main administration building was the true heart, not only because it stood presiding over campus and most of Austin, but because of its recognition and notorious history. However, in terms of volume of foot traffic, nothing surpassed that corner, and when classes let out, it reminded Jake of a Manhattan sidewalk.

Most of the administration for the College of Business—larger classrooms, trading room, and recruiting center—were in the newer part of the college, while the faculty offices were in the older part. The departments were separated by floor, and as far as Jake was concerned, only the sixth floor mattered. That was because finance was the only thing that mattered. In fact, if someone were to ask, he could not name which floor the marketing or management departments were on or who the faculty members were. However, if someone were to ask where any one of the finance professors went to school, what their research interests were, or their number of publications, he could readily supply that information. As was the nature of any good graduate program, or any involved graduate student, total immersion into the subject area was critical so that everything else was trivial.

The elevator doors opened, and Jake walked out, walked through the glass doors into the main office, waved to the secretaries, and then walked through the second set of glass doors to the row of faculty offices. Jake had made this particular walk thousands of times, and he knocked on office 6.270.

"Come in," said the familiar voice from behind the door.

Unlike previous times when he'd walked into this office, Jake felt a nervous energy and a sense of anticipation that could only come with a real breakthrough. In a graduate student's life, there were three major hurdles to overcome. The first was passing qualifiers, which brought an unmatched amount of stress prior to taking the exam until the moment you hear that you have passed. Two years of course work and study boiled down to three days of intense examination. Fail on any subsection and you were invited to leave. There was always one per year who failed.

The second was coming up with a dissertation topic. This was where most students failed, since striving for a unique idea, or at least an idea that was publishable, was the true challenge. In Jake's cohort, Shawn Granger had been smartest throughout their course work and now was still struggling with his dissertation idea. He had fallen two years behind Jake and the other surviving fifth-year PhD student, Audria Kalman. Jake had last seen Shawn Granger, with his bean-pole frame and two-inch-thick glasses, playing online poker in his office.

The third hurdle was finishing that dissertation. This would appear to be the easiest of the three, but if the theory was inconsistent or the data didn't empirically prove the hypothesis, then it was back to the proposal stage, and that meant two years of life wasted. Jake held his breath as he entered, hoping he hadn't wasted two years of his life.

"Jake, how are you doing this fine day?" Dr. Eric Rosen asked. He would say this regardless of what the weather was or how gray the sky looked. There was always a natural happiness to Eric, and over the course of the four years he had known him, Jake had seen Eric upset only twice. The first time was during a job-candidate seminar when the prospective hire hadn't answered Eric's question. Needless to say, that particular candidate did not received an offer. The second was with a graduate student who had incorrectly graded some MBA exams. That student had left after his second year. The messages were few but extremely clear. Do not get on the wrong side of Eric Rosen.

Jake had had only positive interactions with Eric, his advisor for the past two years, and a natural friendship had developed as mentor and pupil had worked closely together on a research topic. As Jake's advisor, Eric would help guide him to the completion of his dissertation and naturally become a coauthor when they attempted to publish the papers that made up the collective thesis. On the surface, this friendship may have seemed unlikely, since the two of them could not be more physically different, but when it came to a passion for their area of finance, there was a natural alignment.

"Well, Dr. Rosen, I saw the new students getting their pictures taken this morning, and it brought back familiar feelings of excitement and uncertainty—although, to be honest, I'm glad those days are over."

"I concur. However, I do long for a fresh perspective every once in a while," Eric said cheerily. "Once you've learned a certain way and gone down a certain path, the view does become a bit parochial. It would be nice to see it again from untrained eyes. You'll understand when you've been in this business for as long as I have. Remember, I was a student when the world started accepting and understanding the Black-Scholes Merton model. That predates the notion of exchange-traded derivatives, options, futures, and everything that you've studied and become so familiar with. Our understanding of how to price assets has fundamentally changed over this thirty-plus-year time span. Along with changing technology, the world of finance has truly evolved. Now, speaking of Black-Scholes, shall we discuss why we're here this morning?" As he talked, Eric made demonstrative hand gestures and wriggled about in his chair. He was a constant whirlwind of energy.

The question was not a question at all but an invitation to sit and listen to what Eric had to say on the empirical findings of Jake's dissertation that he had submitted in mid-July. It had taken three weeks for Eric to return Jake's e-mail, in part because Eric had gone abroad in July, but also in part, Jake hoped, because Eric had taken time to thoroughly read his work and digest the findings. When Eric had sent him an e-mail last Friday asking him to stop by his office at eight o'clock on Monday morning, Jake's weekend had been shot. He had had trouble sleeping, and it had destroyed his workout plans. Needless to say, Haley, Jake's wife, was pissed at him for letting his worries take over, but listening to advice from his wife was as good as giving advice. It usually fell on deaf ears.

"Jake, you're familiar with the story behind the January effect?" Eric asked, somewhat rhetorically. The January effect was the most common and well-publicized anomaly in finance. Hundreds of academic papers had explored why this effect took place, and many had tried to theorize it away, yet it still seemed to persist. At its core, the January effect meant that stocks, especially small-market capitalization stocks relative to large stocks, outperformed in the month of January, such that holding a basket of small stocks in the first month of the year and a market portfolio the rest of the year would provide better-than-average returns consistently through time. It was so popular that the press always loved to bring this topic up at the turn of a new year, and many fund managers had employed this strategy in their portfolios.

"I learned about the January effect back in my undergraduate days, and it was one of the reasons I wanted to study finance further. It's still one of the great problems and challenges facing efficient markets today. This anomaly still persists, and we all know about it. Why should it still be around? It should have disappeared. As to the story behind it, I know only that the paper was first published in the early eighties; I think it was 1982."

"Yes, but what happened to the people that published the findings?"

"They're at Wharton, right?" Jake hesitantly replied. He remembered papers and authors in his area, but stretching to other concentrations in finance and the authors' affiliations was outside of his scope of interest.

"Yes, and they've had extremely successful careers. But they weren't the first ones to discover the January effect, although they were the first to publish it. It was a graduate student at Stanford, one of my own advisor's students. He found the anomaly two years prior."

"Why wasn't it published?" Jake asked.

"This is something that I'm not happy to report, but I think it's worthwhile, given the research you've presented to me. I'm quite fond of my advisor, and, as you know, I think him to be one of the five best minds in finance. His Nobel Prize only validates this. However, while what he did to this student at the time was justifiable, at the same time it hamstrung this student's career. To understand this, you've got to understand what it meant to be a student at Stanford at the time. Stanford is an efficient-market haven, and was especially so back then, and there's no such thing as a violation of that hypothesis. As you know, in an efficient market, no anomalies can persist. Investors should see the excess return relative to the risk and drive the price of the assets up so the excess return disappears. So when this particular student came up with his January empirical anomaly, my advisor told him he was wrong. He told him to go back and estimate the results again and come back in six months with something that made sense."

Jake listened intently, unconsciously shaking his head. There are horror stories and urban legends floating around any graduate-student office or bullpen about conflicts with advisors and blackballing, but he had never heard one directly from a professor's mouth.

"Jake, I see your disbelief, but my advisor thought he was acting in his student's best interest. Anyhow, the student returned six months later, showing that he had rerun all the tests and added other robustness checks, and the results were impossible to deny. There was a January anomaly. Again, he was told to redo everything or risk not graduating. It was at this point that two students from Chicago, whose department was less convinced of the efficient-market hypothesis, were documenting the exact same anomaly. Needless to say, they got their paper to market, published it, and became well established in the profession."

"What happened to your cohort?" Jake asked, trying to mask his concern at where the discussion was going.

"When the other student's results were finally published, his work became moot. He found a lesser topic, finally graduated, and took a position at the University of Wyoming." Eric shrugged his shoulders and splayed his hands apart in the universal gesture of *these things happen.*

Jake got the message. He had always understood the nature of academic work and the challenges associated with it. Finding a unique idea was only half the battle. You still had to convince a gauntlet of people before it would see the light of day in print form. Colleagues, referees, editors, and competitors all sought to reject ideas, whether they were merit based or not. The space for publications was precious, and those few pages would make or break careers. Here was a prime example of how one person had altered three lives, based on an incorrect bias about a belief that was held dear.

"Dr. Rosen, you wouldn't be telling me this without reason. How's this relevant to my work?" Jake asked, knowing the answer but needing to hear it out loud.

CHAPTER 3

The heat in Austin is different from the heat in most of the state. It is humid but not thoroughly overwhelming, as it is in Houston or Dallas. Maybe it is due to the surrounding hills and the lake that runs through the middle of town. The variation in the terrain, along with the young and eclectic demographics, have made Austin a desirable place to live. This has resulted in historic growth over the past several years, such that the traffic has become horrendous. That is why Jake rode his bike to and from campus, trading the inconvenience of sweat for the irritation of traffic lights and difficulties of finding a parking spot. It also meant not paying for gas, and, those little savings added up for a poor graduate student. However, on this particular day, as he rode home from campus feeling the heat pulsating up from the road, he would have gladly traded the stop-and-go traffic for some air conditioning. When there is little wind, the road has been baked all day, and every day in August has exceeded one hundred degrees, riding even five miles is like being cooked in an oven.

Jake had left campus on his four-year-old yellow Cannondale mountain bike. It was a tank but indestructible, perfect for commuting to and from campus. What Eric had told him had left him with the simultaneously feeling of great hope and a fair amount of dread. Eric thought the theory and the underlying model in his research were sound, and some of the empirical findings were worthy of publication. Since publishing is the main goal of any academic, this was a good sign. The problem was the main result—or the attempt at a main result. Eric thought it was too far reaching, and he was highly skeptical of the main statistical findings. Hence Eric's reference to the first January effect findings and his old cohort.

Jake's model and empirical results suggested that the markets were anything but efficient, that the prices for assets—stocks, bonds, real estate, and so on—were all priced incorrectly, and it wasn't a short-term phenomenon. Most people, whether they are academics, professional traders, or the average person on the street, can accept that sometimes prices can be wrong, but the errors can, and should, be fixed quickly. In other words, mispricing doesn't last over long intervals, and the market reacts to information swiftly and corrects that mispricing. That is where real money is made, and lost.

As Eric had said, "Jake, take the case of a CEO resigning, stock splits, a change in interest rate policy, or even a trading-related move, like a large short position in a stock or large derivatives transactions. These cause stock prices to move, and the move takes into account the new information and settles on a new market price. This may take seconds, hours, days, or maybe even weeks—although those are few and far between. We can live with this short-term mispricing. What you've shown and claimed is a level of mispricing over years. I just can't believe that. That means that all of our models are wrong, and everyone who is trading has collectively mispriced all assets. That just doesn't seem possible."

"Dr. Rosen, the results are the results. I've checked the model and the robustness of the results several times," Jake had protested.

"I'm sure that you've been thorough, but look at your pricing or model errors. They're close to zero. This implies almost a perfect model fit and a lack of randomness. There's no such thing in finance because if you had no pricing errors, that would imply a perfect pricing model, and a perfect model implies perfect information with no randomness and way to perfectly price assets. That's just not possible, because it would lead to arbitrage, and there would be no point in trading. No one has perfect information. Look, Jake, you've done excellent work, and your graduation doesn't hinge on this result, but you've got to fix this before the January job market, especially if you want to publish and land a good job."

The simple look in Eric's eyes had been enough to convince Jake that he meant business with that last statement. It was an impressive feat born of years of experience that a simple stare from a man a foot shorter than Jake could have so much sway. Jake was thankful Eric hadn't pulled any punches.

So he now knew he faced a simple choice.

He could either solve the pricing problem and retry to convince Eric of the magnitude of his findings, or he could change his approach slightly, which would result in a less-impactful dissertation. *Fight or flight and no in-between.*

Jake knew minimizing the strength of his findings would allow Eric to sign off on his work because it would be less controversial, and he would graduate. This would be no big deal, except he had been working on this for a year and a half, and the thought of a lesser dissertation was disheartening. The better the dissertation, the better the likelihood of academic placement. Plus, Jake was stubborn as hell.

On Guadalupe Street heading north, Jake reflected back to his prior years in the program, especially the third year, which could best be described as a self-created purgatory. As a third-year student, he had made it through their qualifying exams over the previous summer and, coming off the highs of not flunking out, faced the reality of finding an original, publishable idea. Working on independent research was a daunting task to many coming off the regimented schedule of two years of rigorous course work. There were many reasons graduate students did not finish their doctoral degrees, but the most common one comes down to being unable to find the right dissertation topic. Or working on the right topic with the wrong advisor. Or finding no topic at all. Jake had vowed not to be one of those students early on.

Third-year students are on the bottom rung of the academic ladder. The chaired and endowed scholars sit at the top, followed by full, associate, and assistant professors. Graduate students are last and should be as active and driven as an assistant professor trying to earn tenure. At least, that is the impression they have to give if they want to earn their PhDs. First- and second-year students do not count, since they know nothing and were expected to know nothing. Once students pass the qualifiers, they should know a little something and, as a result, show strong progress toward the goal of finishing their dissertations and publishing in the best journals. Of course, doing these things never guarantees that a good job—or any job at all—will be waiting for them. Hence, the sense of waiting in purgatory.

Jake remembered sitting many hours in his office in the basement of the business building, housed with other PhD students, awash in the uncertainty that he would ever find a topic. After passing his qualifiers he had spent seven months working on research that went nowhere. He had spun his wheels. There had been the three months working on an idea that had just been published in the *Journal of Finance* on information feedback between debt and equity markets. Six weeks in, he knew he hated the idea but gave it another six weeks before cutting bait. The next four months, he had hand collected majority shareholder information to test the impact of how these shareholders affect board decisions, only to realize that that question was only marginally important and the results were uninteresting.

For the next two months, Jake had changed tack. He had gone back to the topic that interested him the most but was the hardest area to publish in: theoretical modeling and the empirical tests of asset prices. He had sat in his office, on the steps of the administrative tower, on the steps by Gregory Gym, all over campus, reading countless papers and searching for the idea. He just read, hadn't programmed code or written a single word. Through the countless papers that he read, there was a consistent theme that tied all these papers together, a premise that was the tenet of finance: *that markets are efficient and assets are priced correctly.*

It was the thought of efficiency, especially the idea of what a *normal* market is, that had triggered something in Jake. Jake just could not accept the idea that the concept of normality, or a statistical normal distribution, played such a large part in asset return and risk.

As he approached Highway 2222, less than a mile from home, he reflected on this moment, almost a year and a half ago, as the moment when he had found his research topic. He had spent the next year and a half building his theoretical model, making sure it was fundamentally sound. After that came the coding. Extensive hours in front of the computer writing lines upon lines, testing subprocedures, compiling, and retesting. Once the code was set came data gathering and the estimation of the model. Testing the model usually meant rewriting the code, maybe going back to the theoretical model, and starting all over again.

There had been moments of frustration, joy, anguish, despair, and elation over that year and a half. Not necessarily in that order, and his emotions certainly hadn't followed a linear path. When he'd finished the first paper of the dissertation and Eric had liked it, Jake had felt that he could actually finish the degree. When he'd gotten decent empirical results on information flows in the option markets for his second paper, Eric had thought the paper would have a chance at a top practitioner journal. That had given Jake the confidence that he could land a good academic job. However, it was the third and final paper for the dissertation, the paper that tied all of his research together, that Jake had thought would give him his best chance at a top-tier publication and a top academic posting. It was this paper that tied his dissertation topic into one collective document, and it was the result and implications of this third paper that Eric was less than convinced about.

As Jake pulled into his condo complex, he realized that he was almost there. All that hard work over the past several years and all he had to do was solve this one problem. He was convinced that the model was right, that he had all the data, and that empirically everything was as it should be. He just had to overcome this final hurdle. Jake knew that solving this problem would be easier than starting from scratch. He understood what Dr. Rosen had implied—that even if he did solve the problem, he might face a similar hurdle as the academic who had first discovered the January effect: that nobody would believe his result. That was a risk Jake was willing to take.

CHAPTER 4

There is nothing sexy about insurance. Walter Matthews knew this, and along with his name, his looks, and his general self-confidence meant that he had almost nothing to offer to the women of Manhattan. Any success that he had always came down to their desperation. He would always target those who looked like they had several drinks in them and steered the conversations away from the question, "So what do you do?" Walter hoped they would assume he was in sales and trading or mergers and acquisitions, since he hung out at the right bars and tried to flash the same kind of money.

Insurance is finance, but it is not the kind of finance job that keeps a woman's attention. At least not the women he was chasing. Maybe he should have visited different bars and settled for a different kind of woman, but Walter always wanted to be part of the cool crowd. He wanted to work on Wall Street, wear the sharp suits, be part of billion-dollar deals, and not remember the number of women he had slept with. As with most aspects of his life, he could see what he wanted but never really got to participate. It was a cruel joke to be surrounded by your dreams and never be allowed to partake in them.

He had to walk past the New York Stock Exchange every day, watching the people walk in and out in their differently colored jackets that represented the different floor brokers or the suits that managed a billion dollars in capital, knowing that he was practically anonymous to them. He worked right next door, on the thirty-seventh floor of 60 Broad Street, processing the claims and policies for Franklin Insurance, a small private property and casualty insurance company. The work was dull and the paycheck small, and it only fueled his need and desire for the finer things.

Even at his office, he got the impression he was considered no different from the furniture; disposable. He existed, and his superiors walked by without even noticing him. Maybe they knew his name, but they probably didn't care. His office was just a cubicle, and his envy extended to those with an office with a door, even if their work was no different from his. He was, by definition, just a cog in the wheel, easily replaceable and relatively unimportant.

Yet Walter Matthews was tremendously important to Franklin Insurance. He would never know his true importance, and neither would the other employees who worked for the firm. They had all been especially chosen, based on a carefully constructed behavioral algorithm and background checks. Franklin Insurance needed employees who were good at their jobs but not good enough to get others, anonymous faces that had desires for success that would never be achieved and enough self-doubt to never question authority. True worker bees.

This was because Franklin Insurance was two firms. The first was what the world and the IRS saw, the property and casualty insurance firm that employed the Walter Matthewses of the world. The second was a covert intelligence-gathering firm that ran the most sophisticated behavioral analysis and surveillance program, one that would have been the envy of the Central Intelligence Agency, Mossad, or the British intelligence agency MI6—if they had known about it. The developments in the private sector always outpaced the public sector, including intelligence gathering. The simple reason was money.

The real Franklin Insurance, the one that could not be seen, employed some of the top analysts and theorists in the fields of game theory, behavioral analytics, surveillance, data gathering and analysis, and information technology. They could earn $150,000 in a government position with little to no flexibility or make ten times that in the private sector. The choice was easy.

Their job was not to analyze market trends, weather patterns, or political outcomes. What they did was analyze people and the decisions people had made and would make in the future. These people also occupied the thirty-seventh floor but were indistinguishable from the Walter Matthewses of the world. They looked the same and worked the same hours but reported to different superiors and had very different security clearances. The assignments they were given were very specific, and the people they analyzed were of critical importance. Their reports were highly protected, and the final reports were seen only by a select few.

The reports these people did helped shape the decisions of the Markov Group and were the real reason that Michelle Lancaster had been chosen. The Markov Group, and, by extension, Franklin Insurance, knew that the best investment was made in investing in the right people.

There was also a special arm of the real Franklin Insurance, a group considered dark analysts. This was a group that couldn't be seen on the thirty-seventh floor but that was critical to the function of the overall work done there. Dark analysts did the dirty work of intelligence gathering and were some of the mostly highly trained and best-compensated individuals in the firm. They followed the potential subjects, planted the bugs, and did the day-to-day surveillance. Without this information, there would have been limited work for the analysts on the thirty-seventh floor to do. Each division was critical to the Markov Group, so that the group could stay ahead of its competition. It also helped that all of the dark analysts were former intelligence operatives and contract killers. The best people go where the money is.

Walter Matthews's day-to-day life was thoroughly dull by comparison to the dark analysts' lives, but that didn't mean that the Walter Matthewses of the world didn't, or couldn't, have an impact on how the world turned. It just so happened that this Walter Matthews would directly influence how the world changed, and the worst part about it was that he wouldn't even know.

CHAPTER 5

The University of Texas campus lies just north of downtown Austin and is known for its distinguishable and infamous landmark administrative tower. The view from the tower to the south is unencumbered and magnificent, stretching past the state capital all the way to the Colorado River. The tower houses the main administrative personnel of the university and is where the final drafts of dissertations are submitted. Jake had never actually gone into the tower and only planned on doing so when he got to that final stage.

Jake walked by the tower after saying bye to his wife, Haley, at her office. He passed Batts Hall before going into the Graduate School of Business Building. He entered the building on the third floor and went around the corner to the main atrium. The business school atrium was an expansive holding area where most students came to congregate, study, and eat. Graduate-student offices were dispersed throughout both buildings, wherever there was available space. The most desirable were on the third floor, contained within a corridor connected to the atrium. These were reserved for fourth- and fifth-year students preparing for the job market. Third-year students were typically housed in the basement with the IT staff and the computer hardware. First- and second-year students got a bullpen in the dark expanse of the fourth floor.

Jake's office, 111c, was one of seven in the 111 corridor. He had been assigned this office after passing his qualifiers and had decided to stay even when a more desirable location had opened up. These five-by-twelve-foot closets were barely wide enough to fit in a desk, let alone big enough for the grad students to hold office hours for their undergraduate students. There were no windows, and being underground had always distorted Jake's perception of time. No matter when he arrived at the office, he always felt that time moved in such a way that when he left, it should be dark outside. In reality this was hardly the case, since he arrived before seven every morning and left before four. Jake found that he was much more productive in the morning hours, in part because that was the quietest time on campus. It also allowed him to get in before the US equity markets opened at eight thirty central time, nine thirty on the East Coast. This was a habit that he had held over from his days working at Morgan Stanley. Through the rotational program and his time spent on the options desk, it was standard operating procedure to get in well before markets opened to digest overnight news and to assess how overseas markets had performed. While that part of his life was behind him, the hours and customs remained.

One office down and across the hall from Jake was Audria. She was housed in office 111d and was the other fifth-year student in this block of offices. She and Jake were two of the three survivors of their initial class of four going on the job market this year. The nonsurviving member had failed at the comprehensive exams, and Shawn was still playing online poker somewhere, not working on his dissertation. Audria kept very different hours from Jake, preferring to come in late and stay late. While they were cordial with each other, they were not friends, and their joint animosity was building due to the pressure of the upcoming job market and perceived favoritism among the faculty. Audria had started working with Sheldon Tacker, the department's most famous and highly regarded researcher. Working with Sheldon was the closest thing to a guarantee of a quality publication and a tenure-track job placement at a prestigious research university. While Jake wouldn't have minded working with Sheldon, Sheldon's area of research focus was different from Jake's interest. This, along with other latent factors, had left Jake with the perception that the faculty was already ranking him second to Audria, which would affect his future placement and ultimately his career.

Jake's concerns were well justified. Audria was well on her way to a published paper. She had a revise-and-resubmit already and was more than ready to present at the upcoming job market in January. Having a published paper or one under review prior to the job market was almost a necessary condition for all PhD students who wished to place well. The job market process was similar to a dating service in that you put out your résumé and were preselected by schools in hopes of finding the right match. You wanted to make your résumé as attractive as possible. That way you could get the most invites for possible dates; in this particular case, a date meant an interview at the AFA conference in January. Second dates would be on-campus visits, and if things got serious, the consummation would be a job offer from a university.

Jake felt he had nothing eye catching to distinguish himself with, and the October deadline for submitting his job-market packet was looming. Well, this wasn't entirely true. It was just that he didn't feel that he was ready to put his best foot forward. As his discussion with Eric had revealed, his results would be met with a high degree of skepticism, and Jake had to be prepared to accept the fact that there would be a low probability of success pushing this line of research. Publishing in this field had become exceedingly challenging, and challenging the idea of why the stock market and all other priced assets moved in a fashion that did not conform to the current paradigm was probably foolhardy.

The concept of randomness was, and is, central to finance. First encapsulated by the eighteenth-century economist Adam Smith, who championed the notion of an "invisible hand" that allows markets to be self-regulating, this concept has been generalized to many other settings. But Jake's focus was specific to the apparent nonrandom, nonnormal behavior in the evolution of stock prices and a direct challenge to Adam Smith's theory.

Currently, stuck in his office for the last five hours, he did not feel any closer to being ready to challenge hat current theory. There were equations all over his whiteboard, Post-it notes with more equations stuck to the walls of the office and the side of his desk, and stacks of paper on the floor with even more equations. The more he stared at the equations, the more unintelligible they all became.

If you can't make sense of them, how are you going to explain and justify them to the faculty? He shook his head in frustration. His computer was still humming from last night's work, and the model simulation had not yet reached convergence. Looking down at his phone, he saw it was close to one o'clock in the afternoon. He was the only one in, and it was depressing sitting in the office with no one else around. While Jake didn't necessarily interact with his office mates, he enjoyed the hum of others working away. It would be another thirty minutes or so until Audria returned from teaching her class. This was probably the perfect time to stop. He stepped out of the office, grabbed the communal phone, and dialed the kinesiology department. It rang twice before the secretary picked up and transferred him to the archives library.

"Archives library. Haley Chamberlain speaking."

"Haley, what are you up to?" Jake asked.

"What am I up to? You should know. We're doing the exact same thing, trying to finish our graduate work. I would be a little bit closer if you would stop interrupting me."

"All true. Listen, can we hang by the tower for ten minutes? My mind is muddled, and nothing is happening," Jake pleaded.

"I'm busy too, you know. I can't just drop what I'm doing because you asked," she said playfully.

"Haley, you're smarter than me, and I need to bounce some ideas off you. Help me out," Jake said. He figured a small amount of ego stroking would be enough to convince her.

"All right. But you'll owe me fifteen minutes of your time later."

"Fifteen?"

"Interest, Jake. You're in finance, right? My time is worth 50 percent more than yours."

"That seems like a heavy price."

"This is a take-it-or-leave-it offer."

"Deal."

"Good. I'll see you there in five minutes."

CHAPTER 6

It took Jake about three minutes to walk from the business school to the base of the administrative tower. On his way out of the business school, Jake passed the student trading center and the stock ticker display that ran along the top of the glass enclosure. The trading center was designed to have the look and feel of a Wall Street trading floor, and the MBA students who were privileged enough to run the McCombs Investment Fund were highly sought-after recruits.

Jake and Haley had left Manhattan in the summer prior to grad school. They had lived through the ups and downs of the market cycle and seen the effects of those market cycles on the people in Manhattan and life in the Northeast. They had been privy to the bull run up through the real-estate bubble, the sense of optimism and invincibility that permeated the Wall Street ranks, and the subsequent crash that followed starting in August 2008. Those were frustrating times, and many friends lost their jobs, along with significant equity. While the market starting improving in late 2009, Jake and Haley had had their fill of Manhattan and the myopic existence of living on that overcrowded island. They had both realized there was more to life than living in a small apartment chasing small fortunes.

It had been Jake's experience working inside a major investment bank that motivated his choice to pursue a PhD. The inside access had allowed Jake to witness first-hand the issues with how equity valuations were done, the frequency with which traders manipulated stock prices, and the poor incentive structure for sell-side analysts. These were interesting subjects, all of which required more research to either solve the problems or at least address the reasons for why the problems existed in the first place. What he really wanted though was autonomy, the chance to work on the things that interested him, and were not assigned to him. Also to live in an area with better weather.

After Jake and Haley talked and discussed their long-term goals, the choice to move to Austin was obvious. It didn't take much for Haley to leave her advertising firm, and selling their one-bedroom was less challenging than they had anticipated given that the demand for New York real estate had started to return.

Haley tapped Jake on the shoulder. She had walked from the basement of the Anna Hiss Gym, where the archives library was located, fighting the undergraduate foot traffic, through the tower to the steps. She took a seat beside him, flipping her shoulder-length blond hair from right to left. With her long legs, defined from years of swimming, stretched out in front of her, she too stared out toward the expanse of downtown Austin.

"Haley, do you think we made a mistake coming here?" Jake asked, flicking the droplets of sweat off his forehead.

"No. And we've been through this before. You should expect this type of anguish. It's completely common. Doing quality research requires patience and persistence. Besides, do you really want to be back in Manhattan, working for someone else? The idea was to come to graduate school, earn the PhD, and become an expert in your field. Not have a boss. Remember."

Jake nodded his head in agreement.

"Well, the same holds true for me. I don't want to work for anyone but myself. Those days of corporate high-rises and political bullshit are over for me."

Jake loved Haley's dirty mouth and quick wit. For many that profanity could be considered uncouth. On Haley it was sexy.

"I know you're right, but I'm frustrated. I feel that I'm onto something great, but Eric believes that I face some significant hurdles. Even if I solve this one problem and convince myself of my findings, I still might not be able to convince others. I'm concerned that all this work won't result in anything, and I'll have spun my wheels for a year and a half. All the while, it looks as if Audria has been gift wrapped a dissertation topic and a future publication, and she will be pushed as the number-one recruit," Jake said, unable to contain the frustration in his voice.

"What does Dr. Rosen say?"

"He said that I had enough to finish the dissertation, and that in small parts the results are interesting enough that we can make a couple of papers out of it."

"Well, that's fucking good."

"Yes, but the main finding, the part that brings it all together, was something that he was very concerned about. He said it's too far reaching and too controversial. I can't accept that. That's the part I really care about, the part that makes it a top-quality publication. The other parts are just not as profound. I mean, they're good, but not *A*-level quality. I won't give up on it. Haley, you know what it's like. You don't want to accept something that's second best, even if it does get you to the end goal. It's not in our nature. Plus, it's hard to share this with your classmates since they're always looking to get a leg up on you, especially now with Audria and me most likely competing for the same jobs. That's why I come to you. Even though we're in different fields, I like to use you as a sounding board."

"I understand." She understood exactly what Jake was talking about since they had spent many hours discussing her research. She was focusing on the influence of the media in the early twentieth century on the perception of the female athlete. "Let's talk through it tonight. Remember, I won't understand most of the equations and the fucking Greek symbols that you scribble down on the Post-it notes, so explain it to me on a normal human level. If you can't explain the research in a simple, straightforward fashion, what good is it anyway?" She had that definitive tone that reminded Jake that she was always right.

"OK. Back to it then," Jake said. "Do you want to meet up at Town Lake before dinner to get in a quick seven-miler? We can run with the Wednesday night group, or it can be just the two of us." Jake's outlook on the day's work was improving with the thought of running on the Town Lake trail.

"Let's decide later. Come and get me at four." She gave him a kiss on the cheek and left for her office through the tower. Jake turned to watch her leave. She still looked the same as she had in college when they had first started dating. Jake knew that the same could not be said of him. While he was still in great shape by conventional standards, he was not satisfied with his current physical appearance. Studying for his qualifiers had added an extra ten pounds to his frame, and given the current state of affairs, it was unlikely to disappear anytime soon. While he had managed to change the extra weight into muscle, he knew he would never be the athlete he'd once been.

"That's why we run, Jake," he said to himself as he headed back to his office in the basement.

"Seven miles, starting at an eight-minute pace," the run leader said at the start of the trailhead. There was a group of about fifteen, and Jake, Haley, and her training partner, Brooke, were at the back of the pack. Brooke was also doing graduate work in kinesiology, but her focus was on the physical-education aspect of the discipline. Brooke had given Haley a ride down to the Mopac footbridge since Jake had stayed later than normal to give some of his undergraduate students some extra help after regular office hours. Brooke was complaining about her fellow graduate students, and although Jake wasn't an active participant in the conversation, he heard the words "lazy" and "deceitful." The running group started out north on Town Lake, running on the hardened dirt surface that made up the trail, past the rowing docks, toward the First Street bridge. As the run began, Jake was grateful for the lack of interaction with the other runners, allowing him some solitude within the group. This would give him time to collect his thoughts.

Jake had left his office with the same unacceptable result that had been appearing ever since he had started, in his opinion, improving the model. The results he had gone over with Eric were good, but they were also three months old. What he hadn't mention to Eric in his office was that he had been working on improving the model ever since sending his preliminary findings to him back in the summer. What Jake hadn't anticipated was that Eric would be concerned that the model was too good, that the pricing errors were too small.

Jake had also failed to mention to Eric that he had been working on getting those pricing errors even lower, to get statistical significance on all his pricing factors, the key variables that determine why asset prices move. However, he had run into an unexpected problem. The model was now failing. Every time he ran the program, there would be no output, no results, no estimation whatsoever. In an attempt to make things better, Jake had made things exponentially worse. Everything he had done had been theoretically correct, yet the empirical test of the model had ended up not only with a worse result but no results at all.

The First Street and Congress Avenue bridges came and went, and the eight-minute pace was keeping the mood in the group jovial. The Congress Avenue bridge was the turning point for the four-and-a-half-mile loop, which was the busiest and had the most foot traffic of all of the water crossings. Jake withdrew from his internal review to look for Haley and Brooke. They were just behind him, laughing about some recent presentation or another. Haley caught Jake's eye and smiled.

"Reflective, aren't we?" she stated.

"Yes, I guess," Jake replied. "I can't help thinking how complicated this has all become."

"By complicated, you mean your research and not our relationship," Haley said between breaths. "Why don't you share your problem with Brooke? Get a fresh perspective."

"Oh, I really don't want to hear this. There could be nothing more uninteresting," Brooke said sarcastically. Brooke was significantly shorter than Haley, requiring her stride turnover to be significantly quicker to stay on pace.

"Thanks for that. Given your obvious interest and acumen for the subject matter, I'll use small words. Everything about stock prices is about risk aversion. The more risk averse you are, the higher the rate of return you require on an investment. The higher the rate of return, the lower the price today. So as people become more risk averse, risky assets fall in price and riskless assets rise. The more risk seeking, the reverse. Every financial model starts there."

"That makes sense."

"No shit, professor." Haley added her two cents.

"I'm ignoring that last comment. I started my model with that simple premise, but then incorporated other factors that are important in pricing. Things like stock characteristics—how big or small a company is, how much debt it has, how long the CEO has been there—behavioral characteristics, political instability, and the Federal Reserve policy all help with fundamental predictions for how prices move. In fact, this was the basis for the first paper in my dissertation, understanding the difference between when financial markets behave normally versus nonnormally, from a statistical point of view."

"That doesn't seem too complicated to me. That's the process we all take as graduate students and researchers. Take a known starting point, a basis for the findings in our field, and expand upon it by asking a relevant question," Brooke said.

"Agreed, and if I had finished my dissertation as a two-paper submission, with that first paper and the second one on option prices and information feedback, I wouldn't have my current dilemma. Maybe I was greedy, but I wanted to make a real splash with this third paper. I wanted to develop a singular model that could explain all asset-price movements in all markets for every time period. A unifying theory of asset pricing," Jake said, noticing a slight pickup in his running tempo that matched his elevated his heart rate. "In doing so, I made the model potentially unwieldy because of the number of pricing factors and the size of the data. When it fails, which it has been doing with some alarming consistency and regularity, it's tough to find where the source of the error is coming from."

"How're you trying to solve the problem?"

"By going back to basics. Removing pricing factors, using less data, a smaller time sample. When I make the market smaller, I can get results. When I use less data, I can get results. When I make the model smaller, I get results. So the problem doesn't seem to be the data or the time period or the model in isolation. Yet when combined together, it fails. When I think back to the summer, the last time it worked properly, the first change

I made after that was adding a specific leverage variable. Leverage is critical because it relates to the potential risk of a crash in the market. Many papers have shown the adverse effect of too much leverage when it came to market crashes, restriction on investment, and asset-allocation decisions. That variable has to be included. Yet when I added it, it coincided with my current run of model failures. I can't take it out and revert to the old model because Eric has already rejected that. Thus my current quandary." Jake shrugged his shoulders.

"Well, I can't solve that problem, especially since my research only focuses on a sample size of sixty-seven survey respondents and no higher-order math, but I'm sure you'll figure it out. You finance guys think you know everything, so one little problem shouldn't hold you back."

Jake smiled in response. While Brooke was clearly mocking him, there was some truth in those words. Those in finance believed they were experts in everything. *Masters of the universe and all that.*

"We don't think; we know. You should know that."

"Typical response. You can't come up with something more creative than that?" Haley said.

"I'm not in marketing. I only speak plain truths." Jake loved this playful banter. It was one of his particular strengths that he was always able to get the final word in. It was also a reason that he had learned to enjoy presenting in the finance-seminar series. The ability to defend your ideas in front of other academics whose intent was to put holes into your theory and empirical work was a key skill for success in the profession. "A quick change in subject: Who were you girls bashing before? Your advisors? Competitors? Students?"

"Nobody you would know. Why don't you keep quiet and fix your problems in silence?" Haley said.

"All right. Plus, this running with you is like a fast walk," Jake said. He sped up just as the I-35 bridge was in sight. This resulted in a minor split of the group, but that was a common outcome, as this was about the halfway point in the run. His heart rate was about 150 beats a minute, and there was very little lactic acid buildup in his legs. The first three miles of the run allowed him to work out any aches and pains that normally existed at the start of any run, and he had reached a nice, smooth rhythm that allowed his mind to clear and focus. Immediately it went back to his current predicament.

There was another issue when it came to highlighting and finding the problem. Each time he ran the model, it took considerable time to finish. The smaller models, with less data over smaller time periods, took the better part of three hours to run. The old model, without the leverage variable, with all the market data, took several days to complete. He wasn't sure how long the new model took to run because it kept failing. Jake believed the program must have entered an infinite loop or resulted in a singular matrix that the minimization function was unable to invert.

Jake knew that fixing these types of problems was fairly simple if the objective function was simple and the number of parameters involved was small. Jake would just put markers in his code that would report back to him the intermediate values of his objective function and the key parameters that were allowed to change over the course of each model iteration. When the program stalled, Jake could backtrack what each value was and determine where the problem lay. However, given the complexity of his objective function, determining the course of the error was now very complicated and time consuming. At this point, Jake was unclear if the problem was with a flaw in the code or the minimization function or whether it was just impossible to solve. Of the three possibilities, the first was the easiest to fix. If it was the last, it would mean having to give up and settle for a second-rate dissertation.

That thought was seriously troubling, and Jake pushed it to the back of his mind. Turning off the bridge and running past the dog park along Riverside Drive, the group began to string out, with some of the lead runners dropping below the seven-minute pace. With just under three miles to go, Jake couldn't hold the front-runner's pace for the rest of the run but held a seven-fifteen pace with two other runners. It was the heart of rush hour, and traffic was building on Riverside Drive in both directions, leading to Mopac and I-35. Jake took the right that led them back to the trailhead. This small stretch was Jake's favorite, especially in the summer, as it was shaded and quiet. The shade lasted until the Hilton hotel and First Street bridge.

The problem must be in the code. I know I can replicate market movements. I just have to overcome the complexity of the problem. Keep it simple. Fix some of the parameters, don't let them vary, and see if the simulation survives. Jake tried to reassure himself that this was the way to go. He relaxed and tried to pick up his pace. Whenever he had a problem with programming, his tried and true way was to reduce what was allowed to vary and slowly relax the assumptions of the model to get to the desired solution. It was time consuming but always got results. Even though he was up against the time constraint of the forthcoming presentation and the job market, using this approach was the right way to go.

The idea is good; don't rush it just because you fear the downside. The upside is too large to ignore. Great research takes time. Maybe it was the natural endorphin high from the run or the sense of a plan, but Jake felt better. There was a mile and a half to go, and he increased his pace close to seven minutes per mile. One of the two runners with him fell off the pace. The remaining runner was slightly older than Jake but had that prototypical runner's body—no shoulders and long limbed. He was also breathing heavily. Jake decided to test him.

"Nice day. Do you think we can catch the three ahead of us?" Jake asked, probing for weakness.

"No. They're at least three hundred yards up the trail." The man had responded quickly but seemed at ease. Jake was disappointed. It was a well-known tactic in running to talk to your opponent to assess his or her current stress level. One-word responses were a typical tell that the runner was close to oxygen debt.

"How far behind is the other guy?" the skinny guy asked. Jake turned his head and almost immediately knew it was a mistake. His fellow runner picked up his tempo just as they came around the bend and over the dip that brought the footbridge into view. He had gotten a gap. There was less than half a mile left, including the footbridge. The head of the group was already on the bridge, and his competitor had about ten yards on him.

The prior six miles were now fully in Jake's legs, and his heart was pumping close to its max. He had never been a gifted long-distance runner but always had sprinter speed. However, today was not his day. His competitor furthered his lead, and Jake's legs felt dead when he got onto the bridge. The finish was slightly downhill, and he finished winded but satisfied. With his hands on his knees and his head down, Jake tried to recover his breath as the guy came over, told him, "Good run," and jogged off. Jake smiled and shook his head. He should never have been outsmarted like that, but there was solace in the fact that the guy was probably faster than he was anyway. An under-fifty-one-minute run for the seven-mile loop was always something to be pleased about.

There were many people milling about, either waiting to go on their runs or just finishing. Jake got a drink from the cooler, which was always filled with some sort of electrolyte drink provided by Run Tex, the local running store, and he waited patiently for Haley and Brooke. They came in about five minutes later, never deviating from the eight-minute pace. They looked tired but happy. The heat was inescapable in Austin, and midafternoon runs in August were the hottest of the year.

They got drinks, and Brooke told Haley she would see her tomorrow. They headed for the parking lot, where their old Jeep was parked. It was just before six o'clock, and the traffic on Mopac was thinning out.

"What should we do for dinner?" Haley asked.

"I thought you were cooking for me. I've had a rough day. Plus, I ran faster than you," Jake said. He kept his face passive but serious.

"You're kidding, right?" She looked at him from the passenger seat as they made their way to the top of Mopac and the on ramp.

"No. I would like lasagna from scratch."

"Balls. How about some dry dog food? I can whip that up in no time," she calmly said back.

"What sort of wife are you? A year plus into our marriage and you've stopped making me dinner. I feel cheated."

"When you marry someone for their looks, you can't expect Betty Crocker in the kitchen."

"I didn't marry you for your looks. I married you for your brains." Jake continued to tease her

"Balls again. You only saw my ass the first time we met. It took you a week before your eyes went above shoulder level. While complimenting me on my superior intelligence is nice, you're still not getting sex tonight. How about some sushi?" She would not be baited.

"Sushi sounds great. I believe sex is still on the table, though."

"I'll be the judge of that. Remember that you owe me fifteen minutes of your time, to be used at my discretion, in exchange for our earlier meeting," she said, smugly playing her trump card. Jake could only laugh. He had forgotten.

"Did you meet with Dr. Rosen after we spoke earlier?" she asked, turning the direction of the conversation back to more serious topics.

"I did, but only briefly. He was teaching two classes today and was between the two. I only updated him on the status of the program, which was still running at the time, and my plan of action when it finishes. He didn't really add much but told me to get back to him when there was more. The program keeps dying, but I'm going to go back to my tried-and-true debugging method to make improvements. I think that I've been so focused on getting this solved before the job market that I forgot that the process takes time. I don't want to rush it to meet some imposed deadline. Better to get it right and reap the rewards over time, even if there's a short-term cost."

"I'm happy for you. I think that's the right approach. Who knows? Maybe you'll find something quickly given the new outlook."

The rest of the drive home was quiet and slow. The top of Mopac was always congested due to the intersection of Highway 183, so Jake wound their way east and north through town to Cullen Avenue and their two-bedroom condo. They had bought the condo over two years ago, three months before they were married. That summer seemed a long time ago, passing qualifiers and heading back to Connecticut to stay with Jake's family for a month before the wedding. The time was so peaceful and relaxing, a great break from the stress of the prior months. Now this new stress had entered Jake's life, and, just as with any prior problem, it was a matter of handling the stress, breaking down the elements of his misunderstanding, and coming up with a solution. Today, unlike the prior month, Jake felt ready to find where the mistakes started and in doing so begin to unravel a solution.

CHAPTER 8

Mr. Jones's name was not Jones, but that did not matter. His identity was not important, because he didn't have a driver's license or social security card or pay taxes. He was paid through a holding company of Franklin Insurance based in the Cayman Islands, with the money then transferred to an account in Switzerland. He was a ghost, both on paper and in reality.

Before he was Mr. Jones, he had been part of the Special Air Service, the elite United Kingdom military forces, and had operated in Dublin, Beirut, Chechnya, and Johannesburg. He had been assigned to 22 SAS squadron—the counterterrorism unit—and had been one of the best assaulters the division had ever had. This kind of specialized training made finding work in the private sector no challenge at all; intelligence gathering was a booming business. The fact that he looked like no one and everyone was a distinct advantage. There was very little point in applying for this kind of work with a large scar across your face.

Not that he had needed to apply. He had been found, and that worked out perfectly for Mr. Jones, since he was born and bred to follow, monitor, and, if need be, take out potential human targets. He could blend in with any crowd and disappear into any shadow, and he always completed his assignments. He was the perfect dark analyst.

His job was to observe Dr. Lancaster: to report her movements, activity, whom she spoke with, whom she fucked, and to assess her daily emotional state. He had been assigned to her many months prior to their meeting in April, ever since she had been earmarked for a potential position with the Markov Group. Now that she was an official member, his assignment hadn't changed, but it had expanded. He was to continue to follow her, report on her movements, and make sure that she was doing as predicted. In addition, he needed to report on the people she interacted with and begin to build files on them. It was critical that her involvement with the Markov Group remain clandestine, and that meant making sure that those people, especially at the New York Federal Reserve, knew nothing about her second job.

Mr. Jones never went into the Franklin Insurance offices. He didn't need to. His reports were filed electronically, along with any surveillance photos or audio files. He never received feedback on the reports, and his communication with his superiors was limited. Unlike many of the employees of Franklin Insurance, Mr. Jones knew his boss. Their interaction was sparse and usually one sided. Mr. Jones didn't care about the motivation of his superior or his ultimate goal. Mr. Jones only ever cared about the assignment.

From his perspective, Michelle Lancaster lived a very boring and predictable life. Other than her involvement with the Markov Group, there was nothing particularly interesting or outstanding about her daily movements. She was an important person doing important-person things, but she went about her day as any other person would. She was prompt and followed a regimented routine. She didn't shop for anything particularly unusual, engage in any bizarre activity, or have any regular, or irregular, sexual encounters. It was a fairly routine assignment, and one thing the SAS had taught Mr. Jones was patience. It had also taught him how to work with a knife. He preferred a knife to a gun. It elicited a better fear response.

He had used the knife twice in the service of the Markov Group. The last time was to extract information out of a junior senator from Ohio. The man had screamed and begged and pleaded. The senator was grotesque, a cartoon of a cartoon. You get to the real character of a man when he is naked with a knife at his genitals. Mr. Jones didn't care. He made no judgments, just did what he was told.

The people Michelle Lancaster interacted with were just as predictable as she was, and from his initial assessment, they didn't appear to suspect anything about her other life. Mr. Jones had targeted the ten people she interacted with the most and had begun his data gathering on all of them. This included the standard computer and phone taps, bank records and credit-card activity, and video and audio recording at their places of work and home residences. The software that received all this information would start to build a behavioral profile that could then be analyzed for potential threats to the Markov Group. If any person started to show patterns of a potential threat, more advanced surveillance and data-gathering techniques would be enacted, and Mr. Jones much preferred that kind of assignment.

If the threat became real, Mr. Jones got to use the full extent of his skills, which hadn't happened for a while. Consequently, he continued to wake up each morning with an orange-flavored acidic taste that was his signal of the extra release of adrenaline that comes with a heighted state of alertness. All of his training and experience had taught him that the most likely time for something to go wrong was when everything looked too good to be true. The routine and commonplace of following Michelle Lancaster over the past year had suddenly brought about the arrival of this taste—his body's way of telling his mind to become extra prepared.

"In 1985, Rajnish Mehra and Edward Prescott published a paper called 'The Equity Risk Premium: A Puzzle' in the *Journal of Monetary Economics*. The authors concluded that the current return on equity assets is inconsistent with general equilibrium models. In other words, the return on stocks is just too high.

"This implies one of two things. First, investors and consumption behavior are not rational, driving the price of equities to be significantly overvalued. We do not like irrational explanations, since irrationality does not fit in general framework for how we think the world works. Second, investor and consumption behavior has not been adequately modeled, and we've been trying to find a model that could explain this behavior." Jake addressed his class, emphasizing a critical and, as of yet, unsolved problem in finance.

He enjoyed talking about the current and important findings in the finance literature to his class after addressing the main topics of the day. Today was a discussion on portfolio formation, the decision to hold stocks or bonds, and how mean-variance analysis is used to construct an efficient portfolio. This led to a question about the returns on stocks in general, which led Jake to talk about the equity premium puzzle.

Jake's investment class was full. He had starting teaching investments in his third year and over the past two years, the news that his class was a must-have had traveled along the student-body grapevine. The rumor was that he was smart, energetic, and exceedingly witty. At least that is what it said on ratemyprofessor.com. The distribution of his class was also more female oriented than most, as most of the female student body had noticed he was better looking than the typical PhD student. This was something Dr. Rosen had commented on after Jake passed his qualifiers, noting that it was a potential advantage he could use in the future. Jake never thought of himself as handsome, but he knew that the girls were looking. Haley always told him that it was his confidence that made him attractive, although she didn't complain about his physique. Overall, he was an imposing figure to his students, who were not prepared for a twenty-nine-year-old who looked more like an athlete than a professor.

Jake always liked to emphasize his physique by wearing fitted shirts to teach in. With his hair shorn down almost to his scalp and no facial hair, he presented a distinct and sculpted figure in class. Of course, this was all part of his act, to initially both scare and endear him to his students. Being a young instructor had some advantages, but most students didn't give young instructors the respect they showed his older, gray-haired colleagues. As such, Jake went into class with energy and aggression, challenging his students as if they were Wall Street traders themselves. While this challenging method unsettled even the most assured students, in the end, even the surliest undergraduates appreciated the style and Jake's enthusiasm for the subject matter.

"So why are equity returns so high?" Jake asked the class. There was a general murmur, a lot of blank stares, and no direct answer. "Am I going to have to randomly call on someone? Well, am I?"

"Because people like stocks," a tired-looking, tall junior said.

"What on earth does that mean?" Jake said in his sarcastic, this-person-is-an-idiot tone.

"Um, because they're always looking for the next Google or Microsoft," the student answered.

"Ok, that is a little better. Go on," Jake urged the student on, rolling his hands over and over.

"Well, investors are buying stocks with the hope of huge returns and are willing to bear the risk."

"Correct. And if I may add to that, a willingness not just to bear risk but to pay for it as well. There was another implication from the Mehra and Prescott findings: equity returns can be explained if investors have a risk-aversion coefficient that allows for risk-seeking behavior. Specifically, we define risk-seeking behavior as a willingness to enter into an investment where the expected rate of return is negative. Can anyone think of an investment that conforms to risk-seeking behavior?" Jake asked.

"There's an obvious one: lotteries," said a slim blond girl who was wearing next to nothing. "the probability of winning the lottery is far lower than the expected payout."

"Exactly. Buying a lottery ticket is risk-seeking behavior. Now, isn't it also possible that there are a number of stocks that exhibit features similar to a lottery?" Jake postulated. "Now, I know that we're out of time, but think about how that behavior relates to investors and if it differentiates them from gamblers at a casino."

It was 10:49 a.m., and the students began the noisy process of gathering their books, bags, and themselves to head for the door. Several students said good-bye to Jake and said they would see him Thursday. No one hung around to ask any other questions since there were no upcoming assignments due, which allowed Jake a clean passage back to his office.

As he approached his door, he noticed that Audria's door was open. He was unwilling to get into a discussion with her right now, especially since the job market was rapidly approaching and their talks would inevitably end on this topic. Jake was tired of hearing about how nervous and excited she was for the upcoming conference, how great the results of her paper were, and how nice it was to have a revise-and-resubmit at a top-tier publication. What was equally annoying was her fishing about the status of his work. It was common for PhD students to dig into the research of others since each student was in competition for placement and publications. The program at the University of Texas was not as cutthroat as, say, Columbia's, but the competition and pressure for success were as high and as stressful as they were at any program in the country.

Jake quietly turned the key in the lock of his office door and silently went in. Teaching was a nice break from the frustrations of his research, but it was time to get back to it.

For the past week, he'd set up thirty separate estimation procedures that could run simultaneously, each run on the full model but with each one excluding a critical pricing factor. At the end of the simulation, if one of the models failed, or had significantly lower pricing errors, then he could identify which pricing factor was causing the problem. Underlying everything in the model was the idea of investor risk aversion. As he mentioned to Brooke, Understanding how investors' risk appetites changed was critical to understanding why certain assets moved up and others moved down. If the world could be split into two types of people, risk averse and risk neutral, and two types of assets, risky and risk-free, you could model how portfolios and prices changed by the change in the risk aversion of the average investor.

However, observing risk aversion, and especially risky behavior, was impossible and could only be inferred ex post. Meaning, it is only when you've broken both legs do you realizes that big wave surfing was not a good choice. From a financial standpoint, only after the 2000 tech bubble burst was it obvious that investors were too risk seeking in buying Internet stocks. In 2007 and 2008, it wasn't obvious the value of real estate was too high, in 2009 it was.

His computer was humming and whining along. It had been doing this for three straight days, and he had maxed out the clock and the CPU so it would run at full capacity. The hard disk spinning away had a soporific effect on him, and his mind would drift back to days prior to grad school—life in Manhattan, the glory days of college, and the first time he saw Haley. Jake remembered that he had excelled at two things in college, soccer and chasing girls. His freshman-year grades were proof of his commitment to those two pursuits. That had all changed when he saw Haley sophomore year walking across the varsity fields.

The noise of the computer's fan stopping and the abrupt silence brought him back to the present. He looked at his screen and saw that each estimation had finished. His left-hand screen showed the following:

CONVERGENCE SUCCESS	Model 1	FIT RMSE	355.9932
CONVERGENCE SUCCESS	Model 2	FIT RMSE	389.7374
CONVERGENCE SUCCESS	Model 3	FIT RMSE	391.8652
CONVERGENCE SUCCESS	Model 4	FIT RMSE	363.2671
CONVERGENCE SUCCESS	Model 5	FIT RMSE	345.6826
CONVERGENCE SUCCESS	Model 6	FIT RMSE	336.5361
CONVERGENCE SUCCESS	Model 7	FIT RMSE	313.1655
CONVERGENCE SUCCESS	Model 8	FIT RMSE	375.1336
CONVERGENCE SUCCESS	Model 9	FIT RMSE	336.3356
CONVERGENCE SUCCESS	Model 10	FIT RMSE	398.7522
CONVERGENCE SUCCESS	Model 11	FIT RMSE	369.0846
CONVERGENCE SUCCESS	Model 12	FIT RMSE	350.0554
CONVERGENCE SUCCESS	Model 13	FIT RMSE	333.3432
CONVERGENCE SUCCESS	Model 14	FIT RMSE	331.2326
CONVERGENCE SUCCESS	Model 15	FIT RMSE	348.9532
CONVERGENCE SUCCESS	Model 16	FIT RMSE	314.5479
CONVERGENCE SUCCESS	Model 17	FIT RMSE	320.5939
CONVERGENCE SUCCESS	Model 18	FIT RMSE	385.2101
CONVERGENCE SUCCESS	Model 19	FIT RMSE	345.5169
CONVERGENCE SUCCESS	Model 20	FIT RMSE	331.1123
CONVERGENCE SUCCESS	Model 21	FIT RMSE	397.8299
CONVERGENCE SUCCESS	Model 22	FIT RMSE	301.4451
CONVERGENCE SUCCESS	Model 23	FIT RMSE	303.5264
CONVERGENCE SUCCESS	Model 24	FIT RMSE	300.9979
CONVERGENCE SUCCESS	Model 25	FIT RMSE	375.8551
CONVERGENCE SUCCESS	Model 26	FIT RMSE	377.9183
CONVERGENCE SUCCESS	Model 27	FIT RMSE	347.8922
CONVERGENCE SUCCESS	Model 28	FIT RMSE	392.8886
CONVERGENCE SUCCESS	Model 29	FIT RMSE	377.9202
CONVERGENCE SUCCESS	Model 30	FIT RMSE	314.6901

The FIT RMSE result, or root-mean-square error, represented the amount of pricing error and how well his model explained the data. A perfect result would be equal to zero or NaN, which was impossible, since there was no such thing as perfect model fit. Each model had successfully converged, but based on the fit numbers, no model was apparently better than another. It was also clear that no model had failed since no NAN appeared.

Jake was pissed. He had expected some variability in his results. He had gotten none. In essence, each model by itself was interesting and had some predictive elements, but looking at all the results as a complete system revealed nothing important. The whole ideas was to try to understand why prices, or the stock markets, moved in the way they did. Right now he was no closer to finding a solution.

One of the key variables that should explain asset price movements was corporate earning announcements. Jake's expectation was that this variable should always matter in the pricing of assets, especially when there was a surprise, regardless of what else was included in the model. The problem was that in model 1 this factor was significant and positive, but in model 13 it was insignificant. Model 1 excluded the measure for industrial production, and model 13 excluded a measure for stock volatility. *How can the exclusion of one factor versus another could have such an effect on corporate earning announcements just doesn't make sense. Not only that, the results are meaningless.* His anger was beginning to build.

Just for reference, Jake opened up the estimation where every factor was included. The screen showed the following:

MODEL FIT	TOLERANCE LEVEL	STEP
NaN	NaN	

When he had included all the factors together, the complete model failed by not finishing, by not converging and giving a model fit number. So he could not get anything of value from the full model, and when he excluded one factor, each of the thirty models finished, but the results were useless. *Maybe I should just write up the results and accept a second-rate dissertation and be ranked second for the job market. UNC-Wilmington, here I come. Damn it!*

The shock that went through Jake's arm lasted for twelve seconds. He had banged his fist so hard on the desk in frustration that the sound had reverberated through the small corridor, leaving him with two unpleasant outcomes: the aforementioned numbness in his right arm and the image of Audria out of the corner of his eye. Unfortunately this wasn't a temporary mirage. She was standing by his door with a large smile on her face, clearly waiting for him to notice her. Audria was used to people noticing her.

Audria's mother was from Turkey, her father from Italy, which helped explain her olive complexion, dark hair, and blue eyes. She had a strong, distinctive face that sat upon a small but voluptuous frame. Her accent was noticeable but not overwhelming. Her voice, combined with her physical attributes, gave the impression of a serene, easygoing individual. However, she was opinionated and strong willed and rarely gave of her time unless it was for her own direct benefit. These qualities had been developed through years of schooling and success and were why she was so determined and convinced of her own abilities.

Jake at times thought her desire outreached her grasp, but this was not necessarily a bad quality to have.

"What's up, Audria?" he asked subtly trying to shake out his arm.

"I was curious to see how your research is coming along. You've been so quiet about it. Are you not nervous about the presentation in front of the faculty before the job market?" She was smirking, trying to sound offhanded. An image of a killer whale playing with a seal entered Jake's mind. He was going to do everything he could to avoid giving her the opportunity to tell him how great her research was, while also not revealing how bad his was at this moment.

"Of course I want to do well. I wouldn't say that I was nervous. I know that it's important to leave a good impression, but I think it's more important to do the research well, irrespective of a set timeline." It was Jake's stock response to this line of questioning. "How are your classes?" he asked, deliberately trying to change the subject.

"Classes? They aren't that important right now. I'm sure Dr. Rosen doesn't ask you about your teaching."

"In fact, he does."

"Well, for us the research is just much more important right now. Would you not agree?" She leaned casually in his doorway, not directly looking at him.

Jake realized she was going to tell him how great things were regardless of how he tried to stall her. Better a quick death than something more long and drawn out. Succumb to the orca. "How's your work coming along? Is Dr. Tacker happy with your progress?" he asked begrudgingly.

"Oh, he's always asking for this and that. You know, he wants to make it just right to give it the best shot at multiple publications," she said. Jake knew that the likelihood that her papers would be published was high given that she was working with Tacker. He was an associate editor with *Journal of Financial Economics*, one of the top academic publications in the field. "He really seems to think there's a significant marginal contribution to the capital structure literature by examining how capital structure has changed through time. I'm looking forward to hearing what other schools have to say." She was almost bursting with enthusiasm.

Jake was skeptical that Audria had come up with the idea herself, but frankly that was between her and Tacker. "I'm sure you'll do well. Listen, I have to get back to this, otherwise I'll have nothing to show at the faculty presentation and American Finance Association conference, and consequently no job interviews." He said the exact thing that he knew she wanted to hear and at the same time would end the conversation.

"Really? Well, I'm sure you'll figure something out." She left the office with a smile on her face and an annoying look of superiority in her eyes. She practically floated to her office.

Jake shook his head. He should be happy for her success, but her voice was beginning to grate on him, as was the way her hair flipped up in the back. There wasn't anything about her not to like, but the pressure of the research and the upcoming job market was definitely not helping their working relationship or their daily interactions.

CHAPTER 10

Duncan Chamberlain was similar to his older brother in many respects, but their subtle differences were enough to make them truly distinct. Duncan had also gone to Emory as an undergrad, played soccer, and majored in economics. He liked to point out that he had gotten a double major in mathematics and was summa cum laude to Jake's magna; Jake liked to point out he was an inch taller. Similar to Jake, he had followed his finance path to New York, and he was a trader at a small boutique firm located in mid-Manhattan. Unlike Jake, he had no intention of leaving. Duncan had the ideal temperament for trading. He was very even keeled, rarely losing his cool, and he always left his work behind when the day was done.

Success as a trader can come down to some very simple, almost cliché rules: Never get emotional about a position. Do not ride a losing position. Be opportunistic when it comes to taking risk. Always be disciplined. Duncan was a very successful trader because of, but also irrespective of, those rules. Jake had the impression that Duncan succeeded because he was just good and not because there was a specific formula in play. Duncan had the ability to assess the emotion of stock movement, and his intuition allowed him to be very successful, especially compared to the other traders that sat in his row. Others could follow him, but it was the notion of timing and the size of the trade that made him stand out. Over the past three years, he had been promoted to junior partner and now had a computer mimicking his trades to add profit—of which he got an additional 20 percent—to the firm.

Jake and Duncan liked to get into spirited debates about the market, with Jake's high-level academic view meeting Duncan's street-level practical viewpoint. There wasn't a natural meeting in the middle, but the exchange was always helpful for both, since it provided Jake with research ideas and Duncan a theoretical foundation for what he was observing.

Duncan wasn't surprised when he received a call as he was walking from the Flatiron District to catch his subway back up to his apartment on the Upper West Side. Jake usually called after the market closed, typically on an active trading day.

"What's up?" Duncan answered with his characteristic emotionless tone after another trading day. Duncan never wasted energy by adding excessive adjectives or flourish when he spoke. Time was money and he got to the point.

"Nothing really. Don't want to take up too much of your time, but I wanted to run a couple of things by you," Jake said.

"OK. I'm on the subway in three or four minutes."

"All right. I'll give you the overview, but this may require a bit longer conversation later."

"OK."

"Have you noticed anything bizarre in stocks with sensitivity to negative skewness?" Jake asked. Jake was deliberately probing Duncan for a reaction to one of his pricing factors. In the thirty-simulation run he had just conducted, negative skewness had been one of the more consistent significant factors across all the simulations.

"I don't know what that means, so I can't say I look at it directly. Maybe I do, and it's reflected in a measure that I do pay attention to, like put-and-call volatility spread differentials. Give me something more concrete so I can understand what you're talking about."

"Well, stocks that are sensitive to negative skewness are going to react sharply to market downturns. If the sensitivity or the factor loading is negative, then the stocks should respond well with a market correction. If the sensitivity is positive, then the stock performance will be very negative. These stocks should behave normally in normal market conditions, but when there's something outsized, they have unusual return distributions, especially when the market tanks."

"So these are stocks that are defensive, held specifically for protection against market downturns?"

"You could say that."

"Well, that's interesting; although I couldn't say I've seen it on a portfolio level. I've seen certain stocks behave, let's say, abnormally, based on their fundamentals. For example, I've seen two stocks, different industry, size, etc., behaving in a way that was very different from their industry peers. Recently, a biotech firm had significant positive performance when there was a small correction in the market. It couldn't have been anticipated. The stock didn't have a high beta, and there was no corporate announcement or liquidity event. It just appreciated in an extreme fashion when the market sold off. Same thing happened with a financial stock."

"How often do you notice this? Are you able to capitalize on this phenomenon?"

"Actually, yes. When you observe an intraday run on a stock, something out of the blue, it usually always trends in the direction of the surprise movement. I just jump on the train and get off by the end of the day."

"Is there a reversal toward the end of the day, or the next trading session?"

"Typically, no. It just hangs at this new level as if it's a correction in the price. Interestingly, it happens across industry, to firms of different size and capital structure and inherent volatility. I haven't noticed any pattern to why it occurs. There certainly isn't a technical marker, such as the firm falling below its fifty-day moving average. But once you see a stock moving in the given direction, and it could be up as well as down, you never fight it intraday."

"That's what I thought. I have a strong loading on this negative skewness factor. It's very strong across most of my models and appears important in the pricing of many assets."

"What do you mean, most of your models? Try to make the answer quick."

"Well, I've run into this problem and am trying to untangle the root cause. I ran thirty models, and negative skewness is significant in twenty-two of the models. Same sign and almost the same significance level. In the other eight, the coefficient is close to zero. The only difference is that in the other eight, I excluded either a measure of debt-to-equity ratio that's firm or country specific, or spreads on investment-grade bonds over treasuries, or the term structure of volatility, or a measure of implicit leverage— you get the idea. The correlations among these variables aren't high enough to cause an econometric issue. Also this isn't unique to negative skewness; it occurs with every one of my pricing factors."

"Time's up. I'm about to enter the station, so I can't offer much more," Duncan said. "I can't help you with your econometric issue, but when I think about the market, whether it's stocks or other assets, I always think about being on the right side of a trade. And that's regardless of the fundamentals of the stock in the short term and holding only fundamentally sound stocks for the long term. For short-term trading, it's really about pain."

"Pain?"

"Yes. Who is receiving the pain when something moves? The more people who are on the wrong side of the trade, the more pain will be inflicted and felt, and the more the asset will move to the point of max pain. The market always finds the point of max pain. I try to always be on the opposite side. Look, we can talk more about this later, but I don't want to miss this train. Bye."

Jake's phone went dead, revealing that Duncan had hung up. In their prior talks, they had always talked about how certain stocks were traded on a given day or why one stock outperformed when the fundamentals hadn't changed. Usually Jake was calling to find out how Duncan had done when there was a significant move in the market. Today was the first time that Duncan had used the word *pain* in describing the trading process. Something about that word stuck with him. *Pain is a human emotion, and the market isn't a person with feelings.* However, even though the market doesn't have emotion, it can certainly be driven by it. Duncan may not have been able to help him econometrically, but the discussion did trigger something in Jake's mind about how to approach his problem.

CHAPTER 11

A s Jake mulled over his brother's words, he thought about how people act when they are put under stress—how their behaviors and actions can result in irrational outcomes, outcomes that would be inconceivable when they are relaxed. He remembered reading about prospect theory, which Daniel Kahneman and Amos Tversky had introduced decades ago as a challenge to the classical view in economics. The idea was that individuals incorporate psychological biases into their decision making, especially the notion that an equivalent loss always hurts more that an equivalent gain. Expanding upon these notions had resulted in an increase in popularity in behavioral finance topics, and these concepts had been used to explain financial phenomena such as the equity premium puzzle. Jake didn't necessarily agree with the behavioral finance approach, since it was typically used in one-off situations and couldn't be generalized, but he believed there could be some benefit if it was used correctly.

Specifically, when people feel pain, they behave in a way that is different from when they do not. Pain is not a variable that can be measured, but normality is. When assets are behaving normally, investors are not feeling pain. When assets experience nonnormal returns, some investors will feel pain, and those investors are on the losing side of the nonnormal move. When lots of investors feel pain the market crashes, the ultimate nonnormal move.

The following day Jake returned to his office ready to dissect the problem by incorporating this idea of different behavior for different markets. He didn't have to teach, so he buried himself in his computer screens. Jake turned on the CPU and faced the three monitors that were connected to his workstation. As the computer turned on and came to life, the left monitor screen was filled with the code, the central monitor gave the updates on the status of the minimization, and the right reported on the values of the parameters. It was times like these that Jake was happy he had three monitors. Having to switch back and forth between programs was annoying and inefficient, plus Jake always liked the way the monitors looked. It reminded him of his old trading desk at Morgan Stanley.

Jake started writing code that would separate data into two minimizations. One minimization focused only on asset movements in normal markets, the non-painful markets, and a second worked on nonnormal movements, or pain markets. Normal markers could be considered boring markets, when the market just plodded along without any large sell-offs or price jumps. These were the conditions most people want; where the stock market wasn't the lead story on network programing, wasn't the number one conversation at the water cooler, or a trending topic on twitter. Nonnormal markets occurred when something unexpected happened, leading to a price outcome that most market participants were not prepared for. Those were the days that always captured national news attention and pundits that had little to no idea about how markets worked would be screaming about another financial collapse. That would induce panic in the average investor, and perpetuate the irrationality cycle.

After incorporating this sorting condition into his code, Jake hit the F8 key to run the program step by step. Going through the code in this fashion would be exceedingly time consuming and immensely tedious, but Jake suspected that he would find the root cause of the problem this way. *I am going to solve this pricing problem today. I am going to write a great dissertation, and I will be the top job candidate.*

As the computer hummed away, his mind drifted back to Haley walking across the varsity fields, the first time they'd met, almost ten years ago. Why this image popped into his mind constantly during this laborious testing process was something he couldn't explain. Every sensation now was almost the opposite of what he'd experienced then. His office was cold, smelled like antiseptic spray and B.O. (many of the grad students had poor hygiene that emanated and consumed the office), and had horrible fluorescent lighting. Ten years ago the sun had been shining on a hot August day, and the fields had recently been mowed. Maybe his mind was compensating with a positive image because of all the stress and failure he had experienced over the past several months.

He remembered catching her walking across the field while his team was playing six versus six small-sided games. He was immediately distracted and stopped playing, tracking her rather than the player who had just dribbled by him. As a teammate was about to yell at him, he'd stopped midsentence, seeing what Jake was looking at. After a second, no one was playing, and all were watching her walk away from them. She then turned back to look, blessed with that instinct all women possess when they know they are being checked out. Most men are cowards, especially college-aged men, and half his teammates had done the quick-turn-around-and-look-the-other-way move that immediately revealed that they were guilty of sizing her up. Jake had just stood there, transfixed, and she had stared right back at him. From that point on, he had known what he wanted in life.

The simulation hummed along, trying to minimize the pricing errors to conform to the structure of the normal and nonnormal models. Jake sat back in his chair thinking about her long legs, shoulders that looked as if they were cut from granite, and the liquid blueish green eyes that left him speechless and in pain. The pain was good. It was the kind of pain that came with longing and patience to truly win a woman's heart. That pain was very different from the *pain* that came from the financial markets.

He rolled his neck and closed his eyes. It was ten thirty, and he had been going at it for four straight hours. Jake opened his eyes and focused on the ceiling, and then on the floor, and finally on the wall. Constantly staring at the monitors was slowly deteriorating his eyesight, and these little exercises helped to prevent further deterioration. At least that is what the optometrist told him.

Jake stood up and walked out to call Haley. He had just gotten through seventeen iterations, and nothing anomalous had happened. He wanted to stay late to at least get to the failure, although he knew it typically took two to three days for a successful simulation. Their conversation was brief, and they decided to skip lunch. She was also in the middle of her research, going through some old newspapers, and had no problems staying late. They said good-bye, and Jake went back to his office. He minimized one of the windows to check how the market was doing, saw it was slightly up, and then checked ESPN and the BBC for any new sports or worldwide news stories. Arsenal had started the premier league season slowly again, but that wasn't surprising, so he went back to the program.

Jake was not looking forward to starting back up again. He had a firm rule about research and was about to break it. He knew that working on the same task for more than four hours usually becomes counterproductive, as more mistakes are typically made than advances because the mind is tired of processing the same information and becomes lazy. He should go hit the weights and not wait until the afternoon, yet Jake would not be satisfied until he reached failure, so he plunged back into the code. This same persistence had finally won him Haley. She had made him work for it every step of the way. *She still does.*

As the hours passed, with each evolution of the code, prices were updated and model parameters were fitted, and Jake checked all of the key indicators. The normal models had lower fit numbers than the nonnormal model. *Good.* This conformed to his expectation and current economic theory; normal markets are just easier to forecast. Jake felt his eyes tiring, soreness in his lower back, and he was regretting skipping lunch. He felt himself getting agitated that he was going to miss his workout, which would make him angry and ultimately cause him to sleep poorly.

What the fuck?

It was two thirty when Jake noticed something with the forty-fifth iteration. The nonnormal simulation now had a *lower* fit number than the normal simulation. He hadn't noticed initially and, scrolling back through the prior model fits, noted that it had first taken place on the forty-third iteration. There was a huge drop in the fit and a massive change in four of the underlying pricing factors: the leverage variable and three key interaction terms related to very specific behaviors of the Federal Reserve, large institutional investors, and market microstructure activity. *This isn't possible. It's contrary to all economic theory.*

Jake hit Escape to stop the program. He had not seen that before, not in any of his prior error checks or any of the prior results. It was a drastic change in the values, and a massive improvement in the model fit. It was his first real breakthrough in solving the problem. *OK. I not sure what this means, but we have something now. There's something special about leverage, the Fed, institutional investors, and how people trade. Let the program run and see what happens.* Jake hit the F5 key to let the program continue.

After an hour, the nonnormal-simulation model-fit numbers were not decreasing anymore and reported the all-too-familiar NaN value. The normal simulation was still running, trying to get to convergence. Sitting upright, Jake looked at the code to find out what had happened. All the pricing errors were at zero, and the simulation was unable to continue. Jake shook his head. *Separating the market into normal and nonnormal movements has shown me something, but I am still getting the same end result.* The foundations of finance suggested that prices were unpredictable, since predictable prices led to potential arbitrages, and arbitrages could not exist for an efficient, well-formed market. *A model that drives pricing errors to zero has to be wrong because it suggests that it can capture all the unpredictability in the market.* Something was causing the error in the nonnormal market conditions that was resulting in this singularity, and Jake bet that it had to be related to the four variables that had had a large change in value in the forty-third iteration.

He got up and walked out of his office. He took a left and walked up the stairs and out of a side entrance of the business building. The sun was starting to set, but the air was still warm. Jake crossed Speedway and sat on the steps of the old gym. The street traffic was quiet now that Speedway had been closed to all cars. The entrance to the new gym was to Jake's left, and students and faculty were making their way in and out on a regular basis. This was the newest of the three main gyms on campus, and it included a climbing wall, the latest weight-lifting and Nautilus equipment, and two outdoor pools. Outdoor pools on a college campus in Austin were popular gathering places, for obvious reasons.

Jake's mind was not on the pool. After several solid months of error checking, he wasn't sure he was any closer to a solution, but something was different. *Everything appeared to be working fine, and then all of a sudden the program failed. There's no obvious problem, but now there's something new, something related to these four variables.* Jake also knew that the answer would not come to him on the steps of the gym. He walked back to the business building, walked in the main entrance, and walked by the old ticker tape that sat in the main foyer.

For the four-plus years Jake had been working and studying in this building, he had never taken the time to stop and look at the old machine. It reminded him of simpler times, when stock prices were read off the tape and information was not instantaneous. With this simplicity also came less transparency, worse valuations, and more speculation. This rampant speculation and excessive leverage were two of the main causes of the October 1929 crash, with the largest price losses on Monday, October 28, and Tuesday, October 29, resulting in a cumulative loss of over 24 percent. While there had been a small recovery, the great bear market in 1931 and 1932 had destroyed close to 89 percent of the equity value from the pre-crash highs.

Jake stood for a moment and reflected upon this. *The crash and the Great Depression's toll on equity prices was immense. It took over twenty-two years for equity prices to get back to pre-crash levels.* While many theories had been put forth on why the crash occurred and the length of time it took to recover, including the fault of the banking industry and Presidential policy, there was no concrete evidence for the exact reason. However, many hours had been spent on the best way to prevent this from happening again. The 1929 crash was the impetus for the establishment of the Securities and Exchange Commission, the federal watchdog over public companies, brokers, dealers, and exchanges on investors' behalf. The institution of regulatory bodies such as the SEC was one way to help protect the public from itself.

Jake knew the economy had natural business cycles, and markets became overvalued and undervalued due to aggregate market perceptions. *Crashes are just a way for the market to correct overvaluation,* he mused. *The 1929 crash was devastating and long lasting, but it brought equities back in line with proper valuations, eventually.*

Jake reflected upon what the idea of proper valuations meant. The underlying assumption was that over the long run, an equity price should reflect the future cash flows of that company discounted at that company's cost of capital. However, it wasn't clear that this happened on the aggregate, and his lecture on the equity premium puzzle had been consistent with that idea.

What is different today? There's more regulation, better information, and more investors. Are investors any more sophisticated? Maybe, but their risk aversion shouldn't be any different. If anything, there is no long-term memory of prior events, and people always revert back to their perception of value. Has the economy changed? Yes, but it still ebbs and flows even though it is now a global economy and US growth isn't based on manufacturing alone. Do we have a better handle on monetary and fiscal policy? Yes, but recessions still occur. What makes now different from then?

As Jake processed his results standing in the large atrium, surrounded by plaques on the walls and the old ticker tape, he'd felt that he was close to the root of his programming problem. It was there; he could see it. Now it was in the details. He realized that in attempting to solve what he'd thought was an error in his code, he had been asking the wrong questions.

What was the right question? If the economy and the market are fundamentally the same as in 1929, and investors are basically the same, why haven't we experienced another 1929?

As he pondered that question, he realized that what he'd thought was a mistake was not a mistake at all. It was like the first time he had seen Haley. Something had fundamentally changed, and a clarity of vision washed over him. He ran down the corridor that led away from the faculty offices toward the stairwell to the basement. He took the steps two at a time, burst through the fire doors, and ran to his office. Opening the door, he smashed the space key to awake the computer from its sleep mode and scrolled through his code. He wrote a one-line command that would output an additional item. He then reloaded the thirty simulations that he had done before, each excluding a key variable, and ran them on the normal and non-normal markets separately. Jake watched the middle screen start to report back prices and model-fit numbers. Jake knew that the program wouldn't finish tonight or even tomorrow, but he felt he was close to the answer. He turned off the screens and walked to the phone. It was five thirty, and Haley was probably anxious to leave. After being transferred to her office phone, Jake heard her pick up after two rings.

"Archives library. Haley Chamberlain speaking."

"Haley, you hungry? I think I've got it."

CHAPTER 12

Houston lies 150 miles southeast of Austin. If Austin is the antithesis of every Texas town, Houston is the embodiment of every Texas stereotype: a large, sprawling city with terrible traffic and rampant humidity and heat, built upon the foundations of the oil and energy industries. Besides Los Angeles, there is no greater urban expanse in the United States than Houston, with a centrally located downtown area right next to I-10. The skyline is dominated by the twin oval towers that were famously inhabited by Enron, the Wells Fargo center, and JPMorgan Chase tower.

Benson Prichard had been in the Houston office of T. B. Worley for just under a year. He worked on the third floor in the high-rise of 1111 Louisiana and was still not sure if he had made the right choice. A year ago he had been the top student at McCombs, working on the MBA Investment Fund, and was being recruited by all the top investment-banking firms. He could not have been happier, but he was nervous. Benson was born in Corpus Christi, grew up in San Antonio, and went to the University of Texas for both his undergraduate and graduate studies. He had done this by choice, because for Benson, Texas had everything a person could possibly want.

In high school, Benson had been heavily recruited for cross-country and track. He'd been running sub-fifteen-minute 5Ks and was on the verge of breaking the thirty-minute barrier for the 10K. However, there were no full scholarships for long-distance runners, and while going to Stanford or Oregon was appealing, his heart was not in it. All the running in junior high and through high school had deadened his legs, but it was his spirit that was broken. The thought of hundred-mile weeks for the next four years was too much for him, and he knew that to be the best, to compete for national and international glory, would require this and more. So he had passed on going west, stayed close to home, and was happier for it.

He had faced this same dilemma finishing up his MBA. Most of the firms interested in him had wanted him for New York City positions. Benson, while smart and driven, did not contain that quintessential New York trait, supreme confidence in his own ability. While born with the gift of Texas-sized heart and lungs, he had been born with humility and self-doubt. Benson had relied on Jake for advice on New York and how well he would do.

Jake and Benson had developed a strong friendship by combining their two main interests, finance and triathlon. They had both happened to work together on the MBA investment fund, Benson as student manager and Jake as an assistant instructor. Through this interaction, they had both begun to run together, which had led to their joint decision to try Ironman. For Benson, this relationship was extremely beneficial, and on long training rides and runs, he would use Jake as a sounding board for his career choices. It was particularly handy when it came to choosing a job, since Jake had relayed his experiences about living and breathing New York finance and what people in the Northeast were like. Ultimately, while Jake had pushed Benson into taking a job with JPMorgan working on the derivatives desk, Benson's heart had not been in it. He just couldn't leave Texas, so he went to work in private wealth management (PWM) in the high-net-worth accounts division at Thatcher, Brooke, and Worley. Jake had thought this the worst of the job offers but knew that Benson's happiness was not derived directly from money, and he was sympathetic to this line of decision making.

Unlike working in sales and trading, mergers and acquisitions, or equity research, private wealth management was less about finance and more about personal relationships. Given the right look, personality, and connections, success in the PWM group was almost assured and required little to no understanding of the intricacies of capital markets. Managing client money successfully was based on two easy principles. First, never be out of the market when it is going up, and second, never lose as much as the market does when it is going down. Clients, in general, were easily satisfied as long as their relative performance was better than a given benchmark, and rarely, if ever, did they switch or leave their initial money manager.

What made the job a challenge was landing the clients in the first place. That was where the pressure lay and why the washout rate was so high. Building a book from scratch was close to impossible, and new financial advisors typically failed within the first six months. At T. B. Worley, Benson was assigned to existing client accounts, and clients at T. B. were always worth over $50 million in liquid assets. So while he didn't have the same pressures of starting a book from scratch, he knew he would eventually be required to go out and expand that book. Associates were not required to be at the office much. They were expected to be entertaining clients on the golf course at River Oaks or Redstone, eating dinner at the Strip House, or having drinks at Marfreless. If the managing director saw too much of a PWM associate, it was a signal that the associate was not servicing his current accounts enough or laying enough groundwork for bringing in new accounts. That's what analysts were hired for.

Benson knew all this sitting at his desk. There were two analysts sitting in his row, busy updating client portfolios and on the phone with the New York valuation team. The two associates who had come in with him were not at their desks, but some senior associates were. The office was mostly empty, and having no cubicles and only one bank of offices on the east wall illuminated the vastness of the floor he worked on. The openness allowed easy communication among the teams in PWM, which the managing director felt promoted the best and friendliest working environment. The only visual constraint was the rows of computer and Bloomberg terminals, giving constant real-time financial information.

Benson had a nice view of downtown Houston, and today the sun was shining. The heat from the sun was accompanied by relentless humidity, which seemed to be ever present. Running in this weather was brutal, and he was looking to escape for a long weekend back to Austin, where the weather was drier. That running was on his mind was indicative of his need for an escape.

He was currently consumed with two problems that he felt were out of his control. First, his portfolio management choices had not gone great, and some of his existing clients were disappointed in that. Second, and more importantly, he was not closing. He was meeting with clients, selling them on T. B. Worley and himself and how they needed to be with the best. This was not hyperbole, given T. B. Worley's history and stature; it was consistently viewed as one of the preeminent investment banks in the world. Yet he was not signing as many people as the two colleagues he had entered T. B. Worley with were. This was pushing his self-doubt into overdrive. He was not looking forward to his next performance review. He knew he needed a new sales approach or a unique product to offer clients to keep the ones he had and to help sign up new ones.

"Jeremy, tell me the value of the Whitman account, year-to-date performance, and the value-at-risk of the portfolio," Benson asked the analyst who sat next to him.

"Sure, give me one second to pull up the account. OK, let's see here. The value is $12.2 million, down 5 percent for the year, with a VAR of 18 percent. Do you need anything else?" Jeremy said.

"Tell me the return of the REIT we bought in April and the energy allocation."

"You're not going to like it. Twelve percent loss year to date on the REIT, 10 percent down on the energy portion."

"Dang it!" Benson hated that shit Jeremy. He had disliked him from the beginning, and the feeling was mutual. He was the smug son of a wealthy client. It was like pulling teeth to get him to do any work. Both of those recommendations had been Benson's call, and both were underperforming. Jeremy must have loved telling him that.

Typically, associates did not make recommendation to clients but relied on equity research and the valuation teams to make those types of decisions. Then the PWM team would go to clients to present those recommendations, allowing the client to see various options. Only rarely would they put forth their own ideas, and if they did, they'd better be right. Benson had felt he was offering his clients the best way to diversify and hedge market risk by increasing their exposure to real estate and energy. He had made a market call and had been wrong, and while clients expected their portfolio values to fluctuate, rarely would the fluctuation be a result of a direct decision based on an associate's choice. Thus, the fault lay with him versus the remote valuation teams, making him directly responsible.

It was two thirty, thirty minutes until the markets closed. Benson picked up the phone and called Jim Swarthmore, a vice president with Shell that he was meeting at the Irish pub at seven thirty.

"Jim Swarthmore's office, may I ask who is callin'?" The voice that answered had the distinctive, sweet Texas drawl that every oil executive's secretary seemed to have. It was standard fare for everyone in Texas to drop the G at the end of words when talking.

"Hi, this is Benson Prichard from T. B. Worley, just confirmin' our meetin' tonight."

"Yes, Mr. Prichard, I have you down on the schedule. Mr. Swarthmore isn't in right now, but I'll let him know that you've called, doll"

"Thank you." Benson hung up. Swarthmore was probably in, but getting past the secretary was not worth the effort right now. He would save the charm and cajoling for later. Jim was one of his first clients, and Benson still had trouble getting by his secretary. The really good ones, the professionals who had been doing it for most of their adult lives, prided themselves on their ability to prevent any would-be caller from reaching their bosses. In one case, it had taken three months of persistence until he was able to talk to an executive at Budweiser.

He turned his attention back to his monitor while ignoring the fact the Jeremy was on Facebook. The market was ticking up for the day with very light trading volume. September was a busy month, as third-quarter numbers were being announced, analysts' estimates and revisions were constantly being updated, and there was the upcoming Fed announcement at the end of the month. Day-to-day market movements were of little concern in his current role, but he liked to stay informed about what was going on in the market as much as possible. It was also a nice reminder of working on the MBA fund. There was something exhilarating about sitting on the desk, following the market, and worrying about all the news and rumors that seemed to float about endlessly. Maybe Jake was right and he should have taken the derivatives desk job.

With running on his mind and the thought of university life, Benson grabbed his cell phone and called the familiar Austin-area number.

"Well, well, what do you want, stranger?" Jake answered.

"What's up, dude? Wanted to see how research is comin'."

"Don't ask me that. I mean, I've got something very interesting but may have some trouble with it from an academic perspective. I may be sitting on some real dynamite, but I know that you're not interested. I'm guessing you're calling because you want to talk big-picture stuff, ask my advice on how to land a woman, and a nice one at that. Am I right?

"Yes on the big picture, not on the woman," Benson replied, his interested piqued on Jake's mention of something interesting.

"I'm shocked. You're making close to $200,000 a year, you're single, have great hair, and are in good shape. You're everything twenty-one-to-thirty-three-year-old females look for, especially since they don't care about looks. Yet you haven't had a date in, what, four months? Honestly, you're pathetic."

"Look, I get laid more than you do, married man. Enough of that for the moment. How's about I come up next weekend? We can run the lake and maybe ride the dam loop. I also want to go over some stuff at work."

"That should work. It would be good to get in some good long workouts, but you better go easy on me. Let me just run it by Haley to make sure it's cool."

"Typical. You're such the married man. Call me when she lets you become a man again."

"Benson, you'll learn one day."

He hung up the phone and smiled. The thought of Austin was very pleasing: to get a break from the monotony of working the phones, the idiot Jeremy, dinner meetings, and weekend golfing. That lifestyle had sounded glamorous initially, but work was still work. Going back and living like a poor graduate student was the perfect break from the routine and a chance to get Jake's view on what the market was doing. Jake's view on the market was different from that of everyone at T. B. Worley because he approached it from an academic viewpoint. Most academics have a pie-in-the-sky view of the world, but it always helped to get a different perspective. Maybe some of Jake's ideas and research could also help Benson with client recruitment, especially if he had found something interesting.

CHAPTER 13

The Federal Reserve Board of Governors and the Federal Open Market Committee, or the FOMC, are the most influential committees in the global economy. It is not a secret what the Fed does, but the ramifications of the decisions are so widespread that the scope of the decisions made is quite uniformly unappreciated. A small change in the federal funds rate or the discount rate affects the valuation of equity securities, the yield curve, which changes the prices of both corporate and government bonds and international exchange rates. All valuation starts with forecasts of the policy that comes out of Fed meetings, and valuations change drastically with unanticipated changes of that policy.

The Board of Governors is made up of political appointees, appointed by the president, except for the members from the twelve Federal Reserve districts, who represent the interests of their areas of the country to ensure fair regional representation. The FOMC includes the Board of Governors and five members from the twelve districts, of whom one is always the president of the Federal Reserve Bank of New York. The other eleven members rotate for the final four spots on a predetermined basis. These twelve individuals hold more power to influence valuation and market prices than any other group in the world. At least that is the perception. It also made Michelle Lancaster, the current president of the Federal Reserve Bank of New York, the most powerful nonelected official in the monetary system.

Since her meeting with the Markov Group, Dennis had formally announced that he was stepping down and that Michelle had been appointed the new president. This had come as no surprise to the staff at the New

York Fed or the other regional governors. Michelle was well respected for her opinions and even judgment on all matters regarding the economy, and while she was relatively young for the position, her intellect and experience were first rate. She had received a call from the current chairman of the Federal Reserve, congratulating her on her appointment to the position and saying he was looking forward to working with her directly in the near future.

The first FOMC meeting that she would have a deciding vote on was scheduled to take place in three weeks. She had attended many of the meetings in the past to give reports on current rates of inflation and un-employment figures but never had been privy to the closed-door sessions of the twelve members. She was nervous about leaving a good impression, excited about the opportunity and the power that come with shaping the US and world economies, and yet fear lingered.

Ever present in the back of her mind was the Markov Group. This clandestine sect of power brokers that she was now a member of was even more elite that the FOMC. Dennis had explained prior to meeting with the Markov Group who was in the group, its purpose, and her role. This had all been reinforced by Frank Lyman, and yet the truth and loyalty of her membership were yet to be tested. Ultimately, she would have to follow, since reason and duty would prevail. Since there had been no con-tact since that first meeting, she had allowed the idea and purpose of the Markov Group to float to the back of her mind.

Michelle sat at her desk and looked out the window. It was raining. Another typical fall day, in that it could be beautiful or dreary. Fall did bring beautiful days, letting the real attractiveness of Manhattan blossom. The brilliant color from the trees in Central Park permeated the city. With summer's humidity a thing of the past, walking the streets was pleasant, and people seemed less ornery and indifferent. Occasionally you would see someone smiling, and that smile would be returned. The streets seemed cleaner, the sun brought a comforting warmth, and the resonating shine off the buildings filled the air with light, hope, and optimism. However, on rainy, gray days, the glow and brilliance of fall would disappear, reminding people that they were only a few days away from a harsh winter and long, cold days. The rain brought a feeling of nostalgia to Michelle, a reminder of graduate school days in Ann Arbor, alone, researching topics long built upon or forgotten.

Those days, while hard and unforgiving, were the ones Michelle remembered most fondly. She had graduated from Michigan's economics department in 1981, when finance was still an undeveloped, misunderstood discipline. William Sharpe and Bob Litner had developed the Capital Asset Pricing Model, or CAPM, in 1964, and Fisher Black, Myron Scholes, and Bob Merton had come up with their closed-form option-pricing model in 1973. But in 1981 the finance world hadn't built the empirical tools yet to effectively use these findings in practice. Portfolio management and trading was still running without a high level of sophistication, relying on gut feeling more than analysis. The world of economics while she was in school was focused on solving adverse selection problems, macroeconomic modeling, and understanding the effects of inflation. At the time, the US inflation rate had been over 10 percent and was considered the biggest problem facing the world economy.

Her dissertation had focused on inflation and asset pricing and how that related to capital investments, real returns, and the effect on the term structure of interest rates. Her research had been very well received and published in the *American Economic Review* and *Journal of Monetary Economics*, and she had been considered one of the top candidates on the market when she graduated. Ultimately, she had gone to work at the University of Chicago, choosing to work in the same department as Milton Freidman and Eugene Fama. She had spent three excellent years there, publishing numerous articles, and was well on her way to tenure but with a growing concern that her impact in academics was minimal. Plus, it was not easy being a woman in a male-dominated profession. If Wall Street of the early 1980s was the old boys' network, academia was its ugly cousin. It was especially hard for her, a young, attractive, single woman. While her colleagues made her feel at home, she could not help but feel that she was an outsider.

It was at a Federal Reserve Monetary Conference in 1984 where she'd first met Dennis Haybert. Michelle had been presenting her work on real versus perceived unemployment and the relationship to the business cycle. Dennis, who was head of research at the time at the NY Fed, had been captivated by her eloquence and her intuition for the effects of macroeconomic changes and the impact they had on the economy. After her talk, he had waited to get her alone and asked her to dinner. At that dinner, he had asked if she was interested in working outside of academia, away from the classroom, and focusing on the true application of her ideas.

The timing could not have been better for her, and while working for the government had never really crossed her mind in school, when Dennis asked her, it seemed like the perfect fit. Reflecting back on her decision to accept his offer now, she could see the true impact of her work and the effect it had had on the economy over these past thirty years. *I definitely made the right choice.* Her rise to her current position was due in part to her intellect and intuition but also to Dennis's favoritism, which had not gone unnoticed. To succeed in this world, one needed intelligence, but luck was definitely a significant part of the equation.

However, those times were in the past, and she was not one to dwell on petty jealousies or perceived slights. Now, instead of worrying about selling her research and ideas to the decision makers of the world, she was one of them. Others now had to present to her, and her say would change future job creation and loss, stock market performance, and foreign governments' reactions to US monetary policy. It was a position of power that carried huge responsibility and one that Michelle relished.

On her desk were several recent reports forecasting inflation, housing development, and the fiscal deficit. On the top of the stack of reports was one on the recent trading activity and prices of the forward market on the federal funds rate. The thirty-day federal funds futures were traded on the Chicago mercantile exchange and were typically used as the substitute for the future expectation of the realized federal funds rate. Research had shown that even if the FOMC changed the federal funds rate and the futures market had priced in the change, there was minimal reaction in the stock market. If the change by the FOMC was unexpected, then there were strong stock market reactions, depending on the direction of the surprise.

Michelle read over the report and reflected on the efficiency of the markets—the interaction of institutional and retail traders, arbitrageurs, speculators, and hedgers, all using different sources of information, driving pricing through buying and selling, coming up with one market price. The ability of the market to price assets fairly, but not necessarily correctly, was still the best system in the world. Michelle honestly believed that the least regulation possible resulted in the best outcome for all market participants. Some regulation was necessary, as demonstrated by the case of the Hunt brothers and the cornering of the silver market in the 1970s, but overregulation was just as bad. In the position she was in, finding that balance was critical for the success of well-functioning markets.

Michelle picked up her phone. "Hi, Wendy, will you please call Chris and ask him to come to my office?"

Things between Chris and Michelle had been uncomfortable for years, and her recent appointment had probably ended any hope of a peaceful working relationship.

After three minutes, there was a knock on Michelle's door, and Dr. Chris Carter came in. Many within the organization had thought Chris would have been an excellent choice to replace Dennis Haybert. More importantly, Chris himself thought he was the best choice, and Michelle knew it. She had joined the research department of the NY Fed a little after he had, but both had been considered stars and had moved up in the bank almost simultaneously. Chris knew Michelle was good and was looked upon favorably. Initially their relationship had been promising, both personally and professionally. They had both succumbed to a natural attraction; however, that was in the past, and that was a pain that neither could forget. Professional jealousy can destroy even the tightest personal bonds.

Once Michelle had been promoted above him, Chris had typically taken an opposing view to hers in seeking acceptance and recognition, and their internal competition had caused friction within the NY Fed. When Michelle had advanced to director of research, his anger, ego, and self-pity were evident to all, and Dennis Haybert had moved him to Credit, Investment, and Payment Risk to minimize their interaction.

While this had been a personal affront to Chris, his talent and skill had prevailed, and he was eventually promoted to run that division. His work and effort were well respected, and he had been very proactive in assessing the opportunities in the credit and risk markets over the past three years. When Dennis stepped down, Michelle knew that she would have to work closely with Chris, and that meant putting their professional competition and personal pain aside. Michelle moved from behind her desk and sat on the couch on the wall facing one of the windows as he walked in. While she was Chris's superior, she tried never to remind him of that fact.

"Chris, thanks for coming up. As you know, we've the FOMC meeting in a couple of weeks, and I wanted to get your thoughts on the real-estate market and the information from the Case-Shiller index," Michelle said.

"Happy to oblige," Chris said as he took a chair and moved it to face her. "The current value of the Composite-20 SPCS20R index is 200.12. The price appreciation over the past month was –0.20 percent, and over the past year, prices have remained fairly flat. The slowdown is fine, and nothing appears out of the ordinary. The fact that prices have stabilized is consistent with our projections, since real estate has recovered significantly since the real-estate bubble burst."

"True, along with the steady decrease in interest rates," Michelle noted. "However, are you not concerned about the appreciation in prices relative to the expansion of the credit markets? Since the trough, prices have appreciated about 60 percent, which isn't that excessive, although significantly higher than the average appreciation over different time periods.

"Nothing bad about that."

"Again, I agree, but you're aware that the size of the credit default swap market is over twice the size of the US stock market. The US mortgage market is one-seventh the size of the CDS market. Do you know what the size of the market was in 2002?"

"Not offhand, but I'm sure you'll tell me."

Here we go. Chris's surly tone did not distract her from delivering her information. She was accustomed to his petulance rising early whenever they were alone.

"It was $2.2 trillion, one-tenth the size of today's market. Along with this astronomical growth, the interest rate derivative market has also tripled. Someone is holding all this debt, which makes the global sensitivity to interest rates a problem. The derivatives market is outpacing the growth in real assets by a ratio of thirty-two to one. That's a significant leverage ratio, don't you agree? We can't have a repeat of 2008." *Get ready for a nasty response.*

"What's your point, Michelle? This risk is disbursed across multiple lenders and institutions, and the paper is backed by real assets. As long as the Fed continues to keep rates low and the demand for treasuries is still high, there's very limited risk. Eventually we'll have to wean people off the lower-interest-rate environment, but how can we be responsible for the leverage in the system if people themselves can't be responsible investors? That's like when the Fed was blamed for the lack of discipline of individual home buyers back in 2008. I'm not sure what your concern is, but I believe it's misplaced." Chris's response was cool and calculated, but the anger in his voice and fire behind his eyes was obvious.

Don't get caught up in his game. "Chris, I don't understand why you're taking this personally. Our job is to assess risk and present ideas that allow the FOMC and the board to make informed, educated opinions. A statement such as 'lack of discipline of individuals' is unsound and borderline irresponsible. I expect more objectivity in a research opinion. It appears you're ignoring the question entirely. We always need to worry about leverage." Michelle's attempt to remain as calm as possible had failed. She knew she had fallen for this obvious trap. It had been the first time that they had talked privately since her appointment, and she couldn't help feeling some lingering emotional tug. *He got under my skin.*

He had always been emotional, but when it came to delivering his research and giving an opinion, he had always been professional. It was what had initially drawn Michelle to him. In his first presentation within the research group, Chris had been addressing the relationship between unanticipated inflation and the recession and had been attacked by a senior fellow about his empirical methodology. He had accepted the criticism calmly but retorted forcefully and with a succinct example that had quieted the fellow rather quickly. Now his opinion was glazed with anger. Michelle had thought she could be objective with him, put aside the emotional component since those days together were a distant memory. She was surprised that the emotions had come so close to the surface so quickly. She stared hard at him, and his expression softened.

"I'm sorry, Michelle, I don't mean to get gruff. I'm just trying to give you an informed opinion." He reached out and lightly rested his hand on her leg. His tone had completely changed that it caught her of guard and she didn't have time to pretend to recoil from his touch.

What is this? He was angry and now he's caring. What game is this? He hasn't shown affection toward me or even been cordial in years.

Chris continued on. "I'm just trying to present the facts to you. You can listen to my research or go with your gut instinct. You never really worried about other people's results, regardless of whether they were right, so I guess you won't worry about the choice you face." He laughed and winked at her.

He is flirting.

Incredulous, Michelle just stared at him. In less than three minutes, a conversation that was supposed to be professional about risk in the markets had become personal, starting in a typically combative way but taking a bizarre turn. Michelle knew that Chris had resented her for years. He had felt cheated and hard done by being passed over throughout his career and had taken his anger out on her. It was why their relationship, both sexual and professional, had fallen apart. Over the past three years, she couldn't remember a time that they were ever alone in the same room. Now here they were, alone, and Chris had actually talked to her and flirted with her in the caring, loving way that had highlighted the best of their relationship. Maybe time did heal all wounds.

"Chris, where is this coming from? I wanted to talk business. We need to be prepared for this meeting."

"I know, and we will, but I can't go on being angry anymore. I'm tired of it. We've been fighting for years, and it's been my fault. I walked in angry, ready to keep fighting, but I've come to the realization that there are more important things than my career. I haven't congratulated you on the job yet. Let me take you to dinner, and we can have a proper conversation, one that we should have had years ago. What do you say?"

Before Michelle had time to respond, Chris had gotten up, kissed her on the cheek, and walked out the door. Shocked, Michelle slumped in her chair. This was not what she needed or expected. She knew that Chris could get a rise out of her, but was stunned that the part that cared for him was still there. Strictly speaking, since she was Chris's boss, entering into a relationship with him would not be prudent, but dinner couldn't hurt. *I haven't been on a date for years.* Michelle walked to her door and told the secretary to call Chris's secretary. She would tread carefully, especially since there were more pressing issues at hand.

He closed the door behind him. Leaning up against the wall, he took several deep breaths before returning to his chair.

Composure, he said to himself. *Breathe in and hold. Close your eyes. Visualize both black and white, and hold that image in your mind.*

Five minutes passed. Ten minutes. At this point his heart rate was below eighty. Staying in good shape and eating right had not been a priority for him, so getting himself to calm down took time. He smiled after his breathing returned to its normal, ran his hands through his salt-and-pepper hair, and took in his first victory. It was a fleeting feeling but one that he cherished.

He had made mistakes. Many mistakes. But now things were turning in his favor. He had let his anger cloud his judgment for too long. He remembered exactly the day when he had stopped being angry; it was the day Dennis had announced that Michelle would be taking the top seat. A calm had washed over him, a clarity, and the formation of his plan. The plan started and ended with Michelle. The best part was that he knew it would work because he knew her better than she knew herself.

He knew how to get under her skin and what made her laugh, blush, get excited, and feel sad. She was an easy mark. Today was just step one, and it was so easy. Get her emotional and get her to drop her guard. Check. Step two, rebuild trust and emotional dependence. Step three, well, he'd worry about step three when they got there. When they were there, that is when he would be in a place of power, and Michelle Lancaster would be ruined. All thanks to his new best friend.

CHAPTER 14

The stock market crashed on October 19, 1987, finishing the day down over 22 percent. Markets all over the world suffered from Black Monday. That October saw London down over 26 percent and Hong Kong close to 50 percent. However, unlike the 1929 crash, which could be considered the starting point of the Great Depression, this crash was more a systematic failure than an economic one. By mid-April 1988, the market had recovered to precrash levels, and from a long-term view, Black Monday was a minor blip on the standard buy-and-hold portfolio. Yet millions of dollars traded hands, and fortunes were made and lost over the course of this day and the next several months. What was more important were the days leading up the crash itself.

The hardest period to trade is when the market is not open, but that does not mean one cannot. The US equity market opens at 9:30 a.m. eastern and closes at 4:00 p.m. It is possible to trade US futures contracts, specifically contracts on the Standard & Poor's (S&P) 500, when Asian and European markets are open, which technically means it is possible to trade at all times except between 4:15 p.m. eastern time, when the US futures markets close, and 6:00 p.m. eastern, when Asia opens. Over the weekend, Sydney opens first, around 6:00 p.m. (EST) on Sunday, which means the greatest uncertainty lies from Friday to Sunday night. Anything can and usually does happen, and market makers, those who set prices, can incorporate any weekend information into the open prints when the market opens. For equity holders, this risk can be huge, since the futures price will reflect all new information and can trade for over fifteen hours before the equity markets open. That can mean significant damage for anyone with large equity exposure who planned on selling, or buying, at the open on Monday.

On October 19, 1987, at 9:30 a.m., most of the damage was done. At the close on Friday, October 16, the market had experienced a significant sell-off from the prior couple of days, there was concern about a change in monetary policy, and there were increased tensions in the Middle East. As Asia opened on Sunday, the sell-off started, and those US investors who looked to protect their equity holdings sold US futures contracts as a type of portfolio insurance. Selling, or shorting, US futures as the price falls results in a positive gain and helps to offset the loss on a long-equity portfolio. Holding this type of insurance seems like a reasonable action to take in the light of a sell-off, but in this particular case, it can be the cause of a larger systemic problem, especially when computers or program trades become involved. Many large portfolio managers institute systematic triggers that initiate trades when certain price or percentage levels are hit in the market. If markets fall 5 percent, they initiate an automatic sell since there are common portfolio risk thresholds that will not allow assets to fall greater than 5 percent before liquidating. The problem with that is that if everyone has the same threshold and it triggers a sell order at the same time, there aren't enough buyers to match the sell order, and the price has to fall further.

By the time the market opened on Monday, futures were trading down around 10 percent relative to the close of Friday. Every program trade, automated order, and short-term trader waiting for the equity market to open was ready to dump their stocks. The sharks were waiting in the wings as well. These short-sellers came in and added to the panic by putting in their short positions as well. This forced the price down even further. In addition, the orders that came in were so large that the equity prices couldn't catch up to the futures price, so it was unclear what the actual price of the stocks was, let alone what true value was. At one point during the day, futures were trading down at a 17 percent discount to equity prices. This led to arbitrage opportunities, since there should never be that great of a disparity between the equity and futures prices. This also forced prices down, since the arbitrageurs were shorting stock. At the end, after a 22 percent drop in prices and trillions in lost value, top portfolio managers, economists, and regulators were left scratching their heads.

From Jake's perspective, the crash of 1987 was fascinating, because with all the noise that occurred and the postmortem on why it happened, nobody really asked *what had fundamentally changed in the economy*. From October 18, Sunday night, to October 19, Monday afternoon, had the economy become 22 percent less valuable? *No*. It was possible that over the course of time, the economy had been artificially creating value, 1 percent at a time, and at that point decided to give it all back. That seemed unlikely as well, but human behavior is quite predictable in these circumstances. As with every major asset bubble, whether it's Dutch tulips, gold, or real estate, when the good times are rolling, everyone buys in, ignoring the risks. When that bubble bursts, there is panic to get out as fast as possible, such that assets are sold well below value. Irrationality always triumphs when uncertainty reigns, thus the predictability of human behavior.

October 1987 also represented a shift in the way the market functioned. Regulatory controls, such as circuit breakers, were put in place to prevent significant one-day falls and limits to short-selling and how short-selling took place. Additionally, a more relevant shift was taking place in the way that assets were traded. From the 1987 crash to today, less and less of the day-to-day trading was done person to person, as more of the operations, both the trading and execution, were handled electronically. While this improved the efficiency of any order, and potentially the information content and price discovery, there was always a lingering concern in Jake's mind that market behavior had reached a critical inflection point that was potentially tipping it over a dire cliff. *While human behavior is irrational, there was always a sense of control that the market was in our hands when each order was person to person. Now, it was just flashing green and red lights.*

Jake was in his office, waiting for his estimations to finish, thinking about the effect of computer trading and how it could drive nonnormal returns, when Audria knocked on the door. This was somewhat unusual, as she just tended to come in whether the person wanted her to or not. Jake expected she wanted something from him, given the heightened politeness in her etiquette.

"Audria, what's up? How's the job market treating you?" Jake asked, trying to be as polite as possible but knowing how distracted he sounded.

"Jake, I wanted to ask you a question. Have you seen the latest publication in the *Journal of Finance*, the one about market efficiency and the impact of ETFs and passively managed funds?" she asked. She was picking at her fingernails as she leaned against the door.

He knew which paper she was talking about. It was a paper that showed that the more passively managed or index replicating funds were in the market, the less efficient the market became. It was an interesting paper because it actually documented an empirical finding that went against modern portfolio theory. Jake hadn't put too much thought into the paper but did think the paper was clever since it showed the results with a simple regression test and used model fit as the measure of efficiency.

"I know of the paper. Why do you ask?"

"Well, it really impacts my dissertation and the paper I have under review. I knew this paper was out there, but I never thought it would be published. I'm now worried that my paper won't be published."

"Why are you coming to me and not Dr. Tacker? Surely he can give you better advice on this than I can. Plus, isn't he an associate editor at the journal?" Jake was honestly perplexed by this line of questioning, and, with his interest piqued, he gave her his full attention. When a paper is published, the findings themselves are about three years old, so it shouldn't have been a shock to her.

"Audria, this paper has been around for years. What's going on?" He dug a little further.

She sat down in the only chair that Jake could fit in his office besides his desk and his own chair. She really did look miserable. Almost on the verge of tears. In the four-plus years he had known Audria, the one emotion he had never seen in her was vulnerability.

"We've never been friends, but we've always been cordial and have had respect for each other, right?" she asked, but said more to herself.

"Of course."

"Well, you know I'm getting a lot of interviews at the AFA meeting, and a lot of them are good schools."

"Yes." Jake nodded, annoyance creeping in at her lack of humility.

Jake's phone rang just as she was about to speak.

"One second." Jake held up his hand. It was a student who needed some extra help on binomial trees, a method used to price options. Jake tried to hurry the student up, but before he could finish, Audria was getting up to leave.

"Hold on one second," he said to the student, cupping his hand over the receiver. To Audria, he asked, "Where are you going? Don't you want to finish this?" he asked her. She shook her head and said thanks as she walked out the door. Jake said bye and went back to responding to the student. After five minutes of painful and meticulous explanation, he hung up with the student and returned his thoughts to his brief and odd conversation with his cohort. Something was amiss, but it was not his job to find out.

Her comments and behavior were certainly out of character, given her almost icy demeanor and oozing self-confidence. Maybe she and Tacker were having an affair, which was disgusting to think about on many levels but interesting all the same. Audria flaunted her sexuality about almost haphazardly, leading to this rumor that had been perpetuated through the PhD corridor for years. Jake seriously doubted the rumor, since Dr. Tacker appeared to be happily married and, beyond his family, cared only about his work.

However, a comment that she made had triggered something in his mind, something related to his work. It was about ETFs—electronically traded funds that have captured the same market replication of index mutual funds but allowed intraday trading. Why did these instruments exist, and what was their purpose if they essentially offered the same return as an existing product? Did they really add to market efficiency, or did they take away from it? The more Jake pondered that idea, the more he lingered on the thought of passive management and how passive management contributed to the idea of normal versus nonnormal returns.

Simply put, it was easy to see that even though these instruments were ideal for the passive investor, they could be used to contribute to greater market distortions and greater nonnormal returns. The more the market moved, the more these ETFs had to replicate the move, further exacerbating the move. So as investors became more passive, ETFs increased not only the probability of another October 1987 but also the ease with which one could manipulate markets to cause a crash.

CHAPTER 15

There are many perceptions of the stock market, this almost living, breathing entity, none of which are entirely true or completely false. Whether individuals are active participants in the stock market or not, most of the country's wealth is tied to the performance and value in the stock market. Yet the size of the actual market, the total value of stocks that are publicly traded, is smaller than the public and private debt market, real estate and the mortgages linked to property, and the derivatives market. However, it is movement in the US broad-based indices, such as the Dow Jones Industrial Average and the S&P 500 Indices, which give direct feedback as to how wealthy most people feel on any given day. This is especially true when the stock market is doing very well and even more so when the stock market is doing poorly. The feeling of loss and fear is simply stronger than that of gain and success.

For those who are active participants, whose day-to-day livelihood depends on the movements and ticks of individual prices, the supply and demand from those on the outside creates a multibillion-dollar business. Whether it is stock traders, investment advisors, analysts, investment bankers, or portfolio managers, being a part of this world feels like the center of the universe. Every Fed meeting, company quarterly report, or macro data release is an opportunity to make money and advance careers. At times this can be at the expense of others, and, in some cases, it can be at the expense of the general public.

Academics view the world of finance and the movement of stock prices as a chance to examine underlying theories of human behavior, rationality, physics properties, game theory, and general equilibrium. After postulating these theories, they then test them, and, unlike in most disciplines, there is almost unlimited data that is easily gathered. The empirical tests verify, refute, and mostly lead to more testing of these theories. Occasionally, significant findings improve the understanding of why prices move, whether regulations are working, and whether managers are truly skillful. Many times empirical findings can lead to profitable trading strategies employed by mutual or hedge funds, improve the public offerings initiated by corporations, or influence how boards are structured. However, for the most part, many on the professional side of the finance world view academic work as useless.

Benson was one who thought that was the case. Most of what he had learned he wasn't really using. Client recruiting had little to do with the fundamentals of finance and more to do with interpersonal skills. Yet, and Benson had to admit this, you still had to know your material, and you had to have a hook. Working at T. B. Worley certainly helped, but you needed to give your clients something special, something that they had not seen or were not getting anywhere else. For the high-end retail clients, the fifty-million-and-higher net-worth group, they needed to feel that they were getting inside access to the markets like the institutions were, especially unique products and exotic instruments.

That was not Benson's core competency, and he knew it. He understood the peripheral information about over-the-counter (OTC) products, such as credit default swaps, binary options, and interest-rate futures, but he did not feel comfortable talking about them in depth. That is why he liked talking with Jake about them. He never viewed Jake as a true academic, more as a practitioner trapped in an academic world, which, coincidentally, was similar to the way most of the faculty viewed Jake as well.

Benson got into Austin late Friday night. The traffic leaving Houston was horrendous, and it took almost three and a half hours before he got to Jake's condo. Benson loved coming back and never really minded the drive. Austin had one of the most physically active populaces for a large city in the country, yet it still maintained a small-town feel. The town had really become a city in the 1980s, thanks to Michael Dell and the technology industry that followed, but from Sixth Street south to the Town Lake trail, the city felt like it must have when it was just a college town with the state capital. It never really felt like a city in Texas since it was so distinct from the larger metropolises, such as Houston and Dallas; there were no oil companies, few large skyscrapers, and no professional sports teams. The downtown area was dominated by local shops and bars, and it was impossible to miss the ubiquitous *Keep Austin Weird* bumper stickers or T-shirts.

Benson wanted to hit the Town Lake trail Sunday and ride Saturday. One of the harder rides was to head west out to Lime Creek Road and do the climb that was called Triple Bitch, named for three pitches that went above 15 percent grade for over half a mile. Benson loved to break most people on this section, given his superior power-to-weight ratio.

There were many people out riding, taking advantage of a cooler, slightly overcast Saturday morning. Haley wanted no part of their ride—her exact words were "Fuck no"—so she went out with Brooke to ride the dam loop, which most people would be riding that day. Jake and Benson rode with several people before they hit Anderson Mill Road and then were own their own except for the occasional car that passed by. Benson pulled beside Jake. The first fifteen miles had been pretty relaxed, and they had been averaging just under twenty miles an hour riding single file.

"Now that we're away from most of the traffic, how's the research coming along? Found out anythin' new? I know you've been workin' on somethin' interestin', but you mentioned you hit some head wind? Given your propensity to go on and on about your research, you better tell me quick before you run out of breath as I kick your ass up Triple Bitch."

Benson had held off asking anything until now, since he'd gotten in late the night before and they had left early in the morning for their ride. Jake wasn't surprised it had come up. Benson had looked anxious ever since he'd arrived.

"I was waiting for you to ask. It looks like you've been on edge ever since you arrived. I must admit I'm curious where this interest is coming from. Anyway, I think I've had a breakthrough, but I'm not 100 percent sure it's correct or what the actual problem is. The long and the short of it is that the drivers of market returns can be segmented into normal and nonnormal movements, and there are distinct drivers for each market. If you're really interested, I can show you."

"That's somethin' I really want to see. It's good to come back and learn somethin' new to change my perspective."

"While I agree with that last sentiment, I can't imagine it would be helpful to you beyond a general curiosity, and I always believed that highbrow academics had no place in your world."

"Dang, it would be and it wouldn't be. The nuts and bolts of what you're doin' holds very little interest to my clients, or prospective clients, but I can use what you're doin' from a high-level approach to drum up interest. It would be a unique selling point to say that I've teamed up with cutting-edge academic research that only I've access to, to help manage risk and enhance returns."

"What happens when they ask you to go into more depth?"

"Well, you're goin' to show me that so I have some of the tools in place."

"Wait, does this mean you're going to use my results to form client portfolios?"

"No. Well, not necessarily. The idea is to try and use what you're doin' as a hook but not necessarily use it. Of course, I may not use any of it at all. It's just that I'm concerned about how things are going at work, and I'm lookin' for a way to change momentum. That's one of the reasons I came up. You know that I think most of what you do as an academic is useless, but your ideas have always had good practical applications."

"Well, I appreciate that. How about we hit this part of the ride hard, get home, eat five thousand calories, and then I can show you some of my results. It'll be nice to show it to someone who is looking at it for value versus trying to tear it down for a change."

Jake had picked up on the subtle comment that Benson had made about work but chose not to address it. He knew he would be more helpful to his friend by going through his results than dwelling on Benson's struggles at work.

With that, they dropped into single-file formation and proceeded to pick up the pace. Besides the seven-mile-an-hour ascent up the climb, they managed to average twenty-two miles an hour the rest of the ride. Benson looked fresh when they pulled into Jake's driveway, but Jake was absolutely spent. They waited for Haley to return before they went and got food. When Haley saw how depleted Jake looked, she couldn't help but laugh.

The rest of the day, Jake went over with Benson what he had been doing and what the research showed. Benson took it in and saw the possibilities. Benson peppered Jake with questions, all the while forming a strategy of how he could use this to recruit clients. *Maybe Jake can't see it, but this is a gold mine. He may care about the why, but it isn't important. The clients are goin' to love it.* He was convinced that if he implemented this for his existing clients, there would be a significant improvement in their portfolio performance. He would start small, just moving small, discretionary portions around, and if the strategy showed promise, he would begin to move larger portions with his clients' permission. Wiping that smug look off Jeremy's face would be an added bonus.

Sunday morning they ran the trail at a relaxed pace as Jake continued to explain the role of each factor, how the sign dictated whether to be short or long a given stock, and how the value of the coefficient represented the size or weight in the portfolio. By the end of the run, Benson felt confident about how it worked and how to use it. He was about to make a lot of money.

Sunday afternoon, after a weekend of excellent exercise and good discussion, Benson headed back to Houston. He was ready to get back to work on Monday, refreshed, ready to make real progress, and armed with a true epiphany. What Benson had seen, and what Jake hadn't realized, was that from a practical standpoint, the model could predict what the stock market was going to do. Jake had been so focused on understanding what was happening that he hadn't seen the model's true potential. Benson didn't need a model-fit number to know that this was something special. He even smiled at Jeremy when he came in fifteen minutes late.

CHAPTER 16

Financial markets are fragile entities. The hinge that provides the stability is liquidity and the access to capital markets. When liquidity disappears, prices collapse and markets break down. The stock market crash of 1929 was brought about by excessive leverage, but the depression that followed was a result of closed capital markets and no liquidity. The same crisis almost befell the global economy in 2008, when leverage in the housing markets almost led to a massive shutdown in capital flows and prompted unprecedented action by the Federal Reserve to pump liquidity back into the system. Regardless of an individual's political views, he or she can view the actions of the Fed as heroic or foolhardy, because at some point the debt has to be paid, either through currency or dollar deflation or excess inflation. The question the Fed answered was whether it wanted the economy to suffer significant short-term pain or a longer, less obvious collection of subtle stab wounds. Given the political life cycle, the Fed's choice was a no-brainer.

Wealth is created and destroyed in periods of upheaval. However, it isn't necessarily a zero-sum game. In normal market periods, when a stock is bought or sold, there is a counterparty that has taken the opposite side, and the gain or loss is determined by the direction of the market. When leverage is introduced, the size of the gain or loss is magnified, but that might result in a one-sided trade, the most obvious example being the amount of deadweight loss that occurred when the housing market collapsed. Excessive borrowing led to inflated prices, and when those prices collapsed, individual borrowers had to sell their homes at a loss, and the banks that repossessed the homes, or the notes on those homes, had to mark on their books real assets that had significantly depreciated. The bond holders who held a collection of these notes, known as collateralized mortgage obligations, or CMOs, lost value, as did the insurance companies underwriting these notes. Everyone lost, and it can be directly tied to the amount of leverage that was built into the fabric of the economy. The higher the leverage, the higher the deadweight loss potential.

Leverage, and how it has been used by individuals, corporations, and governments, was something that really bothered Jake. When he taught his students, he tried to guide them with this simple principle: never borrow more than three times your after-tax income. Use the rule when it comes to the accumulation of all debt, whether it's a mortgage, car loan, or student loan, and never use credit-card debt. Yet it's a rule violated by pretty much everyone.

Now Jake was facing his own leverage problem, except it was not a financial but an econometric problem, a problem that affected his modeling of asset prices and returns. Leverage is attainable in many forms. The simplest from a trading perspective is trading on margin, which allows you to borrow up to 50 percent of the equity price. This allows margin investors to potentially double their expected return but with increased downside cost. The complications of margin and the ability to borrow in greater quantities increase with the complexity of the financial instruments, such as options or over-the-counter derivative products. During the financial crisis, banks had off-balance-sheet leverage ratios of forty to one.

As Jake was deciphering the key components of his model, it appeared that the leverage variable and the three subjective variables related to the Fed, institutional investors, and market microstructure were the key. The results of the thirty simulations that each excluded one key explanatory variable on normal and nonnormal market conditions had all finally finished successfully. The normal model result looked almost identical across each of the thirty estimations, along with the simulation that included all of the explanatory variables. There wasn't much to learn from the normal simulation except that the model could finish regardless of what was included.

The output of the thirty nonnormal simulations showed the following:

CONVERGENCE SUCCESS.	Model 1	FIT RMSE	178.8944
CONVERGENCE SUCCESS.	Model 2	FIT RMSE	171.6958
CONVERGENCE SUCCESS.	Model 3	FIT RMSE	182.1742
CONVERGENCE SUCCESS.	Model 4	FIT RMSE	183.7004
CONVERGENCE SUCCESS.	Model 5	FIT RMSE	180.8553
CONVERGENCE SUCCESS.	Model 6	FIT RMSE	278.7862
CONVERGENCE SUCCESS.	Model 7	FIT RMSE	170.4314
CONVERGENCE SUCCESS.	Model 8	FIT RMSE	176.4152
CONVERGENCE SUCCESS.	Model 9	FIT RMSE	176.8189
CONVERGENCE SUCCESS.	Model 10	FIT RMSE	179.4391
CONVERGENCE SUCCESS.	Model 11	FIT RMSE	182.3472
CONVERGENCE SUCCESS.	Model 12	FIT RMSE	178.9915
CONVERGENCE SUCCESS.	Model 13	FIT RMSE	186.5381
CONVERGENCE SUCCESS.	Model 14	FIT RMSE	188.8867
CONVERGENCE SUCCESS.	Model 15	FIT RMSE	187.2212
CONVERGENCE SUCCESS.	Model 16	FIT RMSE	171.7611
CONVERGENCE SUCCESS.	Model 17	FIT RMSE	174.8951
CONVERGENCE SUCCESS.	Model 18	FIT RMSE	180.2177
CONVERGENCE SUCCESS.	Model 19	FIT RMSE	272.9954
CONVERGENCE SUCCESS.	Model 20	FIT RMSE	180.8755
CONVERGENCE SUCCESS.	Model 21	FIT RMSE	180.6756
CONVERGENCE SUCCESS.	Model 22	FIT RMSE	188.4514
CONVERGENCE SUCCESS.	Model 23	FIT RMSE	178.0748
CONVERGENCE SUCCESS.	Model 24	FIT RMSE	176.3612
CONVERGENCE SUCCESS.	Model 25	FIT RMSE	277.5765
CONVERGENCE SUCCESS.	Model 26	FIT RMSE	182.3998
CONVERGENCE SUCCESS.	Model 27	FIT RMSE	172.6049
CONVERGENCE SUCCESS.	Model 28	FIT RMSE	183.7482
CONVERGENCE SUCCESS.	Model 29	FIT RMSE	288.4833
CONVERGENCE SUCCESS.	Model 30	FIT RMSE	181.6118

This was what he had anticipated. The model could finish on the non-normal returns as long as one of the thirty variables was excluded. Beyond that, he wasn't sure what else this taught him. Jake looked up from his computer and checked the time. It was two minutes to ten, and Jake had to hustle to get to his classroom. He didn't want to be late to teach since he always gave his students a hard time when they walked in late. He could come back to finish the analysis after class.

The third floor of the McCombs Business School had a mixture of offices and classrooms that surrounded the central atrium. Jake was teaching this investments class in room 317, an older classroom with less technology but many windows and a great view across campus. The students in this class were some of his favorite he had ever taught. They were inquisitive and very bright, and many had already landed good jobs. Given the students' input, the class wasn't bound by the typical restrictions of a required class and standard material.

So Jake used this class to share and teach the students his favorite learning tool for success in finance: examining the great trading failures through history. He had already discussed Long-Term Capital Management and bond spreads, Orange County pension and reverse repos, and Nick Lesson and Barings Bank, but today would be slightly different. Today wouldn't be about a billion-dollar trading loss. Today they would discuss the evolution of the markets and trading in the future.

"Can someone explain to me what HFTs are and how they work?" Jake asked as everyone settled down.

Madison, a highly energetic if not pedantic student who had landed a job at Citadel, spoke up. "They're high frequency traders, the computers that trade electronically. They take advantage of speed and positioning of their physical location to get trades in quicker and earlier than human-driven trades. In theory they should help improve efficiency of prices, since more information should be reflected in those prices quicker."

"Are you saying you believe in market efficiency? And that these HFTs are good for average investors?" Jake asked, trying to prompt discussion that would lead to debate.

"There's no way that they're good for investors," Michael said. "These computers don't care about value. They only try to cause short-term disruptions that they can take advantage of."

Jake could always rely on Michael to take to the bait. He was going to Fidelity and believed in long-term, value-based investing.

Jake laughed. "Don't you see the forming paradox between these two ideas, or the disparity between the underlying theory and what occurs in practice? Madison, who believes that more information is better, leading to higher market efficiency, is going to work for a shop that will try to take advantage of short-term inefficiencies in the market. If they're as good as they say they are, then the efficiency should disappear, and you will be out of a job. According to you, Michael, without the HFTs, the market would be better off and would make your search for value significantly harder or potentially moot. How can that be? Let's take time to explore these notions, because this isn't trivial."

The rest of the class delved into the notion of what it meant to trade, placing size in the market, and what led to days such as the Flash Crash of May 2010. Taking that theory into practice was the backbone of making a solid financial professional.

Jake returned to his office exhausted. He loved the teaching, and it gave him great satisfaction, but he had to return to the backbone of his academic career. He hit the spacebar so the monitors came to life and looked at the output of the model.

What the fuck is that? How did I miss that before? Jake hadn't noticed this initially, but models 6, 19, 25, and 29 all had RMSE errors that were an order of magnitude higher than the other models.

CONVERGENCE SUCCESS.	Model 6	FIT RMSE	278.7862
CONVERGENCE SUCCESS.	Model 19	FIT RMSE	272.9954
CONVERGENCE SUCCESS.	Model 25	FIT RMSE	277.5765
CONVERGENCE SUCCESS.	Model 29	FIT RMSE	288.4833

The nonnormal simulations definitely varied depending on what was included and what was not. This was different from the prior thirty simulations that didn't separate normal returns from nonnormal returns.

Jake focused on these twenty-six simulations and was not surprised that each one of these simulations excluded either leverage or one of the three key subjective variables.

The twenty-six simulations that had all four of these variables had the lowest RMSE, and there was little variation in the parameter estimates. This was the biggest breakthrough to solving the problem since he had first run into the issue with the model's inability to finish. By separating out the normality, it was now clear that these four variables were responsible for the asset returns becoming nonnormal. *More than that, these four variables appear to be reducing the uncertainty in nonnormal markets—they're helping to predict asset price movements.* Now all he had to do was figure out why including all thirty variables led to model failure.

He had done all the required econometric error checks and come up blank. It was not a programming or coding issue. There was something in the results.

Jake was stubbornly persistent, a trait that he had inherited from his grandfather, but had enough self-awareness to know when it was time to take a break. He took the next hour to grade some homework, both from his class and Dr. Rosen's. Grading was a tedious part of the job, one that all academics loathed, but it was a good way to take his mind off the research. A better way was to meet Haley for a swim and lunch at Changos, except that he was already five minutes late for their workout.

The pool at the University of Texas was Olympic quality, and had to be, given the number of Olympic swimmers that had called it home. The walk from the business building down to the aquatics center was right down the hill past the Gregory Gym. It was always nice to have the downhill walk heading to the pool, but it wasn't so enjoyable heading back up after a long set.

Haley was waiting at the entrance to the pool, looking fairly unhappy. Her research was as frustrating and time consuming as any other graduate student's, but sifting through old newspapers in the dark, moldy library made her feel as if she were turning into a mole person that was afraid of natural light. It also didn't help that it was freezing, requiring her to wear an extra layer of clothing and do her research with gloves on. Her expression worried Jake greatly, since Haley was a better swimmer than he, and she was going to take her frustration out on him in the pool.

"Where have you been, asshole? I've been waiting for ten minutes," Haley said, quite exasperated with Jake's tardiness.

"Sorry I'm late. I was working on the—"

"Balls. I know, and I don't care. You better be ready to go fast."

Jake could only nod his head, and he knew that for the next hour, he would be in complete oxygen debt.

CHAPTER 17

"Let's have a report on the general market conditions," Frank Lyman's tone was matter of fact with no hint of emotion. As Michelle quickly learned, no names or references to their positions were ever mentioned in the Markov Group meetings. The collective power in this group was staggering and exceeded anything outside of these walls. While other groups in Washington, London, the United Arab Emirates, and Beijing might disagree, their perception of power was only that. Lawmakers overestimated their true clout, since it always took the collective will of multiple incompatible people working together to institute some form of law that typically had little to no impact on the everyday person. The people in this group could change market values and world economies with one collective vote, shifting billions in wealth in a matter of weeks, days, or seconds. The impact of 2008 was evidence of that.

"From a political and policy standpoint, nothing has changed," the man in the charcoal suit and red tie said. "The focus on domestic issues, health care, infrastructure, and immigration is typical pandering and positioning for smaller, less tangible economic impacts. In other words, there's nothing coming out of Washington that should have a material impact. I'm concerned about overseas positioning when it comes to energy. Russia is so susceptible to a drop in oil prices, and Western Europe knows this. I believe there's collusion taking place between the Saudi states and Russia to keep energy prices high. This isn't a problem, but it's something that we should keep an eye on. This does put us in a position of power if we wish to pursue a course of action to weaken global energy markets, but I don't think it's necessary right now." The man in the charcoal suit had no accent. He always wore the same colored suit and red tie. He might have been born and bred in the Northeast, but his international experience was vast, muting his vocal heritage. His experience with dealing with multiple countries and close to a trillion dollars in assets gave him control of capital markets and liquidity that was the largest of any privately held institution. He sat to the right of Frank and was tall and lithe. He had tightly cropped blond hair.

Michelle had always found Michael McQuary to be quite aloof, and his reputation for negotiation was second to none. *Plus he drinks the blood from newborn deer and sleeps in a coffin.* His firm's access to the halls of Washington was legendary and gave him and his firm certain distinct advantages when it came to influence over the US and global political landscapes. By physical contrast, the person to the left of Frank, Harvey Waterman, was short, bald, and significantly overweight. He was pasty and always out of breath and looked on the verge of having a heart attack. Yet his mind was as sharp as any person's in this room. His firm headed up the largest global trading operations across all markets and had the largest market capitalization of any investment bank in the world.

Waterman's firm handled the biggest over-the-counter derivatives operations by a factor of two and thus controlled the most leverage and the flow of that leverage anywhere. The daily volume of the notional contracts that came across the firm's desk exceeded the gross domestic product of all but six of the largest countries in the world. The over-the-counter market could be thirty times the size of the equity markets, and it was this fact alone that demonstrated how leverage could affect the valuation of almost any company or country. In 2006, when the first credit default swap was introduced, it was through the use of these instruments that his firm propped the markets up for an additional eight months before reversing on the contracts that had begun the equity sell-off in September 2008. Through somewhat less-than-transparent marking to market, the Markov Group, through Waterman's firm, was able to position itself to withstand the inevitable bubble burst and initiate a US-based recovery once the dust and damaged had settled. Although propping the market up caused a much sharper decline in the fall of 2008, the actions of the Markov Group made sure the United States could recover and retain its position of power as the world's economic leader. If the tall, blond-haired man was responsible for macrobased decisions, this putrid little man was responsible for the micro-decision that moved capital markets on a daily basis.

Harvey began his update. "So far we can report no abnormal trading behavior from any sector. The amount of leverage we've seen chasing beta has increased, behavior consistent with the slow market drift up we've experienced over the past couple of years. There's also an increase in the demand for high-yield products, which may be extending the risk in the bond markets, but nothing to worry about. The HFTs are not doing anything abnormal, so it's status quo." The man could not suppress his Harvard-educated Bostonian accent. It drove Michelle crazy.

"From the exchange's perspective, there have been no abnormal trades coming through the system. Flows are normal," the man seated next to Waterman said. Jerry Ospry was the oldest of the group and had been front and center in helping with the evolutions of the markets. He had experienced more bull and bear cycles than anyone in the room. From the early days of paper trading to the high-speed nanosecond trading of today's markets, this man had seen it all and had been on the forefront trying to control the damage and panic of the October 1987 crash. Although he controlled no capital flows, without this man, no trade would ever be completed. He had been instrumental in keeping markets functioning when liquidity dried up in the crash and restoring order in the capital markets when people were jumping from their windows. Michelle remembered seeing him on television, his bright-blue eyes preaching faith and confidence in the US economy and the open and free capital markets. Amazing how beliefs can change through time.

"Current lending and borrowing are slower than historical averages," said Victor Panket, head of the largest commercial bank in the world. "It's been important to keep the access to credit limited at the retail level so we don't have a repeat of 2008. This may be causing a wealth gap, but we all agreed that was an alternative we could live with. Some of the European banks' cash positions are weaker than we would have wanted, but that might present an opportunity later. It appears the general conditions are as we anticipated."

The daily lending and overall cash management of this firm exceeded the next two biggest banks combined. Without this bank's liquidity, economic progress could halt in an instant and a repeat of the 1929 Great Depression be replicated. This man had dark hair, translucent brown eyes, and a passive, engaging tone, and his personality was embodied in the bank. There was a reason his firm was consistently rated number one for cash management, reputation, and deposits. He was trusted, respected, and generally considered the man most likely to be the next secretary of the treasury. That title had been available to him for the past two administrations, but he had always declined. His vision had always been to improve the banking community to help improve the lives of all consumers. In part, he felt he had accomplished some of that goal.

The interaction of the people in this group outside these walls was cordial but limited. Any sort of connected relationship could prove detrimental to the goal of the Markov Group. Michelle doubted that anyone could determine a connection between all them, even though they all worked within the finance industry. The finance world was an interconnect web, and the ability for anyone to untangle it would be close to impossible. Personally, besides McQuary, she liked all the men in the group, and especially Victor. Their conversations prior to this group meeting had always been pleasant, and she had always found him to be genuine, almost genteel. There was something about those translucent brown eyes that she always found to be trustworthy. Finding out that he was a part of this group was somewhat of a shock, but, upon reflection, it made a lot of sense given all that he had accomplished. *I know of all of you, except you, Mr. Lyman. What is your story? Why are you here? And why are you the head?*

Michelle knew it was her turn. There wasn't much to add. "Rates will remain close to zero for the next six months, but there's no plan to increase the quantitative easing beyond the next quarter. There will be no surprise statements from the chairman until the formal statement at the next meeting," she said confidently.

"Good," said Frank. "We can adjourn until next month, unless otherwise needed. Remember the protocol for leaving the building. A word before you leave." He looked directly at Michelle.

Michelle waited, watching each member depart in the order assigned. Each waited five minutes after the prior person left before getting up to leave. The first person to leave would go through the main entrance, the second through the service entrance, and then the pattern would repeat. As far as Michelle knew, Frank left using a helicopter that waited for him on the roof, although she didn't know if there was an actual helipad up there.

"How are you adjusting to your new position? I'm sure it isn't too taxing since you've been groomed for it ever since you joined the Fed." Frank answered his own question.

"It's what I expected. As you said, it hasn't been a big adjustment, just a change of title."

"Yet it's more of a challenge because you now have to deal with political appointees and agendas. Yes?"

"Well, that's been easier than I initially thought. I knew all of the FOMC members prior to my new role, and the chairman. The chairman appears to side with whatever the political majority is. It's fair to say that this chairman might be the most malleable we've had in thirty years. That might change, but as of right now, there's very little ego present."

"Good. Good. I didn't think that would be a problem. Now, how about our little group here? Are you comfortable with the makeup and the direction?"

Michelle knew this question would be coming. The meetings up to this point had been repetitive and had required no decisive action. The inaction might have been to get her comfortable with the flow and decision-making process that the group engaged in, but it also might have been to assess her mood through these first couple of months. Her answer would have to be careful, since she did not trust any one of the members completely and was slightly fearful of Frank. *Fear of the unknown.*

"You know my position and the research I've done. The behavioral nature of the markets and the economy requires a suspension of disbelief that free markets are the best mechanism for the allocation of capital. I wouldn't be in this position unless I knew it was up to us to keep that illusion going. We manage the fringe." She was confident. She didn't need to lie, but she also had to remain convincing. *Remember to breathe.*

Frank looked at her without responding, just nodding his head.

After about thirty seconds, which felt significantly longer, Frank suggested they both leave, and Michelle got up and headed to the elevator banks.

Only after the doors closed did she allow herself a moment of reflection. The position she was in was one of significant power, more than most would ever realize, and yet she was beholden to a philosophy that she could not deviate from. *I'm doing the right thing, and it has to be done in this way.* If the general public ever found out, the ramifications would be catastrophic.

Michelle exited onto Broad Street and walked to Wall Street. She passed by the NYSE with its cordoned entryways and huge American flag taut against the building facade. The NYSE was the symbol of capitalism, both good and bad, and the reason so many took the pilgrimage to this part of downtown New York. The fact that Broad Street was a pedestrian street actually added to the ambiance, something Michelle appreciated. It muted the stress and noise typically associated with any typical Manhattan street. Seeing Trinity Church at the left turn on Broadway on her way to catch the number 4 to head back uptown always put a smile on her face. This historic building, like the St. Bartholomew Church on Park Avenue just northeast of Grand Central Station, just seemed so out of place. It was a reminder of the history of this city and all the great accomplishments that had occurred here and had filtered through to the rest of the country. It was always good to reflect on how important a strong foundation was to make a stronger future.

Michelle descended the stairs and pulled out her Metro card to begin her journey home. At the same time she was heading up the street, a man with a distinct cleft in his chin exited the TD Bank building, also took the left on Broadway, descended the same subway stairs, and got into the same subway car heading uptown. The person who followed Michelle was not Mr. Jones, but he did work for Franklin Insurance, filing similar daily reports. Mr. Jones was not following her. He had a more important target, a target that required more of his skill set.

CHAPTER 18

Jake was different from most of his fellow PhD students, and not just in his appearance. He couldn't just sit in his office writing code, reading papers, and generally talking finance and obsessing over publications and the lack of journal space. Jake did his best thinking away from the confines of his office, and on this day, it was out on his bike. As far as luxury went, Jake's triathlon bike was the most expensive item that he owned. It was definitely more valuable than his 1982 Jeep Wrangler, which had rust on top of rust. The BMC TM02 carbon frame with Shimano dura-ace components and Vision Metron wheels was pewter and black, absorbed the road, and exploded when it accelerated. There was no better feeling than being in the aerobars—moving from the traditional seated position to a flat-back, tucked position—going twenty-five-plus miles an hour and letting all worries fly away with the wind.

Door to door, the dam loop, as it was notoriously called, from their condo on Cullen Avenue, was fifty-five miles. It was a relatively cool day, but the sun was out, and it was a perfect day to ride. Haley couldn't ride that day—she had to teach beginning swimming to sophomores and juniors at the swim center—so Jake rode solo. This was probably the best outcome, since he could ride at his own tempo and allow his mind to think freely.

Jake headed out of his complex and went north on Shoal Creek Boulevard. This gave access to Spicewood Springs Road and eventually to 360, the Capital of Texas Highway. This rolling stretch of road had a large shoulder that made riding relatively safe, although the traffic in Austin was getting ridiculous. One could never be too safe on the roads, even with a nice wide shoulder.

The northern part of 360 was downhill until the section of Highway 2222 crossing the Colorado River. Jake took these first couple of miles easy, waiting for the turn onto Bee Caves Road before getting in his aero-bars and holding a more consistent tempo. The rolling hills of 360 allowed for a nice view of Texas Hill Country and a glimpse of the Austin skyline. Focusing on his cadence and the changing pace and effort helped clear his mind, akin to mediation. Jake didn't necessarily subscribe to any type of Eastern philosophy, but he felt exercise was the closest he would get to achieving a sense of nothingness, or whatever the Tibetan monks strived for. That clarity washed away concerns and worries and usually provided a clean alternative view to whatever problem he was trying to solve.

Jake got out of the saddle for the climb up to Bee Caves Road. This climb got his heart rate going and was a great way to lead into a more sustained effort for this nine-mile stretch west before the turn onto the 620. As he climbed, something popped into his mind, something that he had not considered prior to all of his testing, back testing, and error checking.

Reducing drag and weight on the bike always leads to better performance, he thought. He knew that a lighter, more aerodynamic bike will go faster with the same output from the rider than a heavier, less aerodynamic bike. For each marginal gram that leads to weight reduction or shaped tube to improve airflow and aerodynamics, there is an increase in the cost, and that cost grows exponentially. One can buy a very reasonably priced bike that weighs twenty pounds and has no fancy aero components or wheels and ride quite comfortably and quickly. The reduction in weight from nineteen pounds to eighteen pounds and so forth, along with aero wheels, increases the cost dramatically, so a top-end bike could exceed five figures. Yet the marginal performance for the average rider over the twenty-pound bike may not be significant. *Where is the point where the marginal benefit equals to marginal cost?*

As he climbed the 360 Highway, he went into the aerobars. *Just that movement alone improved my speed because it reduced the total drag coefficient, and it cost me nothing to do. All benefit with no cost.* Greg LeMond won the Tour de France in 1990 because he adopted what was at the time a radical position that incorporated aerobars. That changed the way cyclists have raced against the clock ever since.

The parallels to the research academics did were obvious. *Most research tries to improve the bike, and the net marginal gains are very small. Once in a while, someone changes position, and the gains are huge and, in hindsight, obvious.* Jake realized that the problem he had been having with his research was not with the results; it was with the premise of how he was looking at the results.

Jake held 250 watts for the Bee Caves Road stretch, which translated to about an average of twenty-three miles per hour. Satisfied with this effort, he sat up and spun easily for the next twenty minutes before the climb up to the Mansfield Dam and the east descent back down Highway 2222. The dam climb could be broken into three sections, with a slight reprieve between each of the three. The wind had picked up a fraction and was more of a crosswind than a headwind, which could actually be harder to ride through. There was a small group ahead, maybe three or four riders, and he tried to catch them before the climb up.

Passing over the Colorado River again, Jake sat back and tried to hold 280 watts for the two-and-a-half-mile ascent. He figured at that pace he should catch the group ahead before the end of the second section. Riding at a sustained tempo should get him to the top faster than a short, quicker burst and a higher variability in his output. *Again, this same principle applies to the stock market. Investors always demanded higher Sharpe ratios, the ratio of return to risk, and would typically accept it with either higher return or lower risk.* Maximizing that Sharpe ratio was the basis of most financial models and theories of portfolio management. For Jake, riding the dam climb at the highest watts he could with as little variation as possible would result in the quickest time to the top.

However, there are times when this simple and clean theory doesn't work, he thought. *Maximizing a Sharpe ratio doesn't account for all market conditions and makes some very heavy assumptions.* Likewise, he knew that holding the steadiest achievable watts doesn't take into account wind conditions, terrain changes, and other groups on the road. Sometimes putting in an early effort on a harder section with a more controlled effort on an easier section could result in a better overall time up the climb. Jake remembered reading about the power output of Tour de France riders versus the power output of Ironman riders. For the Tour de France stage winners, their power output was much more variable, with specific efforts at key points in a stage. For the Ironman athletes, the lowest variability for their bike rides resulted in the best performance off the bike and in lower marathon times. *Two different styles achieving the best possible outcome.* This also held true for different types of race distances. Shorter distances required different outputs and different race strategies.

As Jake passed the group in the middle of the second hump, the old adage of investing came into his mind. *The market is efficient over the long term, and most investors, whether they're retail or institutional, can't outperform the market. Most investors should hold the market as their portfolio and never trade in and out of the portfolio, hold individual stocks, or make market calls. Yet over the short term, the market is inefficient, and these small deviations are where the true outperformance occurs.* Jake had always held to the belief that the deviations were random in nature and that those investors who were successful were simply in the right place at the right time, having very little to do with skill. It is impossible to predict market shocks—they are truly random events—but the average of these events through time nets to zero. What was best in the long run was to do nothing, not time these events, and hold the market in the long run.

The final of the third humps was the hardest of the three, but not because it came last. It was the steepest of the three climbs and was completely straight, which played a trick on the eye in not showing the full extent of the climb. The peak finished beyond eye level, so the climb actually finished two hundred yards further ahead than where you thought it did. That last section could really hurt, especially if your lactic acid had already built up because of prior efforts. Jake had ridden this climb enough to always keep that little bit in reserve, and when riding with a group and racing for the top, it was those last two hundred yards that would make the difference.

Jake remembered when he had ridden with Benson, when Benson was in prime shape, and he had tried to hold Benson's wheel to the perceived top versus the actual top. He had blown right at the fake top, and Benson had gapped him by fifty yards by the time he actually got to the crest of the hill. The next time he rode with Benson, instead of trying to hold his wheel, Jake rode at his own pace, and while Benson dropped him earlier in the climb, Jake's deficit at the actual crest was less than fifteen yards. Better information led to a better decision and better performance.

This metaphor led Jake to conclude something about the short-term deviations that he hadn't considered before and that could be related to his findings. *What if these short-term deviations are not random? Maybe there's some information out there that actually explains the short-term deviations, the nonnormal returns. In addition, and this is the important part, the information that drives the short-term deviations isn't an attempt to improve market efficiency but actually to make it more inefficient. It's possible that the nonnormal returns have a specific driving force that causes them and have I found the right combination of factors that explain that force?*

I think that answer is yes. The model isn't failing; it's actually capturing why the market experiences outliers beyond the normal distribution. Not only that, it is capturing them...PERFECTLY.

This revelation excited Jake thoroughly because it was beyond a unique finding; it was a finding that would change the current thinking in asset pricing, just like adding aerobars improved time trialing. As Jake rode the last part of 620 and took the right down the hill on 2222, he could feel his heart rate elevate and his cadence picking up. The adrenaline rush was filtering through his body, and he was sure that his Strava time on this section and the return on 360 would be a top time. His desire to get back to his code and assess the data helped him keep his speed up all the way through Spicewood Springs and Shoal Creek Roads.

He got back to the condo in two hours and twenty-two minutes and was feeling a little drained. He had forgotten to eat after the climb on 620 and was beginning to feel the early stages of an energy bonk. Opening the door, he didn't even say hi to Haley but took off his shoes, ran to the fridge, grabbed a Gatorade and a Snickers bar, and sat on the kitchen floor.

Haley walked over and looked at him with a disapproving smirk on her face. She was wearing just a sports bra and running shorts. Her shoes weren't on yet.

"No 'hi.' No 'how was your day.' I'm guessing you forgot to eat, and that's why you're on the kitchen floor. You've got salt caked all over your face. I guess you also didn't drink enough, idiot," Haley said in a mocking yet loving tone.

"Sorry. Hi. How was your day? Yes. And yes," Jake answered, still feeling light-headed. Haley's stomach muscles were on full display in her minimal attire.

"Day was good. You should see some of these kids swim. I swear some of them would drown if the pool was any longer. But they're good kids, and I give them credit for being out there. It's always tough to learn the older you get. Did you have a good ride? Why don't you look at my eyes when I talk to you?"

"The ride was great, especially since you weren't there. Come over here," Jake said, reaching out and trying to hook his finger in the waistband of her shorts.

"I'll remember that bullshit comment the next time we swim together, and given the look on your face, there's no way you have the energy to satisfy me."

Jake balked at that statement and tried to pull her closer. She faux resisted, and he managed to get his hand behind her back and pull her on top of him.

"Your breath smells like chocolate and your—"

He kissed her before she could utter something more disgusting while slipping his hand down the back of her shorts. Getting some calories back in his system had given him the required energy boost. As Haley worked his cycling top over his head, Jake paused and looked into her eyes.

"Haley, listen, I think I figured out the problem, but the solution may result in two larger problems. First, if my model is correct, and I believe it is, the implications for how we think about asset pricing may fundamentally change forever. To get that by the committee and eventually published will take a herculean effort, regardless of the proof I provide. Graduate students are not supposed to have these kinds of breakthroughs."

Haley nodded. "The second problem?" she asked as she removed her sports bra.

"Second is..." She had caused him to lose his train of thought.

"Yes? You were saying?"

It was an important point, but it had gone from his mind. He turned his focus to more immediate matters, pressed his head in between her breasts, and moved his hands further down her shorts.

CHAPTER 19

The first presentation Jake had ever given in front of the faculty was disastrous. First-year graduate students were required to present their summer papers prior to the start of their second year. These first attempts at research tended to be quite awful, from the methodology to the results. The forty-five-minute presentations were designed to be introductions to the difficulty of presenting an original idea to a group of self-important yet highly successful academics. Jake had thought his first year paper was simple and elegant and had been looking forward to explaining it to the faculty.

That presentation had taken place the last week of August right before the fall semester began, and Jake still felt the scars from how badly he had gotten beat up. Presentations took place in the Legacy classroom on the second floor of the business school building. The room held sixty people and had auditorium seating, and on that particular day, the room had been almost full. All the faculty were there, as were the other PhD students. Jake's presentation was the second of the day, after Audria's.

Looking back on it now, he could not remember what she had presented but knew it had gone better than his. The introduction had gone well, outlining the idea, the motivation, the initial problem, and how he went about solving the problem. Then it went downhill very quickly. A couple of assistant professors asked him about investor home bias and the nature of changing correlations, which Jake was not prepared for, which led to him losing the audience. One of the key aspects when presenting is to control the audience, otherwise the talk can get hijacked.

In this particular case, Jake was unable to come back from these questions, stuttered, and gave nonsensical answers. It led to one of the eminent scholars standing up and telling Jake and the audience that this was a waste of time, and he left. Jake didn't remember the rest of the presentation after that incident but clearly remembered how he felt sitting in his office with the door closed and lights off, wondering why he was there. But those scars had been necessary to harden the skin and become better prepared to defend his theories. Reflecting on that experience, Jake was thankful he had gone through it. He knew he could present in front of Nobel Prize winners and stand toe to toe with them. He loved to present and welcomed the challenge.

Jake now stood in front of the faculty in the department conference room, ready to present his dissertation work. After months of concern related to his big finding, he felt supremely confident of the result and the implications of the finding. How it would be received by the faculty was another concern. This presentation was to assess his job-market readiness. Audria was to present her dissertation the next day.

Jake had shown the results to Eric prior to this presentation. He had comprehensive analysis on how the results varied for different models based on different market conditions, the implications of the four factors, and how the model's explanatory variables interacted with one another. Eric had looked at the analysis and had had trouble arguing with the findings. He had relayed to Jake that these results were very impressive, but he had offered a word of caution.

"Jake, you've more than enough for me to sign off on your dissertation, but how this will be received I can't say. I go back to our earlier discussion that it may be met with significant skepticism. I suggest tempering the conclusion. Present the results for sure, but don't conclude anything in regards to the findings. I think it's too controversial."

"Isn't it worth me presenting my conclusion in front of our faculty to get a sense of how it'll be received? I mean, isn't it better to suffer through some adversity here versus with a perspective employer?" Jake asked.

"That's not a bad idea, but if the end goal is to publish the paper, in your case, the least amount of controversy the better."

Jake remembered Eric's words as he started his talk in front of the department. He had about an hour to condense and explain over a year and half of work and hopefully get the feedback he needed to get a sense of how well his work would be received—and, ultimately, his job prospects.

Jake wrapped up his presentation by thanking the participants. There had been the standard type of questions on motivation, methodology, and modeling. These were typical and a test of the faculty to assess his readiness and skill set. When he had gotten to his final table and the results of his large estimation, there had been many questions on the construction of the factors, the design of the empirical tests, and the implications of the results. Jake had answered those questions comfortably without strong rebuttal, and he had never felt as if the presentation was getting away from him.

When he had presented the conclusion, there had been some unease from the faculty. It was definitely met with skepticism but not much in terms of pushback. Jake was pleased by the lack of resistance but also slightly worried. He felt as if the faculty was dismissive of his result. Still, most of the faculty believed he was ready for the job market and had wished him good luck. Eric had come over and told him he had done a good job and asked him to stop by later in the week or the following week to go over some logistics in regards to their upcoming trip to New York.

As Jake was packing, he noticed that Sheldon Tacker had waited behind to have a word with him. Jake knew Sheldon to be direct but also helpful. He wasn't sure what Sheldon would say but assumed it would be some sort of advice for the upcoming job market in January, and his advice usually hit the mark.

"Professor Tacker, thanks for your comments."

"You're welcome, Jake. You've come a long way since that first-year presentation. Eric should be proud of the work you've done."

"I believe he is. I've enjoyed working with him greatly."

"Jake, let me be blunt. I'm concerned with this result of yours. I can only see this being received in one of two ways. One, it is an empirical irregularity such that most will believe that there's either an error in the estimation or with the data. They will assume you've made a mistake, and that's the most likely outcome. Second, if they don't believe that, they will assume that your conclusion is overstated. To believe what you've found, and your conclusion from that result, might border on fantasy. Even if you're right, I don't believe any editor or referee could take it seriously."

Jake suspected this was true, but it still hurt to hear it from Sheldon. Strong headed as he was, Jake would not veer from the path now after so much effort solving the problem.

"Thank you for your input, but the result is the result. I can't draw any other conclusion."

"I know you believe that, but the number of people whose work you would be criticizing, contradicting, and making null and void almost guarantees that this paper will never see the light of day."

"Are you telling me to change the paper?" Jake felt himself getting defensive.

"I'm telling you that publishing is a game. If you don't play within the rules, even if you're right, you can still lose." Sheldon's wiry red beard couldn't hide the concern on his face. Even though Sheldon wasn't his advisor and had a competing student, he cared about all the students in the program and wanted them to succeed.

Sheldon picked up his papers and left the conference room. Sheldon had just told Jake the exact same thing Eric had but had almost threatened him not to present the paper as it was. Jake knew he should heeded the warning, as Sheldon had his finger on the pulse of the publishing world better than almost anyone, but to Jake, the professor's warning only reaffirmed that what he had found was correct. Jake would soon realize that he was right on both accounts.

CHAPTER 20

For a wealth manager, trading a portfolio is a second-order priority. The responsibility of trading the assets should fall on the sales and trading teams, who worry about executing the positions at the best possible price. Benson worked through the sales and trading teams to implement his clients' portfolios, as well as working with his managing director to ensure that the allocations in the portfolios made sense and conformed not only to his client's wishes but the general outlook the firm had for the market. To make drastic portfolio changes usually required authorization from the chief strategist in New York. While clients had discretion over their portfolios and the wealth manager could make recommendations, the firm typically recommended that their clients follow the portfolio allocation that was set forth.

Since this was not the commission-based part of the firm that cared about high portfolio turnover, high-volume trading was not the wealth managers' objective; it was all about raising and accumulating assets. The more assets the firm had under management, the more fees the firm collected and the higher the compensation for the wealth manager. The returns on the portfolios weren't that important as long as the performance wasn't poor enough to have a client leave. Having clients with similar portfolios usually resulted in the best outcome for the firm.

Benson had felt the pressure of underperformance and the deviation from the norm and knew he could do better. He could not revert back to implementing a similar portfolio or approach as the other associates. He needed to distinguish himself to not only retain his existing clients but to recruit new ones. After speaking with Jake and learning about his finding, he had decided it was time to try to use this newfound knowledge.

The process of trading clients' assets was not difficult, but Benson had to do it in a way that would not raise a flag to his managing director (MD). If clients wished to add some individual stocks to their positions, the wealth manager could simply call sales and trading, perform the necessary buys and sells, and make sure the back office cleared the trades. No report had to go to the MD until the end of the month, when a standard portfolio review was required. If a major portfolio overhaul was done, which meant a change in allocation of over 20 percent, then that required the oversight of the MD and a call to the chief strategist.

Benson started slow, shifting a small allocation of his investors' assets out of high growth mutual funds into a collection of stocks that were sensitive to some of the key variables that Jake's model had highlighted. He made sure that the trades never exceeded more than 3 percent of the clients' portfolios and that the basket of stocks never included more than five individual positions. These trades would fly under the radar and would appear to be driven by the clients themselves, at least until the month-end review.

There had been a notable change in performance since he had started, and it was attributable to the shift from the standard client portfolio allocation and Benson's own intuition to trading only discretionary assets using Jake's model. Benson simply followed what the parameters said to do. If certain stocks exhibited strong sensitivities to a positive factor in the model, then he would buy those stocks. If other stocks had negative sensitivities, he would sell. The combination of going long and short, without employing any leverage, had managed to gain significant returns. After news of his performance had leaked out to the rest of the office, his fellow associates grilled him to find out what he was doing.

He had remained coy and told them he was simply doing what his clients asked him to do. There was no way he was going to let on that he had something unique. He had to guard this secret carefully, not only for his own benefit but also because Jake had specifically asked him not to share it.

In fact, Jake never really gave him permission to use the research to trade with, but he hadn't said not to either.

After Benson's monthly review, at which he had the top-performing book out of the entire PWM group, including New York, a sense of security and confidence swelled within him. His MD had no issue with the trades that had been made and told him to keep up the good work. Benson had kept his clients informed of what he was doing, and he hoped through word of mouth from his existing clients that it would become easier to meet with prospective clients and land them. Even Jeremy was showing him some respect.

Given how well it was going and that his MD didn't mind the trades, Benson decided to apply Jake's strategy with more client money, further deviating from the prescribed allocation that came down from New York. He was going to push the allocation to that 20 percent mark. This was easy to justify; his clients would want their capital invested in the best way possible, in fact, it was his fiduciary duty to do so. He would do more if he could, but he didn't want to deal with the T.B. Worley bureaucracy right then.

Benson called up the firm's bond desk, ready to sell several million dollars of US treasuries to begin the shift into buying riskier assets.

CHAPTER 21

The fourth floor of the Flatiron Building was occupied by a relatively innocuous boutique trading firm. As a listed broker-dealer, Griffin Trading Group's focus was finding trading talent and investing in that trading talent. The traditional path most successful finance students took was to be hired by one of the major investment banks, go through a training program, get an MBA, and then be rehired and work their way up to the position of managing director or beyond. Duncan Chamberlain had never wanted that path, and firms like Griffin offered those talented individuals who were willing to bet on themselves a chance for success in the industry without taking the traditional path. If you were good at trading, your chance to make real money would come faster at Griffin than at any other firm. If you could not trade, well, then you had to start at square one.

Firms like Griffin were necessary in today's Wall Street. They filled the gap between the large, longer-term institutional investors and the heavily capitalized short-term HFTs and computerized traders. By investing in human capital, they could find that sweet spot where individual intuition could pick up on behavioral patterns that HFTs could never recognize and the bigger investors were hamstrung to take advantage of. Additionally, the firm's business model was to align its incentives with its traders; if its traders made money, then the firm made money.

Duncan, as a junior partner, was invested in both himself and the firm, and when you had days when you got hammered, it was important not to dwell on them too much. He had always prided himself on his ability to walk away from any day, whether good or bad, and not let it drive his emotions. As he walked to the Twenty-Third Street station, he had to re-flect upon what had happened, because he could not remember a day when the firm had been so wrong on a single trade.

It was one of those gray days in the city where being outside looked and smelled like being trapped inside of a subway station. It was overcast and muggy, as if the underground world of the city had meshed and com-bined with the outside. Duncan always wondered if there was a correlation between the weather in the city and the performance of the overall market. He swiped his metro card and waited for the northbound six to take him home to his one-bedroom apartment. He would get off at Sixty-Eighth Street and take a fifteen-minute walk to his place on East Seventy-Second Street. The place was quite pricey, but it had great views of the East River and across Roosevelt Island.

The day had started off with one of those floated rumors that oil re-serves had been miscalculated and that the new pipeline from Alaska was going to be put on hold. It had started as a whisper, and while nobody could identify the source, most thought it had started with Goldman Sachs. Rumors like this were right about half the time. These rumors were normal, with typical ones being related to one of the big bank's analysts downgrading or upgrading a given stock. Premarket activity typically sent the stock lower if there was a speculated downgrade. If the rumor was false, when the market opened and no downgrade came, or there was a surprise upgrade instead, the shorts would get absolutely destroyed. Duncan knew that following these rumors could be deadly, and he had always believed that firms like Goldman would decide, on any given day, that they would make some small trading firm rich while destroying others.

He also knew he could never ignore the rumors, regardless of how empty they might be, because the rumor always led to unusual trading and greater opportunities. The key was to be positioned correctly, especially if you happened to be on the wrong side of the trade.

The firm had been very active premarket, as were the oil futures and a number of significant energy stocks. The partners had been out on the floor, buzzing about, excited and nervous, making sure that each of their traders was prepared for the day. Duncan could sense that the partners felt this was more than a rumor and that they were excited for the opportunity. Firms like Griffin had their best days when the market was volatile, and over the past year, the market had been quite calm, and their opportunity set had been dwindling. So when short-term plays like this fell in their lap, they were more than ready to take action.

Duncan had also felt the rumor was legit. There was increased conflict in the Middle East and strong production and manufacturing forecast numbers out of Asia, and with the increase in the IMF expectation of global growth, all signs suggested an increase in energy prices. A reduction in US supply could increase oil prices by 10 percent, and premarket futures were already up 5 percent from the prior close. The volatility in the oil and energy markets could be four times higher than that of the equity markets, so while a 5 percent increase was exciting, it certainly wasn't something that was unseen.

Duncan had positioned himself by going long WTI futures contracts, some of the high beta energy companies, and shorting the energy sector spider XLE. The short was a hedge in case prices reversed. He slowly built a position premarket, waiting for the opening bell to increase the equity exposure. As the bell rang, the anticipated liquidity flow went to the energy sector, and from one of Duncan's metrics, he could see that volume was more than double in the first half hour of trading. Trading volumes are always highest in the first and last hour of a market session, but the increased volume was out of the norm.

It wasn't just the energy sector that was rallying; the market was up, with Nasdaq leading the charge. Anyone who had any kind of short exposure was really getting hurt. When stocks go "bid-up," it is usually a signal that someone is caught short and is rushing to cover his or her position. That was the case in many momentum-based stocks in the biotech, technology, and financial sectors, ones that Duncan had held in small proportions overnight and that had strong correlations to the energy sectors. At this point, he was cursing himself a little for putting on his hedge, because the XLE was performing better than the individual positions, and while the hedge was small, it was still eating into his return for the day.

At eleven o'clock, things started to settle down, which should have been expected when the shorts were blown out. The energy on the trading floor was electric while the partners were bouncing from desk to desk to assess how each trader was doing. Duncan sat back and assessed whether it was time to reduce the size of his exposure. His experience suggested that there might be a small sell-off, because blowing out the shorts had driven the price artificially high. His standard protocol was to always take some gains regardless of whether the market continued to trend up. A mixture of discipline and greed was always a successful formula.

The day turned on what seemed like an innocuous move. When prices trade, most of the time the trading is smooth, and the last trade lies somewhere between the bid and ask prices. On the morning rally, there was a gap opening, and the hour-and-a-half price rip up from the opening was a steady, smooth trend upward, even with the pressure on the shorts.

Trading oil was different from trading equity positions. First, there were two choices if one wanted direct exposure to the commodity: WTI Cushing, which reflected North American oil pricing, or Brent, which captured the European and Asian markets. The current market conditions reflected a premium for Brent over WTI because of the US expansion in production and other geopolitical reasons, such as the constant infighting in the Middle East. Most US traders focused on WTI because it affected most other commodities and because it was more liquid. A more liquid instrument is less susceptible to wider bid-ask spreads and potential price legs up or down when large blocks are traded.

So when there was a leg down on the WTI front-month futures contract, it caught Duncan's eye. It was possible that it was some short-term profit taking, which wouldn't have been too surprising given the rally. Duncan kept an eye on it because a full-point leg down meant a relatively large block had been traded. This was followed by another leg down, and in the span of a couple of minutes, the futures were 2 percent of the highs. Duncan reduced his position slightly and began to put in place his trades if things got worse. Another leg down, and he would begin to unwind his book.

At 11:45 a.m., WTI oil futures went down 3 percent from the highs and a "What the fuck?" was issued across the trading floor.

"Be prepared to cover your positions."

"Does anyone know what is happening right now?"

"Is this a standard reversal, or did we miss something?"

Duncan tried to ignore these common phrases shouted by other traders when an unexpected outcome occurred. He began the process of unwinding some of his long exposure. At the same time, he searched his newsfeed for anything related to oil prices and the supply. His Skype chat was active with questions from his colleagues on the floor. He was sensing some real panic from some of them. He estimated they must have ridden some serious leverage through the early morning trading.

At noon, the first news began to filter in that the report from Goldman had been erroneous. Not only was it not legit, but the opposite was true. The United States had an excess energy supply. The US was now essentially energy independent and had enough oil to export to Western Europe. This news would fundamentally change the price in oil. Oil returns went negative on the day, wiping out the positive move in the first hour and a half of trading, and were falling fast. The volume and the profanity picked up over the trading floor.

"Everybody cover now!"

"We're fucked!"

"Can we ride this out?"

Shit. We might be fucked. He could sense the pain on floor but had to put that aside since he was also in a spot of bother. His hedge, which an hour ago had looked like a bad trade, might end up saving his ass. The problem, he knew, was that when there was a large rush to remove positions, liquidity began to dry up. Market makers had no idea what the actual price was and started to protect their inventory by making markets as wide as possible. This was especially true for smaller, individual positions. For positions like WTI and futures on the S&P, traders would send massive order flow to these index-based instruments because they were the easiest to trade and would be used to hedge the smaller, less liquid positions. It would also result in big price drops as traders that were looking to sell their existing futures along with those that were using the indices to hedge converged.

As a result, Duncan had watched as his futures position and his individual longs got crushed, while the short XLE position helped to offset some of his losses. He knew he had to remove the futures right away, but removing the individuals would be a challenge because he needed a slight bounce to be able to unload the size of the position. There would also be the question of timing to cover the XLE. It would make sense to remove it after he was fully out of the futures positions, but his instinct told him to hold on to those because the market would finish on the lows.

There was panic on the floor as his colleagues struggled with their own unwinds. The last time Duncan could remember a reversal of this magnitude was in 2008, when the Fed was struggling to come up with the bailout package and managed to get it through Congress. The market had anticipated the bailout would be accepted, and the day's trading had sent the market higher. When the announcement of the bailout had passed, the market did not like the terms associated with the package, and the prices fell off a cliff.

The offloading of the futures was a fairly simple task that he was able to complete electronically in the span of thirty minutes. Duncan never panic traded, which meant he never dumped his full exposure at one time. He systematically put in his positions without using stops, since in this environment stops usually got blown out as fast as they were put on. He ended up with a small net loss on the futures given transaction costs, which, given the reversal, was not the worst outcome. From the sounds across his desk, it sounded like many of his fellow traders were doing significantly worse.

The individual positions took longer to remove. This would require patience throughout the day. This was tough to do because every instinct you had was to get rid of those positions as fast as possible. In a volatile market, the best course of action was to combine this patience with decisive action. Balancing the two was a challenge, but doing so could be the difference between a small loss and a potentially destructive one. Any tick up in one of the long stocks he owned and he would put in a sell order, while also buying back some of the XLE exposure. This approach was not only smart from a trading perspective but kept him emotionally calm. A spread trade was always the best approach to removing risk because the trade was price agnostic.

Duncan was in an advantageous position in that the demand for hedging in XLE had driven the price of the sector spider down significantly, and it was highly liquid. However, the price drop of his individual positions was horrifying, and the bid-ask spreads had blown out. At this point, his goal was to have a neutral position at the end of the day. There was no point in holding any overnight risk. Ideally he would like to be out of everything by three thirty, because the last half hour usually brought about extra panic as everyone tried to flatten their books and the market makers increased bid-ask spreads even wider.

With twenty minutes to close, Duncan only had a small short in the XLE left in his book that he planned to hold until the closing bell. The market was heading straight down, and the energy stocks and oil futures were driving everything lower. He had become immune to the noise on the floor, as everyone continued to scramble. Today was a bad day for him, and he was going to take a loss, but it appeared nothing like what the firm was experiencing. Oil prices were below forty dollars a barrel for the first time in several years and had reversed over nineteen dollars throughout the course of the day. His row and desk mates looked shell-shocked. Duncan peered behind him and noticed that the partners' doors were closed. He had a feeling people would be writing checks back to the firm that day. Duncan hoped that the firm would not receive a margin call from its prime broker. Most of the traders used a leverage ratio of ten or twenty to one, and days like this could wipe many of them out. It was possible that many shops like Griffin could disappear if they were caught on the wrong side of the trade today.

When the bell rang and Duncan closed his remaining XLE short, a lull descended on the floor. There wasn't the typical activity postmarket, where many traders gathered their things to leave or prepared for an after-hours conference call or earnings announcement. Most people sat in their chairs stunned. You hear stories about people and firms blowing up, but you never think it actually happens or appreciate the emotional impact until you are present for the carnage. Duncan felt fortunate to have had only a small personal loss, and that was because he hadn't deviated from his trading philosophy. Otherwise he would have looked and felt like many of the people he sat next to.

Staring out of his bedroom window at the east river he tried to take a macro view of the day, because when you are stuck in it, your ability to see the big picture is massively distorted. After hours of reflection he realized it was time to start looking at the market from a different perspective.

CHAPTER 22

Duncan called Jake later that night.

"What's up? I wasn't expecting a call from you. How did the trading go today? What an amazing reversal," Jake said, curious to hear what Duncan's take on the day was.

"Yes. That was not cool." Jake was caught a little off guard. Duncan expressing emotion like that must have meant he was furious.

"Listen, we can talk about what happened today in detail if you like, but I had a question regarding your theory and the model." Duncan asked.

"Go ahead," Jake replied.

"Have you run the model using daily frequency?"

"Yes. I've looked at monthly as well. It's pretty robust to the frequency of the data."

"What about tick by tick?"

"Frankly, I hadn't considered it. For the purposes I needed to prove the underlying hypothesis, daily frequency was enough. I can run the model with the Trade and Quote Detail data, but it won't be as comprehensive because the data doesn't go back as far, and frankly, it would take considerable time to run."

"How about over the past ten years, including the crash periods like 2008 and one-offs like the Flash Crash?"

"I could do it. It'll take some time, but I can do it. What are you looking for?"

"Not exactly sure, but today was one of those days when you felt like something was going on outside of your control. I don't want to call it market manipulation, but it sure felt like it. The timing of the news flows, the size of the trades—it all seemed a bit orchestrated. I'm not sure what the end goal is, but given what we've talked about, and some of the predictive components of your model, I want to look at the power of the model for intraday news flows."

"OK. I'll get on that. It shouldn't be too difficult to rewrite the code for intraday data. Plus, the computer is just sitting there doing nothing while I get ready for this conference. It'll-"

"In addition, and I know this is related to your research, but don't discuss the results when the model finishes. If there's any sort of power to the model, I'm hoping to use the information for trading opportunities." Duncan interrupted Jake. Jake could feel the agitation in Duncan even if his voice gave nothing away.

"OK." Jake paused before continuing on. He got the sense of déjà vu that he had had this conversation before. "I must say I'm somewhat in disbelief. You typically don't delve too much into the academic research for trading. Especially with the work I do. Why the change of heart?"

"This is because of our prior discussion and because of the trading today. I think that there are unexplained behaviors that take place when the market has these kinds of days. This analysis may shed some light on it. Call me when the model finishes?"

"Will do."

Jake let Duncan hang up without telling him that his intuition was correct. His brother's feeling that something was off on extreme days was related to Jake's finding on nonnormal market returns. *Duncan's mention of the market being orchestrated may be right. That was what I wanted to tell Haley before she distracted me. If that's the reason for the nonnormality, then the financial markets may be in real trouble.* It also occurred to Jake that this was the second time that someone had now taken an interest in his findings for practical purposes.

Jake went to check what happened in the market that day with a little more intent. With teaching classes and writing up his research, he usually didn't follow what happened in the market on an intraday basis, just checking the closing prices at the end of the day. Now he checked more thoroughly the indices and the key commodities before any individual stocks. The pattern in oil prices was highly irregular, definitely something that lay outside of a normal distribution. It was a potential three-sigma move. Jake would have to call his contact at the New York Mercantile Exchange to see if he could get the daily order flow. The overall volume on the day was five times the normal amount, but Jake was sure that there were some key trades that had definitely triggered the reversal. If there was some relationship between the intraday output of his model and what he had found so far, it was possible that there was a lot of money to be made.

Downloading the intraday data and setting the model up to run on that data would take time. The tick-by-tick data expanded the complexity and time to completion exponentially; however, Jake knew it was necessary to do for Duncan's purpose. From a research standpoint, his empirical evidence was robust to day-to-day movements and was sufficient for his dissertation work and graduation. The results from the TAQ data might fill the gap between academic rigor and practical application. The question was whether he should give the results to Duncan. There were some potentially huge downside risks and implications that he wasn't ready to explore yet.

Jake joined Haley on the couch, their mastiff, Winston, lying at the base, snoring away. Haley was writing some notes on a legal pad, not paying attention to what was on the television.

"What are you working on?" Jake asked.

"Condensing my thoughts on all those old papers I went through over the past weeks. Did you know the overriding adjectives to describe female athletes in the 1920s were *Amazonian*, *brutish*, and *rough*? I suspect that the presentation of these athletes to the general public had nothing to do with their athletic prowess and everything to do with their appearance. Reinforcing a fucking stereotype. I'm not saying much has changed today, but the description of their accomplishments is almost nonexistent. Reading these papers from today's perspective, it almost sounds like they're writing about something foreign, something alien."

"I'm not catching the overt misogyny at all," Jake said sarcastically. He was sensitive to Haley's own self-consciousness about being tall, athletic, and muscular but felt like giving her a little dig anyway. She did not appreciate that comment.

"While this is disgusting and horrible, over the past ninety years, only one thing has changed. Female athletes fall into one of two categories from a public standpoint: sex symbol or brute. Something to be fucked or shunned. Look at Evert and Navratilova as the prime examples. You say those two names together, and a picture is painted in your mind, a yin-yang relationship, one as good and one as evil. That's the way they're marketed and sold to the public. It doesn't just have to be within the same sport. It can be across sports, especially during an Olympic year. And this typecasting of athletes filters down to how women feel about themselves when they work out. Think about how you view a woman who is weight lifting versus cycling versus playing pickup basketball. Each man is going to assign something about that person depending on the activity, and that association is much stronger for a woman than it is for a man. Think about what it's like for you to run without a shirt on and for me to run with just a sports bra."

"Haley, I completely agree with you." Jake shifted out of his more flippant tone. "Men definitely behave and act differently when women are involved in sports. Look at this concept of getting 'chicked.' How many times have you noticed men speed up to try to stay with you or attempt to repass you when you're racing in a triathlon? It happens all the time. I believe men have an expectation that they should be faster, stronger, better than women. Yet there are maybe twenty men who are faster than the fastest woman in Ironman racing."

She put the legal pad down and looked at the television. It was on HGTV and one of their endless programs about home repair.

"Who were you on the phone with?"

"Duncan. He had a rough day in the market and wanted me to run some analysis. It's interesting, but, depending on what the results are, it's possible that what I've been working on can be translated to intraday trading and not just overall portfolio construction."

"What does that mean?"

"Not much for us, but it may show a way for Duncan to use some of my findings to improve his trading. I guess we'll see. I'm not sure I should give him the results. By the way, how can you watch this stuff? It's the same show over and over again."

"I like the homes, and I like seeing people's reactions to the new renovations. I just like real estate. Hold on, why wouldn't you give it to him?"

"Let's not get into that now. Well, how about I show you some existing real estate, with a focus on the bedroom?" Jake winked.

"Seriously. That's the best you can do? I'm not sure I even got the double entendre. You can do better than that."

"That's what she said."

"All right, that's enough."

"That's what she said."

"OK, let's go upstairs just so you'll shut up."

"Deal."

CHAPTER 23

Michelle sat quietly, listening to her staff report on the current bank stress reports. Ever since 2008, when the probability of failure for many banks was at its highest since the Great Depression, bank scrutiny had increased so that a repeat of 2008 could not happen again. It was critical that banks could withstand a liquidity crisis, if and when that occurred again, so their capital reserves and leverage ratio were a constant source of analysis.

Prior to the reign of Alan Greenspan and the actions taken by Ben Bernanke in 2008, the Fed was rarely in the public eye. In the late 1970s, when interest rates had climbed into the low teens, Fed policy had turned accommodative and had begun targeting optimal rates of inflation, so the economy never became too stagnant or too overheated. Starting in the 1980s, there had been a steady trend down in the US interest rates and, not surprisingly, a rapid increase in asset valuations. The lowering of rates and bank reserve requirements had increased the liquidity in capital markets, making it easier for companies and individuals to borrow, which had led to unprecedented growth. This had all capitulated in 2008 when, combined with the leverage in the economy, the housing, stock, and general economic conditions had collapsed. The Fed had then become front and center for those not just on Wall Street but on Main Street as well. Everyone had looked to the Fed to help bail out the global economy from a potential second depression. Some looked upon the actions taken by the Fed as criminal, but most viewed the actions as heroic.

Michelle was preparing for one of the eight yearly meetings of the FOMC. The current monetary policy was a continuation of the 2008 policy of historic low interest rates, but the Fed was winding down its controversial policy of buying US treasury securities and some mortgage-backed securities, known as quantitative easing. These programs had resulted in a two-pronged effect of increasing the liquidity in the system and reducing borrowing rates. The side effect of that was to increase the balance sheet of the Fed holdings to astronomical proportions.

"Right now I would say that our bank institutions are the strongest they have been since 2005," said Sarah Dohanue, who headed up the Financial Institution Supervision division of the NY Fed. This side of the bank had been growing significantly ever since 2008. "The leverage ratios are well within tolerances, and all major institutions have capital requirement well in excess of minimum requirements. It would actually be nice to see more lending, but they're being conservative. The risk-return ratio for lending is low relative to the yield play most banks are participating in. We'll release the semiannual report at the end of the month."

"Good," replied Michelle.

Michelle had a lot of respect for Sarah, especially since the rules and regulations and, along with them, the oversight of all chartered banks had become much more taxing. In terms of prestige, the supervisory role played second fiddle to those on the research and policy side.

"Jim, give me the report on open market operations," Michelle requested.

Jim Tretwell was a lifer at the NY Fed, head of research now that Michelle had moved on, and had seen it all. He could have made significantly more money as a player on Wall Street and, if the cards had fallen more favorably, ended up as president of the NY Fed or higher. It was just the nature of life that some great people never ascended to the positions they were destined for. Fortunately, Jim never seemed to mind, always enjoying the role he was in.

"We've had no need to intervene in the foreign exchange markets over the past quarter. Given the responses by the Bank of Japan and statements from the European Central Bank, I don't think we need to take any action to weaken the US dollar. In fact, consistent with our current policy, we hope the strength in the dollar will actually spur some European growth, which will increase the growth potential globally. A higher dollar means cheaper European and Asian goods."

Chris Carter sat quietly, without really adding much. He had never felt more alive. He had wasted years on anger and jealousy. He knew he was smarter than everyone else, but now he had other prizes to hold on to.

He had a PhD in economics from Chicago and in his double duty made sure the organization behind the NY Fed ran smoothly. The New York Federal Reserve employed more than three thousand people, split into eleven subgroups that included legal, human resources, and communications and outreach. These groups helped the bank operate smoothly, allowing research, risk, and supervision to do their jobs and produce output. Carter hated his job. He didn't do research anymore, just provided reports on global investment and credit risk while acting as the bank's internal manager. It was grunt work without any notoriety. There had been ten NY Fed presidents before Michelle Lancaster, and it was a job that nobody left voluntarily. Chris Carter knew he would never climb that final step. Now he didn't care.

He wasn't really paying attention to the reports and discussions that were going on, but his face showed someone engaged and interested. He could sense that people were more at ease with him—noting that his relationship with Michelle had become cordial, if not friendly, at work. There was more laughing, more small talk. *Idiots, if you only knew.* Michelle was good at hiding it, but he knew people had asked her what had changed. She would never reveal their more personal relationship. Chris really didn't care what people thought, as long as he got what he wanted. *What he wanted.* Well, what he wanted had changed greatly given the opportunity that had been presented to him over a year ago.

"Chris, are you comfortable with our current course of action?" Michelle asked. She caught his eye, and he smiled in response. *Bitch, you will burn.*

"I don't see why we would change anything. I think the financial system is the strongest it has been in ten years. I do think our current policy is too responsive to financial markets, but from a liquidity stand-point, the system is in place to withstand a significant market correction. I'm still shocked by the sensitivity of the markets to each word the chairman says. Somehow we need to get off this particular course. However, that's a big-picture discussion. As for our current agenda, I'm more than satisfied."

"Good. Well, if there's nothing else, let's wrap it up. We're well prepared for the upcoming FOMC," Michelle concluded.

The executive committee got up and departed to their various offices. Michelle's eyes followed Chris as he walked back to his office. She passed her secretary, who was busily typing something in Outlook and didn't look up as she walked by. She sat at her desk, looking at the ornate walls decorated with diplomas and accolades. The power that she could wield as the president of the NY Fed was impressive. The ability to change market prices and the lives of so many with a simple vote was remarkable, and that power had to be used carefully.

This was especially true given the dual role she played within the Markov Group as well. Fortunately, it appeared that her position within the Fed and her role in the Markov Group had a common goal, but this upcoming meeting might test that underlying theory. In the prior meeting, the Markov Group had collectively decided to weaken oil prices to weaken Russia, which had occurred to great effect. That was the right decision regardless of what role she was playing. She wasn't sure what she would do if the two roles were at odds with one another.

Which was why getting into a relationship with Chris outside of the office made little to no sense. Yet it was wonderful to be back with him. He had appeared to have changed. The animosity was gone. He cared for her. Understood the pressures, and gave her the emotional support she needed now that Dennis wasn't there anymore. The physical aspect was also a real bonus. She only wished his eyes didn't look so angry all the time.

Chris did not have any conflicting emotions. Chris was in his office, dialing on a secure phone, plotting her demise. He was waiting to hear his contact pick up on the other end. His report today would not have useful information, as no real policy had changed. Not that his contact really should care that much. He had given them so much all ready.

Mr. Jones never showed emotion, but he was happy. Following Michelle Lancaster had been a boring assignment, but things had changed. He knew he had made the right call bringing in another analyst to stay with her so he could look at this Chris Carter more closely. There was something definitely suspicious about this colleague and current lover of hers. This man was hiding something. He was talking to somebody on a cell phone that would require more than simple cell-phone cloning to listen to. A person like Chris Carter shouldn't have that sophisticated a piece of equipment.

Franklin Insurance was building a full personality profile on Chris Carter, but Mr. Jones knew that more was needed before any action could be taken. He needed to find out whom Dr. Carter was speaking to.

CHAPTER 24

The Annual Derivatives Symposium was held in New York at the NYU Salmon Center. It brought together the best academics in the country who specialized in derivatives research. Some were pure mathematicians who focused on the advancement of models that helped with asset pricing, others were practitioners who looked at the impact of options on firm-specific risk management, but most were financial economists who did research on the impact and information contained in derivative prices.

Jake always enjoyed this conference. Eric had asked him to join him here during his second year, even though his name wasn't on the paper Eric had presented. It was a chance to interact with some of the smartest people in the profession and potentially lay the groundwork for a future academic posting. Unlike the bigger conferences, such as the American Finance Association, which gathered all the top academics together, these smaller conferences allowed professors and graduate students in their individual subfields to interact more closely with one another. It also meant that you could possibly befriend a potential referee, which could mean the difference between a revise-and-resubmit and an outright rejection. It was a dirty little secret that everyone knew: even though the refereeing process was supposedly double-blind, each referee knew who the author was, and most authors knew the referee by the style the report was written in. Publishing a paper had as much to do with how good the paper was as with how good you were at marketing the paper.

The first time Jake had accompanied Eric to the symposium, he had sat next to a quiet, unassuming white-haired individual. He had not thought much about who this person was at the time because he had not yet become immersed in the academic world. During a break between presentations, the man asked Jake what he was working on. At the time Jake was assisting Eric in looking at the premiums in volatility, specifically the difference between volatility inferred from the options market and volatility calculated from equity prices. This perked up the white-haired man, and he had asked Jake some relevant questions related to the findings. One of the questions was whether there was any power in his test when he used the GARCH (1,1) model versus using implied volatility. Jake had responded somewhat flippantly that GARCH (1,1) had no power and was essentially a dinosaur in forecasting future volatility. The white-haired man had thanked Jake for his response and had gone to get some coffee. Eric had been sitting behind Jake the entire time and started laughing after the discussion.

"What's so funny?" Jake asked.

"You don't know who that is, do you?"

"No. I don't know who he is, although he was very nice."

"That's Robert Engle. He just won the Nobel Prize for his work on the GARCH model."

"Wow, I just flat-out insulted his whole research agenda. I guess I'm not getting a job at NYU."

That was idiotic, he thought now, reflecting on his naiveté. In a sense it was a good thing that he had initially been so unaware, because it had increased his confidence in his own belief and the quality of his research. From that point on, he had always felt that he could ask a good research question, answer that question, and defend the answer in front of the most critical audience. Today's presentation would further test this hypothesis. Jake was presenting the second part of his dissertation related to leverage, option open interest, and volatility. He was not presenting the full model and the most controversial findings. Today's presentation would be a good feeler to assess how receptive the academic world would be to some of his findings.

Jake scanned the audience to see how many familiar faces he recognized. There was Gav Burdip, from the University of Maryland; Jorge

Coo, from Penn State; the two guys from Northwestern whom he had never met, Peterson and Sandoval; and Jannu Sada, from Massachusetts Institute of Technology. She was the biggest star in the area and had been tenured early at a place that never gave tenure. There were several other familiar faces, but Jake didn't recognize more than half the audience. He speculated that some of the people were from math departments, especially given their appearance. The others had to be practitioners.

Eric had two papers on the presentation schedule: the paper with Jake, his co-authorship a result of being Jake's dissertation chairman, and a piece with a prior graduate student. Eric was going to present the latter piece, which was scheduled for the morning. Jake's presentation would be coming after lunch. Each presentation was scheduled for twenty minutes, with ten minutes for questions. The shorter time frame made for a nice, smooth presentation and removed the typical intro and backstory that was needed when presenting to a broader audience.

Most professors, especially finance professors who focused on derivatives, were quirky. So the presentations could be a little esoteric, with slides that had only equations on them and a flow that was a little tough to follow. Added to that, most professors wanted to show how smart they were, especially to other professors, so each presentation could be somewhat of a dick-measuring contest. One of the things that Jake liked about Eric was that he cared about his audience and always wanted them engaged. He felt that the more engaged they were, the more intelligent he would come across as being. Jake knew that Eric didn't worry about how smart he appeared to others. Eric always knew how smart he was.

Lunch was a very informal affair, where people siphoned off into individual groups. Established, well-published, semi-famous professors gathered together, unless they were at odds with one another, and then they stood as far from each other as possible. Graduate students hovered around these groups like satellites, hoping to express a smart word or inject themselves into the conversation. Practitioners stood alone and were usually on their phones checking the market or answering e-mails. International presenters or attendees usually gathered together, speaking in their native tongues. Eric was talking with Steven Flaggler, the editor of the *Journal of Derivatives*, full professor at Columbia, and an old graduate-student pal. This left Jake to mingle on his own and go over his presentation.

While Jake was collecting his salad and ignoring the heavy pastries, the man that followed him in line through the buffet asked him what he was presenting. Jake wasn't initially prepared to answer, as his mind was fighting that internal battle for something more satisfying than arugula, carrots, and light vinaigrette. Jake knew he could afford a heavy lunch, especially given the amount of working out he had been doing, but presenting with a full stomach was always a bad idea.

"My current paper is one of the three that ultimately make up my dissertation. They all build upon the idea of information and explaining asset prices. This particular piece is about the information in option markets and how that's related to aggregate measures of leverage in the capital markets."

"That is interesting. And what, if you do not mind telling me, are the findings?"

Jake looked over at the man. It was his accent that caught him out. It was clear that the man was from China, probably Beijing or Shanghai, and the suit was a dead giveaway that he wasn't an academic. However, he spoke with a proper British accent, like the one you pick up when you are educated at Oxford or Cambridge. Every word was perfect enunciated and highly formal.

"I don't mind at all. I'm not sure how the broader academic world thinks about option markets, or asset pricing in general; in fact, I believe that there's a strong bias against this type of work. But I think the work we do here is quite important and revealing. I also believe the practical importance is much more obvious and translatable than most corporate research." Jake answered without answering. It was a typical response that Jake gave to see if the person was actually interested in the answer to the question or was just being polite.

"Oh, I believe that to be most true. But my direct question was with regards to your work. Specifically."

Smart. "But of course. Well, my primary interest is in understanding the risk and return relationship, but more directly I'm concerned with why, where, and how abnormal returns occur. Most of the abnormal returns occur when the market experiences some nonnormal behavior, especially negative skewness. So today's paper is about understanding that general concept in the option markets. In particular, I find that option markets reveal a tremendous amount about the future direction of the underlying stock movement, and the size of that movement is related to the leverage in the market and the amount of open interest at a given strike."

"Has that always been the case, or has it changed through time?"

"Well, that's an interesting question, but a better question is how information flow has changed as the option market's liquidity increased. The more liquid the asset, the more relevant the instrument becomes, especially during periods of turmoil. There's a reason everyone hedges their exposure using the S&P 500, right?"

"This is very true. I look forward to your presentation."

Jake nodded as the man strolled away to speak to some of his more familiar compatriots. Jake didn't think too much of the conversation except to note that the man hadn't injected his own ideas or hinted that his research was more important. The conversation was very one sided, and Jake left it at that.

When it came time to present, Jake felt confident and relaxed. It was a good feeling to know his subject matter well, and Eric had drilled into him to enjoy the sound of his own voice. When a presentation goes well, the time flies by. When it goes poorly, time stands still. As Jake had experienced, a good presentation was directly observable by the attentiveness of the audience, regardless of whether that attentiveness was driven by an acceptance of one's theory or a complete disagreement. As long as the presentation encouraged discussion, Jake felt as if he was doing his job.

That is exactly what he got from this presentation. Given the nature and knowledge of his audience, it was not shocking that some of his findings spurred a reaction. In fact, Jannu Sada was particularly agitated by his finding about the direct and almost perfect relationship between option open interests, leverage, and forecasting future stock returns.

"This result is too strong to be believed," she said. "There must be a cointegration problem or survivorship bias in the data set."

"Jannu, I understand your concern, but the data set is clean. In fact, in some of my robustness checks, I replicated the results of your 2009 paper with this data set. So unless your results are afflicted with the same problem, the data set is clean," Jake replied, somewhat aggressively. It was important to never back down to criticism but to do it in a way that was not defensive.

"I don't believe there's a cointegration problem either," he continued. "I've used a generalized method of moments approach as well as model-free estimation. The results are robust to specification error."

"What are the implications of these results?" Peterson, from Northwestern, asked.

"Well, I believe that they can be interpreted in two ways: First, that there's informed trading in the option markets that drives prices in extreme environments. It certainly appears unusual that this activity picks up prior to nonnormal equity events. Second, there may be some form of manipulation going on, similar and maybe more widespread than the Nasdaq one-eighth dealer collusion in the late 1980s and early 1990s. I'm not sure it's my place to say; I just report the findings."

This led to some internal discussion among many of the audience members and signaled a good point for Jake to end his presentation. It was the first time he had expressed this opinion outside the confines of the University of Texas, and he was very interested to see if this discussion perpetuated or ended in this room. If word of his result spread, that could be a good sign for a future publication, not to mention potential job prospects coming up at the AFA conference. The other part that pleased Jake was that this result was a smaller piece of a much larger finding that affected all asset pricing as a whole, not just the option markets. *If this finding excited people, wait until they hear the result from the larger model.*

The conference finished around four, and lunchtime groups reformed before saying their good-byes and heading back to the conference hotel. Eric grabbed Jake before they took the elevator back down to the lobby.

"Nice job today. You defended your results well. There was certainly good buzz about your findings. I would expect a call from Maryland, the University of North Carolina, and the University of Illinois. If we can push a little more, you may get calls from a Columbia or Northwestern. Maybe we need to step up the timeline and get one of these papers under review? A revise-and-resubmit would certainly improve your chances."

"That's good to hear. I know Audria is being pushed ahead of me, but I honestly believe I'm better than her," Jake said. He would only tell Eric that, and that was because Eric believed it.

"Let's assume today was a win. Enjoy yourself tonight, and let's share a cab back to the airport tomorrow morning." Eric departed the elevator and began the short walk back to the conference hotel. Jake wasn't planning on heading back to his room. He was going to meet Duncan and their parents for drinks in Midtown.

Before leaving the building and heading for the subway, the man from lunch tapped Jake on the shoulder. Jake was surprised to see him standing there, assuming that everyone had cleared out.

"Professor Chamberlain, I very much enjoyed your presentation."

"I'm not a professor yet, not even a doctor. I still have to defend my dissertation."

"Of that I have extreme confidence. I have not introduced myself yet. My name in Benjamin Chen. I hope that we may talk more privately, let us say at the AFA conference in January." He handed Jake his business card.

"Sorry, I don't have any cards of my own."

"Do not worry. We know how to get in contact with you. I look forward to speaking with you soon."

Jake nodded, and the man walked away. It was apparent to Jake that he had never confirmed that he would meet with the man, but the tone of the conversation implied that they would.

I guess I can consider that my first interview. He looked down at the card. It read: Benjamin Chen, PhD, Head of Research, China Investment Corporation.

CHAPTER 25

Jake sat down at the table at Vitae to meet Duncan and their parents. Located at Forty-Sixth and Madison, Vitae was always a popular choice for his parents because the restaurant was so close to Grand Central Station. Vitae offered American food with a four-course option or an à-la-carte choice, and the restaurant promoted itself with an upper-class appearance without being overly stuffy. In other words, it gave their mother the high quality atmosphere she was looking for while allowing his father to eat with his fingers if he so chose.

Buoyed by the strong presentation and the weird but positive exchange with the man from CIC, Jake was feeling upbeat heading to dinner. Additionally, Jake was ready to talk to Duncan about the intraday results. Not only did they confirm the daily and monthly finding, but using the model and keying off the direction of the thirty factors in the correct fashion would result in a trading strategy that would be highly profitable. Having their father there would also be useful in discussing the findings. He had over thirty years of corporate banking experience and was a very good sounding board when it came to any economic issue. Of course the downside was that his father knew everything and wasn't afraid to let you know that..

Heading into the restaurant, Jake saw that his parents were there, waiting to be seated, but Duncan had not yet arrived.

"Hi, Mom, Dad. How was the train in?" Jake greeted his parents with a hug each.

"What is with your hair?" his mother asked.

Jake laughed. It had become an inside joke between him and his brother that his mother would make a comment on their appearance before an actual greeting. It was a shame that Duncan wasn't there to laugh with him at that moment.

"Same as always. Remember I took this journey every day for the better part of twenty years." His father answered the question, short-circuiting the typical back-and-forth Jake and his mother got into after one of her comments.

"I imagine Duncan will be joining us shortly. He texted me and said he was doing some after-hours work."

"Well, I believe our table is ready. Should we sit down and order some drinks?"

The hostess walked them to their table, and the waiter came by and talked about specials and the drink menu. Jake ordered a Guinness, in his opinion the best prerace meal you could have, and even though he wasn't racing, a Guinness was always a good choice. By the time the drinks arrived, Duncan had walked in, had seen that they were seated, and had ordered a whiskey. Jake took pleasure in the fact that they were both carded, even though Duncan was seven years younger.

Jake was starving; since he only had a salad earlier in the day he ordered the pulled pork tacos as an appetizer and the trout for the main course. Jake knew he would be ingesting over twenty-five hundred calories in one sitting, which was something he rarely did. There was nothing wrong with enjoying a fine meal and gorging himself a little after the success of the derivatives conference. He felt he deserved it, especially since the life of the graduate student doesn't pay or feed particularly well.

Dinner discussion turned to Jake's presentation, how it went, and his thoughts on the job market. He relayed the details, the interaction with the other academics, and Eric's view that suggested it was a success. It was tough to contain his excitement. The road to completing the PhD was long and filled with many pitfalls, surviving the first two years of course work, passing comprehensive exams, and culminating with finding and defending a dissertation topic. Once you made it to the job market and the dissertation was approved and mostly written, you could see the light at the end of the tunnel. Jake felt that he was right there and that his results and the defense of his results at the conference and with his faculty would lead to only quality interviews at the AFA job market.

Before they finished their main course and thoughts turned to dessert, Jake brought up the TAQ results. It had taken considerable time for the model to analyze the data, but the results had come in, and Jake was excited to share them, but with a caveat of how to use them. Talking about these findings would be different from discussing his academic results for two reasons. First, this audience would be concerned only about how to use the model. Second, this was about keeping the model between themselves and not sharing the result for the purposes of greater learning. This was all about the chance to make money. *The question is whether we should.* Jake turned to Duncan.

"First, before we get into the findings, I want to make sure that none of this will be shared."

"None of what will be shared?" his mother asked. Jake raised his hand to cut her off.

"Sorry, Mom, save those questions for the end. Now, my dissertation has been looking at the theory of asset pricing and trying to understand price movement but with a focus on nonnormal returns. The reason I want to look at those returns is because it's the nonnormal returns that drive what we think of as alpha, or abnormal or excess returns."

Everyone nodded.

"Well, a couple of weeks back, Duncan asked me to look at the data using intraday frequency, looking at the data tick by tick. This is a considerable undertaking because it multiplies the complexity of solving the problem exponentially. I had to go to the quantum physics lab and use their supercomputers to analyze the data set because of how large it is. It ran continuously and finished two days ago. I didn't call you when it was done because I wanted to show you the results in person and because I wanted to give you this as well. It comes with a condition."

Jake gave Duncan a flash drive.

"What's on this?" Duncan asked.

"Before we get to that, let's look at the results." Jake pulled out a sheet of paper from inside his coat pocket. He placed it between Duncan and his father, and both peered down at the results. His mother grabbed the dessert menu.

"What you're looking at is the output of the model. I'm going to high-light three things on this piece of paper. First is the fit of the model. Note that it says NaN. This means that it could not come up with a number for the model estimation fit, which should be a number between something greater than zero and infinity. You get a NAN when the estimation is un-able to solve for a local or global maximum. You hope for a global maxi-mum, but you would accept a local maximum. Sometimes you don't even care what this number is because some of the models are so nonlinear that fit is almost arbitrary. You typically get a NAN output when the model gets a singular matrix it can't invert, like taking the square root of a nega-tive number or when the recursive nature of the problem only increases because the model has a convex component."

Duncan and his father just stared at him as if he were talking gibberish.

"Sorry. That isn't that relevant, but I just wanted to point out why you could see this kind of output. You can also get a NaN output when model fit is perfect. There's no zero for model fit because you should never be able to explain your dependent variable perfectly. As a simple explanation, let's say I wanted to explain temperature changes using time of day and month. That would explain a fair amount of the variation but wouldn't capture isolated changes and variation captured by weather systems such as nor'easters and El Niños. Thus, your weather-prediction model should have a model fit, or minimizing of pricing errors, close to zero but never fully reach it. In my initial research, I struggled for months overcoming this NaN problem. I believed that the model wasn't reaching convergence. But I found out this isn't the case. The model is perfectly capturing chang-es in asset prices on a tick-by-tick basis."

"Hold on. You have a model that can explain the changes in stock pric-es on a tick-by-tick basis? This doesn't seem possible," his father said.

"Yes, you are right and I'm glad you brought that up. Not stock prices, asset prices. As in all assets. You can't just look at stocks alone. You need to look at all asset classes, and you need to know how to look at them. When I say tick by tick, that's a bit misleading. Assets can move up or down a cent in nanoseconds, driven simply by the size of the order or the type of limit orders surrounding the current bid-ask spread. That's what I consider to be normal movement in the price, and from my perspective what I consider to be noise. In a sense, that's counterintuitive, because, econometrically speaking, anything that lies outside of the normal distribution is considered the outlier. But for our purpose, we care only about the outlier, the nonnormal movement. Why we're able to talk about the results now and not wait a year for the model to analyze the data is because I only looked at nonnormal data, which reduced the size of the sample significantly. What I'm saying is that any nonnormal movement in the market can be fully explained by the model."

"This still seems impossible," his father said again. Duncan remained conspicuously quiet during this conversation.

"I agree," Jake said. "It doesn't seem like that should work. I mean, rationally speaking, there can't be a model that perfectly prices all outcomes. I want to hold off getting to the specific answer until the end, but one reason we don't think about this is that we look at all price movements together, not parsing out normal and nonnormal. So perceiving anything weird in a subset of data is something we just don't look at. A nonnormal event occurs infrequently, and most of us just take it as something that occurred that was outside of our control."

"OK, go on," his father said.

"Duncan, what I handed you contains a program that has the constructed factors and how to use those constructed factors to make trades. This is the second part of the results I wish to highlight." Jake pointed to a column of variables that looked like a list of nonsensical acronyms.

"These are the independent variables that help forecast the nonnormal movements for the data. This is a cross-sectional and time-series analysis, so it holds for all assets through time, and some of the variables are time sensitive and some are instrument sensitive. On the flash drive is the key for what each of these acronyms mean. Now look at the numbers to the right of the names. Those numbers represent the sensitivity for each asset at each point in time to the factor. So the first one is the intercept term, which we typically represent as alpha. It's zero, which means that there's no additional return that can't be explained by the model. The second one is a stock-specific leverage variable. The sign of the coefficient is negative, and the number is 2.3. This means that the higher the leverage, the more negative the response of the asset if there's a nonnormal response."

"That makes sense." Duncan said.

"I can walk you through the other variables, but it should be self-explanatory."

The waiter came by and cleared their dinner plates. It gave Jake time to pause while they pondered dessert. Jake passed on dessert, but his mother got the warm chocolate cake and his father the apple tart. Duncan also passed. Duncan was as health conscious as Jake, maybe more so. Before dessert arrived, they turned their attention back to the piece of paper.

"The last thing I want to point out is the number at the bottom of the page," Jake said. "That number represents the return to using this strategy employing no leverage. Just using the information and letting the account grow by reinvesting profits. Remember, I used ten years of data, and we've been through multiple business cycles."

All of them looked at the number: **$98,162.12**

"How do we interpret this?" his father asked.

"That number represents the dollar value of investing one hundred dollars ten years ago and what that value is today. It represents an annualized return of 115 percent a year. I've checked it over multiple times. It's correct. By investing using the factor model alone and focusing on the nonnormal events at the asset level and employing no leverage, you can make this return."

Jake took the silence to be one of disbelief or shock. Either would be a valid response.

Duncan began nodding. "This has to be correct. I see this every day. This kind of return is justifiable. The markets just behave abnormally on a day-to-day, minute-by-minute basis, and I've come to believe that there was some relationship that tied it together. This confirms my belief."

"Duncan, before we get too excited about this and start trading, I want to point out a potential problem. There are some variables on this piece of paper that concern me." Jake pointed to the last three on the column of acronyms.

"These variables are nonsystematic variables. They're related to very specific behavior of the Federal Reserve, large institutional investors, and market microstructure activity. This also gets back to the point that I wanted to hold off on and the condition. If I don't include these variables, I get a good model output with a reasonable model fit and no NAN problem. That holds true when I look at the daily and monthly data. In fact, it was the exclusion of one or all of these variables, along with leverage, that led me down this particular road. Including them is the key to the perfect model fit and the large returns. These variables' explanatory power is huge, and it seems to have the largest impact around times of the largest nonnormal returns. Interestingly, looking at them individually reveals almost nothing. They all have to be included for any sort of impact."

"Including these variables makes sense to me," his father said. "We know statements from the Fed will cause a reaction in the markets, and the activity of intuitional investors can swing prices. Just look around times of portfolio rebalancing. I'm not surprised that these variables are critical."

"Ah yes, very clever, Dad. This is well known. However, these variables are not stand-alone constructs. These are interaction variables. They're variables that measure a coordinated response, such as having a Fed announcement when there's simultaneous press release from the NYSE on a change in trading behavior while there's a significant increase in hedge fund exposure. The combination of actions has a massive impact on asset valuations, and, as you can see, the sign of the coefficient is negative, and the size is always large. To me, this implies some behind-the-scenes manipulation, and this manipulation is always designed to correct some degree of overvaluation."

Jake paused to take a sip of his Guinness and let that prior statement sink in. "What is interesting is that it's transparent action that's designed to move markets. It's just designed to be difficult to observe the signal. We live in a world where order flow is observed, Fed transcripts and press conferences are dissected word by word, and the cost of a second is the difference between positive and negative returns. Everyone can observe this behavior, and these actions take advantage of that behavior. Now I don't understand the why of what we've found, and I'm a little scared to delve deeper, but it's apparent that by finding this, we can trade it. The question is whether we should. How you answer this, Duncan, will determine whether I let you take that flash drive with you."

Duncan, always reflective and careful before offering his opinion, answered quickly. "It seems obvious, but if someone has the ability to manipulate markets, they have to be exceedingly powerful. Maybe that's something we don't want to get in front of. But if your model does what you say it does, it is the trading opportunity of a lifetime. I think the best thing is to start small. Keep it under the radar. Small-size trades are almost impossible to observe or reverse engineer. The trades would look too random. What do you think?"

Jake looked over at his dad. He was looking for a voice of reason, or at least someone to play devil's advocate.

"I say why not? Test the model, start small, and see where it goes. It's always one thing to back test the data. It's another to see it in practice in the real world." His father answered.

Jake looked at Duncan, and he nodded.

"I'll start next week. First you have to run me through the program, so I can get it into the system and understand how it works." Duncan said.

"OK," Jake replied. *I guess we're going to do this. Please stay small. I don't know what we're truly dealing with here.*

CHAPTER 26

Success in the financial markets can be disastrous for a young associate, and success early on only makes the future problems even worse. The sense of invincibility and hubris from making the right call compounds the notion that you can do no wrong. When something inevitably goes against you, you feel as if it must be someone else's fault or that the universe is conspiring against you. In the world of managing money, early failure can actually be the best outcome for long-term success because it teaches humility and that the market does not care about your feelings.

Managers can get lucky purely by being in the right place at the right time. Managers that entered the market post-2008 have seen their equity, and their clients' equity portfolios, more than double without having to worry about any significant market downturn. Managers that were in the market prior to 2008 had to suffer through a drawdown of over 50 percent, so their perspective of what pain can be caused by the market has come with real experience versus perception. A realized pain is retained in the memory of a manager, and the experience of suffering through those market conditions will always be present, regardless of the time since that pain. For those who haven't experienced that kind of pain, while data and history are easily observed, there is no visceral counterpart or substitute for learned experience.

Finding some success was a thrill for Benson, and, given his prior struggles, he held on to this win tightly. In his office, sharing wins was standard fare and typical of the "look at me" bravado of the private wealth group. Benson had always felt somewhat of an outsider, coming from a small Texas town, the son of a grocer, and he had never felt that he had the starting connections to build his investor book like his more polished and well-connected counterparts. Yet here he was. He knew he was smarter and was determined to succeed. Not from an internal desire for acceptance into a higher social elite, but because Benson's drive was to never fail, regardless of what he did. He also had this new secret weapon.

Establishing trust with his clients had taken time, and maintaining their trust through poorly performing periods had been hard, but he was honest and transparent and clearly explained the goals of the portfolio. No client had left him, but he had, until recently, always felt that he was sitting on a knife's edge. Their faith in him had been rewarded over the past month and a half. Instead of the calls to clients stressing him out, having to relay back the underperformance, each call recently had been exciting and opportunistic. Benson had saved calling his biggest and most important client for last.

"Alfred. Hi, this is Benson at T. B. Worley. Do you have time to speak today? I don't want to take up too much time, but I wanted to update you on your portfolio."

"Sure, Benson. I have about five minutes. We've a board meeting comin' up, so we'll have to be brief. How are things goin'?" Alfred replied. Benson sensed some tension in his voice and could not discern whether it was from his concern over his portfolio or from his upcoming meeting. Long-term, wealthy investors inevitably got worked up about the market and how their portfolio was doing relative to the market performance. What they should have done was file their statements away and not worry about every tick up and down. It was Benson's job to worry about that and to remove the stress from the client.

"Well, I want to point out that since we discussed shiftin' your portfolio, we've seen significant performance improvement with the new allocation. Not only has the portfolio recovered the prior drawdown, but the recent month has seen a portfolio alpha exceedin' 4 percent." Benson tried to keep his voice as neutral as possible, but the excitement was tough to contain.

"Really. Wow. That's great news. I was not expectin' that, given all the yellin' I hear on the news and on CNBC. I was beginnin' to think I should just stick with cattle. You really have made a great call on this one," Alfred replied, with the sense of tension dissipating from his voice.

"Al, you really should stop watchin' that channel. They know nothin'. I can't go into too much detail, but it's related to this changin' portfolio approach that we discussed. I want to keep this approach for a while, and we can circle back to this at the end of the quarter to determine what the appropriate follow-up is," Benson relayed confidently.

"That sounds great. If it's possible to shift more of the passive portfolio to this new style, let's do it. If not, let's keep everythin' the same. I'll speak to you in a couple of months. Talk then." Alfred hung up.

That was exactly what Benson wanted to hear. Having the backing of his biggest client could help sway the rest of his clients to further shift their portfolios when he followed up with them again. Benson's hope was to expand what he had been doing with Jake's model beyond the 20 percent threshold. Having his clients' support would help him when he discussed his proposal with the MD and the bigwigs in New York.

CHAPTER 27

C hangos Taqueria is located on Guadalupe, just north of Thirtieth Street. Haley loved eating there after a swim workout because of the aqua frescas the restaurant had on tap. Today there was a pineapple and coconut mix. Jake loved the tortillas and the freshness of the ingredients. There was no guilt in ordering a Maximo burrito after a four-thousand-yard swim. Again, Jake had been killed in the pool.

It was a week before the AFA meeting. This year it was in San Diego, two days after New Year's Day. Haley and Jake had spent the holiday break in Austin, wanting to avoid traveling to the Northeast during the winter, which meant they would not see Jake's family for the holidays. Instead they hung out in Austin and would visit Haley's family in Los Angeles prior to New Year's. The trip to LA would serve double duty since the AFA meeting was just down the road. Jake and Haley would leave December 30th and stay with her parents for a couple of days, and then Jake would drive down to San Diego for the three-day event.

Jake was in a foul mood. Two related things were contributing to his general anger. First, he had only gotten seven interviews at the AFA. He was shocked by this, especially given how well his presentation had gone in New York and his perception of the quality of his research. Word of mouth was especially important in this profession, and positive outreach from your advisor and the faculty were highly important in landing a good position. Jake knew he had Eric's support, and he assumed that he had the faculty's as well. The problem, of course, was Audria, and this was the second thing that was upsetting him. She had been pushed as Texas's best candidate, and she had twenty-three interviews set up. That was ridiculous. Just as ridiculous was that she had gotten interviews at Harvard and London Business School, and she would not shut up about it.

"I know you're disappointed with the number of interviews, but didn't we limit our sample by deciding we weren't going to live in certain states?" Haley said in between bites.

"True, but I'm still disappointed. None of the Carolina schools called, none in Oregon, none from Colorado. Not even Colorado State. I really thought we would have a shot at those."

"Balls. You can't worry about that now. Just prep the best you can, and present the way you know how. You know this material better than anyone else. Plus, you fucking act like it too. That will come across well in any interview."

"Ture. However something's been bothering me, a little nag in the back of my mind. It has to do with my research and the findings. When I presented it to the faculty, there was some pushback. Dr. Tacker was especially vocal about his concern. He suggested that I would have a lot of trouble publishing the paper. I mean, the results are quite aggressive, and if you've got a set belief, like the idea of market efficiency, then my paper would fly counter to that notion and any research related to it. I can't help but feel like I'm being blackballed a bit."

"Do you really believe that?"

Jake shrugged his shoulders.

"Look, I'm not coming out of Harvard or MIT. I'm coming out of Texas, and while we're good, graduate students from Texas don't write groundbreaking research. Additionally, I'm working with Eric and not Sheldon, so it's possible that people are just too skeptical to believe my results. It's possible I'm getting prejudged."

"Listen—let's not worry about what's out of our control. Let's enjoy the next couple of days, withstand the holidays with my parents, and then you can drill the shit out of the conference."

Haley's matter-of-fact attitude was always soothing. After finishing up their food, they slowly drove back to the condo. It was a rare day in Austin that required pants and an actual jacket, especially since the Jeep didn't have any heat. Jake would try not worry about the research or the job market for the next couple of days. They would exercise, eat, sleep, and do all the things young, energetic, poor graduate students did when they weren't teaching classes, grading papers, doing busy work for their professors, or stressing over their own research.

Jake enjoyed watching movies as a distraction, and this downtime was perfect to catch up on many that he had missed. He used a five-star grading methodology to rate all movies. The movie he was currently watching had three of the five categories required, meaning it was more than acceptable to watch. The highest-rated movie was *Die Hard*, which hit all five categories and was, at this point, the only movie to capture the five-star rating. Jake knew the movie by heart, as did his brother, and they had managed to thoroughly annoy Haley one ski trip by reciting the movie line by line when they were stuck on a ski lift.

Sitting by Jake was Winston, who was like a giant area rug and didn't really move unless there was an opportunity to swim. Winston was the only mastiff Jake knew of that liked the water and enjoyed swimming.

Haley walked down the stairs in her sleeping attire of ratty boxer shorts and a shirt that must have dated back to the eighties. She plopped down on the couch next to him.

"Question for you. How's Duncan doing with the strategy? You haven't really mentioned much about it."

"Well, over the past month, the market has behaved very normally, so the chance to really take advantage of the information hasn't been great."

"So it's not working."

"No, it's working. It's working better than we could've imagined. It appears that there has been some isolated activity that led to some non-normal returns in momentum stocks. A lot of funds were hurt with that correction, but the market itself hardly moved. Our sample account is up 75 percent. That's seventy-five grand. Duncan started small just to test it, using only a hundred-thousand-dollar base and employing no leverage."

"I don't understand anything you just said except that we've made seventy-five grand." Her voice rose an octave, and she punched him in the arm.

"That wasn't necessary," as he rubbed his arm. "Technically, Duncan has made seventy-five grand. It's his money, and the firm's."

"So it's doing what it's supposed to do."

"It appears so."

"Shouldn't you get some of that? It's your research and ideas."

"Don't worry; Duncan will give me 50 percent of the after-tax profits."

"Holy shit. Why are you going into academia again?"

Jake laughed at that. They had had that life and never wanted it again. That is why he hadn't applied to any New York schools. They had left New York to get away from the constant tug and pull of the financial markets. They were planning on having a family in the future, which would mean living in the suburbs and commuting into the city. Living his life commuting on the Metro North was something that Jake wanted to avoid at all costs. That to him was not worth it, regardless of the money that came with it. Academia had its stresses, but he controlled those stresses. Better to have those stresses away from the traffic, cold, and attitude that came with working in Manhattan.

CHAPTER 28

Flying to the West Coast during the winter was always less stressful than flying to the Northeast, but LAX was always a nightmare, and, combined with the traffic from the airport, it felt like it took a full day just to travel door to door. Jake enjoyed staying with Haley's folks. Their place was in West LA, on the hill between the valley and Beverly Hills. The running was always a good challenge because there were no flat streets, and their community had a twenty-five-yard lap pool. So it was easy to get good exercise, and Haley's mom always made excellent meals.

The two days visiting Haley's parents in LA before the AFA conference in San Diego was a welcomed break. Besides the occasional workout, Jake and Haley did nothing but enjoy the LA sunshine and walk up and down the streets of Santa Monica and the pier. It took Jake's mind off the number of interviews he had gotten compared to Audria and allowed him to focus on the fact that he knew his research was right. The quantitative proof through the success of the trading strategy was a huge bonus.

So he didn't mind that the drive down to San Diego took three and a half hours when it should have been an easy two-hour drive. He also didn't mind the difficulty finding parking when the hotel lot was full, or the wait to get checked in, or the obvious smell of smoke in the room when the hotel clearly had a no-smoking policy.

National conferences like the AFA bring the best academics from all over the world to attend the event. Getting a paper on the AFA docket was a real coup and usually a positive signal that the paper would land in a top-tier journal. Submissions for the AFA began early the prior year, so the paper had to be in good working order well in advance of the conference. Jake knew his paper wouldn't have been ready, so he didn't bother to submit it. Plus, given the names of the people who were presenting, it was unlikely that his paper would have been accepted, regardless of how polished it was. Reputation always mattered, no matter how blind the refereeing process claimed to be.

The conference ran over two and a half days, with multiple presentations going on at a time, broken out across the many conference rooms of the hotel. Between job interviews, Jake would stop and listen in on sessions related to his work. The presentations at the AFA could be quite combative, and it was almost uncomfortable at times to see two huge egos go at. It did remind Jake at times of two five-year-olds fighting over the same toy. Walking the halls and riding the elevators, Jake would inevitably run into the competition, other PhD candidates interviewing for the same job. It was a bizarre feeling waiting outside the hotel room to meet the faculty he was interviewing with, knowing that another candidate was in there finishing up. Making eye contact with that other candidate as he or she left the room was just awkward. Jake always smiled at his fellow candidate, but the expression wasn't always returned.

Meeting potential future colleagues and being interviewed in hotel rooms was also a little difficult. Depending on the number of people the university had brought—there were usually three or four faculty members waiting to interview you—either Jake sat on one of the beds in the room or one of the faculty members had to. Sitting comfortably upright on a soft mattress while being peppered with questions was not ideal.

Each interview lasted about forty-five minutes, thirty of which were dedicated to assessing the quality of Jake's research. The faculty probed to discern whether he was responsible for that research or if it had come out of his advisor's research agenda. The rest of the interview was geared to determining whether Jake would be good in the classroom and a good fit as a future colleague. It was key in these interviews for Jake to show how dedicated he was to his research and what his future research ideas were, and to avoid asking the "loaded gun" questions. The two key ones were

"What is the nine-month salary?" and "How many publications do I need to get to make tenure?" Asking one of those questions was a guaranteed way to not get a campus interview.

Jake enjoyed the interview process. The goal of each interview was to show his aptitude and his interest in the school, and the hope was to get an on-campus interview, which would hopefully lead to a job offer. The on-campus interview would mean he was in contention with four or five others. So if Jake could turn his seven interviews here into four campus visits, then he felt his odds of landing at least one job should be pretty good.

Jake's last interview finished the afternoon of the second day of the conference. He didn't plan on spending the last day in San Diego, as he wanted to return to LA for a couple of days before heading back to Austin. So far he had enjoyed his interviews with the University of Arizona, Georgia, Southern Cal, and Montana. Those were his top four, and he hoped each one would land a campus interview. On the elevator down, he ran into Audria. She looked a bit haggard, even though she was impeccably dressed.

"How are things going?" Jake asked. She was almost surprised by the question, and it took her a second to realize that it was Jake asking the question. They hadn't really spoken since that weird exchange in Jake's office.

"Oh, hi, Jake. Sorry I didn't recognize you. I've been running all around this hotel just trying to make each of my interviews. I almost ran over Eugene Fama, I was in such a rush. Well, I still have six more interviews to go. I believe taking on twenty-three was probably a bit too much. I thought agreeing to speak to some of the smaller schools would be good practice, but it's tiring me out."

"You've got nothing to worry about. You'll land a quality position." Jake honestly believed that, and even though he was in direct competition with Audria, he still wanted her to do well. At this point there was no sense feeling any animosity.

"How were your interviews? You look good in that gray suit. I don't think I've ever seen you with a tie on before."

"Thanks. I think the last time I wore a tie was before grad school. I think the interviews went well. Obviously a couple more would have been good, but I've enjoyed the ones I've had."

The elevator hit the ground floor, and Jake walked to the bar while Audria scuttled to the elevator banks that led up to the south tower. He watched her walk away, wondering whether that temporary moment of weakness a couple of months ago back in Austin had dissipated or if it would show itself in her interviews. He hoped for her sake it would not. He had thought of asking about it here but decided it was best to let her bring it up.

Jake ordered a Guinness. He planned on staying awhile to avoid the traffic on I-5 heading north, waiting to drive back after seven to avoid most of the traffic.

"I'll get that," said the man with the perfect Oxford accent as he sat down next to Jake. He sat with his back completely straight, which was impressive on a barstool.

"Dr. Chen. How are you doing?"

"Well, thank you. I hope you've time to talk now?"

"I do actually. I'm done with my interviews and wasn't planning on heading out until later." Jake remembered that Benjamin had said that he would be in contact with him. "I forgot that you had mentioned that you would get in contact with me. Since I didn't hear from you, I assumed it was just a courtesy gesture. I'm glad to see you here."

"I do not usually come to these events, but I came to this one with a particular agenda. You see, ever since your discussion in New York, we've taken a particular interest in your findings. It was no courtesy. Let me ask you, how is your research coming along, and how are your job prospects?"

This is interesting. Let's see where this goes. "Dr. Chen, those are loaded questions, and you know it. Why don't you just ask me what you want?" Jake kept up the formality but decided to be blunt. He wasn't going to play a game of witty banter that danced around Benjamin's true intentions.

"Very true. I like your directness. That is somewhat unusual for some-one in your position, an as-of-yet-unproven graduate student looking for a job. I would have expected a wealth of pleasantries and vagueness. You are a student of game theory, are you not?"

This guy is sharp. Keep playing defense. "I most certainly am. And yes, I know the game and how it's played. I need to appear as if I'm desired by all, but not too much, so as to make myself as attractive a candidate as possible. Yet, I'm not sure what this is. This doesn't feel like an interview for a job. It feels like a fishing expedition."

Benjamin Chen smiled. He was wearing another tailored gray suit, very similar to the one he had worn in New York, but with a slightly darker shade. It was certainly not off the rack. The cut of the suit revealed that the man was fit, probably a runner, but broader than most of his compatriots. His mannerisms and attitude hinted that he was someone who controlled significant amounts of wealth, and he was used to getting his way.

"What am I fishing for?"

"Well, I couldn't possibly answer that. The fish never deliberately jumps on the hook."

That got a laugh out of the man. Jake also chuckled to himself. *Why the hell is the head of research of the largest sovereign wealth fund that's not based on oil reserves sitting next to me in the lobby of a San Diego hotel?*

"Professor Chamberlain, how would you like to take a trip to Beijing and present your research to our team?"

OK. That's why. "Dr. Chen, you know I haven't defended yet. Beijing is a long way from Austin just to come and present some research."

"Maybe it will be more than that. Could you come in, let's say, a week, maybe two?"

Jake tried to hide his excitement. That was an awfully quick turn-around time. Spring semester started next week, and it would mean someone would have to cover a class or two for him. A trip to China would not be an overnight affair.

"You could leave on Wednesday night and come home Sunday. You would meet with the team and present your research Friday, and you and I would discuss other matters Saturday. You will be jetlagged, but an athletic guy like yourself should have no problems whatsoever."

Jake stared at the man. This was considerably out of the norm.

"I can take your silence as a yes. Good. We will make the arrangements. I will see you in Beijing. Enjoy the rest of the conference."

Benjamin got up, shook hands with Jake, gave the bartender a ten, and walked to the exit. Jake watched him leave before returning to his drink. He decided he would have a second after that exchange. He took in the atmosphere of the hotel and watched his colleagues move through the lobby, either to their rooms to conduct an interview or be interviewed or to a conference room to give or listen to a presentation. He could almost guarantee nobody had had a meeting or exchange like the one he'd just had. *He came to see me.* The fact that he was excited by the chance to go to China and find out what was behind these mysterious encounters with Benjamin diminished any lingering disappointment of only having had seven interviews. *I guess I have to consider these AFAs a success.*

He and Haley had never considered an overseas posting, and now he was going to fly across the globe to meet with a nonacademic group who had not exactly courted him but coerced him into coming. In fact, he wasn't sure what he was going over there for, but it felt like more than just a presentation to a practitioner audience. There was something going on, something related to his research, and something that had ties to significant wealth. He had not made public his dissertation findings or conclusions by posting it to Social Science Research Network or his website, and only a handful of academics really knew about the main result. There was certainly no information about the intraday results that Duncan was trading. Yet Jake had a feeling that his interaction with Benjamin Chen and his main results were related.

CHAPTER 29

M ichelle knew today's meeting with the Markov Group would be a long one, and a lot of the focus would be on her. She had been in front of the Senate to discuss recent actions taken by the Fed that seemed to favor a particular US bank in regards to a certain acquisition of shares of a European bank. The deal had allowed the European bank to meet capital and Basel II requirements, and in return the US bank had gotten—well, it wasn't clear what the US bank had gotten—at least to the general public. The uncertainty about what the US bank had received in the deal had drawn the ire of the Senate Finance Committee. The US bank did receive a small fee, but going through the balance sheet of the European bank appeared to reveal that all the deal did was circumvent regulation through creative accounting. The New York Fed had given the deal its blessing, and, given the historic and cozy relationship between the US bank and the New York Fed, Michelle Lancaster had been called to Capitol Hill to explain.

Michelle had relayed in great detail to the chairperson of the Senate Finance Committee and its members that it was the Fed's responsibility to protect the bank's reputation and the transaction fell well within the Fed's handbook on supervision. This televised interaction allowed for some political grandstanding by some self-important senators, while also proving that Michelle could hold up well to scrutiny without actually saying anything.

Now, on the flight home, she realized she knew two things. First, there was a whistleblower within the Fed. The committee chairperson had internal Fed documents and e-mails that had highlighted a particular shady component of the deal. It showed that the deal was just an equity swap and that the European bank had done nothing to improve its capital requirements. Michelle had spent several hours saying that the legal department had deemed the deal legitimate. Convincing the chairperson wasn't the problem. *Especially since most of the senators had no idea what they were looking at.* Weeding out the whistleblower was.

Second, this was a clear action to undermine her. The New York Fed had approved and helped transition many deals more creative than this one and had never had a leak of this magnitude. This particular deal was different in that it fell under her tenure.

Michelle had had a personal stake in the success of this deal because it had been constructed and hatched through plans of the Markov Group and Victor Panket. The liquidity and reputation of this European bank were important to the stability of the European region. If it failed the bank stress test, then there would be significant loss of confidence in the country and the banking sector, and it might result in a contagion across the entire eurozone. Given the European Central Bank's reluctance to engage in a US-style bond-buying program to spur growth, a bank failure could cause massive deflation of the euro and could send the whole area into another recession. That would be disastrous for the global economy.

The actions initiated through the Markov Group were designed to prevent that outcome, and it was Michelle who had facilitated Victor's plan.

The head of the ECB was a vapid, self-serving politician. Francis LeBlanc was not a sound economist and was more concerned with the appearance of European and country sovereignty than promoting growth and improvement. He believed that the global markets were not intertwined. So Michelle had rubberstamped this deal mostly for eurozone stability but also to let this man know that his inaction would result in a response from her. He had said specifically to her at a Basel conference that it was not the role of the ECB to step in and save an institution from itself. LeBlanc had not learned a single lesson from the events and outcomes of 2008. If the ECB would not act, she would. She was more than happy to step on his toes.

Frank Lyman was also happy. Michelle's proactive response meant he would not have to use the pictures of LeBlanc at *Le We Club* to force his hand. LeBlanc's sexual appetite would be excellent fodder for the public, and while it is an antiquated tool, bribery and blackmail were effective weapons. He would save them for another time, just in case.

So while the deal on paper appeared to give the US bank only a small fee for the equity swap, what it actually did was give the US institution a mechanism to control the borrowing and lending from one of the largest European banks to offset the inaction from the ECB. Through this mechanism, this bank could restrict lending, forcing the ECB into the only policy to improve liquidity in the region. Exactly what the Markov Group wanted.

Michelle voiced her concern about the leaked documents to the Markov Group when they met. She felt that the actions had been taken to deliberately hurt her, rather than being a direct attack on the group, but she couldn't be sure.

"This will warrant further investigation. Michelle, you must do everything the head of an organization would do about a potential reprimand when it comes to this in-house action. Find the source of the leak. Depending on who it is and where it came from, we can then discuss the appropriate course of action. Settled?" Frank said.

She nodded, along with the other members. She was unaware that Frank already knew the source of the leak. He was deliberately sitting on this piece of information for use at a later time.

"Excellent job on the hill. No one likes dealing with Washington, but you handled the senators like a true pro. The right amount of deference and stonewalling. OK, I believe we've handled our international problems sufficiently. Russia should relent shortly; the damage to its economy due to the drop in oil prices must be causing significant internal strife. The ECB will start to fall in line as well. Congrats to you all. Let's turn our attention to some smaller domestic issues," Frank said.

"Right now, there appear to be two small but related issues," said the head of the New York Stock Exchange. "One is with an account in a boutique New York trading firm called Griffin, and the other is with a series of trades for client accounts in the wealth management department in the Houston branch of T. B. Worley. Both have had margin requirements increased and have been issued SEC, FINRA, and IRS audits," said the head of the New York Stock Exchange.

"Can you elaborate further?" Frank asked.

"Our algorithms, designed to catch potential inside trading cases, market manipulation, and pump-and-dump schemes, have had a continued red flag. This allows us to see abnormal market behavior, such as when a trader buys thousands of option contracts prior to a merger announcement when they had never bought an option contract before. The algorithm also does another thing, something that it only reports to me. It reports when there are a series of trades over the course of several months that are highly correlated with the actions, or the potential actions, that would be taken by the Markov Group. Up until now, this flag has never been raised. Now it has been raised twice concurrently. It was first raised by a collection of accounts at T. B. Worley under the guidance of a single account representative. Last month it flagged a computerized account at this Griffin trading group."

"Please continue," Frank said, without any emotion. Harvey Waterman stirred in his chair.

"Per our protocol we dispatched monitors last month when the flag was first raised. Since the trading behavior remained correlated with our model for this past month, direct action has to be taken, and further discussion within our group is warranted. This is where we're at. My feeling is that the action of the SEC audit will obviously cause the trading to be disrupted and either hinder or terminate any further correlation. Since this is a new situation for us, I believe further monitoring is required."

All the other members agreed. Harvey began to speak, but Frank cut him off.

"Good. I'll initiate the monitoring process, and we'll review next meeting. Let's end on this," Frank said. Harvey looked agitated but relented on the look from Frank.

With that, each member departed, and Michelle left more satisfied and comfortable than she would have imagined. Her actions and the actions of the group were the right things for the global market. She did not give a second thought to the two accounts or traders that had triggered the red flags related to the Markov Group, thinking this was a small problem compared to the potential usurper at her bank.

CHAPTER 30

The turn of the year is usually met with optimism and failed resolutions. For Benson one of those things held true. His client portfolios were performing the best in the office, his asset raising had doubled because of it, and he was being promoted to senior associate. At least that was the impression his managing director had given him. In fact, some of his moves had attracted the attention of New York, and he was scheduled to head up to the city at the end of the month to discuss his actions and how they might be incorporated across the entire private wealth division.

Earning your clients 22 percent over a six-month period was extremely impressive, especially given a 5 percent return for the market over the same time frame. However, Benson knew that he would have to reach out to Jake, and that it would be best to do that in person. He was always up for a trip to Austin.

When they last had spoken, Benson was struggling and concerned about his position. After their discussion and the use of Jake's model, which at the time had felt like a last-ditch attempt to salvage his career, it was time to catch up and tell Jake about what had happened. It wasn't that Benson had deliberately kept this quiet. He had just been busy working to grow his book, Jake had been involved in finishing his dissertation, and, although Houston and Austin were only 160 miles apart, Benson hadn't had the desire to drive up to Austin just to get in a good ride or run.

He wanted to tell Jake in person how things had been going. This was not an over-the-phone conversation. Plus, he had just starting dating this fabulous girl. She was a former diver at UT and was working as a financial analyst at UBS. He didn't hold the fact she was working as a lowly analyst against her—everyone has to start somewhere—but having someone in the same profession did have its perks. She understood the hours, the lingo, and the demands of the profession. Another perk was that she was a freaking animal in bed. She had retained all of the flexibility from her years of diving and still had the stamina to wear Benson out. That was saying something, given his background as an endurance athlete. Maybe all the years of routine and competition had restricted her inner college wildness, because she seemed to be putting four years of debauchery into one month of activity. Benson didn't think he could keep this up, although he certainly didn't mind trying.

While that aspect of his new relationship was more than pleasurable, it was nice to have a partner as a sounding board. Since she was an analyst, she was not in competition with him. Her job was to assess and value companies, generate reports, and be a general slave to the associates and MD within her division. Working in Houston didn't necessarily come with the horror hours of New York, but she still worked hard and was as proficient with Excel spreadsheets as anyone.

Lying in bed, Benson leaned over and kissed her cheek. He also caught the time out of the corner of his eye. His old college clock radio showed 1:30 a.m. He was really burning the candle at both ends, and yet her hours were worse than his, and she had double his energy.

"I was goin' to head to Austin for the Martin Luther King long weekend. Do you want to come up with me?"

"Sure, I love going back to Austin. Although I'm going nowhere near the pool or the diving center. I dedicated too many years to that, and the thought of going back in the aquatic center gives me the chills."

"I wasn't askin' you to go swimmin'. I wanted to head up and speak to my dude Jake. Maybe get a couple of runs on the Town Lake trail or in Zilker Park, or do a ride in the Hill Country."

"He's the one that helped you out, right?"

"Yeah. He's a good guy. I think he'll be back from his trip. We were exchanging e-mails, and he told me he was heading to present somewhere.

He didn't tell me where, but I'm curious to find out what he's been up to. I believe he's visitin' schools for potential jobs."

"That's all?" She turned over and faced him, her naked body on full display, backlit with the glow of the city lights behind her.

"Dang, no, I wanted to discuss what has happened since I started using his model. I'm not sure he'll be happy about it, but I can't wait any longer."

"He won't be happy about it?" She ran her hand through his tangled blond hair.

"When we discussed the results in the fall, I don't believe he thought I would use them. Or maybe he did but didn't understand the magnitude or what the implications of usin' them would have on my client portfolios. I didn't think it would be a big deal, and I certainly didn't think it would work as well as it has. Given that I'm headin' up to New York, I need to talk to him about it now."

"That's the right thing. Plus, it'll give us a chance to hit Sixth Street and enjoy some Austin nightlife. Now I think we should get some sleep, unless you can give me some of the same effort as you did before we had this conversation," she said with a delicious sparkle in her eyes, working her other hand below the covers.

Benson wasn't sure that he could, but that wouldn't prevent him from trying.

Sarah left the apartment around sixty thirty. Even though it was winter and early morning, it was muggy and disgusting already. She hated everything about Houston—the traffic, the people, the lack of culture, and especially the weather. Benson was a surprising find and not at all what she had expected. She drove from his apartment and headed downtown but was not going to the offices at UBS. In fact, she had never stepped foot inside the building.

She worked for a highly capitalized but highly private insurance firm, a firm that specialized in many products, some of which were nonfinancial.

The firm was headquartered in New York, but could set up satellite branches wherever and whenever needed. There was a small branch in Houston that worked in the First City Tower, but Sarah had never been in it prior to a month ago. She was New York based and had worked there since college but had never actually been on the thirty-seventh floor of 60 Broad Street. She had been preselected because of her accomplishments and, after a comprehensive six-month screening process and two years of training, had been offered the opportunity to work in a field highly suited to her unique talents.

When she walked into the office, she acknowledged no one, and they all ignored her. She had been assigned a nondescript office with minimal furniture. She didn't know what story the Houston staff had about her, and she didn't care, but they knew to leave her alone. She closed the door behind her, sat on the desk, and picked up the phone. She dialed the familiar 212 extension. It was answered after two rings.

"Report."

"The subject will travel to Austin to speak to the academic. I'll be accompanying."

"Good. Continue to monitor and report anything of value."

She hung up the phone and turned on her computer. There was an image of Benson's apartment along with a call log of every call he had made from his home, office, and cell phone. She began to go through each one, looking for any and all details related to the trading he had been doing.

CHAPTER 31

D ealing with an SEC audit is part of the business. It can be the result of a random draw or an actual violation. Typically, investment firms would expect an audit every three to five years, but Duncan felt that the SEC was at Griffin's offices because of the outstanding performance the firm had experienced recently. Given that Griffin was a proprietary trading firm that gave no advice, issued no securities, and did not trade for client accounts, the presence of the SEC gave him no pause. He knew that no fraud had taken place. To Duncan, this was a day just like any other. He couldn't have been more wrong.

The presence of the SEC would not disrupt his daily routine, so he immersed himself in the model and an assessment of the opportunities that were available. The first thing that he noticed was that while his account was fully operational, there was no computer account tracking him. It had been shut down. This caught him unaware and triggered an alarm in his head that there was some relationship between the SEC presence in the office and the account shutdown. His trading had gone extremely well, and judging by everything that he'd heard from the partners, they were ecstatic with the performance. Maybe trading had gone to well.

Looking back over his shoulder, he could see the auditors in the conference room, pouring over their papers with their laptops open and Excel spreadsheets populated. The auditors looked like auditors—nondescript, modest, and meticulous. Duncan had learned this morning from his desk mate that they had initially met with the partners for about an hour before anyone had come in and then had gone off with the chief compliance officer, Leslie Murphy, into the conference room. Duncan had the utmost respect for Leslie, who kept the firm running smoothly, although he didn't envy her for the next couple of days or weeks. Having to go through the firm's trades, compliance manual, and firm documents was a paperwork nightmare.

Leslie got out of the meeting for lunch and called Duncan to her office. The SEC had sent a three-person team, which seemed like a lot to audit a firm of Griffin's size, and all of them had left to go for lunch at the café across the street. She was the only one at Griffin who dressed like she was working in a financial institution and today was wearing a traditional black suit. Most of the people at Griffin wore jeans and T-shirts, even the majority partners.

"Leslie, what's going on? Something tells me that I'm involved in this somehow."

"Duncan, your intuition is right on the mark. First, this isn't your fault. Every firm gets audited, especially the successful ones. Second, it appears that the audit and the inquiry is about your trading over the past month or so, with a particular focus on the computer account that mimics you. I must admit that this is a little weird, but they're going through the entire firm's compliance records, with particular interest in that one account. You obviously saw that it was shut down."

Duncan nodded. "I noticed that."

"What's odd is that your personal account hasn't been closed," Leslie said. "In fact, they haven't even asked about it. Listen, I don't want you to stress too much about this. I know you haven't done anything wrong. Remember, I get paid to handle this type of problem. So far everything is proceeding as normal. They're checking for front running or misrepresentation, and we're going through the computerized trades. So far I wouldn't worry about anything, but they want you to stay late so they can ask you some questions. Just answer truthfully—and, let me emphasize this—don't answer more than you need to. Don't elaborate. Do you understand what I'm saying?" She put her hand on his shoulder and stared unblinking at him.

"Got it. No need to say anything further."

Duncan returned to his desk and waited. He wasn't worried per se, but he was confused. Fortunately, he knew that he had done nothing wrong. At market close, the traders on his row slowly migrated to the doors and made their way to elevators to start their trips home. One by one, his coworkers left the office, including the other two partners. Leslie was still in the conference room with the auditors. At five thirty, Leslie came out looking a little ragged. She came over to Duncan and sat in the chair next to him.

"All right, I'm done for the day. They should be calling you in a few minutes. Listen, something about this doesn't feel right. The timing of it and the nature of the questions just feels orchestrated. I've done enough of these things to know the difference between a scheduled audit and a specific investigation. I feel that these guys are looking for something particular. Be very careful what you tell them. The best part is that I get to continue on again tomorrow, which I'm thrilled about." Sarcasm was a strong suit of hers.

"Make sure you shut off the lights when you leave." She touched his knee before she got up, and like everyone else, left the building.

Duncan waited patiently to be called in. When he looked in the conference room, it didn't appear that the three individuals were in a rush to call him in. The glass doors allowed anyone full access to look inside, and the three of them had their faces buried deep into their laptops. Facing the conference room and away from his computer, he was caught unaware when someone tapped on his shoulder. Two people in black suits were standing there.

"Can I help you?" Duncan asked, taken aback by how they had snuck up on him. He wondered how these two individuals had gotten in the building without him noticing them.

"Mr. Chamberlain, would you come with us? We've got some questions we'd like to ask you." Duncan looked at the two men that stood before him. They didn't look like auditors; they looked like FBI agents with their black suits and tightly cropped hair.

"Sure." He got up from his desk and made his way to the conference room where the other auditors were currently working. As they approached the doors, one of the men asked him to wait outside, while the other went in to speak to the three that were currently working. After two minutes, the three original auditors got up, made their way out of the conference room, and left the building. Duncan was then escorted into the conference room so he was alone with the two black-suited individuals.

"Why were those three excused?" Duncan asked.

"They're assigned a specific task that deals with the accounting and verification of your firm's operations. We're here to perform a duty that's beyond the scope of their mandate," said the first black suit.

"OK." Duncan was going to be cordial and friendly, answering every question without being overly verbose.

"Mr. Chamberlain, I'm Mr. Williams. This is my associate, Mr. Waiters. We're senior investigators for the SEC. We would like to go over with you the trading activity related to your computer account."

"OK."

"We would like a description of the trading process, how and when you made your trades, and the key markers for your decision," Mr. Williams said.

"I'll try to answer that in as much detail as I can. You may have to ask specific questions on specific trades." Duncan remained as vague as possible without sounding defensive.

"OK. Let's go through this day by day."

Duncan now realized he was in for a very long night.

It was two in the morning when Mr. Williams suggested they take a thirty-minute break. Duncan thought this was highly irregular, keeping him here, interrogating him like this, but he stuck to his game plan and answered the questions exactly how Leslie had suggested. Mr. Waiters had left to get them some food while Mr. Williams stayed in the conference room. Duncan returned to his desk to check some e-mail. He was not allowed to leave until they were done with their questioning. He would have to ask Leslie if this was standard protocol, and he almost felt like he should have had a lawyer present. He hadn't been charged with anything, but he certainly felt that this inquisition was leading in that direction.

Mr. Waiters returned with several steaming Styrofoam boxes, along with three cans of soda. He handed Duncan a box and told him he had ten minutes to eat and then should return to the conference room. Duncan skipped drinking the soda but did enjoy the fried rice, which helped give him some energy before returning to the next round of questioning. He hadn't eaten this late since college. So far they had gone through half the trading period since he had started using Jake's model, and he had been able to answer each question in regards to specific trades without revealing too much about the model or giving them any ammunition that would arouse any sort of suspicion.

"Mr. Chamberlain, let us continue going through the trade log. We hope you can explain why you shorted gold at this point in time?" Mr. Williams asked, pointing to a highlighted entry time stamped at 11:35 a.m. on December 17.

"It was because it was overvalued relative to the price of equities that I was long at the time. I think it made complete sense."

"Notice how gold fell quite precipitously after you sold it, and the volume went up. It appears that you may have had inside information. The HFTs and computer algorithms were significantly behind you, or you may have disseminated information that led a short squeeze on the commodity."

"I'm not sure you can draw that conclusion. First, how anyone can front run gold is beyond me, especially since I don't have any clients. Second, Griffin is too small to float rumors and have the street trade on those rumors. Lastly, check my computer, phone, anything; you won't find any information that I've shared. I trade for myself and my firm exclusively. This is the same response I had when you asked me about Nike and about the US dollar and euro trade."

This line of questioning continued for another hour or so, and Duncan continued to answer the questions carefully.

"The timing of your trading is quite fortuitous and highly profitable. Why the change from what you had traditionally done to this new strategy about a month ago?"

"I was trying something new. It was related to some reading I had done, and I thought it made sense. So I gave it a try."

"Can you elaborate further on this research?"

"Sure. It's related to finding the differences between normal and non-normal returns. Specifically, isolating the nonnormality and leverage and trading in the appropriate direction. It makes a lot of sense."

"Who wrote this research, and do you have a copy of the paper?"

Duncan was tired—it was almost three thirty in the morning—but he picked up on the fact they had changed tack, that the line of questioning was now different. More than that, the question itself was oddly phrased. The idea that they had said "copy of the paper" stuck in his mind.

"What paper?" Duncan asked.

"We are referring to the sources that you used to construct the strategy, the trading?"

"It came from various sources, including the *Wall Street Journal*, textbooks, and investing books. No one specific source and all publicly available."

"Mr. Chamberlain, we think you're being evasive. We know that you've changed your trading significantly and that it had to be driven by something very specific."

"I don't know what to tell you." Duncan was putting up a wall. He wasn't going to get bullied.

"When was the last time you spoke to your brother?"

"What?"

"When was the last time you spoke to your brother?" There was some real menace in Mr. Williams's voice.

"What does he have to do with anything? He doesn't work here."

"We hope you can elaborate on any contact you've had with him."

"We talk on the phone. We talk markets, and he tells me about teaching. That's about it."

"Not about his research?"

"I wouldn't understand it."

"You didn't see him when he came to New York in November? The timing of his visit and your trading change seems highly coincidental."

Duncan had had enough. This was beyond the scope of what an audit should be. "So? I can't see the point of this as it relates to Griffin and our trading. So far you haven't suggested or found anything that I've done wrong. These question are pointless, and I'm leaving." Duncan got up and was about to leave.

"Mr. Chamberlain, please sit down. You could leave but we will still be here when you come back. We need to finish going over these trades."

Duncan looked over at the two men and took his seat. He knew this was no regular audit. No auditor behaves this way.

By five in the morning, they had finished up. Mr. Williams thanked Duncan for his time and told him to be on call for further inquiry. The two black suits gathered up their things and were beginning to leave when Mr. Williams stopped at the door.

"One final thing, Mr. Chamberlain. Interestingly, we can't find any algorithm that dictated the trades. Where is the code that programmed the buy and sell orders on the computerized account?"

"Excuse me? I don't understand what you're asking."

"There had to be a program that ran the account. The trading is too systematic to be driven by a human."

Duncan shrugged his shoulders, but the thought that had formed in the back of his mind earlier was now perfectly clear. They were not searching for some mysterious wrongdoing or trying to assess his trading strategy. They already knew about it. They wanted to find it and eliminate it. Their references to Jake, his paper, and now the algorithm could have only suggested prior knowledge of the strategy itself. The questions were too direct, too pointed. They were here to destroy the account, the code, and anything related to the strategy itself. They were here to threaten him. To scare him.

He was scared, but felt a surge of adrenaline. They had missed the crucial piece of evidence in all their searching and questioning. They had no idea that the account they were focusing in on had no information about the underlying model. That information was sitting on his hard drive thirty feet away.

"I'm not sure what answer you're looking for, but everything I do is based on signals in the marketplace, and I just react to those signals," Duncan said, trying to embellish his tiredness and not reveal that he had pieced something together about their motive and what they were looking for.

The two men stared at Duncan. Whether it was the resistance he was putting up or the repetitive answers, it appeared that they were not getting what they wanted. Mr. Williams said good-bye, and Duncan watched him and Mr. Waiters all the way to the elevators. Only after a full three minutes did Duncan leave the conference room and go back to his desk. He would stay in the office until Leslie came in so he could fill her in on the details. It would probably be an hour before anyone else came in. He had always trusted his instincts, and following them had been right most of the time.

He opened up a folder that had the algorithm that Jake had given him on the flash drive back in November. He also plugged in that original flash drive and then executed a full drive delete on the flash drive and the file folder, erasing any copy of the original program. He then closed out the original account the computer had mimicked. He pulled out the hard drive on the computer and put it in his pocket. Jake had been right to be concerned back in November.

Leslie came in at six thirty, before the original auditors arrived. Duncan went into her office and asked her to go outside with him. He didn't trust that any action they took in the office wouldn't be recorded. She didn't resist but thought he was being overly dramatic. He then updated her on what had happened.

"I'm shocked. I've never heard of any kind of internal audit or interrogation like that before, especially since there was no evidence of wrongdoing."

"This isn't about wrongdoing. I've closed out the original account, but I advise you not to reference that account at all when you meet with the SEC team. Just keep acting normal and doing what you've been doing," Duncan said, looking directly at her. She looked very uncomfortable with this suggestion. "Something tells me that my account won't come up through the rest of the audit."

"How can you possibly know that?"

"I can't tell you that, but I want you to trust me. All I can say is that there's something bigger at play here. I don't know what it is, but this isn't about Griffin."

He didn't tell her his thoughts on the true motive for his interrogation by Mr. Williams and Mr. Waiters. At this point it was best to keep that to himself and share it with the only people he could trust.

CHAPTER 32

Flying to Beijing from Austin for a two-day trip can mess with the body and the mind. Fortunately, all the arrangements were made by the CIC, and Jake got to fly business class. Those were some real dollars being spent on him, so he spent the days working up to the trip really honing his talk and presentation. He had been able to work with extra energy because he had received calls from Arizona and USC asking if he would come out for a campus visit. There was also a message from Montana, but he hadn't been able to get back in touch with the person who'd called.

There was no direct flight from Austin to Beijing, so that meant changing planes in San Francisco. The total trip took about eighteen hours, not including getting to and from the airport and dealing with immigration. Added to that was the fourteen-hour time difference, and that meant the disappearance of a day that could never be recovered. The second leg was extremely comfortable relative to what it could have been, but even in business class, Jake found that his ability to sleep and work was highly limited. Jake had reached the point at which he knew his work backward and forward and was now completely sick of all of his research. Reaching this stage usually meant that the doctoral student was ready for his or her final defense. The defense was typically anticlimactic, because once you had a job offer, the dissertation chair and the rest of the faculty could celebrate another placement. As long as you typed up that final document and it conformed to the university's format, your committee would give you almost no hassle in the final presentation.

Jake's inability to sleep on the plane had nothing to do with concerns over his research or getting his six-foot-two-inch frame comfortable in the business-class seats. It had to do with two messages that he had received almost simultaneously. First he'd received a call from Duncan, saying they needed to talk. The second was from Benson, saying he was coming up to Austin. He'd been able to confirm the date and time with Benson, but their talk had been brief. He couldn't get hold of Duncan but had left him a message saying that he would get back to him Sunday or Monday, whenever he got back from his trip.

It was odd that both wanted to touch base with him at almost the same time. It felt more than coincidental that the two people whom he had discussed his results with outside of academic circles were trying to speak with him while he was heading to Beijing to talk to a group that controlled over $650 billion in assets. One of the first rules he'd learned in econometrics was that correlation does not imply causality. It was an idiom that always required checking when drawing conclusions from an econometric test on financial data with no personality. In this particular case, with real people involved, it was a rule that he believed should be ignored.

A car was waiting for Jake after he got through immigration and got his bag. It was a twenty-eight minute drive from the airport to the St. Regis Hotel. As impressive as Beijing had been from the air, the drive in further emphasized the vastness and growth of the city. A mixture of modern and historic buildings was blended throughout the city, melding the new and old worlds together. The hotel was located in the heart of Beijing, about fifteen minutes from the Imperial Palace and five minutes from the address where he was supposed to meet at eight o'clock tomorrow morning for his presentation. On the itinerary he had received with his travel details was an outline with the schedule for Friday and Saturday. Friday he was set to present from eight to noon, lunch for an hour, meet for an hour with the Chief Investment Officer, and then meet with Benjamin Chen for two hours. Saturday was to be determined.

Jake checked into the hotel, went to his room, and laid down on the bed. He didn't even open the curtains to take in the view. He was tired but knew he shouldn't sleep. Falling asleep now would mean waking up at two in the morning. Jake opened his bag, hung up his suit in the bathroom, and turned the shower on to help get some of the wrinkles out. The suit was a Hugo Boss, the color a mortician's black that made a white shirt stand out, and it was tailored. It was probably the nicest thing he owned besides his triathlon bike. Haley had suggested purchasing it after learning of the success of the trading strategy. Her rational for buying the suit was simple: *When you go on the job market, accentuate your finer qualities. It'll make up for your lack of intelligence.* Wearing the suit would always remind him of that statement.

He jumped in the shower and let the heat wash away twenty hours of travel. Jake put on clean clothes and walked down to the hotel restaurant to get some food. After eating a traditional Western meal, he walked around the hotel, checked out the gym and the pool, and decided enough was enough. He couldn't fight it any longer, so he went back to his room and fell asleep.

Jake awoke at four in the morning and considered it a moral victory to not feel overly jetlagged. He got up, turned on the TV, minus the sound, and powered up his tablet. He had brought his phone but hadn't extended his wireless service, so he couldn't receive any calls. It was a little bizarre to feel somewhat disconnected from your contacts and have to rely on free Wi-Fi to be able to check your e-mail. Logging on, Jake used his virtual private network to access his home computer. Given that China censored the Internet, Jake wanted to avoid running into any firewall issues. His school account had the usual e-mails from students, several related to the upcoming speaker coming to present at the department seminar, and some research-related questions from Eric. Jake's Gmail account didn't have much of note except one e-mail from Duncan:

Don't call my cell phone.

Nothing more than that. Jake wasn't sure what that meant but assumed that whatever Duncan wanted to talk about was quite serious. He went down to get some breakfast at six, opted for fruit and yogurt, and took his tablet with him to catch up on some mindless sports reading. Finishing up his food, he went back to the room, took a shower, dressed in his suit, and waited patiently to walk to CIC headquarters. He had brought an overcoat since January in Beijing wasn't exactly warm, but at least it was dry. He left the room at a quarter to eight and walked to the office building. There was nothing unique about the building, especially since it was surrounded by the twin structures of the Poly Theatre. Jake walked to the reception desk and announced who he was and whom he was visiting. He signed in on the ledger and was instructed to take the elevator to the top floor. The elevator opened to a wide atrium, and he was greeted by the receptionist, who offered him some water and asked him to take a seat.

"Professor Chamberlain, good to see you again," Benjamin Chen walked out and greeted him. "I hope your travel was good as well as the accommodations." He was as formal as ever, keeping his left hand behind his back as he walked. It was a very British mannerism.

"Yes, thank you. I'm not sure I would be in this good a state if your arrangements hadn't been so comfortable."

"Excellent. Well, please come this way. We are all very interested to hear your presentation."

Benjamin brought Jake to a corner conference room. There was a table that could seat fifteen comfortably, a large projection screen on the front wall, and a food spread in the corner. The windows had been shaded gray so no one could see in or out. Each seat at the table was taken except for the one at the head of the table, which Jake assumed was for Benjamin. Below the projection screen was a USB port for Jake to insert his flash drive. His drive was password protected, as was his research, so he needed access to the computer to open his presentation. Having a double-password-protected document felt important somehow.

After Jake finished getting the document open, Benjamin introduced him, first in Mandarin and then in English.

"Jake, the floor is yours. Take your time. This is not a typical academic presentation. Think of it more like you are teaching an MBA class. There is no pressure. We are here to learn from you." With that, Benjamin took his seat.

Jake started his presentation with a slide that had two powerful charts. He liked these charts because they had immediate impact on the audience and led to a nice discussion about market efficiency and asset valuation.

"First, I want to thank you for your time and inviting me to come and present my work to you. It's a pleasure to be here, and I look forward to your comments and discussion in regards to my underlying theory and the results. Please let me know if anything is unclear. Now, what I have above my right shoulder are two charts, and both should be very familiar to us. The first is the stock market crash of 1929; the second is the stock market crash of 1987. They're similar in that they resulted in untold losses and economic destruction, but the cause of each crash was wildly different. That's what we're going to discuss today. We want to understand the fundamentals of why asset prices change and lead to nonnormality in returns."

Jake paused and looked around the room to assess his audience's attentiveness and see if there were any questions. He had his audience's attention, but no one stirred. With that, he continued on, gearing himself for a four-hour monologue.

CHAPTER 33

L unch was an odd affair. It was held in the communal lunch room on the second floor of the CIC building. It seemed that all the employees who worked within the building gathered there at the same time, and there was an assortment of exotic choices. Jake recognized the Peking duck and some mutton dish that was part of a Mongolian hot pot. He passed on anything with seafood and anything that had *Sichuan* in front of it. He wasn't afraid of spices—in fact, he quite enjoyed them—but eating a potentially unknown spicy dish prior to meeting with the CIO was probably not the best course of action.

Jake was guided through the lunch process by the head of the alternative division, Bing Ho, who spoke excellent English. It probably helped that he had earned his MBA from Wharton. They sat together after the food had been acquired.

"We rarely have speakers come in unless they're trying to pitch us an investment idea. I don't believe we've had a presentation quite like yours. I enjoyed it."

"I'm glad you did. It's rare for me to give a lecture with such limited feedback." *Code speak for 'that presentation sucked.'*

"That's a cultural thing. Our approach is noncombative. Additionally, we were looking for information. This was not about your academic credibility. This was purely about the results. Benjamin has never made a recommendation like this."

"Good." *It still sucked.* Jake nodded as he ingested some flavored lamb.

"Listen. Enjoy your meal. I'll leave you to eat and relax, and come back to take you to the CIO when you're done."

"Thanks." Jake watched his guide walk away and noticed several other people glance back in his direction. He greeted each of these glances with a nod but got no nod in return.

The presentation was definitely odd. Jake had built in time, as he always did, for questions and interruptions. There were almost none in this presentation, except for a couple of questions about clarifications on the construction of the factors and some interpretation of the results. Besides the occasional person coming in or out of the room, there had been almost no break in his four-hour lecture. *Why the hell am I here?*

This was not going to lead to an academic posting. It seemed to be a presentation for presentation's sake, and his desire to leave was quite strong. He was halfway across the world when he should be back in Austin teaching his class, finishing the writing for his dissertation, and preparing to send his papers to the journals—although the hot tea was very good.

Bing tapped Jake on the shoulder as Jake was finishing his tea.

"Jake, will you please follow me?"

He finished up, returned his tray, and followed the man to the elevators, where they ascended to the top floor. They walked to a corner office, and Bing knocked on the door.

"Jake, when you go in, just sit and listen. Don't make any judgments. You'll know when it's time for you to talk. I hope for the best outcome."

With that, the man left, and Jake felt a sense of utter confusion. *Well, this is most bizarre.* Oddly, his comment had given Jake a weird sense of hope, like the visit had not been a total waste.

A noise from the other side of the door indicated it was time for Jake to enter.

The office was large but not overly lavish. There was a couch against the back wall and a table and set of chairs in front of a large mahogany desk. A painting depicted warriors from the Ming dynasty (Jake's best guess) on the Great Wall fending off a northern herd of horsemen (probably Genghis Khan and Mongol warriors). History was never his strong point. Jake stood by a chair facing the desk, behind which sat the CIO of the CIC. Lao Keping was a no-nonsense man who believed in the old ways but who also understood the changing economic shape of China and its status as a world power.

"Professor Chamberlain, please take a seat." Unlike his compatriots, Lao spoke English laced with a strong Asian accent.

Jake sat.

An hour later there was a knock on the door. It was Benjamin. A few words were exchanged in Mandarin, and Jake stood, gave a slight nod to the man, and thanked him for his time. He wasn't quite sure what the appropriate custom was to say good-bye, so he didn't reach out for a handshake. They walked out of the office, and Benjamin closed the door. Jake's head was spinning from what he had just been offered.

"Jake, shall we go for a walk? I think it's best to digest this information outside, even if it's cold. When it's cold, the air quality is best."

CHAPTER 34

"Let us walk to the Dongyue Temple. The street is tree lined, and it is a good reminder of our history and culture among all this progress. I find being in the presence of the Old World allows me to think clearer." Benjamin said.

"I find the same with exercise. Riding my bike was how I got my biggest breakthrough."

That got a short laugh out of Benjamin, but not because he thought it was funny. "I think it is time we speak clearly. No more need to dance around our true intentions."

"I could not agree more. I don't feel like myself, and my witty banter may result in some great insult. Maybe it's the travel or the presentation or that last meeting, but I feel somewhat outside of myself, like I'm watching my actions from five feet away."

"I understand. That feeling will take a while to go away. It will be better flying west, although you will be traveling in an easterly direction." Jake nodded in ascension.

"All right, Benjamin, what am I doing here in Beijing?"

A cold wind blew as they made their way to the open area that the temple and surrounding gardens overlooked.

"Do you want to know a dirty secret about the investing community? It is controlled by a group of people so small you could fit them inside the Olympic Swim Center and still have seats remaining. The size of the global pension market is over $35 trillion. The global insurance market has a $600 billion surplus. Sovereign wealth funds have over $7 trillion, of which $4 trillion is tied to energy. US foundations have capital that exceeds $400 billion. That's at least $43 trillion controlled by maybe two thousand people who truly matter. The size of that capital is massive compared to the people whose job it is to allocate it. By comparison, Fidelity employs over forty thousand people to manage $4.3 trillion.

"Now I am ignoring the retail space when it comes to the capital figure because, frankly, that capital does not matter. It is controlled by individuals that, as a collective group, could not come together to make an informed decision on the color of the sky, let alone have any meaningful impact on capital markets—"

"Benjamin, did you just make a joke?"

"I did. Do not mention it to anyone. Shall we continue?"

"Of course."

"The retail investors are also second movers, so once prices move, they tend to be net followers. That becomes important only when the markets move, as you say, in a nonnormal fashion. I am also ignoring investment managers, because these managers are dependent on investment from one of the four groups I just mentioned. Blackstone is big because it has received capital from many of these groups. If four or five of Blackstone's largest investors pulled, Blackstone could fold. The reason that there are investment managers is that pension funds, foundations, etc., do not hire people to make investment decisions; they hire people to evaluate managers. So each pension fund has a small team whose job it is to evaluate managers and then distribute their capital to those managers. Or they hire consultants to tell them what to do."

They reached the temple and sat on a bench that looked back in the direction they had just come from. The view showed the expanse of the city as one office tower blurred into another. The sun was beginning its descent below the horizon. Jake knew it was cold, but his adrenaline was pumping. He was feeling almost the exact opposite from how he had felt at lunch.

Benjamin continued. "Now if you look at the investment landscape, you can see that most people, firms, and countries allocate in the exact same way: about 50 percent allocation to equities, 30 percent to fixed

income, and 20 percent to alternatives and cash. There is some small variation across countries and managers, but everyone follows the same model
and tends to invest with the same managers. Most do it because it is easy
to send money to the biggest firms and that requires the least amount of
due diligence and oversight, or because they have strict portfolio mandates
about who they can invest with and limitations on the size of the manager.
So you've highly correlated portfolio allocations and highly correlated security selections."

I know where this is going. He gets it. Jake added to Benjamin's point.
"We know that return attribution can be broken down into three specific
categories. Market timing is the most important, followed by asset allocation, and then security selection. In fact, security selection has a very minor
impact in terms of moving the return needle. So you're suggesting that
the most significant global capital, which we know is sticky because of the
investment process, is causing a huge correlation problem because capital
is being invested in very similar ways. I imagine it takes significant time
for you to change your investment managers just because of due diligence.
So your ability to market time your capital is highly limited. Additionally,
most investment managers have career risk, so they're not willing to take
a chance on having a different portfolio. They'd rather lose money with
everyone else than take the proper risk-reward choices."

Benjamin nodded. His attention was focused solely on the sunset, but
it didn't appear that he was actually looking at it, but beyond it.

"It is a problem that I have been thinking about for a while, and it is
a solution that I did not believe had an actual answer," Benjamin said. "I
believe that our general approach to portfolio management is causing a
significant problem when it comes to a potential tail-oriented event. There
are too many assets in the same place, meaning that selling those assets at
the same time would cause a catastrophic fall in prices and require a reboot
of the entire economic system. That should have occurred in 2008, but it
did not. It could have happened in 1987 for the United States but did not.
Your research may have shed some light on why it did not. As you noted,

there were significant signals prior that pointed to the nonnormal events, and coordinated actions that followed to get the world out of that event."

"For example, the crash of 1987 was precipitated by an increase in volatility, especially downside volatility, and an increase in the short position of futures contracts on the S&P 500, a pre-event signal," Jake said. "One of the responses to the 1987 event was to change the circuit breakers to prevent the market from going down over 20 percent in a day."

"This is true, but why did 1987 take place?" Benjamin asked. "Why did 2008 take place? Why at those points in time? The market was propped up artificially for a year. The housing data was available in 2007, and the correction took place in August 2008. I believe there was some manipulation behind the scenes. John Paulson, who famously won biggest for betting against the housing market, even outright said it, saying how the valuations at the banks were deliberately higher than they should have been," Benjamin said, accentuating every word more than usual.

"I'm not comfortable answering that, yet the data seems to suggest it. In fact, I'm really uncomfortable with that because it rocks the foundation for everything we do. We believe in free capital markets, and this suggests otherwise," Jake said.

"There is one other thing to consider. The world survived the 2008 financial collapse by the skin of its teeth because there was a worldwide disbursement of risk. However, I do not believe there are any more safety nets. Another shock, another larger nonnormal event, and there is nowhere to shift the risk. The Fed cannot take any more action, and leverage is still a problem. We never learn." Benjamin was speaking with conviction. Jake detected real passion in his voice, and he could see Benjamin's muscles tense through his suit. *He's not really talking to me. He's expressing his opinion freely, maybe for the first time ever.*

"That's a little outside my area of expertise, since I don't focus on monetary policy."

"True. Shall we walk to your hotel?" Benjamin said, with a little more peace in his voice, coming out of his own personal universe.

They got up and started to head back to the St. Regis. The wind had picked up significantly. Everyone who was on the streets was bundled up, walking with their heads down, keeping their faces out of the wind. Benjamin remained upright and as ridged as ever, his right arm swinging freely with his left still at the small of his back.

"Do you know the size of the equity market is $70 trillion, the bond market is over $150 trillion, and the size of the OTC market is $655 trillion?" Benjamin asked. "The notional amount of derivatives far outweighs the underlying value of the instruments. The gross value is about $20 trillion, and that speaks to the leverage built into the system. This confirms your findings about the importance of leverage and nonnormal returns. What this tells me is that it does not take a large amount of capital to move markets. Right now, a smallish fund could in fact trigger a significant market event. The Flash Crash started and built momentum because of 80,000 short contract trades in the e-mini S&P 500 futures contracts. That means a $10 million capital outlay caused the markets to lose almost $3 trillion at the trough. That, in my opinion, should never happen," Benjamin said.

They reached Jake's hotel. Benjamin walked into the lobby with him.

"Benjamin, I've noticed that while we've been talking, you haven't really made a point. You've just been giving me facts and some conjecture," Jake said.

"Very true. Jake, I want you to seriously consider the offer from us. The point I want to make is that I think what you've found is a solution to the problem we have just discussed. It could result in a two-step solution that would be best for the global economy. Together we can solve a major problem and advance the world forward." Benjamin paused to let that statement sink in, his eyes laser focused on Jake's.

This heavy discussion of the world and markets had temporarily allowed Jake to focus on something other than the offer from CIC, but now it had been brought squarely back to the forefront, and with that, the corresponding light-headedness he was feeling earlier. In response, he could only nod.

"Good. Now for some enjoyment. Tomorrow we have prepared a full tour of the Imperial Palace, as well as a tour of the Great Wall. Is there anything else you would like to do while you're here?" Benjamin asked.

"I want to swim at the aquatics center in the Olympic pool." *Haley will be so jealous.*

Benjamin smiled. "Of course. Expect a pickup at 7:30 a.m. Enjoy tomorrow, and let us talk before you leave Saturday."

With that, Benjamin left. Jake realized he was in a position that he could not have dreamed of while working on his research in his tiny office back in Austin a month ago.

CHAPTER 35

Jake got back to Austin Sunday morning. Benjamin had given him a week to decide his course of action. This didn't mean Jake couldn't go on his campus visits, but Benjamin was anxious to move forward.

He had thoroughly enjoyed his Saturday tour of Beijing. The pool had been almost empty when he swam. Swimming in the same arena where the historic Olympic Games were held was thrilling. While his times would never compare—in fact, it was quite humbling to think how slow he was relative to those great athletes—it did not diminish the experience. Finishing up, he looked at the arena, taking in the beauty of it and reflecting on how a group of individuals could get together in this facility and change the investing landscape.

The tour of the palace and the Forbidden City was beautiful, even though it was cold. It was so grand that it was almost impossible to take it in in one day. Jake could not walk across Tiananmen Square without thinking of that notorious day in 1989 that could be considered an inflection point on how China and the world viewed the country. It was also a shame how much smog engulfed the city, a result of the massive industrial expansion and population growth over the past fifteen years. The weather on the Great Wall was better, as it was far enough outside of the city that the smog didn't reach eyesight. How anyone ran a marathon on the wall was beyond Jake. The best times were about three and a half hours, which was mind-boggling. The wall was more impressive than the Forbidden City, in Jake's opinion, spanning thousands of miles and millions of man-hours. The scope and size of the wall were remarkable, even by today's engineering standards.

As Jake looked over the wall into Mongolia, his thoughts returned to the painting in Lao's office. The wall was an engineering feat designed to keep people both in and out, expand and regulate trade, and control transportation. At its core it was a physical means of regulation, a way to control population, goods, and information. It might have served to protect royal dynasties from Mongol invaders, but it probably restricted the growth of the people contained within its walls just as successfully, if not more so.

Can an impediment to trade and growth really be a good thing? Jake wondered. *Is it important to knock down the wall to improve conditions for all, and at what cost? The wall could almost be symbolic for the economy, which gives a sense of freedom, a sense of openness. Should any market be truly free and open? And what the hell should I do with this offer from CIC?*

Landing stateside was fantastic because it meant that he had cell-phone service. Interestingly, he had only one voice mail, from Haley, asking how the trip was going. He texted her that he had landed in San Francisco and would be home in five hours or so. There were no new e-mails worth replying to, so he wasted time reading various social-media sites and reviewing Arsenal's performance in the FA Cup match as he plodded through immigration. Getting through immigration, retrieving his bags, and then rechecking them and going through security again was a royal pain. He found that traveling back home was easier on the body because he hadn't lost the day crossing the time zones. That didn't mean it was easy, and Jake believed that there had to be a better way to streamline the plane-transfer process. It took a herculean effort to act like a normal human being after international travel and then have to go through the airport protocol again.

By the time the flight for Austin boarded, Jake was really irritable, especially because Haley hadn't responded. The flight to Austin felt longer than the one from Beijing, and by the time he deplaned, Jake was beginning to worry. Haley had still not responded.

The traffic back home wasn't bad at all, which was saying something, given how bad I-35 had become. Jake pulled into their condo complex and saw that Haley's car was parked under the awning. He parked in an open spot, got his bags, and walked to the front door. He put his keys in the lock and heard Winston's bark. There was something very relaxing knowing you had a two-hundred-pound mastiff protecting your home and loved ones when you left. Even if Winston was a gentle giant, that bark alone would be enough to deter any would-be home invader.

Jake opened the door and was greeted by his brindled beast. Haley was standing on the landing by the kitchen smiling, and the TV was on at a higher-than-normal volume.

"Hi, babe. How was your trip?" Haley said in greeting, but Jake sensed that it was forced.

"It was great. Why didn't you answer my—"

She interrupted him with a finger wave. "Sorry, I must have misplaced my phone." She was keeping up this weirdly forced, overly happy tone. "I missed you so much. I want you to tell me all about it."

"Babe, what is going—"

She ran over and hugged him before he could finish his question. She held him tight and brought her mouth to his ear. She was practically hyperventilating.

"We can't talk about any of this now. Let's go to dinner tonight. Maybe the Salt Lick. Somewhere outside the city. Just act normal now. Take a nap, Watch TV. Don't talk about the trip or anything related to what you're doing," she whispered in between breaths in a barely audible voice.

She pulled back and returned to her prior cheery tone. "You must be exhausted. Go lie down, and let's get you back to neutral."

"OK. I'm tired. Wake me in two hours." *What the hell is going on?*

The Salt Lick was south of Austin, and it took about twenty-five minutes to get there in the beat-up Jeep. Jake and Haley talked about exercise, her research, and the pains of travel, but nothing about China or his research. He wanted desperately to talk to her about Beijing but was waiting for a cue from her that it was all right to talk. She had kept up this oddly cheerful but clearly disturbed appearance after he'd woken up.

They parked, walked into the old brick building, and lined up to order. Jake ordered the brisket plate, Haley ordered the turkey plate, and they found a bench toward the back of the building.

"Is it OK to talk? What is going on?" Jake asked.

Haley looked around and leaned over the table. The tension in her was physically evident in how fatigued she looked.

"Duncan called me Thursday. At first I didn't know it was him because I didn't recognize the number. He was very brief and sounded rushed. He told me not to use our cell phones to speak about your research or anything related to it. Nothing in e-mail, and not to speak to anyone about it, even the most trusted confidant. He wouldn't elaborate beyond that over the phone. It was very odd. Later that day he sent me the following message through Google Hangouts." She handed her phone to Jake and showed him the text.

I will be there next Friday.

She took the phone back, erased the message, and turned it off.

"I thought that was extremely weird. I replied but got no response. I assume he's coming to Austin, but I'm not sure, and I don't know why."

"This is what has gotten you so spooked?" Jake asked. *Alarm bells are ringing.*

She shook her head. "It was weird for sure but only made me curious. Then Friday happened." She seemed visibly shaken. It was unlike her to be rattled unless something truly awful had occurred.

"Haley, this isn't like you. Tell me what happened. Are you hurt? Were you hurt?" Jake was getting really worried.

She shook her head, but that did not relieve Jake's anxiety. He almost forgot about his own news.

"You know my office in the basement of Anna Hiss Gym? It's so poorly lit, and my desk is surrounded by those stacks and rows of books. This semester I teach that Monday, Wednesday, Friday swim class at ten."

"Right, I know. And—?" Jake said. His impatience and worry interrupting her. She reached over and rested his hand on his.

"Stay calm and just listen. Last Friday, the pool was closed, so there was no class. I think they were cleaning the diving well or something. So

I stayed in my office to do some research and was in the stacks when the door opened. You know the layout of the office. My desk is in the front, off to the right. If you're in the back of the stacks, you can't be seen by people that come in the door because the lighting is so bad. Well, it was about ten after ten, and I was in the back of the library, and someone came in. Normally I would have said hello or asked who was there, but a man came in and walked right to my desk and sat down. That really confused me. He then inserted something into my computer, turned on a flashlight, and started walking the stacks. Given where I was, I ducked under the shelving. Unless you were directly looking, you never could've found me. He seemed to just do a cursory check to see if anyone was there. It scares me every time to think about it because of what he might have done if he had found me."

"I know you would have given him a hard time," Jake said, trying to sound reassuring.

"Maybe. Shit. I don't know. The man walked like he knew how to handle himself, and something just told me he had a weapon. After he returned to my desk, he waited five minutes, took the flash drive out, or whatever he put in the computer, and left. Jake, I didn't leave my hiding space for thirty minutes."

"Did you call campus security? The police?" Jake felt a rage building inside himself, knowing that Haley had been threatened and he could do nothing about it.

"No. When I finally crawled out, I went to my computer. There was nothing missing. No trace of anything I could see. Nothing had been taken from my desk. It was as if it hadn't happened. There was nothing to report. My door hadn't even been locked. What could I tell them?"

"What do you think he was doing?"

"I'll tell you in a sec, because there's more to the story. After checking my desk, I got the hell out of there. I practically ran to the car. I'd taken the Jeep into work that day. You know what a piece of shit the car is, right? You know your old stereo and how we could never get it to sit right, and that it always seemed to shake when you went above thirty-five miles an hour?

Well, it wasn't shaking on the way home. I took a look at it, and someone had moved it, or reset it. I could tell that someone had been in the car. Did you notice it when we drove here?"

Jake thought back to the ride. He hadn't even thought about or noticed anything. Yet as she was talking about the stereo, he remembered that as he'd turned on the radio, it hadn't moved.

"You're right. It was fixed. There was no shimmy."

"Right. Well, when I got home, Winston was freaking out. I could hear him before I even turned off the engine. When I got in the house, he was barking and growling. It took me ten minutes to calm him and get him away from the front door. Someone had tried to get in our house. I've taken Winston with me everywhere I've gone since Friday. I know that it meant leaving the condo unguarded, but I don't think that matters anymore. Jake, someone is watching us. They're monitoring us. I imagine your computer is bugged, and your office phone. I wouldn't be surprised if Eric's phone was also bugged. Combined with what Duncan said and how he's acting, I have to ask, what the hell is going on? Are you guys doing something illegal? Who are these fucking people, and what do they want?" Haley was on the verge of tears, the stress of the past couple of days finally coming out.

Jake reached over and grabbed her other hand. He could see the fear in her eyes. He also suppressed his anger. Now was not the time to get angry. Now was the time for calm, rational thinking.

"We're doing nothing wrong. I'm a little unsure of what is happening, but I hope Duncan will be able to shed some light on it. The timing of this is too coordinated to be coincidental. I'm sure that it has something to do with my findings, but I'm not sure it has anything to do with my trip to China. What I learned over there tells me something about the why of this. I want to hear what Duncan has to say, but if I were to speculate, I would think we're upsetting some important people, people that don't want to be found."

"Can't we just stop what you're doing?'

"It's not that simple. My research is somewhat public since it has been traded on, and whoever is doing this knows that we're out there. It's possible that they don't know the specifics, but it's clear that they have now taken an interest in us. We'll need to construct the timeline to assess the what and the how of their knowledge, but this requires us to be very cautious. We must continue on with our lives as normal as possible to not let on that we know. Agreed?"

Haley nodded. "Do you think this is why you've had trouble getting a favorable academic response to your research? Could there be some pushback because these two things are related?"

"I guess that's possible, but I doubt it. I still have good campus interviews coming up. I need to consider what CIC has offered."

"Balls. I completely forgot to ask about your visit. And what do you mean 'offered'?" Haley perked up.

"I noticed you hadn't asked, but I forgive you, all things considered." Jake laughed, trying to introduce a bit of levity into their discussion.

"I thought the presentation was one of the worst I had ever given. There was no discussion, feedback, or comments. Nothing. I went to lunch so depressed because I had no idea what I was doing there. Then I had an interesting meeting with the CIO and a nice discussion with the head of research, Benjamin."

"The guy you met in New York and San Diego?"

"Right. That guy is sharp and gets it. I think he sees the same thing my research shows. Anyway, Saturday I did the tourist thing and went to the Forbidden City and the Great Wall. Oh, I also swam at the Olympic aquatic center."

"You lucky bastard." Some of the tension seemed to be leaving her body.

"That's right." Jake had deliberately left that juicy tidbit for last, a cheeky smile accompanying the statement.

"OK, tell me about your talk with the CIO and Benjamin, and then you can tell me all about the city and the sights."

"They want to set me up and run the model using some of their capital. They know there's an inefficiency in the marketplace, that the marketplace can't correct itself properly, and that there may be some coordinated actions that are causing the market to ebb and flow outside of normality. They feel comfortable that my model has found where the inefficiency lies. One thing did strike me as odd. Before I left on Friday, Benjamin said that I could provide a two-step solution to the problem. Initially I didn't understand what he meant, but now I think I know. I assume the first would be to take advantage of this market inefficiency and improve information flow in the market. We would make money on this inefficiency, but eventually it would lead to better portfolio allocation and better global diversification. Consequently, the size of a nonnormal event should be minimized. In other words, it would lower the likelihood of another market crash event like we had in 2008."

"The second?"

"I just figured that out when I heard what happened to you. Benjamin mentioned manipulation, and I also conjectured in my research that something or someone had to be driving the nonnormal events. I think it's this point that's caused me so much distress with the academic community. It's this result that would cause fifty years of asset pricing to be rethought. Nobody really wants to accept that point, especially from a graduate student. Yet I digress. I believe Benjamin wanted me to implement the model to reveal who is behind these market forces. Something tells me that we've already alerted them to our presence."

"You haven't told me what their offer was."

"They want me to manage a billion dollars."

CHAPTER 36

Chris Carter was in the dark. He wasn't sure where he stood. Ever since he had been approached, he had followed protocol to the letter. Each task had been performed with absolute precision. Now his contact had gone dark. They had been speaking every week consistently. It had been a month now and nothing.

It was possible he had been blinded by greed. It was tough to admit your career had run its course. He should have been satisfied, but he wasn't. He could have made more money, but he didn't. He should have gained more notoriety, but he was just another cog in the machine. Now he had sold his integrity too. He had been given an opportunity, one that had come in a vulnerable moment in a meeting in Switzerland, and he had taken it.

What was he supposed to do now? He couldn't pursue the contact; he had to sit and wait until he was contacted. The promise of money and a senior position at the International Monetary Fund had seemed so close a couple of months ago. Now it seemed miles away.

He had deliberately undermined his superior and threatened the credibility of the Federal Reserve, even if the action the Fed itself took was questionable. He couldn't go to the press with what he had done because all he would do was reveal his duplicity. He couldn't tell Michelle since it would undermine all the work he had put in to get on her good side. *And front side, and backside.*

If the contact was really gone, there was nothing he could do about it. He could still destroy Michelle without them. *Fuck it. There is another option.*

He had leverage and could use it. It was time to partner with the firm down the street. Since his integrity was already gone, he might as well sell some data and information along with it. *And get paid.*

CHAPTER 37

The week moved slowly. Jake continued to finish up the writing for his dissertation, which required two versions of the document. One would be presented as a complete document to be submitted for approval, and the second would be separated into three papers, two of which he was sure he was submitting to journals, the third of which he was less sure. The semester was in full swing, so students were omnipresent, and the faculty were adjusting to the demands of a new semester. Those first couple of weeks of the spring semester were always challenging because everyone was playing catch-up from winter break. That was fine with Jake, because Eric was teaching two sections of energy finance this semester and hadn't even called him in to discuss the AFAs or his trip.

Jake had been coy with the faculty about whom he had seen. They just assumed he must have been on a campus visit, and Jake would do nothing to change that assumption. Jake saw Audria on Monday and Tuesday and did not have a chance to speak with her, and then she left on Wednesday for a trip to Louisiana State University. Haley was still spooked about going to her office, so she worked in the atrium in the College of Business. They rode in together and left together. This wouldn't have been normal protocol, but their schedules were similar enough that waiting an extra an hour for Jake to finish teaching or for Jake to go in with Haley on a Friday for her swim class wouldn't have seemed too peculiar. They kept up a normal workout routine and had Winston sleep in their bedroom.

Jake was teaching just one class, a senior seminar on derivatives. It had gotten off to an uncomfortable start with him missing one class the first week, but after Wednesday's class, he had learned the students' names and had starting building a decent dialogue with them. The interaction with the students brought some normality back to his world, and getting into the routine of teaching and writing and working out reduced the uncertainty and stress he'd felt since the AFA meeting and Haley's revelation of the break-in. Duncan's visit would hopefully bring further clarity and an appropriate course of action. That could also help with the decision he had to make regarding Benjamin's offer. Right now he really did not have enough information to make a choice.

When Friday came, Jake hung out at the café next to the aquatics center, waiting for Haley to finish her class. It was cold for Austin, and everyone was bundled up. Jake still didn't know when, or if, Duncan was coming in. He hadn't provided any details, so they stuck to their normal *modus operandi*. It was eleven fifteen before Haley joined Jake. She came over smelling of chlorine, even though she hadn't gotten in the water.

"How was class?" Jake asked.

"Good. I think they have absorbed enough now that they won't drown swimming a fifty." She handed Jake her phone.

Jake looked at the chat on Google Hangouts.

Meet me at the Driskill at 7:30 tonight.

"What time is Benson coming in?" Haley asked.

"He should be getting in around the same time. Let me give him a call to confirm. I'll call him from the office phone in the department. I'm curious to meet this girl he's dating."

"She isn't staying with us?"

"No, she's staying with some of her college friends."

"OK. Let's stop by the office and head home."

"Hold on, make sure you tell Benson to call you back from an office line that isn't his. We can't be too careful."

"Will do."

The rest of the day passed without incident. Jake and Haley both worked on their dissertations at home while Winston slept peacefully on the couch. Benson had confirmed that he could make the meeting at seven thirty and was curious as to why they were meeting downtown and why he had to switch phones. Jake hadn't provided any details but stressed he should come alone.

Getting parking on Sixth Street on a Friday night was going to be a nightmare, so Jake and Haley left at six to get food at Stubbs before walking over to the hotel.

The Driskill Hotel was quintessential Austin. It had retained the strong historical Southwestern culture and fe el while the city expanded and grew around it. It was a go-to place to stay when visiting the city. Jake and Haley walked in, didn't see Benson or Duncan, and waited on the leather couches that sat under the longhorn head. Benson came in about five minutes after them and joined them on the couch.

"Dang. What the hell is goin' on? Why are we here?" Benson greeted them in a boisterous, overt manner that was atypical for him. He was clearly excited.

"A little less loud, please. We'll get to that," replied Jake. "We're waiting on my brother, Duncan, to join us."

"Your brother is here? Now I'm really confused," Benson said, a little quieter.

"Go and order a drink for yourself and get me one too," Haley ordered Benson.

He got up, looking a little bewildered. Benson returned with two bottles of Dos Equis and a Guinness. They were about to start small talk when Duncan came over.

"You finally got here," Jake said, getting up to greet his brother.

"I've been here for an hour. I just wanted to watch you guys for a while to see if you were followed. I was nervous about sending those texts, but I think we're in the clear."

"Now somebody better tell me what the hell is goin' on," Benson said a little too loudly.

"Goddamn it—keep it quiet." Duncan was clearly in no mood for histrionics.

"All right. It's time we shared all of our information, because I believe we're in trouble. I'll tell you my story first, and then, Jake, you need to fill us in on your trip," Duncan quietly stated, looking over at Benson as a reminder to keep his voice low.

"A little reordering first. Haley will have to tell you her part as well, because she is now directly involved," Jake said. "Then Benson, you have to tell us what you've been up to. I'll go last."

Benson looked thoroughly confused. "I'm not in trouble. I'm going to New York to speak with our chief market strategist. I believe I'm gettin' promoted."

"I doubt that," Duncan said. "Hold on to that for a while. Let me tell you my story first."

Benson was taken aback.

"I started implementing the model right after our dinner in New York," Duncan said. "It didn't take long to get the program up and running, and it started making money right away. As we discussed, we started small, just using the hundred-thousand-dollar base to start. It was able to isolate the nonnormal movements across the asset classes and take advantage of any misallocations when it came to leverage."

"None of this is new so far," Jake said.

"It's to me," said Benson. His curiosity had started to outweigh his confusion.

"Settle down. After three weeks I got a call to come see the partners. They were really curious as to what was going on because the performance was outstanding and, well, different from the way I typically trade. I told them I was trying out a new strategy, an algorithm that had come from some unique research. I didn't mention your name. Now, here's where the problem began. You know I have a computer that tracks my trades and follows what I do?"

Jake nodded. Benson and Haley just listened.

"Well, they asked me if I wouldn't mind having the computer track and follow the strategy. I thought about it and said it would be OK. It was fucking stupid, and I didn't call you because I didn't think it would be a big deal. I just didn't think they would commit a lot of capital to the strategy. Normally a parallel computer trading system would run half of what the trader would have at risk. So it would still be small enough to test the theory without too much downside risk. When I called you back in December to tell you the account was up 75 percent, that wasn't entirely accurate. That was 75 percent on a notional basis, not including the leverage we employ. I was employing a leverage ratio of five to one."

"Holy shit. That's $375,000 in under three months."

"Yes, we all know you're good at math, Jake," Haley injected.

"So much for starting small." Jake said shaking his head.

"Wait. I haven't gotten to the troubling part yet. The partners had implemented the tracking-computer account to follow along. Initially they put in a hundred thousand but had a stipulation that each day money was made, they would add 5 percent additional capital. It's standard firm policy to follow the money. The computerized account has been trading for sixty days, and this is how much the account is worth." Duncan handed them a piece of paper that read the following:

$53,913,950.99.

"If you take away the capital contributions, the account is up over $30 million."

Jake took a long sip of his drink. *Damn it. This was exactly what I wanted to avoid.* Haley was the first to break the silence.

"Let me get this straight. The strategy has made lots of money. A ridiculous amount of money, and this is a problem, right?"

Jake and Duncan nodded.

"Why is this a problem? Your bosses should be over the moon. Hell, you both should be over the moon." Benson was so utterly confused he forgot to keep his voice quiet.

"Jesus, Benson, keep it down. This is working too well too fast." Jake punched Benson in the shoulder. "Duncan, was nobody monitoring the computer? Don't they reconcile every day?"

"Since the trading is all done electronically, the trades are all time stamped and verified through our compliance software. Since there were no trade breaks, there was no issue. At the end of the month, the account values are verified, and the profit and loss numbers are tallied. Just due to the compounding nature of the strategy, the last twenty days have seen the highest absolute growth. So when the monthly reconciliation was done and they saw the account values, they were more than shocked. Since I don't know the notional value of the account the computer controls, I didn't find out until they did. Needless to say, I was shocked as well. I know this is exactly what you wanted to avoid." Duncan echoed the exact same thought that had entered Jake's mind seconds ago.

"Dang, so what happened next?" Benson asked.

"We did nothing. For a firm of our size, that kind of return makes the year. Hell, it's worth two years. We kept both accounts open—at least we did for one more day. The next day, the firm got a notice from the SEC that we were being audited and were on watch for suspicious trading behavior. Almost simultaneously the margin requirement increased for the account across all exchanges. The computer account was shut down almost immediately."

"Whoa. You did nothin' wrong," said Benson.

"True, but the SEC can audit you at any point in time for any reason. When you've got an account that does as well as our account did in that amount of time, you're going to get flagged for some potential action. Who can be that right, that often?"

"Duncan, this actually explains a lot. I won't say why yet because I want you to finish, but the fact that the account got flagged is highly telling," Jake added. *Puzzle pieces are coming together*

"I'm glad you think that, because it was a shock to me. The partners and I were pretty pissed about what happened. We had this huge financial win, and then we had to deal with the SEC. The SEC can shut you down for any irregularity or technicality they find. It doesn't even have to be related to what we've been doing. It could be on a small compliance ir-regularity or some sort of marketing misrepresentation." Duncan shook his head as he proceeded to fill them in on the events that had transpired once the SEC arrived and how he was interrogated.

"Duncan, that's crazy. Those people don't sound like auditors to me," said Benson.

"I don't think they were. Just from a big-picture perspective, have you ever heard of an account being restricted on trading because it was up with no clear evidence of wrongdoing? And why the great concern over Jake's work? This just felt wrong. It just felt like someone was watching for this particular strategy or trades, and once we started using Jake's model, we were targeted and reported to the SEC and the exchanges. Plus, there was the focus on just the computer account and not my personal account. A true audit wouldn't have missed that."

"How so?" Haley asked.

"I think whoever was watching us confused the fact that my personal account and the computer traded simultaneously and thought them the same account. An order must have come down to increase the margin lim-its for the account responsible for the trade without realizing that they were two separate accounts. You see, Griffin is a prop trading firm and doesn't run client capital. We've individual accounts that feed to a master account that logs the ID with the exchanges. Trades are then allocated ac-cordingly to the individual trader. Each trader is linked to his or her own account, and all are registered, but the exchange only sees us through the master account. So when you've got two accounts trading separately, both are registered as separate accounts and trades are cleared separately; how-ever, the exchange only sees one trade for both accounts." Duncan paused to take a drink and scanned the room again before continuing.

"Since there was a massive difference in the size of the accounts, no-body thought to ask about the second account. They assumed that the only account trading was the computer account. There must have been something in the size of the trades and the trades themselves that caught someone's eye. Otherwise the individual account would have been restricted as well. It is a little odd to have two accounts trading identically and have such a size differential. Anyway, my personal account with the algorithm was still running, but I shut that down on the day of the interrogation. I erased everything from the system. I have a new computer now but the same account, and nothing has happened to my personal account—no notice, no margin change, nothing."

"Forgive me, but I'm fucking confused," Haley said.

"A $50 million account is nothing. It's chump change on the street, but the ability of that account to potentially move markets is possible," Jake answered, thinking back to the Flash Crash of 2010.

"Correct," Duncan said. "So what you have is a small account that certain private wealth shops wouldn't take on because it's too small, yet it's causing distress to all the exchanges and the SEC. And it's not because of leverage or a violation of any margin requirement. There has been no evidence of insider trading because the trades are over a variety of different instruments, and it's too small to corner a particular market. Additionally, they're focusing on a single account when a sister account that's doing the exact same thing run by the same trader has not been flagged. There's no clear violation, and the rules they have used to target one account are not being applied across the whole firm. It doesn't make sense."

"Could they have just missed the second account?" Haley asked.

"Not likely," Duncan answered. "They caught somebody the other day who sold their shares with inside information that made $170,000 before a negative-earnings announcement. They're always watching for illicit activity. The size of the illicit activity doesn't matter. However, in our case size certainly mattered."

"So what you're saying is that someone is watching for these types of trades using certain amounts of money," Haley said.

"Again correct," said Duncan. "Now the reason I think this is something on a grand scale is because they missed the second account, they focused on the strategy, and they were concerned about Jake's work. The fact that my personal account was too small to raise any flags even though it was doing the same thing suggests that the computer account was targeted because it hit a certain size threshold. If both accounts were shut down, I would have thought we had done something wrong, and I wouldn't have thought twice about the reason. Additionally, the way I was interrogated and the focus on Jake's research suggested a very specific desire to learn about what I had been doing. Someone was watching for these kinds of trades, and that someone is very powerful. To be able to initiate an SEC audit like that, so quickly, along with the margin increases— that's serious clout."

CHAPTER 38

People lingered about in the lobby of the Driskill, and, as time passed, the bar area became more and more crowded. The seats across from Jake, Haley, Duncan, and Benson were occupied by a rowdy group of drinkers completely oblivious to any conversation but their own. The noise level in the hotel had picked up noticeably, but Jake's group was too engaged to pay attention to anyone else. Everyone except Duncan, who kept scanning the bar every other minute. Satisfied no one was listening, he continued on with his timeline.

"That's when I called you and left the message. It was a risk, but I had to get in contact with you immediately. That was before you left for your trip. By the way, you never told us where you went. I assume it was a campus visit?"

"We'll get to that," Jake said. The only person who knew that Jake had been in China was Haley. At least, that was his hope. The fact that he had been so quiet about it was fortunate, given everything that had happened. Duncan continued.

"So, two days later I'm staying late, listening to a conference call, when the chief compliance officer, Leslie, comes and gets me. She knew what was going on peripherally but hadn't seen the two guys, Williams and Waiters, who had interrogated me. However, she told me that someone had logged into the system late the prior night, and it appeared that two SEC officials had come in the office and accessed the system and downloaded some of our data. That's technically illegal, but let's ignore that for now. They stayed for about fifteen minutes and didn't come back. Leslie told me that the only machine they accessed was mine—the one I had hard deleted the morning before. That's when I stopped using my cell phone and computer except to send those two messages to Haley, which, again, was a risk. I even booked my whole trip through Mom's friend who works with American Airlines. I can't verify it, but I think I'm being watched. You wouldn't believe the precautions I took to get here."

"Dang, now I'm officially spooked," Benson said. He was looking a little ill.

"Benson, just wait. Haley, it's time to relay your story to the guys," Jake said.

She proceeded to repeat what had happened to her. She told them she thought they were all probably bugged.

"Haley. I'm sorry. I wonder if my calling you led them down here. Besides us being related, there should have been no direct link." Duncan was looking pretty ashen too.

"Remember, they had made the connection with you and Jake in November, and even though you denied it, it appears these people are thorough. Regardless of how they got the information, they're looking at us now. I certainly don't blame you." Haley tried to reassure him. "I'm also sure they have been in Jake's office as well. Oh shit, now I'm worried that they know where you took your trip, Jake." She met his eyes with a deep look of concern.

"I think we can safely assume that we're all bugged; beyond that I don't know," Jake said. *I really hope they haven't tracked my trip. If they have, we're in some serious peril. What I've planned may not work at all.* "OK, Benson, tell us your news. I believe what you may have considered positive initially may not be positive at all."

"Shit, Jake. It's worse than that," Benson said.

"Let's have it."

"I've been trading the model since our talk in the fall. I implemented it for the client accounts using a monthly rebalancin'. I started small and then eventually grew it to the point that I had to inform my MD and the chief portfolio strategist in New York. It's done very well. Sound familiar?"

Benson said, looking over at Duncan. "Given the success, I've been invited to New York to discuss how to implement it across all our high-net-worth accounts. I've been given the impression that I'm being promoted."

"Benson, you should have told me, but I kind of expected it. However, I don't think you're going to New York to be promoted. I think you're getting fired. What is the size of your client book?" Jake asked.

"It's now over $175 million. It was around $50 million, but with the return and some new accounts, I'm in excess of the magic $100 million mark. That's the key number for our division and why I thought I was gettin' promoted. Dang, things were going so well. I was killin' it at work and had met this fabulous girl."

"What girl?" Duncan asked, his head snapping back quickly to look over at Benson.

"I met Sarah about a month or so ago. She works at UBS and was a former diver at UT. She came up with me this weekend."

"How much have you told her about what you've been doing?" Duncan said, his eyes alert and unblinking.

"Not that much, just that things have been goin' well. No, um.., I did tell her about our connection and that it was the reason we were comin' up, but nothin' about your model and the specifics of what I do." Benson defensive tone was almost apologetic.

"Where is she now? What does she look like?" Duncan continued to stare down Benson. To the uniformed, Duncan appeared quite calm. Jake knew this was not the case. The look in Duncan's eyes revealed he had entered into full paranoia mode.

"It's OK. She doesn't know I'm here." Benson gave away his uncertainty by scanning the room for her.

"How do you know that? Call her; find out where she is immediately." Duncan said as he got up.

Benson pulled out his cell phone. He called, and it went straight to voice mail.

"Did you tell her where you were going? Did she tell you what she was going to do?" Haley asked.

"I don't remember…meet some friends. She said we could meet up at the hotel later. Shit." Benson's voice revealed the extent of doubt about her whereabouts.

"We better get out of here right now." Jake said.

CHAPTER 39

Jake and Haley left the hotel ten minutes after Benson. Duncan stayed behind. He didn't tell them where he was staying or where he was going. They agreed to meet at four in the morning on Kirby Lane. Jake had written down the directions, and no one had said anything. Duncan was convinced that Benson had some sort of listening device on him.

Benson walked his way back to the Hilton on Fourth Street. On his way back, he got a text from Sarah. She apologized for missing his call and was looking forward to seeing him. She said she was a little drunk and ready for him to do bad things to her.

Benson hurried up to the room and closed the door. He sat on the bed and started to go over his person, trying to feel for an imperceptible bug that was on him. He then went through his suitcase, opened his laptop, and took the battery out of his phone. He couldn't find anything. On the other side of the bed was Sarah's bag. He walked over and brought it up on the bed. He dumped the contents out and searched along the lining for any secret compartments or hidden pouches. Nothing. He then went through the contents. Clothes, shoes, and a small bag for toiletries. He opened that up and searched the bag. Nothing in there either. Then he heard the click of the automatic lock opening.

Sarah walked in as he finished throwing her clothes back in her bag and tossing it back on the floor. She hadn't appeared to notice what he was doing as she turned her back to close the door. She looked back at him and smiled. She wore a sleeveless blue blouse with a plunging V-neck collar, jeans, and cowboy boots. Her black hair was down, and it went almost to her lower back. Walking up to Benson, she kicked off her cowboy boots and kissed him hard on the lips. She pressed herself against him, and he could feel her firm breasts thought the thin fabric of her shirt..

"Why don't you take a shower? You stink." She played with the buttons of his jeans.

"Where were you tonight?" he asked, trying to stay relaxed.

"Out with the girls. Living it up. But I can only take so much before I need my man. Go get in that shower."

Benson debated with the emotions he was feeling. This girl was perfect, but what he had just heard had really made him wary. There was no evidence that she was just here to monitor him. *The stuff that we've done, the emotions that have been expressed—no one is that professional*, he thought. *Plus, given what she was wearing-she would have been spotted miles away-it was highly conspicuous.*

"I'll clean up. Are you goin' to join me?"

"Oh no. Just get clean. I'll be waiting for you."

Benson let the water run over his face for a good five minutes. *Have I missed somethin'?* The seeds of doubt were growing. If Jake and Duncan were right, he was caught in a game that was way over his head. It also meant that he had put everyone at risk. Maybe there was a way to confirm this suspicion.

He came out of the bathroom with a towel wrapped around his waist. The bedside light was on, and Sarah stood by the window with the curtain partially open.

"Come here," she said. "Come and take my clothes off."

"In front of the window? Everyone can see."

"Yes."

"Man, you're into some kinky shit. I love it."

"Start with my top and go from there. Go slow."

Benson did as he was told. When she was fully undressed, she asked him to press her up against the glass and hold her there. It was some of the weirdest foreplay he had ever engaged in. She then told him to turn off the light. He turned around and found the switch, and the room went dark. That is when he felt something slip around his neck, and he couldn't breathe.

Kirby Lane was empty except for Jake and Haley. It was 4:05 a.m., and they were tired as hell. Duncan came in five minutes later. He looked ragged.

"Where is Benson? I've been waiting across the street for over half an hour," he said irritably.

"Don't know."

"I really hope he's OK. Maybe one of us should have stayed with him," Haley suggested.

"How long should we wait for him?" Jake asked just as Benson walked up to them.

"Jake, you were wrong about me gettin' fired. Sarah just tried to kill me."

The three of them looked at him in shock.

CHAPTER 40

"I don't know how much time we have or what we're goin' to do, but you better get on with your story and you better have a plan," Benson said, looking at Jake. He had changed his clothes and was wearing a jacket that was fully zipped up. It didn't cover the cuts and bruises on his face. Thankfully they were sitting in a dark corner of the restaurant.

"Balls. We need to get you to a hospital right now. Look at your hands." Haley reached over to him and saw the red line around his neck. "Holy fucking shit, look at your neck. What the fuck happened?" Haley was in hysterics.

"Keep calm. Time is of the essence. Jake, get goin' with what you've got to say. I need to understand this," Benson said. His voice sounded like he had gargled with acid.

"OK, I'll try to make this quick. We're going to have to deal with whatever situation has now arisen. Let me quickly summarize to paint the picture. Both you and Duncan have been targeted. The question is, why? Think about the influence and power one needs to target a particular strategy, monitor that particular strategy, and then be able to decipher and isolate who is running it. You need to have access to all kinds of data and to be friends with the right kinds of people. Remember what I found in my research, about some key variables that seem to be critical in driving nonnormal returns? It was the interaction of large institutions, the Fed, and some effect of margins through the exchanges. Well, it would make sense that if that's the model used to either cause a distortion in the marketplace or correct a distortion, then whoever is running it is going to closely monitor trades that are similar to that model. Especially if those trades are of a certain size. The larger those trades become, the less effect their model has, and it then reduces the ability for whoever is running this model to drive market forces. Again, whoever 'they' are, they're willing to do everything in their power to protect this resource. Benson has just witnessed this firsthand. Now, we don't know why they're doing this, but think about the implications of what we've found. This is what I've been so concerned about. Someone is controlling the capital markets, and it's a coordinated effort."

"We're in real fuckin' trouble," Benson said.

"Yes, but we've got a way out, and we'll have to move fast," Jake said. "Let me tell you about my trip to Beijing."

"As in China?" Benson asked, pressing his hand against his neck.

"As in China," Jake replied.

"Were you speaking to Chinese National University, or whatever the name of the university is out there?" Duncan asked.

"No. I was presenting to China Investment Corporation."

Duncan and Benson looked at each other.

"That's right, boys. The China Investment Corporation. I met this guy in New York when I presented at the derivatives conference, and he liked my research and said he would be in contact. Then he caught me at the AFA conference and invited me out. I thought it was a good idea since I didn't have that many interviews or potential campus visits. It was arranged quickly, and it meant I would have to miss only one of my classes. I was there for two days—one day to present and one day to see the sights. Honestly, it feels like a year ago."

"What did they want?"

"To hear about my research and understand it."

"Could they be behind what's happening? They certainly have the resources," Benson said.

"True, but they don't have the motive, plus what they offered me is in direct opposition from that theory. They want to back me to run some of their capital. To do what both of you've been doing for the past couple of months."

"Why?" Duncan asked.

"They see the opportunity, but Benjamin, the head of research, also believes that there's something illicit going on. I believe he thinks by doing this, they can smoke out the relevant players. I think he has known something was wrong for a long time but didn't know the root cause, let alone how to solve the problem."

"How will tradin' accomplish this?" Benson asked.

Jake looked at Haley. They had spent a lot of time discussing what the appropriate action was, and they knew Jake was butting up against the deadline for a decision. They both had a view of what Jake should do, and both had agreed on discussing it with Duncan and Benson. The events of tonight only further cemented that this was the right course of action.

"They want me to trade it on a billion-dollar capital base."

"Dang, that'll certainly get noticed. Won't you run into the same problems that have shut Duncan down?" asked Benson.

"It's possible, but it'll be set up as an offshore hedge-fund vehicle, backed with a team of lawyers and the weight and power of the CIC. They have picked the legal and the administrator, neither of whom are US based, and they exert significant influence over both of them. So if and when the hammer comes down from the regulatory bodies, the uproar and pushback will cause more stress than the initial audits themselves."

"What is the effect of running this strategy on such capital?"

"Duncan, that's the right question. I mean, I've asked myself that same question, and the answer is very scary. It has massive market implications and may also speaks to some ulterior motives from our friends in the East. So I wanted to ask both of you a question. Should we do this? I want your honest opinion, because I have to let Benjamin know in about eight hours. Oh, and the compensation structure is a 1 percent management fee and 20 percent of profits."

"Why did you say *we*?"

"That's easy—because if we do this, I'll need both of you to help."

Jake could see that both of them were doing the math in their heads to figure out what a 1 and 20 percent fee structure on a billion dollars would pay.

"Jake, I don't see that we've got a choice. I don't know what happened to Benson, but something tells me we all better disappear, and fast," Duncan said.

"Jake and Haley won't have to," Benson said.

"How can you know that?" Duncan asked.

"I'll get to it. Finish up, Jake."

"OK. This actually works out better. Since both of you have been directly identified, it would make sense if you disappeared. Haley and I are just graduate students, and I'm the one that's done the research. As far as interested parties are concerned, all I did was do research, and nothing so far suggests I've had any contact with the CIC. *I hope.* There was no information on my CPU about it, or on my phone. If Haley and I left along with the two of you, I think that would look more suspicious. Duncan, you have to quit Griffin this week. Now, Benson, you better tell us exactly what happened to you."

Benson relayed the details of what had happened in his room. "All of a sudden, I'm being strangled with a telephone cord and bein' pushed down on the bed. This girl is naked with a knee in my back stranglin' me. But she isn't pulling the cord too tight, enough for me to get these little gasps in. She's askin' about your program—if you told me anymore about it, or if there was a file or paper with the algorithm on it. She wants to know where the program is, if I knew, or if you had told me. You see, they don't know where it is. She then tells me it was a mistake to go into her bag and that she can't risk me knowin' the truth. The thing is, I didn't find anythin' in there, but she must have seen me lookin' through it. She then asks if I knew where you were since you were gone for three days. They don't know you were in China. I think the CIC may have covered your tracks for you. I mean, Immigration may have stamped your passport, and maybe they tracked you that way, but it seems unlikely. Anyway, she is pepperin' me with these questions, and I can hardly fuckin' breathe. I'm on the verge of blackin' out."

The three of them looked on in disbelief. Benson paused to drink some water. Clearly talking was irritating his throat.

"Anyway, before I came out of the shower, I'd thought about a way to test her. I was going to tell her about our meeting but tell her it was for 3:30 a.m. Then I was goin' to wait and follow her to see if she came to the restaurant. It felt like the right thin' to do, to test her, but it also spooked me. So I went into my toiletry case to grab my little Swiss Army knife. I don't know what told me to grab it, but my instinct was right."

"And where did you put this knife during your, um, activities?" Haley asked.

"Initially it was in my left hand, but I slipped it in the waistband of the towel when she called me over. So when I was on the bed and the lights were off, she couldn't see me reach for it and cut the cord loose from my neck. So when she pulled tight again, she slipped off my back, and I turned and hit her flush in the face with my right hand. I hit this girl hard, and dang, she came right back at me and clawed for my eyes. Then I felt a knee in the groin, and then I think she hit me with an elbow." Benson instinctively reached for his jaw. "That's when I swung out with my left hand. I still had the knife in my hand, and she was on top of me. I must have stuck her in the stomach. Her hands went slack, but she didn't scream. I rolled on top of her and looked into her eyes. She was still breathin', but I saw nothing in the eyes. No emotion, no carin', nothin'. I grabbed my stuff and bolted."

"Is she still there?" Duncan said, somewhat in shock.

"I couldn't say. Now, I'm not worried about the police or the hotel. Sarah and whoever she works for have much more to lose than we do. They will cover up what happened in there. I don't want to call the police or go to a hospital. Too easy for me to be found. The key for me now is to disappear as fast as possible."

"Right. Right." Jake was thinking as fast as he could. "Benson, we better get you some cash right away. I want you in the Virgin Islands as fast as possible. There will be some down time because it takes a while for an offshore fund to be set up. This will give Duncan a chance to effectively disappear with a different timeline. It'll look like two distinct events. Hopefully, no one knows Duncan is down here."

"I don't even care about the money. What these people are doing goes against the fundamentals of free markets and capitalism. I've seen so much manipulation that I'm sick of it. We almost have a responsibility to do this," Duncan said.

They all agreed with that statement.

Benson's departure from Austin required a quick detour to Jake's place for clothes and cash. He had to move quickly, but his getaway required some very careful and meticulous planning. He didn't use any credit cards, bought two burner phones, and drove as fast as he could to Houston.

Time was working against him, but he had to take two calculated risks. The first was using his car to drive back to Houston. He had to assume there was some sort of tracking device on it, which meant he could easily be followed. His hope was that he could get back there before Sarah or whomever could track him down. It was critical to draw any attention away from Jake and Haley, which required leaving no trace of himself in Austin. Fortunately, he had walked to Kirby Lane, so if there was some GPS tracker on it, there would be no record of him at the meeting or Jake's condo.

The second risky action required Jake's help. He had written the instructions down and given Jake one of the phones. Jake was to make a call and then discard the phone after everything had been confirmed. Benson didn't dare use the phone in the car, so this required a bit of faith on his part. If he got to Houston and no one was waiting for him, he could be in big trouble.

Benson made it back to Houston by six thirty in the morning. He parked his car a mile from his condo complex, took any info that may have identified him, and left the keys in the car with the door open. He then ran four blocks west and another three north and hailed a cab. The cab arrived at the David Wayne Hooks airport at 7:05 a.m. Jim Swarthmore was standing outside his limo, with a look of deep concern. Benson could not have been more relieved.

"Jim, thank God you're here."

"Benson. I'm glad to help, but this is very odd. You look awful. When I got a call at five o'clock in the mornin' from someone I'd never heard of, I was not happy. Then he started explaining what happened. What's goin' on?"

"Jim, it's best that I don't tell you anymore than you already know. I really appreciate you steppin' up like this. Listen, I can't tell you details, and I don't want you to ask, but I'll wire the money and cost for this as soon as it's safe."

"Don't worry about it. You've made me so much money recently it more than covers it. Just be safe."

"That's exactly what we're tryin' to do."

He shook hands with his client, thankful that developing personal relationships had been at the heart of his business and that Jim had been proactive in getting the plane ready. The small Cessna took off at eight thirty and headed southeast. In just over four hours, Benson would land and would have to start making the arrangements for the rest of the team. He used the opportunity to sleep.

CHAPTER 41

As far as Michelle Lancaster was concerned, the economy and the markets were behaving well. All the data were in-line, there was no worrying line item on any bank's balance sheet, and the Fed had begun its exit strategy from the QE programs. She had integrated nicely into the Markov Group and had added value and felt relied upon. The work she was doing kept the machine running smoothly and moving forward.

Today's meeting was to discuss the tools and strategy the Markov group was using and how to minimize any potential correlation if a similar strategy started trading simultaneously. They would also review the outcome from handling the two accounts that had recently been halted.

"The two accounts that raised the red flags have stopped trading," said Jerry Ospry. "The initiation of margin increases and the SEC investigations have had the desired effect. I've learned that both of the individuals have left their respective firms. There's also no evidence of the trading strategy in either firm's computers. Each firm was issued a fine, and it appears that both have gone about business as usual since the resolution of the notice. The New York trader has quit and appears to be living a normal life. We can't seem to locate the Houston manager. We aren't exactly sure what happened in that meeting in Austin, but since he doesn't have access to client accounts and isn't currently employed in the finance field, I think that threat has been minimized."

"Don't worry about the Houston manager," Frank said. "We know he initiated the meeting in Austin, and it appears that the Austin academic didn't know his strategy was being traded. I believe the academic knew about the New York trader's efforts but probably wasn't cognizant of the size. There has been no contact between the brothers since the New York trader was notified and left the firm."

"What about the Austin academic? Is he showing interest in pursuing this further?" Victor asked.

"He appears to be working hard to get an academic job," replied Frank. "After the report of their meeting in Austin, we were concerned that he was more involved, but our Houston contact relayed information to suggest his travel was all academic in nature. We've a copy of his research, and it's quite provocative. I would suggest that this never gets published. I would press your academic contacts, although, from what I understand, most in the academic community don't believe the findings. There was also no evidence of a trading algorithm on his office or home computer," replied Frank.

"Shall we continue to monitor?"

"We're continuing to monitor electronically but have removed any direct observation except for the New York trader. Given his difficult and combative nature during the interview process, we think it best to keep an eye on him."

"I agree," Michelle said. "I think we may need to review the process if a similar situation arises. I'm concerned that the line of questioning was too transparent."

"I'm of the opinion that this is a unique situation," Harvey said confidently. "The combination of factors we use and the way we use them is almost impossible to reverse engineer. The fact that the academic found a nonlinear, nonnormal result that captured a part of what we do is unfortunate, but nobody can actually fully replicate what we do because they would need to be privy to what goes on in this room. The threat that we recently had was of small probability and was handled well within the protocols set. I also don't believe we'll hear from these three again."

"I hope so." Said McQuary.

"Fortunately, we're still monitoring, so if any threat becomes real, we can quickly handle it. I can live with this outcome. What's everyone's opinion?" Frank asked.

There was no need to elaborate on what had happened to one of the dark analysts. It was information that the rest of the Markov Group didn't need to know about. Frank had never met this operative, but the money and time spent on her had made her a valuable asset. The report on her had showed she was the ideal candidate for this kind of work. Intelligent, adaptable, morally neutral, and with no inhibitions. She had a penchant for masochism, but it drove her focus. She had made a mistake, and that mistake had had consequences. After her call, Mr. Jones had sent a colleague down to Austin. He was at the hotel in six hours, and she had explained everything. He had handled the hotel cleanup, the resignation letter that would be sent to T. B. Worley on Benson Prichard's behalf, and the thorough and exhaustive search of Benson Prichard's apartment in Houston. Benson's car had been found abandoned in south Houston, completely stripped of its parts. If Benson popped up on the grid, they would find him. The girl who had been called Sarah would never be heard from again.

The meeting adjourned with a general consensus that no other action was needed. Each member then went through his or her monthly updates and followed protocol in leaving the building.

Michelle left the building and made her way back uptown. She had starting using a car service, which made it easier to get around town and allowed her more privacy when on the phone versus the subway. It was always easiest leaving one of the Markov Group meetings when no deliberate action was planned. Letting the markets run freely was always the best outcome, until it wasn't. That was what they were there for, because they had to protect people from themselves.

The taxi that followed her would have been impossible to notice among the hundreds that drove alongside it. Trying to identify a unique New York City cab is a fruitless exercise, a fact not lost on Chris Carter. That made following Michelle very easy. When she had left the office earlier, Chris had followed her to 60 Broad Street. There was little reason for her to be going to a building right next to the NYSE. Chris had waited on the steps by the George Washington statue for her to return. He had plain view of her town car, which was waiting up the street, as well as the doors to the building. He just had to be patient. She emerged from the building an hour after arriving.

Who did she meet with, and what was it about? Chris needed to find this out. His new partner cared only about his access to the New York Fed reports, but Chris wanted to know more about her and what she was doing in this building. His obsession was growing.

Chris Carter wouldn't have made a good field operative, thought Mr. Jones. He was easy to see and pick out, if his target was choosing to pay any attention. Fortunately for Mr. Jones, Michelle Lancaster wasn't looking for a tail, which meant dealing with Chris Carter would be easy. Mr. Jones now believed more direct action would be required for Chris Carter. He would wait for confirmation.

CHAPTER 42

It took about a month to get the offshore fund papered up correctly, have the accounts established, and then fully fund them. It took two weeks to set up the office, get the systems up and running, and gain access to the accounts. Once that was all in place, they were ready to begin trading. While the logistics and paperwork of fund construction was taking place, Jake had arranged to meet with Duncan to go over the operations. They would start two weeks after Duncan left his job. Benson was already busy with the minutiae of setting up the office.

Jake had recently bought a new phone and a laptop that were dedicated for one thing, communicating with Benjamin, Duncan, and Benson. He had explained to Benjamin that all contact had to be done through the management company e-mail and through Skype. The new phone wasn't even connected to a cellular carrier; he would use the Wi-Fi connection only to make calls. The management company was registered in the Cayman Islands and was called Charon Capital Partners, an homage to the ferryman that carried the newly deceased across the river Styx. Jake had always liked Greek mythology, and although he'd gotten a C in his classics class, he felt the name was appropriate for what they were about the do. They were providing a transition from one market state to the next. At least that was his hope.

Jake was the only one who knew where Benson and Duncan were. Haley didn't know, and neither did Benjamin. He had informed Benjamin that he would need two partners to handle the operations and trading responsibilities, to which Benjamin assented. Jake had also outlined some specifics as to how he would like the accounts structured. While CIC controlled the capital and who was the administrator and the prime broker, Jake needed control of the trading operations and requested that multiple accounts be set up. In fact, he requested thirty unique accounts and asked for them to be primed across multiple banks. Benjamin was curious as to why, but Jake wanted to keep the real answer to that as vague as possible. He had told him it was about protecting his intellectual capital, which was true but only part of the answer. He didn't elaborate on the real reason.

After his return from Austin, Duncan had informed his partners that he was taking a leave of absence. They were disappointed but understood. Following his resignation, the firm suffered minimal interruption, as the SEC team did a three-day follow-up audit. The auditors had left satisfied and had noted that the firm would probably be fined due to the inappropriate actions of one trader. They had commended the partners for resolving the issue quickly with the given trader and said having him leave the firm reduced their liability. The fine the firm received would be $30 million, or the net profit from the computerized trading of the strategy.

The day Duncan resigned, he closed all his trading accounts, including the one he had used to trade the strategy on, and asked the partners to wire his capital to his personal bank account. He had already erased any traces of anything he had done and wiped clean his hard drive. Technically, that was a major compliance violation, but at this point nobody would care or notice. He spent two weeks running in Central Park and eating out and one weekend skiing in Vermont. After the two weeks, he left his place, took a cab to LaGuardia, and got aboard a plane. He had also bought a new phone and laptop. He took one backpack and a carry-on, no credit cards, and $10,000 in cash.

Jake met Duncan in the Miami airport to go over their communication strategy and the roles that Benson and Duncan would play. Jake had used his trip to the University of Georgia as cover, flying an indirect route through Miami. Jake told Duncan he wanted him to control the trading operations, running the model and making sure the fills were good. Benson would handle the back office, reconciling the trades and dealing with the account representatives of each of the prime brokers. Given the model and the way the program worked, it was fairly easy to run a billion dollars using only three people. Jake opened up his laptop and showed Duncan their contact info and usernames. This would be how they would communicate among themselves outside of Charon Capital. Each would establish a unique ID and chat through Google Hangouts. Adding another layer of protection was something they all thought necessary.

"Benson will be Tantalus; Duncan, you're Ixion; and I'm Sisyphus."

"Why these names?" asked Duncan.

"In keeping with our Greek mythology theme, these are the three highest-profile prisoners of Tartarus."

"Couldn't we have more uplifting characters, maybe a god or a hero?" Duncan proposed.

"No. These are more appropriate. By the way, did your bosses buy why you were leaving? What about friends and the family? Did you make it convincing?" Jake asked, wondering how Duncan had left things.

"Nobody doubted my sincerity when I left. I'm not sure what Benson's fallout has been, but I imagine T. B. Worley won't follow up. Hopefully his friends don't go looking too deeply. What about his folks?"

"It was the second call I made on that burner phone before I got rid of it. They're freaked out but are staying put."

"Have you spoken to Benson recently?"

"Very briefly and only to pass along instructions. He has been busy taking care of the logistics and the setup. I left him to it. You should be walking into a fully functioning operation when you get there."

"Good. OK, let's review again."

After a third review of how to get in contact with each other and the daily roles each would play, Jake headed for his flight to Georgia, while Duncan headed for the gate that had the plane waiting to take him to Saint Croix.

The flight from Miami to the US Virgin Islands boarded at 5:30 p.m. and arrived at 9:17 p.m. The plane sat four to a row in a standard two-by-two formation. Duncan sat in the window seat of an exit row. The plane arrived on time, and he deplaned and took a cab to King Street to the office block that would house Charon Capital. He went to the lockbox, punched in the code, and took out the key. Using the key, he unlocked the door to the second-floor office. It wasn't much. It was about eight hundred square feet but had a dedicated T-1 line. There were four large unopened boxes in the middle of the floor. Duncan opened all four, went through the contents to make sure all of what they needed was there, closed the boxes, locked the door, and left.

He then took a cab to Northside Road and a place called Colony Cove. They had a fully furnished, two-bedroom apartment that looked out on the Caribbean waters. The décor was similar to what you would find at any other beach-resort apartment—lots of pastels and wicker—but they weren't there for the furniture. The views were spectacular, and the apartment would be an acceptable place to be for the next couple of weeks, months, or years. Duncan wasn't sure how long they were going to be there, but it certainly was a change from being in New York in the winter. He went out on the balcony and took out his phone. The Wi-Fi at the condo was excellent, and he logged on to his account. There were only two contacts, Sisyphus and Tantalus. He clicked on the Sisyphus contact and typed.

"Ixion has arrived. Will come back to you when we're fully set up."

Duncan sat on one of the chairs and waited for Benson to arrive. Ten minutes later Benson came through the door.

"You're finally here. No problems, right?" Benson asked.

"No. I see the office has all our gear."

"Yup, arrived yesterday. We can set it up tomorrow. I'm tired from my run. Needed to get out. Been on the phone all day with the primes making sure they are ready."

"Good. I'll go over protocol with you tomorrow. Which bedroom do you have?"

"The one on the right. Both have views of the ocean, so I didn't think it really mattered."

Duncan nodded in approval. "The scar around your neck has faded."

"Yup, I don't think it'll ever disappear, but it could be confused for irritation or a trick of the light. I'm goin' to bed."

Benson went off to the right bedroom and closed the door. Duncan headed off to the left. Tomorrow they would begin the construction of the trading operations, testing of the systems, and completing all the prep work required to run CIC's capital.

While Benson was helping Duncan settle in on Saint Croix and building their base of operations, Jake had come back from Georgia feeling pretty good. The presentation with faculty had gone well, he had enjoyed the group, and everyone had been cordial. Athens was a small town, but it wasn't that far from Atlanta. He liked the department better than the one at USC, but he still had his Arizona trip to make. He was expecting an offer from Georgia based on the signs he had received.

His spirits were also up because his dissertation defense date had been set for early April, and there were only some formatting issues left with the document itself. That allowed him to focus on getting a job, teaching his class, and checking in on his team on the island. He should have been more stressed, but he wasn't. The specter of what had happened in January had diminished, and as long as he stuck to the protocol, there was no reason for any of those people who were watching them to have their suspicions aroused. He avoided any phrasing in general e-mails or conversations that had the words *trading*, *research*, *strategy*, *China*, *Duncan*, or *Benson*.

Jake and Haley fell into their everyday routine. They resumed their activities as if they were normal graduate students. Haley wasn't as concerned about going to her office anymore, and Winston had resumed sleeping on the couch downstairs versus in their bedroom. Yet both Jake and Haley couldn't help but feel excited and nervous as they waited to hear that everything was set up and ready to begin. Although Haley had been a part of this from the start, Jake tried to keep as much information from her as possible, keeping her in the dark for her own protection. That is why he didn't tell her exactly where Jake and Benson were. There was no need for her to worry, plus he wanted her to be able to concentrate and finish her thesis. They avoided talking about anything related to Charon Capital at home or in their campus offices, but she couldn't help but ask when they were away from campus and the house how things were progressing or when trading would begin.

The Friday after Jake had returned from Georgia, he was going over his presentation for his upcoming trip to Arizona when he got a call on his regular cell phone. It was the department head at UGA offering him a tenure-track position. The chairmen went over the details and asked Jake if he could have his decision in a week. A week was a short turnaround time, but Jake felt confident that he could make a choice by then. He would have returned from Arizona and could use this offer to force Arizona's hand. He was elated and went to meet Haley at the stadium. They were going to run from the stadium to the Town Lake trail, do the four-mile loop, and then run back.

On the way down the hill, his other phone chimed. There was a message from Benjamin.

"Everything has been finalized. You can begin trading. Best of luck. Let us talk in two weeks to review."

Jake replied and then opened his Sisyphus account and sent a message to Jake and Benson. *You should have access to the accounts and are set to trade.*

Thirty seconds later a message from Ixion said, *Confirmed. We will officially start Monday.*

Jake replied and shut off the phone. He saw Haley waiting, already in her running clothes.

"I need to change before we go."

"Balls. Hurry up. It's beautiful, and I want to run fast."

"OK. By the way, I got an offer from Georgia."

"That's great. Oh, I'm so excited. All that hard work has paid off." She came over to him, hugged him hard, and bit his earlobe.

"Ouch. I know. That's a good feeling. It'll make me so much more relaxed going to visit Arizona. I'll be back out in a minute."

Jake went into the stadium to change, rubbing his ear as he walked. He wanted to tell Haley that the fund was ready to start trading as well but decided against it. She knew that they were probably close to beginning, but he stuck to his guns and decided to stay quiet on the subject.

CHAPTER 43

There has always been speculation about the way information has been passed around Wall Street. Who gets what information and when they get it has been the catalyst for making and losing fortunes. Ivan Boesky has almost become immortalized due to his role in the insider trading scandal of the 1980s and in part was responsible for the fall of Michael Milken. While these actions were blatant, predatory, and profitable, they were also poorly conceived. There are many ways to get access to privileged information that skirt the lines of legality.

Chris Carter realized this when he had reached the apex of his monetary policy career. He saw an opportunity to potentially salvage his dreams, only to realize he was being used. He wasn't going to be used anymore. Chris had gone to school and was close friends with a partner at Rising Tide Capital. Rising Tide had assets in excess of $50 billion and had its fingers in many different markets. Whether it was stocks, credit, real estate, or commodities, Rising Tide had a presence. However, the problem with being so large was that the alpha of their aggregate portfolio had fallen, and they had underperformed the market for the past three years. It's tough to justify charging your clients a 2 percent management fee and 20 percent of profits when you consistently underperform. So when Patrick Stinson got a call from his old friend, he was more than happy to take the call.

They had first met at Shenorock Country Club in Rye, New York, to discuss what Chris could do for them. Chris hadn't reached out by chance to his old friend, who was well connected in the industry. He had reached out to him because he knew of the firm's underperformance and because

Patrick was going through a divorce. A very public, messy, and expensive divorce. When people feel pressure, they are apt to take rash and desperate actions. Chris knew what that felt like, and the deal he offered Patrick was one that was easy for him to take.

Chris highlighted that Patrick would not need to do anything but listen, and how he chose to act on the information that was passed on was up to him. Patrick saw the opportunity and seized it. Rising Tide's macro fund was essentially a catchall for any type of investment strategy. Patrick could use the fund to capitalize on the information Chris supplied about the actions the Fed was taking by correctly positioning in interest rates instruments, government paper, or financial securities. For his assistance, Chris received a consulting fee paid through an offshore management company, so no direct connection between Chris and Rising Tide could be established. Patrick did ask how he was able to get such sensitive information, especially right off the Fed chairman's desk. Chris only smiled.

So far things were working well. Rising Tide's macro fund had started outperforming its benchmark, and their investors' concerns had somewhat abated. Chris was enjoying his new capital injection, which had brought back his smile after his prior contact had gone dark. Michelle had expressed concern for him the past month, worried that the old Chris had returned, but had not made mention of it since. She was such a wonderful source, so oblivious to his pilfering. The self-confidence she expressed in the real world masked the insecurity she felt in the bedroom. He gained such great pleasure taking advantage of it.

The little tidbits he was able to provide Patrick that came from his own desk and the information he gleaned from Michelle were more than satisfactory, but he needed to know more. Chris's obsession with finding out what Michelle was doing felt critical to further success and further money, and for his ultimate goal of destroying her. Besides their private interludes, she had an almost nonexistent personal life. Michelle did nothing extravagant. She occasionally went out with friends; she liked walking in the park, even when it was cold; and she read at her local coffee shop. The only new personal hobby he had really learned of was that she went to hit

Dr. James Doran

golf balls early Saturday morning, and she had a decent swing. So besides this bizarre meeting that she went to at random times that weren't on her calendar, nothing she did was out of the norm.

Finding out whom she met at 60 Broad Street and why became very important to Chris, and he was always hyperaware of times she was leaving the office so he could learn more. Chris had his door open and saw that Michelle was leaving the office. It was four o'clock and probably a little early for her to be leaving, but it was Friday, and people always try to get a jump start on the weekend. Why should the head of the New York Fed be any different?

Chris closed up his office and beat her to the elevator banks. He wanted to be out of the building before she was so he could follow her at a distance. Given the time she was leaving, he felt there was a good probability she was going to one of her secret meetings. Chris was across the street when Michelle came out. She spoke to her driver, who was at the front of the building, but didn't get in the car. She took a left on Nassau Street and continued to walk toward the exchange. Chris was ahead of her and got to the building first. He had already scouted who worked there so that when he got to the security desk, he could say whom he was visiting and be prepared to see what floor Michelle went to. Chris initially planned to wait toward the back of the elevator banks and watch which elevator Michelle went into to see what floor the elevator stopped at. At the time there were more people coming down, and many were taking their time leaving the building. This would provide a degree of anonymity that Chris was hoping for.

Unfortunately, the security officer was being overly diligent in his job. Nobody was allowed to linger in the lobby for long, and Chris was one of the final people escorted out. Nervous he would run into Michelle, he darted to his left and hid in the small alcove between the two buildings. That is when he noticed a tall man whom he had seen multiple times on TV. He had been in the same room with this man but had never been introduced to him. It was very unlikely the man knew who Chris was. Chris watched him walk up to the entrance of 60 Broad Street and walk in. Confused, Chris looked around for signs of Michelle—*where was she?*—and, not seeing her, made his way to the entrance. There was no security guard there anymore. *Where had he gone, and why was the head of the NYSE in this building?*

He didn't dare linger in case Michelle saw him. He would have to come back another time. There would be time to explore the building, but for now he would wait and see who else might show up or leave.

An hour and a half passed while Chris waited. Nobody else had gone in, and he hadn't seen a glimpse of Michelle. He was ready to give up when he recognized the person who was just exiting. In fact, when he saw this person leave, he had to do a double take. The man was tall, wore a charcoal suit with a red tie, and was head of the largest private equity firm in the world. His offices were in Midtown, and there was absolutely no reason for this man to be here. The fact that the head of the NYSE, president of the NY Fed, and the CEO of the world's largest private equity firm were in the same building at the same time was more than coincidental. *Something big is going on, and Michelle is part of it. This is exactly what I need.* Chris felt a surge of exhilaration similar to the time he had been approached about the IMF position. Fortune was smiling on him again.

Chris followed the man with his eyes before the man turned up the street and headed to Broadway. He waited another half hour, and no other person he recognized came out. He sensed that he had missed Jerry Ospry and Michelle but was unsure how. He headed back to the Federal Reserve building and saw that Michelle's car was gone. How she had left the building without him seeing added to his confusion. As much as he was consumed by his desire to make money, he was even more fixated on finding out what Michelle and these individuals were up to. Lamenting his ability to successfully tail someone, Chris gave up for the day, catching the train back to his apartment. Maybe he would call Michelle later and invite her to dinner. Sex with her tonight would be twice as pleasurable.

Frank was in his helicopter watching the video of the man watching the entrance of 60 Broad Street. While he had been in the meeting, he had been alerted to the person's presence by Mr. Jones. Without interrupting the meeting or drawing the attention of any other members of the group, he had sent a one-letter text to Mr. Jones.

Mr. Jones was angry he hadn't taken matters into his own hands earlier. The acidic taste in his mouth never let him down, but he had to wait for the go-ahead. Usually a report would come from Franklin Insurance after his initial assessment giving him the authority to act. Chris Carter's actions had escalated quicker than the analysts at Franklin Insurance had predicted, but the path was still the same. Mr. Jones would be waiting at the end of that path.

CHAPTER 44

C hris knew he was in trouble. He had asked the wrong question at the right time. She was most vulnerable right after sex, freely talking about her emotions and fears. She was careful in what she told him and always had been, but there was trust. When he had asked how well she knew Michael McQuary, she had hesitated for the slightest second and said she hardly knew him. It was not the reaction he had wanted; he had been hoping for a much more defensive reaction. That would have led to a more heated exchange and then maybe a breakthrough into what was happening. That would have been the beginning of the end for her. So when she turned away and became icy, he should have read the signal. He hadn't. He had pressed further.

"Chris. Please stop. I don't know McQuary well at all. Besides his reputation, I've no clue what he's like."

"Bullshit. I saw you with him yesterday going into 60 Broad Street." It was a guess, it hit the mark—but was the wrong target. Her expression changed, and it shocked him.

"Oh, Chris. You're such a fool. I hoped and hoped and hoped, but I knew you could never let it go. You don't know what you've done." *I fear for you.* There was true hurt on her face and a look of deep concern.

"What I've done. What I've done!" Chris's face was almost purple and his clenched fists were white. His anger painted an array of colors over his body and face. There was no holding back now. "You're colluding with people you have no business being with."

"I don't think I can help you anymore. I wish you were the man you could've been. It would've been great. You're so transparent, it hurts. I gave it a go because it felt good, and I thought it would change you. You couldn't hide the hurt in your eyes. I hoped we could get that emotional connection back, but you never let it happen."

"What are you talking about? I've been playing you for months." There was no point holding back now.

"I'm so sorry you feel this way. You'd better leave."

"I'm not going anywhere. I want to know what you've been up to." He stood defiantly in front her.

"There's nothing to tell you, Chris. Last warning. Go now."

"Get out of that bed and make me."

Mr. Jones had had enough. He didn't bother knocking. It wasn't personal, but this guy was a coward, and Michelle was a good person. He walked in silently, the training keeping him a ghost. To her credit Michelle didn't scream as he approached the target's back. Chris never turned around, never sensed Mr. Jones behind him, and probably didn't feel the needle inserted behind his ear into the superficial temporal vein. The barbiturate mixture worked with alarming speed, and Chris bent at the waist and hit the floor headfirst. Mr. Jones leaned over him and checked for a pulse. The dose wasn't fatal, but Chris would wake in an hour with a massive headache.

Mr. Jones proceeded to gather Chris's things. "Dr. Lancaster, what other items does this person have in your apartment? We need to remove all trace of him. Can you hear me?"

She nodded. She climbed out of bed, walked to the bathroom, and put her robe on. She felt slightly embarrassed walking around in a University of Michigan T-shirt and underwear with Mr. Jones in her apartment. The task took less than twenty minutes. All traces of Chris's presence in her apartment were removed, including the actual Chris over the shoulder of

Mr. Jones. He closed the door and left her with the silence and the dread of what was about to happen.

Chris awoke with the taste of vomit in his mouth. All he could see was black. That was when he realized he was facedown with his hands tied behind him. His head was throbbing and he was moving.

"Where am I?" his voice was barely audible. No response. The monotonic thumps of the road made Chris look up. He was able to peer out the window. They were crossing the George Washington Bridge and heading into New Jersey.

"Where are we going?" Chris's throat hurt, so the words were scratchy and again got no response. He was confused. *Why would we be heading into New Jersey?* His mind was cloudy. He couldn't remember why he was in a car. *And why am I tied up?*

Chris closed his eyes to think. The last thing he remembered was being in Michelle's apartment. He remembered yelling at her, then nothing. He tried to look at the driver and his passenger, but the back of their heads told him nothing. The way they were dressed suggested they could be Federal agents.

"Hey, I'm talking to you. Who are you guys? If you're Feds, you have to identify yourselves. Am I under arrest?" *Could this be related to Rising Tide and insider trading? God, I hope not.*

The car passed MetLife stadium and headed along Route 3 West until merging onto Highway 80. It continued west until they got to the New Jersey and Pennsylvania state line. Chris tried cajoling, bribing, yelling, and threatening the men in the front and got no response. He could feel the fear that had always been there, hidden below the surface for so many years, come front and center. He was not an imposing figure and had almost no physical strength or personal willpower when threatened. The two men in the car looked as if they were made out of steel. All of a sudden, he started to cry.

The car pulled off the highway after entering Pennsylvania and worked its way to River Road, which was typically closed during the winter. After several miles they finally stopped. The man next to the driver got out and pulled Chris out by his restraints. Chris yelped as he was tugged backwards, pain shooting from his wrists all the way up to his shoulder. The driver came around the car with a flashlight and a gun with an extended barrel on it that Chris assumed was a silencer.

"Walk," the driver ordered, pointing Chris into the woods that were highlighted by the flashlight.

Chris stood frozen with fear. The man who had been standing next to him punched him in the gut. Chris doubled over and fell to the ground, unable to breathe, tears streaming down his cheeks.

"Why are you doing this?" he managed to get out between gulping breaths. It came out as a whimper, and Chris was ashamed of the lack of strength of his gutless and juvenile reply.

"Walk, and I'll tell you,"

Chris was yanked up, dirt and gravel caught in his hair and clothing. He started down a makeshift path through the half-frozen woods barefoot, following the directions of the two men behind him. He must have walked half a mile before he was stopped by one of the men and ordered to walk off the path, deeper into the woods. The two-hundred-yard trek into the thick Washington State Forest took another twenty minutes. As Chris walked by two huge trees, they reached a small clearing. The passenger had brought a shovel with him.

The next thing he knew he was lying on the ground. He head was now bleeding, and he was having trouble focusing. He must have been hit from behind. His trousers were wet as well. His bladder had finally let go. Before he was lifted of the ground, the passenger put a foot on his back, lent over him, and cut his restraints. He was then ordered to dig.

Chris wasn't strong, and with the ground half frozen, the digging took forever. Chris thought about swinging the shovel at his captors, but it looked as if they would be ready for that. When the hole was three feet deep, he looked up and made eye contact with the driver.

"Tell us why you've been following Michelle Lancaster," the driver said.

"What?"

The driver shot Chris in the foot. He screamed out in pain.

"I won't stand for non-answers. You've got a choice here, pain or no pain. Answer the question."

Chris wished he was braver but knew he was a coward. He was smart and brilliant but also a liar and a petty and unscrupulous man. He wanted to hold out, to make one defiant stand, but he succumbed to the likely outcome. He told them why he was following her—his jealousy, the goal of revenge, and selling information to Rising Tide.

"Good. You've made the right choice," the driver said. "Now, who have you told about this?"

"Not a single person."

The passenger took the shovel and smashed Chris's foot with it. Chris screamed again, sobbing uncontrollably. Any pride that was still buried deep within Chris left with that last scream.

"I told no one. No one. Please stop hitting me," he wailed.

"I believe you. One final thing, who is the Markov Group?"

"Who?" Chris questioned with wide eyes. He had never heard that name before, and the driver could see it. The driver smiled and put his gun away.

For the briefest second Chris's hopes rose, a momentary reprieve from the fear of pain of a certain death. Then he saw the knife. The swing from the glimmer of hope to the thought of the knife entering his body was too much for his mind to bear. Chris collapsed in a heap, unconscious, making Mr. Jones's job easy and wholly unsatisfying.

The knife, designed for deep and lethal penetration, entered close to the jawline and was thrusted upward, piercing the brain cavity. Chris's already limp body, with a trickle of blood running down his neck, would never move again. He was rolled gently into the small three-foot grave. Mr. Jones looked at his companion, who began to shovel the dirt onto Chris and filled the hole. Mr. Jones was satisfied with a job well done. He had gotten the crucial piece of information that Frank Lyman had requested. The Markov Group was safe.

Neither Mr. Jones or Frank Lyman could have known that a couple of minutes of further questioning would have revealed a much greater threat to the Markov Group—a threat that was gathering power and momentum, ready to take them down.

CHAPTER 45

Monday morning at ten thirty Atlantic time, the machines started working. Benson and Duncan had the office set up so that each of them had access to four monitors and two TVs on mute, one with Bloomberg TV running and the other with CNBC. Each of them had access to Bloomberg Professional, which imported the portfolio, so Duncan could run shock and sensitivity analysis while Benson used the Bloomberg OEM system to make sure the trades were sent to the correct accounts. There were thirty accounts that would hold securities: some were dedicated short accounts, some were long-only accounts, and some had combined positions. Some accounts handled only option contracts, others held derivative instruments related to credit, and still others strictly held fixed income.

Duncan's responsibilities were to make sure the model traded appropriately, to get the liquid assets filled electronically, and to get non-liquid assets or OTC instruments filled via voice. There were times that he was extremely busy and other times that he just sat and waited. When he had traded the model on the small capital at Griffin, he had focused on trading only exchange-traded products. Now everything was in play. That meant calling desks to get pricing and fills for credit default swaps, mortgage-backed securities, and illiquid-traded corporate and sovereign debt.

Once a trade was completed, it was up to Benson to make sure the trade was assigned to the correct account. This meant maintaining a good understanding of the cash in each account, what margin was required, and where potential exposures may lie. For instance, an account dedicated to only short contracts could easily receive a margin call if the market steadily went up. If they faced an account with that potential liability, it could restrict the overall strategy and lead to a significant problem. So Benson had to make sure that when a trade was assigned, it was always assigned to an account that would never face a shortfall. This added a layer of complexity, was time consuming, and required Benson to be right next to Duncan when a trade was made. To make sure that they were SEC compliant, whenever a trade was initiated, Duncan would start the process, but Benson would always send an e-mail to the various account representatives or traders that a trade was coming their way. When a trade was done electronically, the OEM system had a default program about the assignment and always logged when the trade was initiated and who the counterparty was.

This was why it was so critical to get the system set up correctly and test it for two weeks prior to running live. Jake had explained that they needed the thirty separate accounts because both of them had been flagged when they traded in the past. The trading they did was not unique, and the instruments that they were buying and selling were not unique either, but the combination of trades at the times they were doing it was. So they needed a way to mask the trading, and the best way to do that was to make it look like the trades were done by different people through separate accounts. Jake was banking on the fact that whoever had discovered what they were doing had tied the trading activity by the unique trader or account identification number. If they traded this way with accounts that were all unique, whoever had found them out before would have no way of telling whether there was a problem now, even if the trades were done in the exact same fashion as before and on a much larger scale. All the system would see would be a trade from one account that might be short inflation-linked bonds and another account that could be long financial stocks. It would not be able to discern that the two trades were linked from the same firm.

Trading this way only worked if you had one client. The client had 100 percent ownership of all the accounts, and CIC cared about the sum of the accounts and not the performance of any one of the accounts. The shifting of cash and the differences across accounts would never have been allowed if Charon Capital had more than one client. Putting winning trades in one account and losing trades in another is the best way to get sent to jail for fraud. Fortunately, Charon didn't have to worry about this problem.

The initial trading activity was slow at first, as the market was experiencing a period of low volatility and normally distributed returns. The algorithmic part of the model found some nonnormal components in biotech and energy, and there was some weakness in Western European debt, but other than that, it was a nice week to transition into live activity. Duncan and Benson got their feet wet, which allowed them to refine the trading process and get into a regular groove. By the end of the week, they felt good about the process and were happy to see that the combined account was up thirty-five basis points. Besides a couple of trade breaks, it was so far, so good.

Duncan texted Jake and gave him the return for the week, along with the Greek symbol ψ. Psi meant all good, while omega meant there was a problem. If Jake received an Ω, they would speak at 10:00 p.m. Atlantic time, 9:00 p.m. central, to discuss the issue. This was a detail that needed to be double checked since Atlantic time doesn't observe daylight saving.

At market close on Friday, Duncan and Benson closed up shop. They had improved the security of the office with a keypad lock, and to log in to each computer required a thumbprint scan.

"Dang, not a bad first week," said Benson. He looked tired but happy. "How crazy is it that we're down here? It feels so surreal."

"I understand completely." Duncan was also tired.

"Say, you know how we can make it real? Let's go hit the Cliff Restaurant and maybe see Kiki and the Flying Gypsies. Maybe we can catch some of that island fever."

"You know, that's not a bad idea. Are you sure it's good to go out?" Duncan said with a smile.

"Look, I've been down here for over a month. I've been careful. As long as we don't make a scene, I think we're in good shape. No one knows us down here."

CHAPTER 46

When looking at trading volume by quarter, the first quarter of the year is typically the most active, with the third quarter the least. There is an old saying to trade through May and stay away, and most of the time that is not a bad idea, especially since October has typically had the worst performing months and the most nonnormal events historically. However, when bad news comes, and when investors are unprepared, overleveraged, or underhedged, those old adages fly out the window. It doesn't take much for panic to start, and when it does, the effect of widespread contagion filters through the marketplace very quickly.

So when certain senators started stalling on signing the government spending bill, a shudder was felt through the marketplace. This was not surprising to the Markov Group, especially since its members had suggested at the last meeting that recent proposed presidential initiatives would result in a significant increase to entitlement programs, further debt, and an inevitable increase in taxes. The increase in taxes was the worst outcome for future growth. The man in the charcoal suit and red tie had exerted some political influence, knowing that the threat of a government shutdown would likely lessen or destroy the president's health care agenda.

The market typically reacts negatively to anything out of Washington, so when a calm market that had been running smoothly got an unforeseen jolt, such as a potential halt in Washington, most participants were caught unaware. Charon Capital was not caught unaware. So far the model had been steadily seeking out opportunities from cross-section nonnormality in certain assets, but two weeks prior, one of the major interaction factors had started to flag an opportunity. It had suggested that political instability had increased relative to overall market volatility, meaning that the cost of volatility was too cheap relative to macro uncertainty, lying two standard deviations outside of normal parameters. So the model said it was time to go long short-term VIX futures and shift the portfolio to have a long volatility, short market exposure. It was the first time they had flagged a true macro-oriented shock and the chance for a correlation-one event.

Jake had just finished teaching class when his phone chimed: Ω

He closed the phone, finished up work, worked out, had dinner with Haley, and went to a corner coffee shop at ten to nine and waited to receive the call from Tantalus and Ixion. He was not too concerned that there was a problem, since the market had been chill and the operations had been smooth up until this point. Yet you never know what problems will occur until the problems arrive. Right at nine, he got the call and clicked on the accept call button. Both were on the video chat.

"What's up, Tantalus, Ixion," Jake asked. When talking on Hangouts, they had agreed to speak using their usernames only. Jake felt that Hangouts was secure, but you could never be too careful.

"Well, it's nothing to be too concerned about, but the model has flagged a potential macro event. It's the first time we've seen it."

"Give me the details."

They proceeded to explain what the model showed and the actions that the model suggested they take. Duncan and Benson just wanted to confirm the findings and follow through with the correct actions.

"Let the model run. If you're concerned with the directional component, reduce the exposure a bit, but let it run."

"I'm just worried that if the model is wrong, we'd have some exposure to upside losses."

"I see. Let the model dictate the direction, but cut the exposure in half. If the model is right, we'll still do very well, and if it's wrong, the damage will be small. Agreed?

"Agreed. It's just the first time we've had this signal, and I want to be careful," Duncan said.

"I understand. Keep me informed how things progress."

They signed off, and Jake left the coffee shop and returned home. Over the next several days, Benson and Duncan slowly moved capital in the direction the model suggested, and at each day's end they sent a ψ with a return update. The day-to-day returns were not that impressive until the Republican senator started making statements about a government shutdown and threats about not signing the spending bill. The market began to sell off, and volatility started to rise.

From Tuesday to Thursday, volatility increased from 11 percent to 20 percent, and the market fell over 4 percent. It was the biggest two-day move in over two years, and the behavior and risk appetite of market participants changed. The model was able to pick up on the changing risk aversion through shifts in leverage and open interest and started to increase the long-vega/volatility positions. By close of Thursday, the portfolio was long eighty thousand VIX contracts and short thirty thousand S&P contracts. Charon Capital was up 10 percent, and Jake received another ψ with the return number for the fund and sent an Ω back.

"Talk to me about what's happening," Jake said to his colleagues that Thursday night.

"The portfolio is doing what it's supposed to do. It actually increased the long-vega position going into tomorrow's trading day," Duncan replied.

"We've been managin' the positions to spread them across the accounts," Benson said. "I was skeptical when the model suggested we increase size today, but the model really saw some strong anomalous positions. If people are starting to unwind risk, they have only just started. Remember the market isn't even down 5 percent from the highs. Once we hit 5 percent, then we'll see some real action."

"OK. Let's not let things get too crazy," Jake added. "We've been doing very well. Let's not throw it away by getting greedy."

Although the US markets were closed, Asia was open, and Europe would open early in the morning. All markets are correlated, and the correlations tend to increase when there are extreme events. Asia was down over 2 percent in the overnight session, and Europe opened down 1.5 percent.

US futures were down about seventy basis points and were trending down. When US markets opened, the market gapped down a full percent and broke through the 5 percent number, and volatility jumped to 25 percent. Duncan watched the model increase the short position, and the market continued to fall. Duncan wasn't surprised by the sell-off; nobody would want to hold anything long going into a weekend. With so much uncertainty, any long-leveraged position would be scrambling to cover. Each time the model increased its exposure, the market went with the trade, almost as if the model was driving the price.

At 10:00 a.m. Eastern time, the model parameters started to change signs, which suggested that they should start covering their short exposure. Duncan checked the factors and noted that the level of volatility relative to macro uncertainty had become positive. The market had overreacted, and the model now was adjusting the exposure. The market was down almost 10 percent from its highs but hadn't quite reached it. Ten percent is a critical number, more so than 5 percent, because it represents a qualitative market correction and may lead to a bear market.

Volatility had spiked to over 30 percent. Volatility had not gotten to that level since the 2011 sovereign wealth crisis. However, the model was now suggesting neutralizing the exposure and recommended shifting to a long position. Duncan was talking to multiple trading desks at the same time attempting to remove their OTC positions. Benson was in awe at how calmly he managed this insane task.

Slowly and steadily, the market started to recover, and volatility started to fall. For the remaining trading hours, the market drifted back up and finished down only 2 percent on the day. Volatility finished lower on the day than it had started, and Duncan and Benson were exhausted by the close. It took over two hours to reconcile the trades. Benson checked the expected value of the cumulative portfolio once they were done and showed it to Duncan.

"Benson, is that right?"

"We'll know for sure Monday, but I would say it's correct, plus or minus 1 percent. Dang, it's a big number."

"Let me text Sisyphus." Duncan pulled out his phone and sent a text.

Jake was waiting patiently all day for the text. He knew the market had been crazy and was eager to find out what was happening. The phone dinged. He clicked on the Ixion contact: 20 percent, Ω

Jake broke protocol and texted back. "Was that return for today alone?"

"Yes. Will review tonight."

Jake closed out of the chat. The model had made 30 percent over the week. Once the full reconciliation was made, he would expect a call from Benjamin on Monday. Duncan and Benson would have to give him a full debrief tonight.

In New York, a short, fat, bald man was very worried, as was the head of the NYSE. Their model had done what it was supposed to do, but the market had moved in a way that they were unaccustomed to. The size of the trades that had matched them had caused markets to sell off and become more volatile than they had forecasted. Worse was that they were unclear how things had gotten out of hand. It was a series of trades that appeared random, which meant that their market control was compromised. It wasn't possible for anyone to mimic them without them knowing, but that was exactly what had happened.

CHAPTER 47

Jake's discussion with Benjamin had taken about thirty minutes. He detailed what the model had identified, how it had traded, and what the risk profile of the fund looked like at the close of Friday. There was an expectation about the performance of the fund, but to see actual realized returns was always a welcomed surprise.

Jake and his team were awed by the amount of return and what those earnings meant for them. If they closed the fund today, he would have made more money than he ever could have as an academic. *It doesn't seem real.* It was as if they were operating in a vacuum or some financial lab. Charon Capital was a part of his life he tried to separate from what he was doing in Austin. That way he could still teach class and do his research without questioning why. It would have been very easy to just stop doing the research and give up on the academic lifestyle, but he hadn't put in four-plus years and all that pain and suffering just to give in at the finish line.

Jake had gotten an offer from Arizona and had decided to take it. It was tough turning Georgia down, but Haley and he had both decided that the dry heat would be better than humidity. He would start in the fall teaching two sections of investments and then one section in the spring. There would be full summer support for three years, which was a standard offer for a new assistant professor. This allowed new professors the chance to get a good start on their research agenda and fight for precious publication space since most academic contracts are written for nine months.

Eric was happy with Jake's choice and felt that he had done well given the limited opportunities that he had at the AFA. Eric had initially been disheartened with the limited response from the schools but felt the final outcome was very favorable.

"You know, Sheldon told me he was happy with how you did on the market. He realized you were fighting an uphill battle with your research topic, especially with the department pushing Audria, but that placement is very good," Eric relayed to Jake in his office.

"I appreciate that. It's still a little frustrating thinking about what happened, but Haley and I are both happy."

"Good. Do you know if Audria is close to a decision? I don't speak with her, so I don't know where she stands," Eric said.

"I ran into her last week, and she had narrowed it down to North Carolina, Boston College, and Georgetown. I think she wants a big city, and her boyfriend has some influence. Beyond that I don't know where things stand. Frankly I was astonished when she mentioned a boyfriend. I didn't know she had one or that his influence would matter." Jake didn't mention the fact that she was also considering a position with the SEC. She didn't come out and say it directly, but she implied that she hated the research. *It happens.* He knew that after almost five years of rigorous work, many students became disillusioned.

"Interesting. Any of those positions would be good, but I think the department would prefer Boston College or North Carolina. It would look better."

"I would pick UNC. I always liked the Tar Heel blue."

That got a laugh out of Eric. Then his tone turned serious.

"I'm afraid that the final paper on your dissertation topic may not see the light of day. I've heard that the editors of the top three journals have seen your paper and discussed it at length. I think they feel it's too controversial."

"Why would they say that? Isn't our job to publish research without a subjective bias? Let the profession decide the merit of it."

"Jake, I agree. This particular paper appears to have some strong opinions associated with it, and publishing has always had a political component to it. It's possible that your findings make many other findings seem moot. There are too many people that are impacted by it and too many referees willing to reject it."

"That's ridiculous." *Especially because I know the results are true.*

"I agree, but unfortunately, publishing a paper today has less to do with the quality of the findings than finding the right hole to fill."

Jake left Eric's office quietly fuming. He had suspected something like this would happen ever since Sheldon had warned him. It might also have been related to the success of the trading strategy and the people they were trying to avoid. They were powerful people, and he had been naïve to assume that their influence would not have extended to academic circles. He badly wanted to tell Eric about the strategy and what it had accomplished, but knew it was in Eric's best interest to not know.

When Jake spoke with Duncan two days later, his mood had not improved. Over the past two days, the market had continued to improve and had slowly reverted back to normality. Jake griped for about five minutes with Duncan about the ridiculousness of the refereeing process and how it could make or break careers depending on how the referee was feeling that day. Duncan listened patiently on the other end, waiting for Jake to finish his rant.

"This shouldn't matter as much to you as it does. You know you're right; we have the physical proof to justify your research. I guess I'll never understand why this is so important to you, but I would like to discuss something slightly more pressing."

"Yes. Sorry. I just needed another person to vent to. Haley is sick of me complaining about it. OK. Talk to me about what is going on."

"I think we've a problem. It's not a problem with the model or the operations. It's a fundamental problem with the market. When we ran the strategy at first, back when I was at Griffin, I never concerned myself with the trades or getting the fills or what followed. We were too small to be noticed; even the computer was too small. Now we're over $1.3 billion. That's the sort of capital that moves markets. I've got a feeling that the floor guys know something when we come in—not that they're front running us, but positioning after one of our trades. I also feel that the HFTs compound our moves. We may know something they don't, but once we put on a position, our information is revealed, and others may be piggybacking off of that."

"No one can know the full extent of Charon Capital's positioning. That's why we've spread it over multiple accounts," Jake said, still irritated.

"This is true, but an informed trade is an informed trade. Let's say the market is ambivalent about direction, and then a large directional trade comes in, and it forces market weakness or strength. All the behavioral models, HFTs, and computerized programs are going to pick up on that and compound the direction."

Jake took an introspective pause before replying. He leaned back and looked toward the ceiling, the thought coming to the forefront. "Just like Flash Crash or Black Monday."

"Exactly. Now here we are, filling in the mispricing in nonnormal returns, a place that wasn't filled before. We either reduce the nonnormality or make it worse, potentially much worse, depending on what the model predicts. We saw some of this on Friday."

Jake could see where this was going. Duncan continued.

"It's possible that depending on the size of the aberration, we could be the catalyst of a major market meltdown. We could see the mispricing, trade the mispricing, have all the other market participants' jump on the trade, and then have Black Monday or worse. I know about the circuit breakers, but that doesn't extend to the other markets. It could result in a massive liquidity crisis. We never thought about this problem before because we didn't think about the size. Now this is a legitimate concern. You should bring this up with Benjamin."

"It's funny that you brought that up. I spoke with him Monday, and he's obviously very happy with how things have gone. He was considering adding to our allocation. I told him to hold on that, but he seemed anxious. In fact, he almost seemed distracted."

"You readdressed how size is the killer of great strategies, right?"

"I did, but that didn't seem to bother him. It was odd, but Benjamin is very smart and should have understood that. It was like he almost didn't care what our returns were. He was very happy about the performance on Friday, and our talk was mostly about that. He reiterated how happy he was with the model. Then he pushed for us to take on more capital."

"Normally I wouldn't turn down money, but we've made more than our fair share. In fact, we never need to work again, which is why your anger over the research is so perplexing to me. I think we need to build an exit strategy. We may have two parties to worry about." Duncan said, emphasizing the last statement.

You're absolutely right. Jake understood what Duncan was talking about and was coming to the realization that it wasn't enough to have a model that worked; it was how you ran the model within the landscape of the investing world that mattered.

CHAPTER 48

The Markov Group had two agenda items. The first was to address a security concern that had been solved but still needed to be addressed. The second was a much more complex problem. Frank spoke first. There was a real edge in his voice.

"In the past we've had certain individuals poke around the dealings of our group, and it has required decisive action on our part to deal with them. We've multiple means to take care of these people, and in each case it was handled swiftly and quietly. The situation we face today can be handled in one of two ways. The first is to launch an SEC insider trading investigation into the actions of one of the partners of Rising Tide Capital. This would be highly public, and the person would end up in jail, but the nature of the investigation could potentially lead to an avenue that may open doors to information we don't want revealed. The link is dead, but we don't want people looking beyond the link and making conjectures. The second method would be to ignore the infraction publically but address it in a more personal manner."

Michelle had been briefed on the infraction days earlier. An unmarked envelope had been on her desk waiting for her when she got to work. It contained pictures and a report of the activities of Chris Carter. The information he had been giving to Rising Tide and the extent to which he had been following her were all detailed. Michelle had initially reacted with numbness. Chris' actions were so transparent, but the extent of his deviousness was abhorrent. She had never stopped caring for him, even when he was at his worse. When the numbness faded, only an emptiness remained. She wasn't sure what would fill that void. She would never understand his motivation. Whether it was money, jealousy, or revenge, the motivation was always more relevant to the person conducting the action than to the person who received the action.

Sitting in her chair, listening to Frank talk, she knew Chris was dead. The suicide note had been found. It was tough putting on a brave face at work, but not because of his death; what hurt more was the extent of his betrayal. He had put her and the Markov Group at risk, and the protection and anonymity of the Markov Group was paramount. All the members knew this, and that meant an ancillary connection that might be a threat would have to be removed. That was bad news for Patrick Stinson.

Frank continued. "It's clear the link knew nothing about the group, but he definitely witnessed several of us enter the building. The link did not pass information about us to the person at Rising Tide but did pass on sensitive material related to people in this room. I have a strong opinion on what we should do. Shall we open it up for discussion, or are you confident in my judgment?"

Michelle knew that Frank had chosen his words carefully. He wasn't giving them an option. There would be no discussion, and the group's silence meant they would be all complicit in the death of a man. Chris's actions had forced the Markov Group's hand, taking the choice away from the members. This would be different. Patrick Stinson's crime was one of greed and desperation. He wasn't a direct threat, but there was enough of a connection to make eliminating him worthwhile. It was a basic cost/benefit analysis. Michelle could see Mr. Jones slipping into Patrick's home, injecting the needle behind the ear while he slept. The mixture of barbiturates and adrenaline would cause a massive heart attack, ruling out suspicion of any kind of foul play. The group remained silent.

"Good. That was easy. Now, to a much more pressing issue."

The man to Frank's left began speaking. Michelle noted that Harvey Waterman's Harvard accent was even more accentuated and annoying given his agitated state.

"Let's start with the good. After the senator's initial speech that led to the disruption in the markets, we got the desired effect, and it appears that the presidential initiative will be softened. That was the outcome we planned for, along with the markets returning to a normal, low-volatility state. Now here's the bad.

"The market fell more than the model predicted, and there were trades taking place that were similar to ours. In combination with our trades, it caused a simultaneous reaction from the algorithmic traders, which ultimately led to a significant market sell-off. There was a point that we could've lost control. When the market was getting quite unstable and liquidity was drying up, there were significant trades that halted the equity slide. This brought liquidity back to the market, and things started to improve. We didn't initiate those trades. They were done by a large player, or a series of traders, that drove the market. Here's what concerns me. We had two traders run a version of our model over the past six months. That's the first time that's ever happened. We dealt with the problem, and everything seemed fine. Now we've almost the exact same thing occurring on a much larger scale."

The head of the NYSE, Jerry Ospry, spoke up. "I want to echo these concerns. Unlike last time, when our algorithm picked up the anomaly and gave us forewarning, there was no forewarning this time. We can't isolate any one account that's doing something similar to our model. Obviously we can look at key trades, but on a trade-by-trade basis, they appear to be isolated and coming from different prime brokers and different accounts."

Frank interjected at this point. "The fact that we can't find the two traders who were responsible for the action the first time has to be more than coincidental. The Houston manager disappeared right after the Austin incident. The New Yorker trader, after he left his firm, disappeared from his apartment, and, it appears, the United States completely. There's no record of them leaving the country, but no evidence of them here either. Our team can't seem to locate them. The initial analysis of the data from the Austin academic doesn't show any contact with either of them, and he doesn't appear to be involved. The fact that he's still here is confusing our behavioral analyst. Suggestion?"

The man to Frank's right, Michael McQuary, spoke up. "I expect that these three individuals are involved somehow. It's the academic's research that's the driver. Somehow he must know something. The disappearance of the two traders is highly suspicious."

Frank was seething. The models had missed this. Benson Pritchard disappearing made sense given what had happened in Austin. But his data scientists hadn't even suggested that the New York trader would also disappear. If they had, he would have beefed up surveillance, and they wouldn't be in this mess.

McQuary continued on. "I would also suggest that we get hold of the individual accounts that made the key trades during this period and see if there's some link."

The group looked over at Michelle.

She replied, "Done." As head of the New York Federal Reserve, getting access to that information was well within her power.

"Excellent. The quicker we solve the who of this problem, the quicker we can solve the how. It's imperative we find this out immediately since we're dealing with real money that can affect our long-term economic goals. Meeting adjourned," Frank concluded.

He waited for all the members to leave before issuing commands for Franklin Insurance to do a full work-up and behavioral analysis on the two traders and the academic. He also contacted Mr. Jones about heading down to Austin.

CHAPTER 49

O ver the past two weeks, the model had continued to run, but Duncan and Benson had reduced any leverage in the account to dampen the returns. They also did not invest any of the additional profits. They kept the base at $1 billion since Jake considered that number to be of utmost importance when it came to running an effective strategy. Duncan and Benson had fallen into a relatively easy routine and seemed to be enjoying island life. However, Jake was left in a quandary.

For him, this had all started as an attempt to understand the fundamentals that drive asset prices, to explain the nonnormality in returns. Now it was a legitimate trading strategy running significant capital. He now felt that it had become a tool used by two masters. It was clear that what he had discovered was a method used by some powerful people using a combination of trading, influence, and leverage to move markets in a certain fashion. In discovering this, he had entered a world that was beyond him, a realm of unimaginable wealth and power. He knew he, Duncan, and Benson had been, or currently were being, watched, but he only realized the full implication of what they were doing when he stared at his screen.

Jake had gone to campus only to teach, attend office hours, and check in with Eric. He was enjoying that bit of a lull in a graduate student's life when the dissertation is done, but the defense hasn't happened. He was just waiting to present to get the necessary signatures so he could submit the final document to the administration. This blissful purgatory allowed Jake to work on the problem that had crept into his mind after his discussion with Duncan.

For two weeks, he aggregated macro data and combined it with exchange data and information on over-the-counter trading. He then formed a simulated market and underlying economy and ran scenario analysis. He would shock his market using two factors. The first was a metric that measured risk aversion. The second was an implicit leverage variable, a gauge on how much wealth was invested in the capital markets relative to actual cash. The model was simple in its design but was set up to be able to try to replicate the ebbs and flows in the marketplace and the way they translated to overall economic conditions. By changing the risk-aversion variable with leverage, it was possible to simulate crashes and market recoveries. High leverage in the system combined with a small change in risk aversion could lead to quick and potentially violent market sell-offs.

Once Jake was able to replicate a good pattern that duplicated the time series of the stock market and overall asset performance, he replaced the risk-aversion variable with a portion of his asset pricing model. This was critical because risk aversion is not directly observable, especially contemporaneously. Even more important was to understand how risk aversion changes, because when investors become more or less risk averse, regardless of the level of their aversion, is when asset prices change. Jake needed to know specifically about the nonnormal changes and what leads to large crashes or recoveries. Given what he had found prior, he knew his model could capture these risk-aversion changes; it was what had led him to the discovery in the first place. However, the purpose of this exercise wasn't to reaffirm his findings but to assess the damage that came from them.

Following his conversation with Duncan, Jake had realized that what they were doing could be very disastrous, especially if it was used in the wrong way. He had been working furiously over the past two weeks to assess how bad it could get. The model was a proxy for human risk aversion, and it could drive people to be more risk seeking or change their aversion all together. Trading in a certain way, using certain assets, with the right amount of size, can alter the behavior of the markets and thus ultimately people's behavior. That was what Jake had found. *I've found a tool to control human emotion.*

What is the market but a collection of individuals with a view on the price of a given asset? he mused. *Each individual brings in his or her own intuition, biases, and emotion. Individuals can have different views on value and on the holding periods and can be in different stages of the life cycle. The combination of all these people together creates a price and the invisible hand that moves the price. Even with the introduction of computers, algorithms, and HFTs, we can never remove the human element, and each computer trade is based on the perception of value assessed and programmed by a person. The interaction of each unique trait of each individual who participates in the market represents the aggregate risk aversion for the economy. If you can control that risk aversion, you can manipulate the markets.*

Jake knew that was what he had found and that it had been used for years o control the flow of capital and make significant wealth changes. However, the results in front of him showed that if used incorrectly, if the model was pushed to certain limits, this tool could result in a market crash and a destruction of wealth greater than what was experienced in 1929.

Holy shit. Jake felt anxiety swelling in his stomach to a degree that he had never experienced.

We face a real fucking problem. It was far greater than publishing a paper, finding a job, or even being watched. He realized that he could be responsible for the start of another Great Depression. Stopping the model wouldn't make the problem go away. There were too many parties that knew too much. Jake opened up Hangouts and texted Ω to both Ixion and Tantalus.

Haley walked in later that afternoon and crashed on the couch. She had reached a point of extreme frustration with her advisor. It was always better to have an overbearing dissertation chair than a nonexistent one, and Haley was dealing with the latter. She had voiced her frustration over the past several months, but over the past couple of weeks it had become a daily occurrence. *Balls, shit, fuck, fucker,* and some words so dirty that Jake didn't even know what they meant had come out of her mouth. She often reminded Jake of how lucky he was to have Eric. Jake always agreed.

"I swear, I should have worked with Dr. Chitworth. Do you know how many times he asked me to work on a project with him, but I passed because I thought it was best to remain loyal to Dr. Trent? She's never around and is utterly hopeless. Balls, I really feel that I might not finish this." Haley's agitation was coursing through her body. She had trouble sitting still.

"I have full faith that you'll get this done, but you may need to switch advisors. Maybe that sets you back six months, but I don't think you'll progress any more with Dr. Trent. It's a hard choice, but it's the right choice." Jake didn't have it in him to be sarcastic. *It's time to tell her.*

"You've told me that many times. Maybe one day I'll listen."

Jake gave her a kiss and went to the kitchen to get Haley and himself a glass of water. He came back over to the couch, handed her the glass, turned on the TV, and leaned over to her ear.

"I want you to join me at the coffee shop tonight," he whispered. Her eyes widened, and she nodded her head. Ever since they had begun trading, Jake had not mentioned anything to Haley about how things had been progressing, and she had not asked, even when he disappeared and subsequently returned from the coffee shop. All their conversations at home were about school, working out, where to eat, and how bad Winston's breath smelled. Jake had intentionally pushed that part of their lives away, and they had fallen into a nice routine. Now that routine had been broken, and Jake could see the panic behind Haley's eyes.

Jake pulled back from her and said, "If you're up for it, let's do a long loop around the lake. The weather is nice, and it won't be long before it starts to get really hot. Let's take advantage of this afternoon."

Haley agreed, and they got into their appropriate running attire and drove the Jeep down to the Town Lake trail. They parked close to Mopac footbridge and decided to head east. They opened up at an easy 8:30 pace, passing the rowing commune, the Lamar, First Street, and Congress Avenue bridges, and proceeding to the wider, less-traveled part of the loop. Given that a small percentage of people did the seven-mile option that crossed over the lake at the I-35 bridge, and even fewer did the full loop that crossed the Pleasant Valley Bridge, meant that on this weekday afternoon, the eastern part of the trail was practically deserted.

"Haley, it's time I caught you up on what has been happening," Jake said between breaths, looking around before he spoke to make sure that no one was around.

"To borrow a phrase from you, it's about time!"

Jake proceeded to fill her in on the performance, what had happened around the peak in volatility related to the potential government shutdown, and the conversations he'd had with Benjamin. They had passed the three-mile marker and were past I-35. He did not bring up his concern and the potential problems until the impact of what they had already accomplished set in.

"When you told me you wanted me to join you, I thought something terrible had happened, or that you had lost money. I know you're the one that's good at math, but it sounds like we've made $50 million." Haley was so shocked by the number that she didn't realize she had picked up the pace.

"Give or take a rounding error, yes," Jake said, looking at his watch and seeing a 7:45 pace.

"And no one suspects anything?"

"Good question. Over the past two weeks, I've put a lot of thought into that. Whoever found us before must suspect something is amiss, but I doubt they're able to point any fingers toward Charon Capital. They would have noticed some trades similar to theirs, but none of them can be linked to the same account. However, when things got highly volatile, Duncan believes, and I agree, that we were moving the market. Even with how small we are, relatively speaking, our position caused a herding behavior that drove the markets in the direction we wanted."

"How's that possible?"

"The model that we have implements the finding from my research. Using the thirty factors as markers for how to construct our portfolio is a proxy for human emotion. In trading the way we do, we can push or change the underlying behavior in the markets, causing the market to become more or less risk averse. Depending on the leverage on an asset and the size of a trade, we can cause swings in that asset price or the overall market to be triggered with very little capital. That's what I found in my research, and that's the tool that whoever we're copying has used for several decades to manipulate markets. Now, we're much smaller than they are, and we don't have their power or influence, but we've got enough size and can extract out the nonnormality in the marketplace to really cause change. Remember, it's the fringe, the nonnormality, that leads to over or underperformance."

"So this is what this is really all about. Somebody has been manipulating markets, and you've stumbled onto it, and they'll do what is necessary to keep it. We really are in some deep shit now. I kind of knew it back in January, but I guess I had let time dampen that feeling. It's funny, but everything you've said sounds more like psychology than finance."

God, I love this woman. She's fucking smart. "Exactly. This is all about emotion. That's what the market is. Finance just wraps the math around what this is all about. It's all about emotion. These people, the ones we're hiding from, have been controlling people's emotions through sophisticated means," Jake said excitedly.

"But why?"

"I hadn't really thought about that until I ran the model in my simulated market and economy. I believe I've got an answer to that, but there's one other thing we need to talk about."

"What's that?"

"I don't believe Benjamin's motives have been entirely transparent."

This caused Haley to stop. They were at the most eastern part of the run, about to cross over the bridge.

"That doesn't sound good at all."

"It's not. Let me explain."

Jake proceeded to tell Haley everything that he had learned and what the problems were. During the five miles back, which they ran at seven minutes per mile, he laid out what he was planning on telling Duncan and Benson tonight and the course of action ahead. They had to play this very carefully, and they had to time it exactly right; otherwise the consequence would be catastrophic.

Mr. Jones had been following them at a distance over the past several days, not noticing anything out of the ordinary except for that one visit to the coffee shop and the use of a different computer. He continued to send reports back to Franklin Insurance. He was starting to taste orange in the back of his throat.

CHAPTER 50

Chen is a powerful last name, with ties to past emperors and dynasties. The surname can be traced back to an eastern province lying halfway between Beijing and Shanghai. Chen Jie couldn't speak to his past ancestors or their migration habits, but his father was a powerful commander in the Chinese National Army. He grew up in a traditional household that held strong ties to the Communist Party and the old ways. Jie was a gifted child and excelled at school. He was identified early and was pushed into the best programs, and, given his family patronage and his father's position, he was earmarked as a future leader and member of the politburo for a growing and powerful China.

Jie was on the verge of finishing high school when the Tiananmen Square protest occurred. It was eye opening to a smart, privileged, and indoctrinated teenager. The swelling of unrest had been present for some time, but to see the hostility leveled on such a grand scale was horrific. If anyone could attest to the understanding of both sides, it was Jie. He understood that the world was changing, and China's role in the new world would be defined by how it adapted, but there was no need to change China's identity. They couldn't grow and establish themselves without a strong ruling party, but the party had to reduce its xenophobia.

Jie's choices would prove prophetic. He learned English in high school and chose to do his university studies abroad, changing his given name to Benjamin, studying economics at Oxford, getting a master's at the London School of Economics, and then changing tracks to pursue a psychology PhD at Stanford. Along the way he published several papers on the psychology of the markets and wrote an unpublished piece on the role of China in the world's future economic expansion. That paper never was accepted because its main conclusion was that China would ascend to the top of the economic landscape at the expense of, and as a result of, a massive implosion in the United States.

After finishing his degree, Benjamin went to work at Goldman Sachs, where he was on a team that exclusively dealt with Asia. His role was to act as a facilitator between Asian governments, companies, and banks, which would help smooth the road for Goldman gaining access to an untapped gold mine of consumers and opportunity. This experience taught Benjamin not only how to work on and close billion-dollar deals but the route and path from which China could ascend. There was no need to change the political landscape to become an economic power. Benjamin had realized long ago that true power came from the flow and management of capital, not who was ruling. This was the mistake Russia had made. It wasn't the Communist Party that was the problem; it was the implementation of a short-sighted economic plan. Russia tried to change who it was because its economic model was wrong, and this caused a failure on both the political and economic fronts. China had succeeded because it never changed who it was or how it ruled. The country had just adapted to a global growth model that circumvented the ideals of the ruling party, without the ruling party ever giving up control.

After Goldman Sachs, Benjamin returned home, but instead of taking a position that would probably have led to a politburo placement, he went to work at the Bank of China. Being able to influence and direct capital flows gave him much more influence and allowed him to use his insights into where the future growth was coming from. However, as time progressed, Benjamin came to realize a hard and undeniable fact. China's growth was driven by its people and its relative youth. The size of the population meant that labor was cheap, and as a consumer base, a base that had been relatively untouched meant new markets for all products that previously had never dealt with China. As the world expanded and companies began to use China and its labor force, China fueled global consumerism, and its economy became dependent on that consumerism. China sup̶p̶l̶i̶e̶d̶, and the world bought. Nowhere was this more apparent than in the relationship between China and the United States. As the world's leader and the dominant economic power, the United States was a debt-riddled mess. It funded its projects and its growth with an ever-increasing and potentially insurmountable amount of leverage, and China was responsible for fueling that frenzy. The United States issued debt, and China bought it, and it bought it because it had to. If it didn't, consumer spending stalled, and with that, China's growth.

The idea that China was slowing buying the United States was false. The United States was slowing owning China. Benjamin reflected on a statement one of his old professors had said to him: "Owe the bank a million dollars, and the bank owns you; owe the bank a billion dollars, and you own the bank." As China accumulated more and more US debt, the United States held more and more power over China.

As time progressed, Benjamin had seen two problems for China. After the 2008 crisis, as the US interest rate had fallen close to zero, China's accumulation of US treasuries over the next six years had become highly susceptible to interest rate hikes. This also meant that China couldn't sell part of its holdings without also causing a massive loss to its total portfolio. This left China in the position of having to continue to buy US treasuries without the ability to sell them. Additionally, China's labor force was becoming more skilled and more expensive. As China developed, it started to import more while the cost of exports increased, which meant that the country could not rely just on the comparative advantage of having lots of cheap labor. India, Indonesia, Thailand, and other Asian countries could provide a similar service. Benjamin knew that things would have to change.

He had made the switch to CIC because change would have to come from direct investment. Benjamin knew the longer this relationship with the United States continued, the more detrimental it would be for China. Through time China would never become fully independent from the United States. The two countries would forever be economically linked, and the United States would always hold the upper hand. So Benjamin sought a means and a method to break this link, returning to his old research for the answer.

The key was 2008. There was a valuable lesson to be learned in dispersion of risk that many did not appreciate. The United States was responsible for the inflated home prices, an asset bubble driven by easy capital and limited oversight. However, in many US banks' infinite and uncalculated wisdom, the packaging of mortgages and bonds priced on the value of real estate, and credit derivatives that were a function of a borrower's ability to pay, were sold across the globe. Most of the US banks also had tremendous exposure to this leveraged risk, but the fact that it was sold overseas made it a global problem versus one isolated to the United States. So when the crash happened, it had affected the globe.

When the best economic minds were deciding what to do, Benjamin had felt that there was an opportunity for China to damage the United States further and step in to become the dominant economic power. However, his superiors had balked, and the United States had recovered and, as a result, gained further strength, while Europe and most everyone else had lagged behind. The US recovery had been led by an accommodative Fed, which deliberately enticed investors to buy risky assets, which had buoyed asset prices, brought liquidity back to the markets, and eventually led to a real-estate recovery.

The psychological impact the swing in prices took was remarkable. What was more remarkable to Benjamin was that the crash had taken place in 2008 versus 2007. There were clear forces that kept assets inflated before they crumbled, and it appeared that the extra year had allowed certain firms, US firms, to be better positioned for the crash and to take advantage of it when things finally settled. This realization led Benjamin to make his switch to CIC and focus on investing China's wealth to make an impact. He had realized that the market did not behave consistently and seemed to be driven by a force that was deliberate and manipulative.

If Benjamin could replicate that, if he could find a similar method, then he could influence prices in a way that would cause an isolated loss in the United States, one that China could gain from. When you control over $600 billion in capital, you have a lot of sway over how capital is distributed, which ultimately will affect prices and risk aversion. He had the capital; now he needed to find the method.

He began to search for anything that resembled a clue into what was happening in the markets, whether it was behavioral or economic. He had tried various methods, including recruitment of Federal Reserve employees, but his search ended in New York when he read a paper and met a graduate student from the University of Texas. Here was a tool he could use, a tool that would allow him to push asset prices to the point of collapsing. He believed that doing so would force such a devaluation of the US dollar that, given the right timing and removing the float on the yuan, the yuan would become the world currency. *The key was the yuan.* The Fed had essentially printed so much money that, given the right circumstance, the value of the dollar would crumble to zero, and the world would be forced to hold the yuan. This would make China the global economic power and remove the stranglehold the United States had over them.

Benjamin thought the start of this was less than two weeks away.

CHAPTER 51

"If we thought we were in trouble a couple of months ago…" Benson trailed off.

"Yes, but this mess is somewhat self-inflicted," Haley said.

"What is the game plan now?" Duncan said, getting them back on track.

"I see only one possibility. We have to destroy this anomaly; it has to become an untradeable strategy. We talked about January and why the January effect still exists, but with this, we have to trade it so that it can never be replicated or repeated. We need to run the model to full effect but without causing a market crash of epic and unrecoverable proportions," Jake said.

"Dang. How'd we do that?" Benson asked.

"Before we discuss that, can we all agree that this has to be done?" Jake asked. "There can be no half measures; otherwise, we face the possibility of significant market turmoil, jail time, and potentially death. I mean, we still don't know all the players, but let's assume they could make us disappear. Additionally, and on the opposite side, we're dealing with a person and a motivation that can change the global economic landscape. So, let's all agree that this has to be done. This isn't about making money; this is about fixing a long-overdue wrong and preventing worse from happening." Jake paused to let the gravity of the situation sink in.

On the other end of the connection, Duncan and Benson agreed simultaneously. Haley nodded.

"Good. Now let's discuss the process that it'll take to accomplish this. It'll require three critical steps. First, I don't believe that we can wait for a market disturbance to take advantage of. The originators of the model are smart and connected. I don't think we can stay anonymous for much longer, so we need to act fast. We'll need to nudge the markets. Fortunately, this won't take much. The US market is in a bit of lull and has such a short-term memory problem when it comes to current global risks that investors may be caught unaware. From what the two of you have told me, Russia appears to be in real trouble with its currency, and European debt and growth concerns have returned."

"This is true," Duncan said. "The model has been increasing its exposure to FX markets, especially the US dollar versus the euro and the ruble. Objectively, if Russia doesn't do something with its interest rates, the value of their currency is going to crumble. They have taken such a hit with the loss in oil prices that started last year that the ruble is essentially worthless. I would bet they're going to increase rates. That means bond prices are going to get crushed. That could lead to a long-term capital management situation for stat arb funds."

"Excellent. Depending on the leverage, that could be our starting point. Now what do we think would be the best outcome for those that are running our model? I guess it's more accurate to say *their* model," Jake said.

"Well, if we believe these people are using markets to drive economic or political outcomes, we need to see who has the most to lose or gain for spread and dispersion trades," Benson said.

"That's true. I think we also need to frame it in terms of what the best outcome is for the United States. Look at the effect the falling oil prices have had in causing Russia to stop rattling its saber," Duncan added.

"Once we identify that, we can plan for the right trades to get this started," Jake said. "We need to run the model so that it causes a big disturbance—one that will cause an immediate response from the other algorithms that will overrun the possible fail-safe procedures and tools their model has built in. In other words, we need to cause such a systematic shock that the price movement and drop in liquidity will render whatever size these guys have behind them moot," Jake said.

"What kind of price move are you talking about?" Haley asked.

"Enough of a move to blow through the circuit breakers and kill liquidity in the OTC markets," Jake replied.

"Hold on, I thought you wanted to avoid that."

"We need to cause that kind of movement to force the hand of the originators of the model. I think our action will provoke them to come forward. If they don't, it'll cause a complete market shutdown. At some point they'll have to use their capital to reverse markets, and if we've got enough momentum, we can overrun the trades. At that point we'll reveal ourselves."

"What?" The other three said.

"This is the second part. We'll send out a press release to Bloomberg, CNBC, the *Financial Times*, etc., outlining exactly what we're doing. We'll suggest that everything is just vapor—that nothing has fundamentally changed. I don't believe that this will change the outcome in the markets. It may cause the downward trend to pause, but that's not the desired effect. What I believe it'll do is force the originators of the model to reach out to us. Given that we would have control over the model and momentum at that point, they'll come to us."

"Right. So then we can learn who they are and what they're doing," Duncan added.

"Yes. We need that information more than anything. Once we know that, we don't need the model anymore. We can reveal these people, and that should end the manipulation."

"They could just shoot us and continue on," Haley said.

"Dang no. They'll still need us. There's still the problem of the market and returnin' order to it," Benson noted.

"This is step three, and it's obviously conditional on step two. This is a game of chicken. We essentially want the same thing as the model originators at this point, but we can't show our hand until they do. However, we can't push the market to a place where neither one of us can get it back. This is the part I'm most worried about. We need to reverse every trade—and by that point we should have built up significant capital—and start to short everything that would benefit China at the expense of the United States. We'll need to go long the United States in everything we can—equity, credit, currency—except one instrument. We need to short US treasuries across the curve. I mean hammer them. And we'll need the Fed to announce a rise in rates."

"How are we going to do that?" Duncan asked.

"Well, I think that's very simple. I'm almost certain that the Fed is involved and has been for a very long time. Look at our four key variables. Leverage, institutional investors, market microstructure, and the Fed are the critical factors that drive the model fit. Fed policy, statements, and actions are a coordinated result of this organizaion, and those actions are intertwined with institutional buying and selling. Let's end here. We'll talk in person tomorrow."

Mr. Jones watched them at the coffee shop, seeing that both the academic and his wife were there this time. He would really like access to that laptop but was still in the evaluation stage. He also noted that the behavior of the academic and his wife was out of the norm, which was something that he would send in his new report. The taste of orange was not going away.

In front of her, Michelle had a list of the accounts that were linked to the trades that had caused the market to crash more than predicted several weeks ago. The group had identified eighty-seven key trades of a certain size at certain points in time. The list had about twenty-five unique firms, with several appearing more than once, but one firm had over fifteen accounts associated with it, a firm called Charon Capital.

Michelle looked up the firm's ADV and saw that it was a newly registered management company, less than four months old. The principle owners of the fund were three names she recognized.

CHAPTER 52

The Markov Group was scheduled to meet Thursday. Michelle knew they would outline a plan to remove the concern created by Charon Capital Management. She assumed they would follow a similar procedure as before, a shutdown of trading privileges, SEC investigation, the works. However, there was something that concerned her greatly that was unclear. Where had they gotten the capital? The size of the trades they were making were on huge notional amounts, meaning the Markov Group wasn't dealing with three small fish anymore. Somebody with real clout was behind the trades.

Jake's dissertation defense was less than a month away, but his focus was only on the objective at hand. His academic career would have to wait for a couple of days at best. At worst, well, it could be on indefinite suspension. The plan was simple, and he had to take advantage of the small incongruities that were built into the system.

Jake and Haley got on a plane from Austin to Dallas early Wednesday morning after dropping Winston off at Camp Bow Wow. From there the plane went to Miami, and then they took a private plane to Saint Croix. Mr. Jones saw the plane they boarded in Austin and that it was going to Dallas. Beyond that he knew nothing else. Since he was there just to observe and no more, he would have to backtrack through passenger manifests to find out where they had gone. It troubled him that there was no record of them buying an airplane ticket in any of their credit reports. He tasted more acid than orange.

Benjamin sat in his office, looking out on a beautiful April Thursday. On his desk sat a report from his team. Based on the analysis of the trades done by Charon Capital and the understanding of the research, he felt confident that they could have a model in place that would replicate everything Charon Capital had done. Benjamin ordered his team to back test the results one more time. It might not be a perfect match, but he now had an intraday model that had to be similar to the one Charon Capital was using.

Frank knew they were dealing with something timely. It would not be enough to just shut down certain accounts and initiate an SEC audit. More drastic measures would need to be taken. They needed to find out who the client was immediately. The rest of the group agreed with Frank's concern about swift measures. Frank messaged the security team to move in on Jake.

He received a message back almost instantaneously that said Jake wasn't in Austin anymore and that the subject had flown to Dallas. Additionally, there were no eyes on him at this point. Frank was furious and ordered the team to find him at all costs. This led to a simultaneous operation. The first was a ground operation that went through the personal effects at Jake and Haley's home and their campus offices looking for any information. The second was a cyberattack, which scoured the Internet for any information related to their whereabouts.

On Thursday, Charon Capital went over the plans for Friday ad nauseam. Friday morning the four of them were prepared and wired for the day. A trading station had been set up for Jake, and Haley had her own terminal to assist Benson. They would start Friday at noon and hopefully be finished by Monday at close. Friday they needed to set up the bait without attracting attention. Since their intention was to create the nonnormality, it had to be done in such a way that the model would flag a problem right at the close on Friday.

Nothing in the search of their home revealed anything about where Jake or Haley were or what they were doing. Additionally, nothing in the cyber search had come up with any hits, but that was a more extensive process. The computer that Mr. Jones had wanted was not in the condo.

Benjamin went to bed Friday night satisfied with the results of the back test and prepared to let the model run at the first sign of a nonnormality. Before that he would have to pull the capital from Charon and shut down their trading operation. Monday he would notify Charon and begin the unwind process. The tool was now in his control, and he needed to eliminate any potential conflict with Charon before he could launch a full attack on his real target.

Right at noon on Friday, Charon Capital started to slowly acquire front-month S&P 500 put options that were 5 percent out of the money, long US treasury futures contracts, long credit default spreads on Greece, Russia, and Spain, short US dollar and euro foreign-exchange contracts, and long gold. This was done in small quantities and in a way that masked the trades so it didn't appear there was a large accumulation of a given position. By 3:45 p.m. eastern, Charon Capital had built the downside protection it was looking for and then started to push some bigger trades, which led to an increase in bid-ask spreads. Volatility started to increase, and the market began to sell off, along with that, and although liquidity was thin, CDS spreads started to increase. Volatility was above 20 percent, and skew was approaching a yearly high. Gold had a little bounce in price, and the equity market was down almost 3 percent on the day. Russian bonds were trading at a yield of 25 percent—the yield that the bonds needed to get to put pressure on the dispersion traders and statistical arbitrage hedge funds.

Jake watched the model and the market-risk-premium-versus-volatility flag light up two minutes before the close. There was a large sell on close orders, and the futures, which traded fifteen minutes after equity markets closed, fell another 1 percent. The groundwork was set. They would have Saturday and most of Sunday morning to prepare for what would be the longest twenty-three-hour stretch of their lives. Starting at 6:00 p.m. Sunday, when the Sydney market opened, through the close of US equity markets at 4:00 p.m. Monday, the four of them would try to undo the greatest market manipulation and fraud that had been perpetuated in modern history—without causing irreparable harm.

CHAPTER 53

Jake and Haley sat on the beach, looking out over the Caribbean and not speaking. He was wearing his knee-length board shorts and his Oakley running shades. She was in a white bikini top and floral-print sarong wrap. The cool breeze coming over the water mitigated the heat that radiated off the sand. It almost felt like a vacation, and there was no better place to be to help soothe the stress that they were all feeling. Duncan and Benson were at the beachside bar and were also quiet and contemplative. Duncan was the only one who had gotten a decent night's sleep, but he still wore a concerned expression on his face.

The sun was beginning its long arc toward sunset. The island had increased in traffic and people over the past couple of weeks, but the beach was fairly empty. Jake got up from his chair and asked Haley to walk with him along the shoreline. They waded out into the water knee-deep and headed north up the beach. The water at their knees was a brilliant turquoise, and stretched to a sapphire and finally a rich cobalt as the water met the horizon.

"I know what we're about to do is right, but I have no idea if it'll work. We could cause no impact, we might crash all international markets, we could make a lot of money, or we could lose it all. This is so different from searching out the inefficiencies in the marketplace. We're now going to be causing them. We're going to be the catalyst for causing change. I honestly don't know what the outcome will be. I mean, I know what the most likely result is, but there's a wealth of possibilities." He stopped and looked out at the ocean.

"Jake, we trust you. This is the right thing. Fuck, I don't really understand what is going on, but I don't think we've got a choice. You found something, and that something has led us down this path. We've to take it to the end." From behind him she wrapped her arms around his waist and bit his ear.

"Do you know what I'm truly afraid of? What happens after, if we're successful? The potential effect on the confidence of the investing public could be catastrophic."

"Shall we cross that bridge when we get to it?"

"I guess that's our only option, but I'd like an idea of what the right path is and what will happen on Tuesday after everything plays out."

"Isn't that the idea? Nobody knows the future; you just have to do the best you can with the information you have. After Monday, your ability to see what will happen will disappear. That's what an efficient market is all about. That's the goal."

Jake looked back over his shoulder at Haley. "What have you been reading? You sound like a finance professor."

"I've been living with one for the past several years. Didn't you think I was paying attention? Plus, what you do is easy compared to my work. I just let you believe you were as smart as you thought you were."

He turned and faced her, pulling her close. She was almost as tall as he was, probably taller at that point, given the slope in the beach. He kissed her deeply. "I love you. I know you know, but it's important to say it out loud," Jake told her.

"I know, and I love you too. Now get your head right. Let's end this."

Google Hangouts is a great way to conduct either video or audio calls without using a phone or a cellular provider. However, nothing is fully secure. Hangouts doesn't use OTR, off-the-record, or end-to-end encryption, and if you don't delete your chat history, it is archived in Gmail. If Google receives a government court order, it can actually tap into individual user conversations. Using this access late Saturday night, the Markov Group, through Franklin Insurance's cyber patrol division, stumbled on a recorded conversation that mentioned Charon Capital. In searching the route of the call, two users were identified, one called Sisyphus and the other Tantalus. Sisyphus's IP address was in Austin, Texas, and Tantalus was located in the US Virgin Islands.

This was the first positive hit that the Markov Group had on the possible location of the Charon Capital partners. The Markov Group members would learn of this information first thing Sunday morning. Each member received a message to meet Sunday at 8:00 a.m. to discuss what would be the best course of action. Frank called the meeting, ignoring standard safety protocols. It was agreed upon that two representatives of Franklin Insurance would head to the islands to find the location of Charon Capital. Frank would also be heading down. Something in his gut told him it was important for him to be there.

His private plane was to leave from Westchester airport at 1:00 p.m. and arrive on the island in just under four hours. The problem was that the plane didn't leave until 2:00 p.m., and that was because of Walter Matthews. Franklin Insurance prided itself on telling its employees that they were not allowed to work weekends, that the company valued the quality of life of its employees. That usually meant that the floor was inaccessible, but not today. So when Walter Matthews went to the office at noon that Sunday, desperate to get the business card of a junior analyst he had met at a bar that Thursday with her cell phone number on the back, he didn't run into the security that would have normally been in place. He had waited the mandatory two days and now would call, hoping for a proper date. It just so happened that the Markov Group was in its conference room at the time, and the members had to wait for Walter to leave before they left. This five-minute delay caused a chain reaction that lead to an hour delay in the takeoff of Frank's plane. Walter Matthews had played his unwitting part, and played it well.

By the time they arrived in Saint Croix, it would be Sunday night. Frank doubted that any office or apartment would be under one of the three individuals' names, or Charon Capital, so it would be pointless looking at property records. They phoned ahead and got a private investigator, Dennis Shaw, to start gathering any information on people who fit the description of Jake, Benson, and Duncan. The man bristled, given that it was Sunday, so Frank threw out a figure that quashed the man's concerns. He immediately went to work. Frank wanted something by the time they arrived.

When the plane taxied down the runway, a car greeted them on the strip and took Frank and the two security personnel to their hotel. Mr. Jones had made commercial arrangements from Austin and would be joining them shortly. Dennis Shaw was waiting for them in the lobby of the hotel and was invited up to Frank's suite. Dennis had been able to learn where the members of Charon Capital were staying. It wasn't hard. The island is small and friendly, and when people have extended stays, they become integrated into island life. Additionally, it was hard to miss Benson. While his scar had healed, it was still evident. Once Dennis got Benson's picture, he tracked down someone from a local running club who had met Benson outside of Colony Cove to go for a run. Dennis relayed that information to Frank, who sent out his two travel companions to retrieve any and all members of Charon Capital.

When the Franklin Insurance representatives got to Colony Cove, found the correct apartment, and knocked on the door, no greeting was returned. They listened for any noise, but none was coming from inside. Looking around and seeing no one, they picked the lock, which was preposterously easy, and went inside. The apartment was clean and orderly and looked like it was well lived in. There were drawers full of clothes in both bedrooms, and there was a bed pulled out in the living room. It was clear that both Duncan and Benson were there on the island but just not in the apartment at the time. It was also evident that someone had come to visit them. Looking through the personal effects, they learned that Jake and Haley were there as well. There were no phones or computers in the apartment, and nothing to indicate where they were or where Charon Capital's office was. They left the place as they had found it, called Frank, and waited for instructions. He told them to wait for an hour for any of the members to show up, and if they did not, to return immediately to the hotel.

It was 7:30 p.m. They had missed the principals of Charon Capital by less than an hour.

CHAPTER 54

A sian markets opened lower, and US futures were leading the charge. The markets were thin, and the bid-ask spreads were wide, but the volumes were twice the normal overnight average. Russian bond yields had crept up to 27 percent. US treasuries were getting action, as the "flight to quality" trade was starting to happen, and the ten-year yield was heading below 2 percent.

In Hong Kong, which was the headquarters of Asian Pacific operations for Harvey Waterman's firm, traders were scrambling. The Hang Seng was down 5 percent, liquidity was disappearing, and phones were ringing at every desk and in every office. Stop losses were being triggered, and client anxiety was audible in every conversation. It was 10:00 p.m. in New York, and multiple factors had been flagged in the Markov Group's model. Harvey had been alerted to the activity and was concerned. The model was designed to anticipate these risks so they could then put in their position to drive the markets in the direction they wanted. Now it appeared that the market was ahead of the model. If they traded the way the model suggested, this would create further market distortions. Harvey had always allowed his firm to operate in a vacuum and then use the capital when the Markov Group needed it. Now his firm was facing market losses, and the model was telling him to contribute to the market slide. Harvey called the executive vice president in charge of Asian Pacific operations and ordered him and the traders to reverse out of their exposures immediately. He knew this would cause massive market distortions and losses, but if he didn't, the losses could be catastrophic for his firm.

He then called Frank to let him know what was happening. The probability that the market was going to experience a day like October 19, 1987, was now in play. Frank was highly distressed. There had been no sightings of the members of Charon Capital, and Frank was convinced that they were the drivers of what was happening. He recalled Dennis Shaw and his security team to scour the island to look for the group. Mr. Jones had arrived and joined in the search. Frank also called the other members of the Markov Group. They would need to react quickly to what was happening. Michelle Lancaster would be critical in stopping this.

Benjamin sat in his office watching his Bloomberg terminal. It was eleven thirty Monday morning, and he was watching a precipitous dive in asset values. Credit-default swap on all country debt was souring, and US treasury values were approaching all-time highs. He had planned on calling Charon Capital today before implementing the CIC's in-house model, but it appeared it would not be necessary. He had dismissed his research team to their offices and just sat back and watched the carnage. Everything that he wanted to happen was occurring without him having to lift a finger. He was shocked and elated at his good fortune. Maybe he wasn't the trigger and would not benefit as much from the price free fall, but the end result would be the same. Benjamin would wait until US trading hours and then start the systematic sell, starting small and then time the massive sell along with his historic announcement.

There was a lull in the Asian markets after the first several hours. US futures had also stabilized, and it appeared that the market was waiting for Europe to open. Europe opens at 3:00 a.m. (EST). Futures on the DAX and the FTSE 100 were down about 4 percent, so when Europe opened, a flurry of activity was anticipated. Frank had sent a message to the members of the Markov Group on what the best course of action would be. With Harvey's somewhat preemptive trades, it was possible that they would need to follow the market. All indications suggested that there was no bottom. In outlining how to stop the free fall, Frank said Michelle Lancaster would need to make a statement about the Fed helping to meet liquidity demands—to supply the world, through the big banks, a line of indefinite credit. This statement could not be made until after close on Monday. They would have to ride this out through the trading hours.

At the same time, Dennis Shaw, accompanied by Mr. Jones and the two other members of Frank's security team, were searching all over the island. It was early Monday morning, so there were few people about. Since it was a waste of time to just scour the island aimlessly, they staked out the apartment at Colony Cove. Hopefully they would get lucky and one of the members of Charon Capital would return to the apartment in the next couple of hours.

Predictably, Europe opened down, fell another 2 percent in the first two hours, and then leveled off. All credit risk had increased, and the spread between US treasuries and investment-grade corporate bonds was close to 7 percent. High-yield bonds were down over 12 percent. US futures were down almost 4.5 percent. Combined with the loss on Friday, the market would be down about 7.5 percent by the open at 9:30 a.m. There would be a flurry of activity, and if that activity meant a 10 percent drop from the prior market highs, it could send the markets into further free fall. The Markov Group knew that was going to happen, and so did Benjamin. At this point there was nothing they could do to prevent it.

CHAPTER 55

When investors hedge, they go to the most liquid asset possible, which is the futures contract on the S&P 500. The S&P 500 is an index, not an actual equity that can be bought or sold. It is a composite measure of five hundred underlying stocks. Futures and options can be bought and sold on the index as well as ETFs that replicate the S&P 500. When the futures on the S&P 500, which can be traded on overseas exchanges, fall in price, the five hundred stocks that make up the index have to fall in price as well; otherwise, the price difference can be exploited or arbitraged. The selling pressure on these stocks leads to further selling pressure and brings the whole market down. That is why when markets fall, the price drops are aggressive and precipitous.

The US market opened with an absolute frenzy. People waking up to the carnage overseas and the gap opening were caught unaware, and all investors had to play catch-up. Computerized algorithms were searching out weakness and positioning for further sells. What was most disconcerting for investors was that the move was driven on limited news. Yes, there were concerns in Europe, but there was nothing wrong in the United States. Or was there? The business channels on TV did no one any favors by perpetuating the panic. Every stock was down, and stop losses were blown through. Selling was taking place for retail and institutions investors alike. Sometimes, regardless of fundamentals, short-term concerns overwhelm long-term rationality.

There are price limits that certain stocks can trade within on a given day, but no actual market circuit breakers for the Hang Seng, the Nikkei, and most Asian stock markets. This is the same for Europe as well. Only the United States has well-defined breaks in trading depending on market movements. Specifically, the circuit-breaker halt for a level 1 (7 percent) or level 2 (13 percent) decline occurring after 9:30 a.m. (EST) and up to and including 3:25 p.m. (EST), or, in the case of an early scheduled close, 12:25 p.m. (EST), would result in a trading halt in all stocks for fifteen minutes. If the market declined by 20 percent, triggering a level 3 circuit breaker, at any time, trading would be halted for the remainder of the day.

At 10:00 a.m. (EST), the market was close to being down 7 percent, triggering a circuit breaker. This was a critical marker, because not only would the market halt for fifteen minutes, it would also be down 10 percent from the highs and that indicated that assets had entered into bear market territory. It hovered around this value for ten minutes, as it appeared that investors started to jump back in on the buy side, seeing the relative value in stocks. The Markov Group knew better. Everything in the model suggested that further selling would take place. The level of risk aversion was too high, as was the leverage. At 10:10 a.m., the level 1 circuit breaker was triggered.

The fifteen-minute break was designed to reduce panic. Investors hoped to have some reassuring statement come from the Fed or someone important that this was a temporary disruption and that everything was fine. Nothing came. The ten-year US treasury yield was at 1.8 percent.

When the market reopened, it fell 5 percent almost immediately. There were no buyers, and market makers had no idea where true market value was. By 11:30 a.m., the market had hit the second circuit breaker. News agencies were looking for quotes from any portfolio manager about what was going on and what they were doing. Reuters picked up a newswire from a small firm that no one had heard of called Charon Capital, who believed everything was computer driven and that nothing had fundamentally changed. The group claimed that there was no reason to sell, that this was all panic driven and caused by a systematic problem in the investment process. This statement was picked up by Bloomberg and others, who tried to get in contact with the portfolio manager.

Benjamin and Frank both saw this statement at the same time, right before the US markets opened again. The statement could not prevent the continued sell-off, since it was only one positive statement in a sea of negativity. Benjamin didn't understand the purpose of the statement. He was going to speak to Jake today anyway, but he knew he would not pick up the phone until the market closed. He wasn't sure if anything was wrong, but his intuition said something was off. Addressing that would have to wait.

Frank knew exactly why the statement had been made. The press release had the location of the firm's office. Frank called his team to come and get him, and they headed directly for Charon Capital's base of operations.

Benjamin started the slow selling of US treasuries. Regardless of what Charon was doing, it was time to unload some of China's exposure to the United States. There would never be a better time. In about an hour, he would press his contacts in the politburo to announce that they would let the yuan float against the US dollar. They would also allow countries to hold bonds backed by the yuan. Gold prices had soared relative to the dollar, so it was at the weakest level since 2008. Benjamin believed this would be the start of the yuan replacing the dollar as the world currency, but it was critical that China reduce its US treasury holdings. If countries started using yuan-backed bonds versus dollars, the United States would not be able to finance its operations, would succumb to its massive debt problem, and would fall into an unrecoverable depression. China would be inoculated from this free fall, and the world would have to turn to China for help.

Frank and his team headed up the stairs on King Street and knocked on the door. They noticed the reinforced lock and the keypad. They heard the mechanical sounds of the locks, and the door opened. Haley stepped out and greeted Frank and his two companions.

"We were expecting a call." She looked directly at Frank, and then noticed the woman behind him. "She can't come in," Haley said, trying to keep the emotion out of her voice.

"I'm sorry—you don't have a choice in that matter," Frank said. He stepped aside, and the woman that was formerly known as Sarah stepped forward, grabbed Haley's left wrist with her left hand, and pulled it back and down in a smooth motion. This caused Haley to become unbalanced, allowing the woman with the long black hair the opportunity to get around her and hold the six-inch blade, which was in her right hand, at the base of Haley's neck, just below the jugular. The tip of the blade broke the skin, letting a single drop of blood hit the floor. This took less than two seconds.

"Now, let's all go in, shall we?" said Frank.

They all walked into the eight-hundred-square-foot office. Jake and Benson looked up; Duncan kept his eyes firmly on the screen. Benson was shocked to see Sarah staring at him and almost jumped across the desk at her. She showed no emotion at all. Jake held him back, along with the rage he was feeling. He had known this would be part of it.

"Stay focused. We're about to get to the point of no return," Duncan said, his voice a little louder than normal, which was practically shouting for him.

Frank walked over to the empty seat and took it. Sarah walked Haley to the opposite corner of the room. Mr. Jones stood serenely by the closed office door. The third associate had taken a position on the roof of the building across the street, looking through a telescopic lens on the rifle supplied by Dennis Shaw, the crosshairs fixed on the entryway. He would wait for the signal.

Inside the office, Jake turned in his chair. *Keep your emotions in check. Don't look at Haley. Keep it together.* Then he addressed Frank directly: "We've three hours until the market closes, but I think we've less than an hour to fix this."

CHAPTER 56

"Right now we control $50 billion in notional capital that's leading a charge in the free fall in the markets," Jake said, staring directly at Frank. "We're long gold, volatility, treasuries, and credit default swaps, and short equities, the dollar, and high yield. Gold is close to a price of $2,000 per troy ounce, volatility is 70 percent, the market is down almost 16 percent, and the two-year is 1.73 percent. You know this already, but I wanted to reiterate the position of strength we're in."

Frank could not remember the last time somebody had spoken to him in that fashion or looked at him with that kind of loathing.

"We could break you like that," Frank said, snapping his fingers. "We can erase you from existence, and we're in the position of power." Frank flashed his eyes over to Haley in the corner.

"Yes. We know, but you won't. You could make us disappear, but you won't. Right now the market is beyond your control. You have to ride out the damage and then rebuild. You know the damage this market shock will cause, but you think you and, more importantly, the US economy will survive. You probably have the Fed lined up to help with market liquidity and restore market confidence, but it won't help. You have more capital than we do, and you think that you can break us, but the market is with us. There's also something else that we know that you don't." *Hold on to it just a little longer.* Jake was stern. His tone didn't change, and the menace didn't leave his eyes.

"And what is that?"

"All your plans, all your actions, will be useless in about thirty minutes. Look at the model; look at the risk. The dollar is at a point of absolute weakness. People are terrified, and money is leaving the market at a rapid rate. They don't know where to put capital. Everyone is holding either cash, US treasuries, or gold."

"We predicted that. And we can easily get that cash back into the risky assets and restore confidence."

"True, if the model plays out as predicted. Your model is wrong."

"Not possible. An idle threat. We've accounted for everything. I'm going to give you one chance to fix this and reverse your trades. If you don't…" Frank made a subtle hand gesture, and the woman who was called Sarah stuck the knife a little deeper into Haley. Haley gasped as blood ran down her neck.

"You'll pay for that. I should have stayed to finish the job." Benson couldn't contain himself. He was looking directly at Sarah.

"Benson, enough! Stick to the task at hand." Jake scolded him. He returned his attention to this man who held his wife's life in his hands. "For the first time since it has been in existence, your model has finally missed something. It was inevitable that the model would eventually fail, as I'll explain shortly, but we've sped up the process."

"You're bluffing and playing with your wife's life. We control the flow of capital, we keep the markets running smoothly, and we're more powerful than any government or investment entity. We control the decision from the Fed, to the IMF, to the Bank of Japan. There are no surprises."

Now drop the hammer. "Wrong! China!"

Frank's expression changed, and a puzzlement flashed across his face. "What about them?"

"They're going to crash the US economy."

"They can't. They need us. They depend on us. If they don't buy our bonds, their country can't grow. If the US dollar collapses, then every country's reserves would deflate, and purchasing power would collapse. Hell, China would lose so much in value with any kind of interest rate increase in the United States; they couldn't afford any destabilization in US markets. We dictate their fiscal and monetary policy."

"I'm going to give you something, and you better read it fast. Then you're going to do exactly as I say."

"No one has ever spoken to me that way before. I'll take what you give me, and after I look at it, Ms. Fletcher will partially sever an artery in your wife's throat. It won't be fatal, at least not instantaneously. She will bleed, and it'll be up to you and how quickly you reverse your trades on whether you can save her. It'll be painful, and Ms. Fletcher is good at administering pain."

"Read."

Jake handed him a fifteen-year-old unpublished paper by Benjamin Chen on how the world could survive a US market collapse with China stepping in. It outlined how the collapse could happen and the steps that would be taken. The world would enter a period of transition as countries transferred US-dollar-backed assets for yuan-backed assets. The recession would last for about a year, but the world would recover—everyone, that is, except the United States. The devaluation of the US currency, soaring interest rates, and crippling debt would leave the country bankrupt. Companies would be forced to relocate to Asia, as the power of consumerism would shift east. The American way of life would end. Frank flipped through the article as Jake explained the findings.

"How can you be sure that this is what is happening? There has been no aggressive selling of US treasuries. Buyers far outweigh the sellers," Frank said.

"Who do you think is selling? I would have expected the ten-year to be at 1.5 percent, but it's 1.75 percent because there's an active seller. Look at the spreads. They're still tight, much tighter than any other security. China is the one selling. It's reducing its US exposure across all assets. Now let me guess. You plan on having the Fed cut rates and provide an open-door policy for banks to borrow to make sure liquidity is available. Guess what? Right when you announce that, China will sell as much if not all of their

US holdings. They will crash the market and reduce and reverse the intended impact of the Fed. Once that happens, it'll be the beginning of the end." Jake looked at the clock on his screen. "I think we've less than twenty minutes. If we get to that third circuit breaker, it could all be over."

"How could you know this?" Frank's confidence was wavering.

"Who do you think funded us? China Investment Corporation. We were backed by the author of that paper."

The market was down 17 percent. For the first time in his life, Frank was afraid. Everything had been so carefully planned and controlled, and now it looked like it was going to blow up, more so than in 2008, 1987, or 1929. It was possible that the United States was looking at a true economic abyss, and there was nothing he could do about it.

Jake could see the fear in the man's eyes.

"Are you ready to listen?" Jake asked. Frank nodded and motioned for the women who was now called Ms. Fletcher to let Haley go. Benson was ready to go right for her, but Haley motioned him to stop. She put a hand to her neck to feel for the blood and looked back at Ms. Fletcher, who showed no emotion. In one swift motion, Haley pivoted to the left and hit Ms. Fletcher flush in the face. Her nose exploded in a shower of crimson as her head snapped back against the wall. The combined blows sent her eyes rolling into the back of her head, and she collapsed in heap on the floor.

"Nice girl you chose to date, Benson," Haley said. Benson's mouth was on the floor. Jake, who couldn't have loved his wife any more, turned to the scared man in the chair beside him.

"I don't know who you are, and I don't know who your friends are, but you better call them now," Jake ordered.

CHAPTER 57

Frank had been in contact with every member of the team and linked them through the video conference connection in Charon Capital's small office. Jake was now in discussion with every Markov Group member and had gotten the details of who they were and what they controlled. Jake instructed each of them to perform a specific task. First, Jerry Ospry was to make sure that no margin was called on any account for any reason. The exchanges had to be open and had to maintain liquidity. Second, Victor Panket's bank had to be ready to lend to any firm or bank that was experiencing a run on capital. Third, it was critical that Harvey Waterman's and Michael McQuary's firms combine to sell gold and buy the dollar. Fourth, it was time for everyone to sell US treasuries and interest rate futures. They needed to lower the price as fast as possible.

There was some initial balking at Jake's instructions, but Frank held up his hands, quieting the conversation, and told them to do it. Lastly, and this was critical, Michelle would have to call a press conference now and talk about how the Fed was considering raising interest rates—the exact opposite action of the one taken in 1987. She would have to reaffirm that this was because the economy was in great shape, and raising rates would actually bring money back into risky assets. This would tell people that tying up their money at 1.7 percent interest rate for ten years was a ridiculous return for the level of risk, even if the perception of the asset was risk-free. This would help investors see the value in stocks. It should cause a massive risk reversal.

"This will cause more pain," Jerry said over the conference speaker. "Michelle would be crucified if she said that."

"To restore market confidence, she has to do this, and it'll prevent an even more catastrophic sell-off," Jake replied.

"But this goes against the model. The model actually says the opposite," Harvey warned.

"The model is wrong. It has a missing variable, and that omitted variable means the signs are all backward. We've maybe ten minutes. Michelle better get moving," Jake barked.

"What is this missing variable? We control all the variables," Harvey retorted in a confused voice.

"China is what is missing. You don't control China. They control the largest asset, US treasuries, and can kill the economy. It goes beyond the scope of anything you could've accounted for. Now we don't have time to argue. You better do what I say, or we'll be in an unrecoverable situation."

"Do what he says. Now!" Frank ordered.

They got off the phone and got to work. Trades were put in motion by both Charon Capital and the Markov Group to reverse out of their shorts and start going long. The shift in capital was noticeable. Market makers noticed huge order flow on the buy side that hadn't been there all day. It was confusing for all involved. There was still significant sell-side size, but the prices started to stabilize with the market down 18 percent. The dollar stopped falling, and gold flattened its upward trajectory.

Michelle called her press secretary, who issued a press release and sent messages to all the news services that the New York Fed president was going to make a statement at 2:00 p.m. (EST) on the state of the markets. Reporters from all the news services rushed to the Federal Reserve, since most of them were at the NYSE anyway. It was like the start of a 5K race, watching reporters take-off up the street. Jake watched as the breaking news banner flashed across the bottom of the Bloomberg screen that Michelle Lancaster was about to talk. The market pundits on the screen started speculating about how this would probably be about lowering interest rates and increasing market liquidity.

This seemed to bring a halt to the selling, and there were some small ticks up in the market prices. There was some aggressive buying of US treasuries as the thought of lowering interest rates meant an increase in bond prices.

It was the middle of the night in Beijing, but Benjamin was waiting for this moment to begin his massive selling programs. Once the Fed announced the interest rate decrease, the CIC would sell large lots of US treasuries and then enact a full-scale sale of US securities. China would then issue its statement that it no longer had faith in US-backed treasuries, and this would bring the stock market to a halt, but credit, exchange rates, and treasuries would continue to trade and enter a free fall. Investors who had initially bought US bonds because they were considered risk free would sell them like there was no tomorrow, which would not be too far from the truth. Yields would explode when there were no buyers. With the stock market closed and all US assets in massive price decline, China would step in and start offering its yuan-backed bonds. From there, the rest would be history, as would the United States.

CHAPTER 58

Michelle stood in front of a room of fifty reporters and hundreds of crewmen. This was going to be the most important news conference she would ever give, and possibly her last. She was here because she could be. She wasn't a political appointee and didn't have to answer to Congress or the president. She didn't need their approval to enact economic policy. She wasn't the Fed chairman, but she was more powerful.

"Today has seen volatility in the marketplace that's reminiscent of 1987 or 1929. We believe that this is nothing like those times, although the outcome could be far worse. There's no cause for concern. In fact, we believe that with the right actions, this should be viewed with optimism. The US economy is stronger than it has been since the 2008 crisis. It's stronger than it was prior to the technology and Internet bubble burst. Growth has been consistent, and there's little personal or business leverage. Unemployment has not gotten to 4 percent, but we may never get there. If we do, that's great, but for right now, 6 percent is a more reasonable target. The labor force is different; the need for skilled workers is higher than it has ever been. It's my belief, and it's shared by some of the other Fed governors, that the time to raise interest rates is now."

There was an audible shock in the press room. Hands went up, and voices screamed over each other to get questions in. The reaction was almost violent. Michelle raised both her hands to silence the crowd. Her heart was beating faster than it had ever in her life.

"What the markets need right now is a sense of rationality, a sense of calm. The market isn't the economy; it's a reflection of attitude about price, and one that's currently widely distorted. The Fed will be there to provide liquidity, but lowering interest rates right now is the worst thing that could happen. The premium for risky assets versus riskless assets is at historic highs. We don't need to enhance people's risk appetite with lower rates; investors just have to use their eyes and see the opportunity. From our standpoint, we believe that it would be shortsighted for people to buy US treasuries at the expense of more fairly priced investments. I'll now take questions."

The reporter from Bloomberg shouted out the quickest. "Why this course of action now? At this point in time? Do you really believe that's what the markets want to hear?"

"I don't care what the markets want to hear. What people want to hear and what is best for them aren't necessarily the same thing. This is clearly one of those times. The Fed's job isn't to placate market participants; it has been too accommodative for too long. This is best for the economy. People will continue to buy US bonds. Wouldn't you prefer a higher yield on your risk-free asset? This is just a sign of how much strength the economy has right now. We're looking to the future and don't want the economy to overheat. The stock market will rebound. It has to because there's real value in those companies."

The CNBC reporter got in next. "This is the most hawkish sentiment in years. Why the reversal?"

"That's because the Fed does not need to support the risk appetite of the market participants. That's not our job. The market can take care of itself. It has to stop reading so much into the statements we make for short-term positioning. It needs to think about the longer-term picture. Today could not have been a better day to announce this. We were going to make a statement at the next FOMC meeting, but why wait?" Michelle knew this was a lie, but knew here was little downside to it. *If this works, the Fed chairman has to follow. If he doesn't, we're all out of a job. On the bright side, the economy will be dead as well so not having a job won't matter.*

There was more screaming and hand waving as reporters tried to get questions in. Michelle took each question and handled them all like the pro she was.

Frank, Jake, and the members of Charon Capital watched the TV as this was going on. While Michelle finished that last statement, Duncan was watching the model and noticed the sign on the US treasury and S&P 500 risk metric turn from negative to positive.

"Jake, the risk aversion is changing," Duncan said, making sure everyone heard. "Make the call now."

Jake picked up the phone and dialed Beijing.

CHAPTER 59

B enjamin was watching what was happening with utter confusion. The United States raising interest rates was the last thing he was expecting. It made no sense. How would that give the market confidence? It also caused him to delay his mass selling of US treasuries. He was expecting rates to collapse while the "flight to quality" trade continued. He couldn't enact the rest of his plan until he sold China's US treasuries holdings. The idea was to let the yield get as low as possible and then dump China's holdings. Over $1.2 trillion worth, almost 25 percent of the international market. Selling that amount would crash the treasury market.

Now it might not be possible to cause a US economic collapse without a simultaneous crash in the value of their own assets. Each percentage point increase in US treasury yields could mean hundreds of billions in losses. If the flight-to-quality trade disappeared and the demand for US treasuries disappeared, as much as he would have liked to sell the securities, there might not be any buyers. Effectively, if the ten-year yields started to creep back up to 2 percent and the market recovered, then this would all be for naught.

Still, it was worth a shot. It would hurt China more than he would have liked, but the United States was severely vulnerable. China would be able to recover faster because, while there was a growing middle class, the wealth divide was still significant. The large wealth divide meant that when prices fell, there was actually less damage because the rich could sustain the loss and the poor were poor to begin with. It was always the middle class that suffered the most when a recession hit, and the United

States had the biggest middle class in the world. The loss in value would disseminate throughout the population resulting in falling prices, home values, and wages. However, a recovery would occur in China because labor was cheap, and, unlike in the United States, there was nothing as punitive as a minimum wage. Benjamin was convinced his original plan could still work. He called up his traders and told them to increase the selling of US treasuries.

He put down the phone and waited. He watched his screen and saw nothing was happening. There were no large orders and no significant price changes in the US treasury markets. He wasn't getting any trade confirmations from his traders. After three minutes he called back, but no one was on the desk. He was furious. He got up from his chair and was ready to head out to the trading desk when Bing Ho walked in.

"Benjamin, you better follow me. I've just learned of something quite troubling. Lao would like to talk with you."

"What is this about?" Defiance radiated through Benjamin's body.

"We know what you have done. You have violated our institutional trading protocol. More so, you deliberately tried to manipulate the markets. Fortunately, you were unsuccessful. We have the program, and we know what trades you had planned. Hopefully, this never comes to light, because the implications for US-China relations could be set back centuries. What were you thinking?"

Benjamin stood there, realizing Bing was in possession of the program and had effectively shut down everything that Benjamin had planned.

"You do not have the foresight or the knowledge to even begin to comprehend what I was doing. I was doing what was best for China. Do you not see the problem? We will never get out from under the United States. Do you always want to cower to their economic policy, their political instability, their lack of history and culture? I for one will not. We have the infrastructure, the manpower, and the capital to lead the world away from this democratic tyrant to a true utopia. Bing, you must let me continue for the sake of our people."

Bing realized he was watching a tormented but brilliant man. He was sympathetic and knew that in an earlier time, a different time, this man would have been a general, leading men into battle to protect and grow China's way of life. Yesterday's general is today's investment manager, since it was through the influence of money, and not the sword, that lives and the existing power structure changed.

"Benjamin, it's time to leave. Your loyalty to this country won't be forgotten. This is a new China, a China that will become the world power and leader through proper channels. Not by undermining and destroying the world economy. I hope you're able to live to see that, but for right now, it's best that you come with me."

Benjamin got up from his desk and followed Bing to Lao's office. Benjamin knew now he would never see a dominant China, a China that was the pinnacle of the economic and cultural landscape. He was probably going to jail for life or would be sentenced to death. Given that he came from a prominent family with a rich history, he would be given a choice. As he walked into Lao's office, he was unsure of what he would choose.

"Jake, I think we're in the clear. I don't see a massive dumping of US treasuries. The buyers have left the market, and rates are climbing. The sellers are there, but I don't think it is China. Whoa. Have you seen volatility? It's crashing," Duncan said, barely able to contain his excitement.

There was about an hour left before the close. Michelle's statement had done the trick. Of course, it was completely speculative, as she had not consulted with any other Fed governor or the actual chairman. The head of the Federal Reserve would be apoplectic, but it had to be done. While Michelle was talking Jake had simultaneously finished a conversation with Bing letting him know what Benjamin had been up to. They had gotten there just in time before Benjamin created the massive short and collapsed the treasury market.

Charon Capital had completed two of its three goals. It had flushed out the Markov Group and prevented Benjamin from collapsing the world economy. Now Charon had to help repair the damage. From initial appearances, the market was already coming around.

"Are you surprised? We just sold off fifty thousand put contracts. Look at the model; signs are changing across the board. Frank, get your guys to leak info that everything was computer generated, triggered by a fat-finger trade that accidently went long a hundred thousand VIX futures contracts," Jake ordered.

"That's not necessary. They're already on it," Frank said.

While a market that is in free fall can fall precipitously, a market that has been oversold can bounce back just as fast. All it takes is a change in risk aversion and an understanding of fundamental value versus price. When the market realizes there are no sellers out there and that there is no leverage to concern itself with, and when this is combined with an asset price that is ridiculously low, investors jump on it as fast as they can. It was as if the market participants all came to their collective senses at the same time when prices stabilized. Consequently, there were only buyers for all assets, and prices went bid up.

For the next hour, everyone sat back and watched the market recover a record 15 percent of the 18 percent lost over the course of the remaining trading day. It was the biggest one-day move ever. Volatility, which had gotten above 100 percent, finished the day at 32 percent. Charon Capital removed all of its exposure by the end of the day and had a completely neutral portfolio at the close. The model showed some slightly elevated risk flags, mostly on volatility, but all other key risk metrics were back to normal. The market was essentially back to where it had been at the start of the day. Jake knew that there had been some significant damage done, and major wealth transfers had occurred, but hopefully, for those who were long-term, rational investors, this day would have been a minor blip on their overall wealth.

Benson finalized the trades. It might take a month to do a full portfolio reconciliation. He was looking at his screen in absolute wonder. He called all of them over, except for Frank and his team, and showed them the figure:

$5,120,486,997.32

"What is that?" Haley asked.

"That's the value of our account," Benson replied to her. They all started laughing. It was an unreal figure, and 20 percent of the profit was theirs.

Jake turned to Frank.

"Now I know who your partners are. Who the hell are you?"

CHAPTER 60

In the late nineteenth century, the Vanderbilt family had amassed a fortune that exceeded the US treasury, owning one in every twenty dollars in the United States. When the twentieth century rolled around, and transportation peaked in the 1920s, the Vanderbilt money had been dispersed to the next generation, but this generation didn't follow in Cornelius Vanderbilt's footsteps. Instead of further accumulation and growth of the family fortune, the fortune was spent, so much so that by the 1950s, the Vanderbilt family was no longer on the list of America's richest and most powerful.

The Lyman family was not a household name such as the Rockefellers, Fords, or DuPonts at the turn of the twentieth century. They never had a patriarch such as Cornelius Vanderbilt, who took a risk and created a fortune. They married into it. Frank Lyman married one of Cornelius's daughters and, although never participating in the expansion of the railroad, managed and invested part of the Vanderbilt fortune in the stock market and grew the inheritance. Prior to the stock market crash of 1929, Frank Lyman had foreseen the exuberance that took hold of the country and the potential damage that was coming. He had sold all of his and his wife's investments and bought agricultural commodities. When the crash came, and the subsequent Great Depression, he was shocked by the extent of the economic destruction. He also became a man of substantial power. He controlled a needed resource, food, and was quietly sitting on one of America's largest fortunes.

At the same time, he was witnessing the descendants of Cornelius Vanderbilt quickly throw away an unimaginable fortune. To Frank this was abhorrent and shortsighted. Wealth was to be protected and grown, and if a powerful family couldn't understand that, then how was the average person to? Frank was friends with powerful and influential people and met with them to discuss a growing concern. Given what had happened leading up to the stock market crash and with his relatives, Frank realized that people needed to be protected from themselves. He called a meeting with John Maynard Keynes, John Morgan Jr., George Harrison, and Richard Whitney, and together they devised a plan to prevent another Great Depression from ever happening again. The world's leading economist, the head of the biggest New York bank, the president of the New York Fed, and the head of the NYSE, along with Frank Lyman, were the original founders of the Markov Group.

Keynes named the group after the work of Andrey Markov, who developed a process in which the future path is independent from the present state and all prior history. This was apt to describe the stock market, where all future returns should be independent from past returns. Of course, this name was, as Keynes said, "somewhat cheeky," since what they planned to do was the complete opposite of a Markov process.

With the establishment of this group, with Frank as its de facto head, they were able to control the flow of resources and the growth of the economy in a silent, more efficient way than the government ever could. They did all they could do to contest the destructive economic policies of Roosevelt's New Deal, flow capital to the right resources so the United States could prosper and grow after World War II, and position the United States and its allies to combat and eventually defeat communism from an economic front. They did this in the presences of the poor economic, social, and political choices made by the government and individuals alike: inflation, unemployment, the Vietnam War, civil unrest, the tech bubble, the housing crisis—government- and individual-made problems that lacked the foresight to see where the country and world were going. The Markov Group felt a responsibility to correct these problems and direct the country to a place that would always be best for the future, independent of its past.

Frank Lyman believed in the scarcity of resources. As a result, he only had one child, a son named Frank Lyman II. Frank felt that the most important thing he could pass on to his child was his experience and philosophy. While the other members of the Markov Group were temporary and would eventually either retire or change positions, a member of the Lyman family would always be part of the group. So Frank passed his responsibilities on to his son, who eventually passed on the responsibilities to his son, Frank Lyman III.

This was the man who sat in the office of Charon Capital with Jake, Haley, Duncan, and Benson.

CHAPTER 61

Frank looked at the four individuals in the room and smiled. He had hung up the conference call with the other members of the Markov Group after the market closed. The Markov Group had been satisfied with where the market finished and the risks going forward; the current threat had abated. Less than three hours ago, they had been in a place of vulnerability not seen since the inception of the group, but now they were as strong as ever. At least it appeared that way to Frank. Michelle Lancaster looked like an economic savior, and her word would be considered gospel from here on. She would hold sway over markets similar to Alan Greenspan's influence. The concern from China had been revealed and could and would be dealt with. Finally, the Charon Group had been found, and all four members who were a threat to the Markov Group were sitting right in front of him. Frank knew what he had to do.

Frank addressed the four of them with a renewed confidence. After explaining who he was, he nodded to Mr. Jones and Ms. Fletcher, who had picked herself up from the floor and regained her steely, but somewhat damaged exterior. No one moved. Frank smiled and continued with his talk, looking directly at Jake.

"Now, I believe we're back to where we were before you discovered the model. The only difference is that you know about us, and no one knows about the Markov Group. I don't believe you're in a position to be making any more demands, but I'll give you a choice. You're all smart, thoughtful people, and since we've some time, let me first tell you a story.

"Economic systems are as fragile as the human psyche, so much so that the two are interrelated. Economic exuberance leads to inflated asset prices, and fire sales are a result of panicked decisions that lead to undervaluation. In a world where long-term rationality should dominate short-term foolishness, it's the latter that tends to result in the most consequential outcomes. That and leverage. The greatest investors of this generation have had long-term success for two main reasons.

"First, they understand the value of an asset over the long term and don't worry about short-term disturbances. Preaching and finding value are the fundamental tenets of consistent long-term performance. The evidence of this is overwhelming, and the fact that value stocks have been better performers than growth stocks is further proof of people's short-sightedness. Look at how people bid up the latest, greatest tech stock even when that stock has negative earnings. Why do people ignore the evidence right in front of their faces? Everyone knows the anomaly exists, yet they continue with this inconsistent behavior. This speaks to the lack of rationality among the investing populace more than anything else.

"The second reason is that when opportunity strikes, rational investors have enough cash on hand to make any opportunity profitable. The management of cash and misuse of leverage are the main drivers of extreme returns. Warren Buffet invested in a warrant on Goldman Sachs at the height of the 2008 crisis not because of the long-term value proposition but because he could afford to, and the short-term return potential was so attractive. That's how you win big when there's a crisis. Conversely, Long-Term Capital Management—LTCM—didn't fail because their strategy was wrong; they failed because they were leveraged at the wrong time. They were on the wrong side of a dispersion trade that blew out, they were too large to unload their position, and they received market calls. In 1998 LTCM almost brought down the market and the economic system with it. This process was repeated in 2008 with much greater effect. Yet if you look at the long-term growth of the economy and the upward trend of the stock market, these are but small blips caused by leverage and short-term irrationality. It is the role of the Markov Group to provide oversight so this positive growth continues in the face of short-term exuberance. If we did not, the world economy would have failed long ago. The crash in 2008 was unavoidable, but our actions allowed the world to escape mostly unscathed."

Frank paused to let what he was saying have its effect, but from the look Jake was giving him, he assumed that Jake had understood this from the start.

"Mr. Lyman, this is market manipulation. You're presenting the world with the illusion of free markets when it's the furthest thing from the truth," Jake said.

"Absolutely. People need to believe that the market is just and fair, dictated by an underlying process where capital flows to the resources with the most demand. Communism failed because people always try to maximize their utility—their usefulness—and that can occur only in a system that allows them to maximize their talents and wealth. However, people are not rational and don't have preferences that conform to normal distributions. So, in an attempt to maximize their preferences, their utility, they usually make the wrong decisions. Why do people buy insurance and gamble? They pay for life, home, and car insurance and gamble their money in Vegas when both have negative expected payoffs and are done for two completely different reasons. On the one hand, they buy insurance because they're too risk averse, and on the other hand, they gamble because they're risk seeking. How can the same person do two actions with such opposite rationales with the exact same payoff profile? And yet this is considered normal behavior." Frank's intensity was fully apparent.

"That's simplifying the argument. You can't aggregate human nature like that," Jake countered.

"Why not? Look at aggregate debt levels and consumer spending. I would say individual habits are reflected on the macro level. Let me present another argument. When regulation to prevent short-term irrationality is implemented, what happens? When exchanges ban short selling, asset values become too high, creating a massive bubble and greater leverage, so when prices fall, they fall more violently and cause more damage than if the ban had never been there. A short-sighted and reactionary government put in Sarbanes-Oxley legislation to provide more oversight, and it made banks more restrictive and reduces the liquidity and credit available to the general public. Politicians preach about increasing the minimum wage and instituting global health care, and it leads to lower employment and a reduction in growth. These are just recent examples, and I could go on and on. People are flawed, and regulation doesn't work. People need to be able to make the choices they want, as long as they think they're doing it freely and it's the right choice."

"And it's your job to make sure they're making the right choice."

"Damn right it is. The people that have been a part of the Markov Group have been benevolently guiding the country for decades, and what has been the result? Massive economic growth, technological advancement, improved living conditions, and so on. At no point in history has the world prospered more than when the Markov Group guided it. The people in the Markov Group didn't need to do this. They were wealthy and powerful to begin with. They did it because they cared. If we weren't there, the country would never have survived Roosevelt's New Deal or Carter's administration and stagflation. Yes, we flush out the market sometimes, like we did in October 1987 and 2008, but these are necessary tools to help improve the overall economy for everyone. Everyone!"

"And you kill and threaten people."

"Don't be myopic. This is about the greater good. The morality of what we do comes from a place of sustaining what is good for the masses, not the individual. We all have to make hard choices, and when the time comes, it's best to be decisive."

"There's another solution, a solution that doesn't require a deity to oversee, eliminate, or guide people," Jake replied calmly, ignoring the fact that Ms. Fletcher had worked her way behind him. The man at the door hadn't moved since he walked in

"I'm all ears," Frank said skeptically, leaning back in his chair.

"Frank, I agree with everything you've said, but it only takes one non-benevolent person to destroy this utopia you've created. The law of averages suggests that this will come to pass, and then everything you've created will be destroyed. It is something that can't last. What happens then? Also, what happens when everyone finds out what you've been doing or someone replicates my research or China or India or another developing world power starts to non-conform? The world is changing; the economy is global. As the world economy grows while simultaneously becoming smaller through technology and synergy, your ability to control markets will fall. Assets are becoming more and more correlated. An event will occur that the Markov Group won't be able to correct. It's basic math.

"In the 1930s there was limited correlation between the United States and Europe and Asia. In the 1970s it was trending up, and now those correlations are almost one. I've tested the market progression through time, and the effect of the model in the not-too-distant future wanes once the correlations exceed 0.75. Since the growth of technology and the speed of information dissemination have grown exponentially, the model has been reaching the limit of what it's capable of doing. It's as simple as this: Your ability to maximize the risk-return trade-off through diversification falls to zero when you get above twenty or so assets. Additionally, this return falls drastically as correlations among your assets increase. As such, the model becomes too similar to the market. Whether you like it or not, the Markov Group's control mechanism is gone because you will become the market."

"The model can and has changed through time," Frank said. "Plus, the model is only one aspect of what we do."

"But your model is the mechanism that controls the market. Without that everything else is moot. Even your Fed connections won't be able to manipulate the markets without a way to deliver the capital. Mr. Lyman, it's time to let the Markov Group go. You have to let people make mistakes, even if the choices are poor. The problem isn't the people. The problem is how capital is used."

"What do you mean?" Frank asked.

"The greatest threat for a potential economic collapse is how correlated the world's assets are and how we invest our assets. We've created, through multiple mechanisms, an investment protocol where most retail and institutional investors have portfolios that look identical. Either through consultants, investment guidelines, or internal constraints, everyone has similar allocations and invests with the same investment managers. Several large investment banks and several large hedge funds dominate the landscape. The ability for investors to arbitrage inefficiencies and make money effectively requires capital to be small and nimble. The bigger you are, the harder it is to find alpha, to find true opportunity. So all the money that's invested with the largest managers looks just like the overall market, which brings us back to the correlation problem. To reduce the world risk, you need to reduce the size of the biggest banks, the biggest hedge funds, all and any of the investment managers over a billion dollars. For a firm to effectively trade without moving markets it can't control more than a billion dollars. That is the key figure for a firm to remain nimble. Anything above that, and it starts to become the market itself. You need more firms with less, not less firms with more.

"This is the opposite of what the Markov Group is about. You don't need more control; you need more options, more ways to disburse capital. Will breaking up the big banks and fund fundamentally change the industry? Of course. It'll require more people to conduct research to find where the alpha exists; it'll require more people to do due diligence on managers; it'll require more people to assess portfolio risk. The industry would grow and become more efficient, more dynamic, and less likely to become overly correlated. It'll take away huge systematic crash risk," Jake said, finally finished. *I've played my last card.*

"That's against the fundamentals of capitalism. If you have success, there shouldn't be a limit on how successful you can be. You should grow to the maximum you can become!" Frank exclaimed.

"Wrong," Jake shouted back. "We don't live in a Keynesian world. The world is governed by our individual maximization of personal utility, our desire for happiness and the reduction of sadness, conditional on the environment we're in. It's basic game theory. My approach is the approach that's best for the individual and the whole. Yours is best for the individual. As a collective body, the world can take care of itself, but it needs limits.

These are limits that would work. It doesn't need an Oz character, a man behind the curtain controlling outcomes."

"It won't work. We can't break up these firms. It wouldn't be possible. The outcry would be huge."

"Over time you could. You also have the person who can get this started." Jake pointed to the image of Michelle Lancaster on the screen. "It's time to start this now. Meet with your group and start planning how this will work. If you truly are benevolent, and this isn't about power, then you should realize that this is the best outcome for the global economy. Your control would have been lost whether I found it out or not. We just sped up the process. The choice isn't ours; the choice is yours. You could silence us and everyone else that's now privy to the model and try to keep up the illusion, or you could use your influence one last time to create a lasting change that your grandfather would be proud of. Mr. Lyman. I understand what his intentions were, and even though I don't agree with them, they came from the right place. The world has changed, and the Markov Group should actually live up to its name. It's time to let the future truly be independent."

Jake stared at Frank Lyman, knowing that only one of two outcomes was possible. He knew Frank Lyman was a man of power, a man that got what he wanted, and a man that would kill to keep what he had. He also knew he was a man that had tremendous foresight and cared about the greater good, even if it was misguided. Jake had made a choice, appealing to the man's sense of rationality, hoping that long-term wisdom would overcome short-term instincts.

The acidic taste in Mr. Jones's mouth was gone. He was trained to show no emotion, but a flicker of surprise briefly flashed across his face before his typical inexpressive face returned. He opened the door and signaled to the third man to come down from the roof. He took out his knife and went back into the office. He needed to complete his assignment.

CHAPTER 62

B reaking up huge investment firms was a complicated task, not because of the ownership structure but because of people's unwillingness to give up power. There was significant resistance from major mutual and hedge funds. They argued that it would be impossible for large insurance companies and pension funds to allocate capital, and the restriction on size would limit their ability to participate in the bond and credit market. These resistances were quickly squashed when Michelle Lancaster increased the power under the Volcker rule and simply suggested that these resisting firms would be forced to return capital to their investors and disband if they didn't comply. Major stakeholders in these firms were given interests in the smaller firms that came out of the larger ones, under a specific mandate that interest did not mean control. A manager of one firm could not have a controlling interest or management stake in another firm, and each of the firms had to be managed independently.

With the breakup and disbursement of assets across many different firms, tens of thousands of jobs were created because of the new shortfall of financial professionals. Pension funds, endowments, and trusts had to hire more professionals to do due diligence, regulatory bodies had to hire more people to help manage the influx of new firms and the resulting paperwork from new regulations, and the new firms had to hire more people to do research and manage client relations. The resulting increase in employment led to a significant uptick in growth in the economy.

An added benefit of smaller managers was that the control of large asset allocators had diminished, along with a systematic correlation in the market. The reduction in size of financial firms actually led to a growth in assets and a reduction in global risk. Michelle Lancaster spearheaded this charge; she was relentless in pushing this agenda through. She believed in it and thought it would bring a new and improved efficiency back to the markets. More importantly, it was a way for her to suppress her guilt and fill the void left by Chris Carter. The Markov Group had been wrong. It had been wrong to provide this shadow oversight from the investing public, to dupe investors for their own good. While she'd been part of the group, she'd felt it necessary; now she was not so sure. While it could have been argued that her actions in the Markov Group had been done for the greater good, she had clearly been a willing participant in the death of Patrick Stinson, and no one could argue that what they did was right. Every day she thought she should probably be in jail for her role in his murder, and she pushed every day to improve the global economy as a reminder that she had a second chance to do things right.

Bing Ho was eventually promoted to CIO of the China Investment Corp. Benjamin was escorted from the building and was never heard from again. Bing didn't know if he was executed or imprisoned, and frankly it didn't matter. Lao was forced to resign, as his shortsightedness for not realizing what was happening was considered almost as bad as the action Benjamin had taken. CIC had done very well in the brief period the market had almost collapsed, in part due to the investment of Charon Capital, but also and in spite of the actions Benjamin took. He had sold the CIC's treasuries when yields were at all-time lows, so when Bing bought them back when yields had increased, CIC made a nice profit. The potential economic attack on the United States was never revealed, and the economic ties between China and the United States strengthened as a result.

Frank Lyman III quietly disappeared. He'd been the overseer of a shadow group that had had power that only a few knew about when the Markov Group was active, and, once it disbanded, he became just a shadow. Frank had known only one thing: to protect and preserve the global economy. He'd never had to worry about a job or wealth or repercussions from his actions. Now he just had wealth and nothing to do. For almost a century, the Lyman family had been a quiet, munificent economic over-lord. Now that role was gone. It was gone not because they had failed but because the world had evolved and a new solution had been found. Frank wondered whether his grandfather would have been happy or disappointed in the outcome.

Franklin Insurance continued to operate as usual, and Walter Matthews continued to be a solid and reliable employee. He continued to hope for a better life but knew his station was probably set. He continued to reach too high when it came to women.

Mr. Jones never worked for Franklin Insurance again, as was the case for all the dark analysts and the whole behavioral division. Mr. Jones didn't care. A man with his skill set was never too far away from his next paying job. That time would come. There still was some personal unfinished business with his protégé, Ms. Fletcher, to take care of.

She had been trained well, maybe too well. She was responsible for the loss of feeling in Mr. Jones's left hand. She had bettered him in Saint Croix. She had been prepared. Once Frank Lyman had let *them* go, her instincts had kicked in. She would not forget. She would wait. She had no master. She could choose. Jake, Haley, Duncan, Frank Lyman, and Mr. Jones. As she watched Benson from a far she knew she would save him for last.

Jake got off the phone with Duncan and joined Haley out on the terrace. He looked at the views of the Santa Rita Mountains, baked in a pink after-glow from the early morning sun. She wasn't dressed yet, lounging about in the same ratty boxer shorts and paper-thin T-shirt she had been sleeping in for years. Jake came up to her and ran his finger across the half inch scar on her neck, a gift from Ms. Fletcher's knife as an ever-present reminder of what could have happened.

"Who was on the phone?" she asked.

"Duncan. He was just giving me an update. He's moving to Boulder, and Leslie is going to move in with him."

"That was fast. They only started dating when he got back to New York."

"I expect there was more going on back at Griffin than a working relationship between the two of them. He told me he was done with the city. He just wants to ski and live by the mountains. Oh, and he got a bulldog."

She just shook her head.

"He also said that Benson is racing cyclocross now, trying to become a professional. I guess Duncan spoke to him during the week."

"Benson always had the lungs and heart for it. Still can't believe he moved to Portland."

"He needed a change of scenery, just like the rest of us. From what I understand, he will only date blond women now."

She turned to him, her hand instinctively going to her neck. "We don't talk about the incident much, and there's no need, but there's something I wanted to ask you."

"OK."

"Right after the market recovered and before they let us go, Lyman said he would give us a choice. What was he talking about? I figured it was about us staying quiet or killing us, but that doesn't seem like a choice at all."

"That's correct. The choice was death or work for the Markov Group. It was either help perpetuate the manipulation or get out of the way. That was how he saw the world, and in the end, in a weird way, he was doing everything he could to protect and help people. In his heart, he really cared about the greater good. He could've just killed us, but he saw value. It was up to us to make him realize that the world was changing. And had changed."

"It doesn't seem real."

"I know."

They stood there together, silently watching the pink afterglow burn off. After about ten minutes, she grabbed his hand and looked at his watch. "You'd better go. Otherwise you'll be late for class." She kissed him on the cheek and went back inside. She was a month away from her PhD defense and had a position waiting for her when she was finished.

He made his way to his car, a BMW X5. It was a nice upgrade from the old Jeep. He headed into campus with a smile on his face. His latest article had just received a revise and resubmit at the *Journal of Finance*. *Maybe it'll be next to Audria's article*, he thought. She had gone to the SEC, deciding she was done with academia. For Jake, given up the academic world had never been an option, and he felt good about his prospects of making tenure.

Little did he know that he was about to face a much greater, much more personal challenge.

ACKNOWLEDGMENTS

There are many people to thank, including my editors, my wife Heather, Leah Doran, and close friends who read the multiple drafts I gave them. Special thanks is reserved for my brother David, who provided invaluable insight, reviews, and corrections when it came to the intricacies of day to day trading and the readability of the more dense finance topics.

AUTHOR BIOGRAPHY

Dr. James Doran founded and served as the chief investment officer of Implied Capital LP, a volatility arbitrage hedge fund. He previously worked as the Bank of America Professor in Finance at a university in Florida. He has published numerous academic and practitioner articles in the areas of option pricing theory and portfolio risk management, both in the equity and energy markets. Currently he is the financial dimension leader at Get Fit Enterprises, a health and wellness firm.

Dr. Doran earned his bachelor of science degree in economics and computer science from Emory University and a doctorate in finance from the University of Texas at Austin. He is married with three children and currently lives in Boulder, Colorado.

Made in the USA
Middletown, DE
01 August 2016